Paranormworld Book One

Voodoo Moon

A Moon Sisters Novel

DJ Westerfield writing as
June Stevens

THIS book is a work of fiction. Names, characters, places and incidents are the product of the authors' imagination or are used factiously. Any resemblance to actual persons, living or dead, business establishments, events or locales is entirely coincidental.

NO part of this book may be reproduced, scanned, or distributed in any printed or electronic form without permission. Please do not participate in or encourage piracy of copyrighted materials in violation of the author's rights. Purchase only authorized editions.

Voodoo Moon
Copyright ©2014 June Stevens
All rights reserved.

ISBN: 978-1-63422-021-7
Cover Design by: Marya Heiman
Typography by: Courtney Nuckels
Editing by: Cynthia Shepp

For the love of my life, my hero, my husband, without whom nothing I do would be possible.

And for my mother, who always wanted to write a book but life was too short. This book is for you Mommy.

PROLOGUE

*I*T ONLY TOOK MILLIE A FEW MINUTES TO TALLY UP THE DAY'S BUSINESS AND PUT the money in the safe for Mr. Fegley to find the next morning. Quickly wiping down the counters, she made sure everything was tidy. She went into the back room, removed her apron, and took a quick look in the mirror that hung next to the back door. Wisps and strands of tawny hair had escaped the ribbon she tied it back in this morning, forming a messy halo around her pale, freckled face. In the threadbare, brown tunic and pants that were her normal work uniform, she looked drab and washed out. If she weren't so clean, she could almost be mistaken for a beggar. She swiped at her hair, but it did no good. No matter. She didn't have time to pretty up, and she wouldn't be graded on her looks today, just her powers.

She jumped as the clock on the wall chimed the hour. There was less than half an hour left to get across town in order to make the evening test. If she were even a minute late, they would turn her away and she would have to wait six more months for another test date. Luckily, she'd saved up a whole buck so she could take the trolley.

Being sure to lock the door behind her, she ran out into the early evening twilight. She had just a few minutes to make it two blocks over to the magi-trolley line. Glancing down the street, she saw it was crowded with daytime shoppers hurrying home to dinner and the beginnings of nighttime shoppers coming out. Dusk and dawn were always the busiest time in this part of Old Nash City. The vampires who stayed out of the daylight to avoid severe sunburns and allergic reactions were venturing out and mingling with the norms and paranorms who had no such allergies to the sun. The shops and streets were usually crowded for the first hour or so past dusk.

Even as small and fast as Millie was, it would take her forever to slip through the crowd. She eyed the narrow alley to the right. The light from the blue-tinged crystal streetlights didn't make it into the alley. It was dark and dirty. She hated walking through it even in the daylight, but she didn't have much choice. Some things were just more important than her fear of the dark.

He leaned against the stone wall, deep in the shadows cast by the setting sun and the solar-crystal lights that illuminated the bustling street. This body was awkward and cumbersome. He'd used it too many nights now, and it was starting to get stiff. No matter. He would pick another from his store tomorrow. But for now, he needed to find new food—another worthy enough to fuel his body and perhaps become a vehicle for his spirit.

He scanned the crowd, using his second sight, his divine sight, to view the magical auras that pulsed around the unsuspecting people. They had no idea he was there, hunting, waiting for the perfect specimen. Of course, none of them had anything to worry about. Their auras were all dull and muddy. All no-to-medium powers. Not one bright aura in the bunch. None were worthy. He was just about ready to give up his search and move on to another street when a bright light caught his eye at the other end of the alley. He turned his full attention to the young girl moving quickly down the alley, as if she were afraid. Her magic burned brightly around her. Most people, common people, wouldn't know what was inside the girl. But he did. Brilliant shades of purple and blue pulsed and shimmered around her. The colors of her aura were so dark and bright they were almost tangible. His fingers itched to reach out and touch it. She was brimming with untapped power. Oh yes, her power would be filling and delicious. She was worthy. He would have her

ONE
Fiona

I PULLED THE CLOAK TIGHTER IN AN ATTEMPT TO PROTECT MYSELF FROM THE WIND and rain. With short, stumbling steps along the uneven road, I used the stick in my hand like a cane to avoid rocks, holes, and other obstacles. There was a full moon tonight, but the dense storm clouds hid its light. I'd tossed my useless lantern aside over an hour ago when I'd had to dismount my horse and lead him along the treacherous path.

Though I knew Mal could see better than I could, and that he had nerves of steel, the weather and pitch black was enough to send even the steadiest of equines into a tizzy. But I didn't dare use magic to light our path so I trudged through the mud and grime, Mal following along reluctantly.

Lightning sliced the sky less than a second before thunder crashed. I hit the ground with a thud, knocked off my feet as Mal reared back, a shrill whinny voicing his dislike of the situation.

"Oh, come on, you big baby!" I shouted at the massive, black beast as I struggled to rise out of the slick mud. Stabbing my stick into the ground, I used it to leverage myself up. After a feeble attempt at wiping the grime from my hands onto my even filthier pants, I grabbed Mal's lead. Pulling his head down, I ran my hand over his nose and put my lips close to his ear.

"It's ok, Big Bad. I hate it out here too," I soothed. "But we've got things to do and places to go. We can't let a little rain get in our way."

Mal snorted.

"The faster we get down this road and get this done, the faster we get somewhere dry with some nice, crunchy oats."

Mal snorted again and nudged my shoulder as if trying to push me along.

"Okay, you big, bad baby." I laughed. "You'll do anything for food, won't you? Let's go."

I turned and resumed my slow progress down the muddy road, Mal following behind. The rain began to let up. By the time we made it about another half a mile, the rain had gone completely and the moon was starting to peek out from behind the clouds—just in time for me to see a massive shape across the road about ten feet ahead.

"Stay here," I whispered to Mal. Dropping his reins, I sloshed through the mud to inspect the tree. Not too big. On a dry day, I could pull it out alone. With the mud to contend with and the inability to use magic for fear of being discovered, it was a good thing I had Mal.

I returned to Mal and patted his neck. "Well, big boy, looks like it's time for you to get to work. We are going to pull that little stick over there out of the road, so we don't have to walk through the woods. Okay?" I said in a loud voice that could be heard over the wind and rain.

Mentally, I spoke to him, *Be on the lookout. I don't think the storm had anything to do with that tree.*

Mal snorted acquiescence.

"This is the stupidest thing I've ever done," I groused loudly as I dug through my saddlebag in search of the rope I always carried. "I should be at home in bed, not skulking along a dark road alone in a storm."

"You're right," a deep voice intoned at my ear. "But since you are, it would be my pleasure to relieve you of some of your burden by taking your horse and any valuables you have hidden under that cloak."

Shit! I folded my fingers around the stick I'd leaned against Mal's side as I felt the point of a knife dig into the skin under my ear.

I turned my eyes to look at Mal. "You couldn't have warned me?"

Mal snorted. While he could use our mental link to communicate with me, he seemed to think himself above it and only deigned to do so under the direst circumstances. Apparently, he didn't feel this qualified.

"I don't want to have to hurt you, so let go of that little stick," the voice at my ear intoned menacingly.

A crack of laughter alerted me to another thief. "As if that little twig could do any damage in the hands of a little girl!"

Oh, so that was how it was going to be then? No problem. I could play that game. I let go of the stick, raised my hands above my head, and turned around slowly. "Okay. I'll do whatever you want. Just, please, don't hurt me," I whined, my voice tremulous.

"That's more like it!" Thug number one pulled the knife away from my neck with a lecherous grin. "Be a good girl and we won't hurt you. Now, let's see what you've got under that cloak, sweetie."

I took quick stock. The first one was in front of me, the other behind him and to the left about six paces. There had to be more, though. I pasted on a naive smile. Slowly, I began to lower my arms as I opened my senses just enough to pull in enough energy to get a read on the immediate area. These two punks didn't have any magic. Shifters, most likely. I could feel a fluctuation of energy coming from the woods. Someone was using power. I pulled in a little more energy as my hands reached the clasp of my cloak.

"I just have one question before I do," I said. Silently, I asked, *Come on, where are you hiding?* I pulled a little more, stretching out threads around them like a web. There he was. Lurking behind a tree was a mage—low level from what I could tell. Time to make my move.

Thug one grinned. "What is that?"

I smiled sweetly as I began pulling more and more power, holding my hands out, side by side, palms out. "What took you guys so long to attack? I've been out here, trudging back and forth, for three hours."

"Shit! She's a mage!" a frantic voice called at almost the same instant I clapped my hands together and pushed forward, palms out, forcing a wave of energy outwards.

The thug in front of me flew back four feet, landing against a tree at the edge of the road, but the second stood still, staring openmouthed at his unconscious buddy. Damn! I had underestimated the power level of the mage behind the tree. He'd detected me in time to throw up a barrier around himself and Thug two.

It only took a moment for Thug two to snap out of his stupor and charge. He was fast, but not fast enough. My hand shot behind my back and closed around the stick, whipping it around in time to jab the end into his solar plexus.

"Humph!" Wind whooshed out of him, mixing with a moan as he

doubled over.

"By the way, this isn't a stick," I said as I smoothly twirled it so that the other end slammed into the side of his head. "It's a hanbo."

He hit the ground with a thump and a howl. Letting out another howl, his skin began to crawl and shift. Suddenly, it wasn't skin anymore, but curly, brown fur. Within seconds, the thug's body was no longer recognizable as human. When he rose, he was a strange mixture of man and beast.

Shifters had three forms—their human, animal, and were. The were-form was something between human and animal. In were-form, a shifter had all the best characteristics of both human and animal. They were fast, strong, fierce, and terrifying looking. Shifters, especially those whose animal form was small, usually chose to do battle in were form, as Thug two had chosen to do now.

He stood a good six inches taller than he had as a human, his clothes hanging off him in shreds. His arms and legs were lengthened, and sharp claws jutted out of paws that had only moments ago been hands. Strangely enough, his face had morphed into a strange mixture of human and...

"Poodle? You're a were-poodle?" I couldn't stop the snort of laughter I let out as I spread my legs, bent my knees slightly, and gripped my hanbo in a defensive stance. Despite my derision, I was still cautious. Shifters had superhuman strength and speed, no matter what type of animal DNA they were fused with. But a poodle? That had to be as humiliating as being a were-mouse. It was hard to take the fluffy beast-man with floppy ears and a long snout seriously. Especially when the curly fur was matted and caked with mud.

The thug snarled, his lip curling back from long, sharp teeth. He let out a sound that was part howl and part bark, and charged at me. I held my stance until a second before his teeth made contact with the soft flesh of my shoulder. Effortlessly sidestepping, I brought my hanbo around to smash across his huge, muscled back. The force from my blow and his forward momentum sent him flying face-first into a tree. He collapsed to the ground unconscious.

I heard the other thug start coming to. "Oh no, you don't. Stay!" Spreading my arms out, I sent thin ropes of energy out to spiral around each of them. "That should hold you...oomph!"

Stumbling forward, I fell to my hands and knees, my hanbo flying out of my hands as a ball of energy hit me square in the back. *Damn!* I'd forgotten about the mage. Rolling to my back, I threw my hands up in front of my face.

"Shield!" As I screamed out the word, a field of protective energy encased me just as another burst of power snaked out of the trees. I felt the physical jolt as the shining, blue ball of energy hit the shield. If I'd been on my feet, it would have knocked the shit out of me. As it was, it sent me sliding back in the mud and grime a few feet. The mage must have cast an energy-cloaking spell earlier because now I sensed much more power.

In the now-full light of the moon, I could see a figure encased in a cloak moving from behind a tree and advancing on me, hands raised. "Get back!" I shouted, my hands pushing a wall of energy out. The mage toppled backwards with a grunt. While I didn't have to use words to manipulate energy, when I didn't have my staff in my hands, it helped me focus defensive magic. I had to get to my hanbo. In addition to being a powerful hand-to-hand combat weapon, the oak staff helped me focus my power and made it easier to draw and concentrate energy for use as a magical weapon.

Keeping the temporary shield up with one hand, I frantically searched the ground for my weapon. It was lying on the edge of the road about a foot beyond my reach. I was about to send out a rope of energy to float it to me when I felt a burst of power strike my shield. The mage was still down, but he was sending small balls of energy at me in rapid-fire succession in an attempt to weaken my defense. I couldn't split my focus to get the hanbo magically. Pulling in energy from the surrounding air, I focused it through my hand to bolster my shield. Using my feet, I pushed closer to the staff, letting out a disgusted groan as I slid through the mud and grime, rocks biting into my skin.

The balls of energy came faster and harder as the mage rose and began advancing. I pulled my legs up, dug my boots into the mud, and gave one last hard push. Gravel tore at my cloak and flesh as I slid across the road. Pain shot through me. Straining and stretching my arm out as far as I could, my hand searched through the grime as I kept my eyes focused on the advancing mage. His cloak had fallen back, and I could see his face. He was nothing more than a boy, barely of age, if I guessed right. He had a lot of power for a kid, and he was pretty good at focusing it. He was using offensive magic as well. The ability to form energy into visible bursts that could be used like a weapon was rare. I had only met two other mages besides myself who had the ability, one being my mother. We could both form energy into shining streams using a focusing tool. My mother had carried a thin, wooden wand to focus the energy. I preferred my hanbo staff. It was larger but could be used for fighting, and I could focus larger streams to blast out of the end. The other mage was a Blade in the Atlanta city-state division. We'd worked together on a case of gang smuggling between the two city-states. He hadn't used anything to focus the energy flow, but instead of a steady stream, he produced small, lightning-like bolts that appeared in the air and struck the target.

This was the first time I'd seen a mage able to form a ball of pure energy that could be thrown. Though there were many that could form and throw fireballs, this was very different. Fire magic was common. This kid was forming and throwing actual balls of pure energy. Rare indeed.

He was only a few paces away. Though I could tell by the strain on his face and the diminishing size of energy bursts that he was starting to tire and run out of energy, one good blast like the last one would disintegrate my shield, leaving me defenseless.

As he took another step and raised his hands for another assault, I felt the smooth oak of my hanbo. Gratefully, I closed my fingers around it. Bringing the staff around, I shifted all the energy I'd been using to shield myself directly into the thirty-six inches of smooth, carved wood and out the end. Just as the mage was bringing his hands down in what would have been a knockout blow of energy, a bolt of lightning shot from the end of the hanbo and struck him square in the chest. He let out a pitiful cry and crumpled to the ground.

Using the hanbo for leverage, I vaulted to my feet and hurried over to him. He was out cold, but still breathing. Lying there, he looked like a peaceful, sleeping child. He looked even younger than I first thought. Even in the dim light, I could see the smooth skin of his face with no sign of facial hair. Was he even sixteen?

He would likely be out for a while, but I didn't want to take any chances. I carefully wove a shield of null energy around him. It was a temporary measure and would dissipate in about an hour, but if he did wake up before I got him tied up and neutralized, he would be unable to use any magic.

Exhausted, I flopped down onto the ground next to him. For someone so young, the mage was strong. Fending him off had taken a lot of energy. Add that to the power I had just expended to neutralize the other creeps, and I could have gladly taken a long nap, even in the cold, wet mud. But, napping wasn't a part of my job, and the energy fields keeping them contained wouldn't last forever. I gave myself a few moments, rose to my feet, and, once again, wiped mud off my ass.

I whistled, and Mal calmly walked over to where I stood. "What happened to you?" I asked the horse as I rummaged through the saddlebags. "You couldn't kick him? Or even warn me he was behind me? What kind of partner are you?"

Mal stared at me silently, flicking his tail from side to side.

"Okay, I get it. He wasn't worthy of you unleashing your considerable badness on him." I laughed as I retrieved a thick, strong rope and three hanging crystals from the packs and went on with my business.

I used the dagger that rested on my hip to cut two lengths. First, I tied the mage's feet and hands. Then, I tied two of the crystals to the bindings and looped the third around his neck. Each crystal was charged with a powerful binding spell. The ropes would keep him from running, and the magic in the crystals would keep him from working magic.

With him secured, I moved on to the other two. The first thug was awake and just starting to struggle against his magical bindings. Now that I had more visibility, I could see that he, too, was barely more than a boy. I had no way of knowing if he were a shifter or not. He hadn't shifted, but the magical bonds I had wrapped around him would have prevented the change. He glared at me as I tied him up.

"What's your name?" I asked.

"Fuck you."

"Well, Mr. Fuck You, you are bound by law under my authority as an agent of the Black Blade Guard under the jurisdiction of the Paranorm Council of Elders." I almost felt sorry for him as the blood drained from his face. He was smart enough to realize the trouble he was in.

It was apparent they thought I was nothing more than a random traveler with a few fighting skills. He'd likely figured he could escape or bribe me into letting him go. Even if I were a guard from Nash, or one of the small villages in the area, sent out to hunt down the highwaymen that had been plaguing the travelers on the road for the past three months, the most they would face was a few months in prison or on a work crew. But the fact that I was a Blade changed their fate considerably. They would be taken into Nash City, but they would not be handed over to the City Guard there.

The Blades fell under the jurisdiction of the Paranorm Council of Elders. The Council and the Blades took a much grimmer view on paranorm crime. They would be tried by a tribunal of Blade judges and, if found guilty, they could face years of hard labor on a work crew, or even execution. Because they attacked a Blade, there would be no doubt of them being found guilty. What he didn't know was that I had been sent out on a mission to find and capture them. This meant they had become enough of a nuisance to draw the attention of the Blades, and it reduced the likelihood of a light sentence. I almost felt sorry for them. *Almost.*

"Ralph." His voice shook. "My name is Ralph. Please, we didn't hurt anyone. Don't kill us!"

I bit back a smile. A scared kid. "Well, it's not my call. You guys stole a lot of merchandise. That can't go unpunished."

"We only stole from merchants. They are rich enough to replace their stuff!" His tone was defiant.

"Really? Did you know that many of the merchants that use this road come from deep in the mountains? That they work for months to dry the meat and create the handcrafts they bring in to market? Did you know that the money and food they get in return will have to feed their clans for months until they can make the next trip to the market?"

"Umm. No. But…um. We only stole enough to sell to feed ourselves."

He was near tears now. Though I was feeling sorry for him, I didn't let it show in my voice or demeanor. There was more to this story, and I wouldn't be able to help them if he didn't tell me. The only way to keep his tongue loose was to keep him scared.

"Is that so? According to reports, you've stolen enough to feed you three scrawny boys for several months."

His face went white, and the reality of the situation dawned on me.

"How many of you are there?"

The defiance was back in his face, if not in his voice as he visibly struggled to be believable. "There is just the three of us. Do with us what you will, Blade."

A pang of sympathy slammed through me. I knew what it was like to be young and have people who depended on you for food and comfort. The truth was in his eyes.

"Look, Ralph, I can't make you many promises, but I can make this one. If you tell me the truth, I will make sure that whoever it is you are protecting is safe. I give you my word as a Blade. Think about it this way… who is going to take care of them if the three of you just disappear?"

His expression was stony.

"Okay, don't tell me right now. I'll let you talk it over with your buddies once I get you back to Nash City."

Leaving him to ponder on the deep shit he was in, I moved on to

Thug two and groaned. He had changed back into human form and was now lying naked in the mud. I grabbed the mage's cloak and wrapped him in it before binding his arms and legs. He had shaggy beard and looked to be a couple of years older than the other two, but he was still just a kid.

Once they were all tied, I used my magic to float them to the middle of the road, side by side. I didn't dare remove the strands of energy that encased them. The mage was pretty well neutralized, but the ropes were not close to strong enough to hold a fully shifted were-beast of any kind. The thin strands of energy were the only thing keeping them from shifting. Now I had to figure out how to get them back to the city.

"Mal, watch them. Stomp on them if they move." The eyes of the conscious boy went wide as the horse snorted as if in agreement.

"He won't really stomp us, will he?" he stammered.

"We'll never know unless you try to escape. If I were you, I wouldn't test him. He's in a bad mood over having to be out in the rain tonight." We had that in common.

Leaving Mal to watch over the three boys, I headed into the woods. There had been a time when this area had been a highly populated suburb of the metropolis of Nashville. But that had been over two hundred years ago, when the city had spanned over five hundred square miles and boasted almost a million inhabitants just within the city limits. Now, most of the buildings and homes were gone and the woods had overtaken everything. The nearest village was more than ten miles away. That meant the gang had to have a hideout or transportation nearby. Though they were young and stupid, I doubted they were attacking people close to where they lived, especially if they were providing for children younger than themselves, as I suspected.

Horses were expensive, and most petty thieves couldn't afford them. But this gang had been preying on merchants for months. Reports said they had stolen dozens of horses, mules, and oxen. It was likely they had sold most of their ill-gotten gains, but odds were they'd kept some of the animals to get around.

I tromped through the overgrown brush, my senses open to detect if there were any more of the gang hidden somewhere. The reports consistently indicated there only being three of them, but I couldn't be too careful.

About a mile from the road, I felt the presence of three more beings. I knew immediately they weren't human. I'd found the gang's horses. The underbrush was too thick to ride through, so I had to lead them to the road on foot. By the time I got back, it had started to rain again.

Well, I thought. *At least the rain will wash away some of this mud.*

As quickly as I could, I loaded the now-awake gang onto the horses, tossing them over the saddles like sacks of grain. I tied their reins together and then attached a longer lead rope. Climbing onto Mal's back, I leaned down and rubbed his neck.

"Come on, Big Bad; let's go get some of those crunchy oats."

He was off like a shot. This time, I used magic to keep the rain off Mal and me, as well as to light the way. I didn't bother covering the gang.

TWO
Fiona

A LITTLE OVER TWO HUNDRED YEARS AGO IN THE YEAR OF TECHNOLOGY CALLED 2012, the North and South Poles started shifting. It was gradual at first and lasted a couple of decades. When it was over, the shift wasn't exactly ninety degrees, but it was close enough that east became north, north became west, and so on. The shift caused a climatic Cataclysm that pounded the world with storms, earthquakes, and other natural disasters for more than forty years.

Damn Mayans.

Whole cities were destroyed, and governments crumbled. Famine ran rampant. Widespread panic caused wars, which killed even more than the natural disasters and starvation. When the smoke and weather finally cleared, the world had changed drastically. What had once been the Eastern United States was now a peninsula called Appalachia made up of a range of mountains in the west and bordered by the Atlantic Ocean in the north and east, as well as the newly formed Mississippi Sea in the south. Only two major cities, what had once been Nashville and Atlanta, remained partially standing. From those ruins rose the autonomous city-states of Nash and Atlanta. For more than fifty years after the start of the Cataclysm, every city, town, and community was at war with each other and internally. Finally, the Paranorm Council of Elders stepped in to bring peace and unity. While the two city-states were completely autonomous in rule, they were allied under the Council of Elders along with three other city-states—Okie City and Sanlou to the south, and New Winnipeg in the west. Many areas in the south and west had resisted the Council. Some set up legitimate governments of their own, but many others were ruled by warlords and tyrants.

The city-state of Nash claimed jurisdiction over several small fishing, farming, and industrial villages throughout southern Appalachia, but the main part of it was built around the heart of the original city and separated into two main parts—Nash City and New Nashville.

The walls of Nash City rose up out of the ground like a lumpy, gray fortress. Sentries marched along the top. The path and most of the materials for the walls of Nash City had once been a vast highway that looped around downtown Nashville. But when the Cataclysm began, mages and other paranorms used it as the building blocks of a wall to protect the people who huddled within.

The road up to the North Gate was crowded with travelers and merchants waiting to get inside the city. I scanned the crowd discreetly as I moved through.

There were a few travelers as well that carried only themselves and a pack. Others had horses or donkeys, and some were on foot. Some of them would seek a job and housing in Nash, but most of them would stay a night or two and then move on. Those who chose traveling as a way of life usually formed gypsy caravans because it was safer to travel in a group.

Most bands of gypsies were harmless and could provide market wares from far to the North. But there was one group I always kept an eye out for. They hadn't ventured back into Nash City in more than fourteen years, but I still watched for them. I wasn't a child anymore, and I now had the power of the Blades behind me. If I ever laid eyes on any of them again, I would make them pay for what they had done to my sister.

None of the travelers I saw looked like they were together. Satisfied, I wove Mal and the gang's horses past wagons and carts loaded with baskets of assorted fruits and vegetables, bolts of cloth, wood and clay dishes, and other assorted goods. Smiling, I nodded to the merchants as I passed. I recognized most of them as inhabitants of nearby villages who came to the market several times a week. Others, the ones that were much more roughly garbed and looked a bit unkempt, I knew were from much further away. They only ventured from their mountain dens every couple of months to bring their wares to the city to sell.

I reached the gate and approached the guard tower where the gate guard sat in a tiny room. Behind him, a large window opening allowed him to be on eye level with anyone requesting entrance to the gate.

"Fiona Moon of the Black Blade Guard requesting entrance," I called, raising my arm to show the tattoo of black-bladed crossed swords beneath a fleur-de-lis on my right wrist.

"The gates open in one hour," the guard called back.

"You will open them to me now," I replied in a slightly raised voice.

"I can't. The crowd is too thick. If I open, they will all rush in. I have strict orders from my captain to let no one in before the dawn bell rings." His voice was young and nervous, and I could see the distress on his face.

"Okay. Apparently, you're new," I said, trying not to get too pissed off. "I'm going to repeat myself one time, and one time only. I am Fiona Moon of the Black Blade Guard, and you *will* open these gates, now."

I nudged Mal several paces closer to the guard's tower and held my arm up again. This time muttering a spell to illuminate it in the pre-dawn haze just to make sure he saw it.

"I have three fugitives that I need to take into Blade Headquarters," I continued, my calm tone edged with steel. "Because you are new, I will explain this to you. This tattoo identifies me as a Blade. As a Blade, I have a higher authority than your captain and every other officer in the City-Guard, for that matter. Protocol dictates that you immediately let me enter, no matter the time of day or night."

A hoot of laughter echoed through the air, and I looked up to see a mage-guard I recognized as Carter on top of the tower. He had been the gate guard for many years. He must have gotten promoted when this newbie took his place. Only the best mage-guards were assigned to the towers. He wasn't even trying to hide his laughter.

"Burke," he called down between guffaws. "If you don't let her in, you will have much bigger problems than the captain!"

"Um... okay. Sorry. You can pass," Burke said nervously. I could tell he was horrified at his mistake. In a much stronger, authoritative voice, he called out, "Everyone, stand back. Only the Blade has permission to enter the city. Anyone attempting to pass will be arrested."

Clearing his voice, he called out to the guards behind the wall. "Open the gates a quarter."

There was a loud creak and groan as the intricate pulley system worked to slide the heavy gates. It stopped when the opening was wide enough for a horse to fit through. I led the horses through the narrow opening without another word to the guard. Once we were through, the gates creaked and moaned again as they closed with a thud.

I called an absent "Thanks" to the guardsmen on either side of the gate, who were pulling the heavy ropes, but I didn't feel the need to thank the gatekeeper. As I rode away, I heard the laughing tower guard let out a hoot and call down to the gatekeeper.

"Wow! Of all the Blades to piss off on your first day on duty, you had to pick Moon! You are lucky she wasn't in a bad mood."

"She didn't seem so tough!" the gatekeeper called back, either thinking I was out of earshot or not caring.

"Stop a minute, Mal. I need to teach someone a lesson," I whispered so that only he could hear. He pulled to a stop and turned slightly so I could clearly see the guard tower.

I pulled my hanbo from its sheath across my back and pointed it towards the tower. Concentrating, I pulled in power and then shot it out of the end in a visible line of white light. The energy shot straight through the bars on the gatekeeper's room and hitting the stone wall barely three inches above Burke's head. The gatekeeper stared openmouthed as I moved the line of energy in a pattern. When the energy bolt dissipated, there was a Blade symbol identical to my tattoo permanently etched into the stone.

I held back the laughter that threatened to bubble up as the look on his face went from shock to fear.

"There, now. The next time you see that mark, you will know to let the person in. Have a good day," I called back, loud enough for Burke, Carter, and all the guards in the vicinity to hear.

Mal snorted, clearly amused, as we resumed down the road. Behind us, I heard peals of laughter erupt from several of the guards. Poor Burke wouldn't hear the end of it for a while. I almost felt sorry for him. But I had a reputation to uphold and if I'd let his ignorance and rudeness go unpunished, I would have been opening myself up to ridicule from the whole City Guard.

One didn't become a member of the elite Black Blade Guard by being kind or easy. Blades were the toughest, most powerful paranorms in the world. A Blade had to be willing to back that reputation up with action. That went double for women. Though there were many female City Guards, there were few female Blades, and even fewer of those were non-vampires. Having super strength and speed commanded a certain amount of respect, but I had to gain and keep respect by the demonstration of my power and ability to use it. And I had done just that.

Since starting the Academy ten years ago when I turned fourteen, and being appointed to the Black Blade Guard years earlier than any other mage in history, I'd worked hard to obtain and maintain my reputation as the toughest mage in the Blades. It was the same reputation my mother had before me, and I intended to keep it.

The lower part of the Black Blade Guard Headquarters building held stables and a temporary prisoner holding area. Nine floors beneath the main building were made of concrete and steel. They had been built to house the huge metal, gas-burning cars people had once used to get around. Now the top two levels were used to stable the horses and mules owned by Blades or, like the three I'd hauled the gang in on, had been confiscated from criminals. Those animals would be temporarily stabled here, and then taken to the public city stables to be sold.

I paused at the stables, handing off Mal and the other horses to a stable-hand to be brushed and fed the promised oats. Luckily, all three teenagers were awake so I didn't have to float any of them along on a current of magic. Untying their feet, I used the rope as a lead. I wasn't surprised they followed along meekly. Fear was a palpable cloud hanging around them.

I led them down a flight of stairs to the processing area of the temporary prisoner holding facility. While the upper level of the stable areas had wide-open spaces between the walls that were covered only with wire mesh, the lower levels were completely underground, making them perfect for holding the dangerous paranormal criminals the Blades apprehended.

The criminals were held here until a tribunal was convened to decide their fate. Then they were either executed or transported to one of the prison compounds outside the city in the Outer Zone to work off their sentence.

I looked back at the squirming boys shuffling along behind me. As strong and powerful as they were, I doubted they would survive long in prison. The Blades established the work compounds as a way to contain paranormal criminals while making them contribute to the welfare of society. Each compound had a specialty: farming, manufacturing, or mining. The inmates worked to produce food or goods that were made available to the city-state district the compound was located in. The conditions were barely livable, the guards were cruel, and the prisoners were more so.

While there were other work farms established by the city-state's senate and ran by City Guards, the criminals housed there were norms or non-violent, low-level mages. The prisoners at the Blade Compounds weren't the worst paranormal criminals society had to offer. The worst offenders were executed with little delay, but they were only about one step down. You only went to a Blade farm once. If you offended again and were caught, you were executed.

While they had robbed dozens of travelers and merchants over the past few months and made quite a nuisance of themselves, these were not hardened criminals. They had only caught the attention of the senate when the wealthy merchant cousin of one of the senators was robbed. Normally, the City Guard would have taken care of such a minor offense, but the senator had thrown such a fit that the Black Blade liaison to the senate had agreed to send one of the best Blades out to investigate.

Thus, I had mucked through the mud and rain for hours tonight. As annoyed as I was, I couldn't see condemning these kids to death, and I was sure that a council work farm would be as sure of a death sentence as execution.

Once I got them to the processing area, I split them up and interrogated each of them separately. The were-poodle was Georgie, the mage was Simon, and they gave the same story as Ralph. They had also clammed up and become defiant when the subject of others in their gang came up. The fear energy they gave off ramped up a few notches at the same time.

That, in itself, wasn't uncommon. A lot of the gangs roaming the Outer Zones kept their members in line using fear and control. Ratting out your gang was a death sentence. That wasn't the vibe I got off these kids, however. It was fear, but more like a concern for, not fear of.

I couldn't explain why I was sure of that. It was one of the more peculiar manifestations of my power. I wasn't an empath; I didn't feel the emotions of others. When I concentrated, I could see the energy patterns that radiated from them, almost like an aura. While I'd met only a few mages with the ability to channel energy into offensive bursts, I'd never met another that could "read" the type of energy people gave off. But then, I hadn't asked either. Even in this day and age, where magic was a scientifically proven fact and a part of daily life, having an unusual power could be dangerous.

It took me almost two hours to get the three of them questioned, processed, and into holding cells. Once they were settled in, I headed upstairs into Blade Headquarters. Though I sorely wanted a long, hot soak at a bathhouse and a clean change of clothes, I needed to report the success of my mission to my boss, Sam. I also needed to talk to him about the fate of the three boys I'd hauled in.

The building had been built in the height of the Tech Age and was thirty-three stories high, in addition to the nine underground levels. The building housed the headquarters of the entirety of the Black Blade Guard for the region. There was a headquarters in each of the Paranorm Council allied city-states. While a few Blades from other regions visited Nash occasionally, I had never been to the headquarters for any other region.

The headquarters' offices were on the top five floors. The levels between held rooms and apartments for Blade operatives to use when they had to visit headquarters as a home base when not on assignment. Some, like me, chose to live in their family homes within the city, but many did not live within the city-state or did not have permanent homes elsewhere. The building also housed a healing clinic, a bathhouse, combat training facilities, and barracks for Blade Cadets.

I used the stairs to get back up to the ground level, and then crossed to the stairwell to go up to the main entrance of the building. From there, I crossed over to the crystal-powered lifts. The staircases were used primarily by cadets who lived on the first few floors and did not have clearance to access other portions of the building and by vampires that didn't get winded just by the prospect of trudging up thirty flights of stairs.

I pushed up the barred gate that served as a door to the lift. Once inside, I pulled down the gate, flipped open the smallest pouch on my leather belt, and pulled out a small piece of intricately cut crystal.

On the wall, there was a series of numbers. Beside each, there was a hole. I pressed my crystal into the one next to the number thirty. The etchings on the crystal and the special spell charged into it by Blade Chargers worked together to activate the clockwork gears that pulled the lift car up and down via thick ropes and pulleys. A series of clicks, then a loud grinding, filled the small chamber before the lift lurched and slowly began to rise. After a few moments, the lift rumbled to a shuddering stop and I stepped out.

"Moon! Get in here!" Sam Harrison's voice rumbled through the scry-crystal mounted on the wall next to the lift.

I hated when he did that.

Muttering under my breath, I made my way down the hall. Though the glow had gone out of the scry-crystal—meaning it was no longer activated—I knew that even over the clicks from typewriters and ongoing conversations in many of the offices on the floor, he'd still be able to hear me.

My boss used his keen were-leopard senses to monitor the comings and goings on the floor. It was a good practice, I supposed, but it always felt weird, especially since there were two long hallways and ten offices full of people between the elevator and his office.

I opened the door to Sam's office without knocking and walked in without an invitation. His office, though the biggest on the floor, seemed small with the massive wooden desk in the middle of it and the just-as-massive dark-skinned man sitting behind it.

Sam appeared to be in his mid-thirties. But I'd known the big man all of my life and he'd never looked any different. I guessed he was older. A lot older. Shifters usually aged a little slower than norms and had a life span of around 150 years or so, but there was something different about Sam. One of my best friends was a five-hundred-year-old vampire that had been trained as a Blade shortly after he'd been turned. Sam had been his trainer. Everyone knew he was different, but no one knew exactly how, and no one questioned it. Even in a world of magic, vampires, and shifters, no one dared question a six-foot-four-inch two-hundred-pound man with super-human strength and the speed and senses of a leopard.

"You've really got to stop doing that! You're never going to get a woman if you make us all feel like we reek," I said as I plopped down into the wooden chair in front of his cluttered desk.

"You do reek. Did you take a mud bath?" He scrunched his lean, olive-toned face in mock distaste.

"As a matter of fact, I did. Courtesy of the highwaymen on the West Trade Road."

"Don't tell me they got away."

I rolled my eyes. "You know me better than that!"

Sam's laugh was rich and deep. "I take that to mean they are safely in the prison hold awaiting tribunal."

"Yes." I shifted in the chair, leaning forward to rest my elbows on the edge of Sam's desk. "They are in the hold, but I'm not sure a tribunal is the best thing in this case."

A tribunal only had two possible outcomes—execution or council work compound.

Sam let out an exasperated sigh and leaned back in his chair, his hands clasped behind his head. "Okay, what is it this time?"

"They are kids, Sam. And don't sit there and look at me like I'm some sort of bleeding heart. You know every time I've ever had a gut feeling about something like this, I've been right."

Sam sat up straight. "I don't think the feeling comes from your gut, but you usually are right. Tell me about these kids."

Sam was one of the very few people that knew about my ability to read energy, but we rarely spoke about it aloud. One never knew when a paranorm with super hearing would be lurking nearby.

"Three boys, half brothers, all under nineteen. The two eldest are shifters, the youngest is a mage. Sam, this kid has offensive energy magic, and he almost kicked my ass with it."

Sam pushed books and papers to the side to clear his desk a little and jotted notes down on the blotter.

"A lot of power, even a rare power, isn't a reason to give mercy. Actually, it could be an argument for the opposite."

I sighed. "I know, I know. But I think that would be a mistake. This kid has mega potential. He forms and throws balls of energy for fuck's sake! I've never seen anything like it. I can't get that much energy together without a wand to focus through and Cramer, that mage from Atlanta, could only form weak lightning bolts. This kid has power and a modicum of control over it. With training, he could be one hell of a Blade."

"Okay," Sam said. "But why do you think he would work for us? He's been robbing merchants for months. You think he's going to give up his gang? They rarely do."

I detailed the reactions I got from each of the boys during interrogation and my ideas about what they may be hiding.

Sam stopped making notes. "So, you think they are protecting younger siblings?"

"Yeah, that, or younger and weaker orphans. Families don't always share blood."

Realization slowly spread across Sam's handsome features. "I suppose you would know that better than anyone." He paused, as if trying to decide whether to give in right away or make me work for it a little. "Okay, what do you propose I do?"

I smiled, knowing I had gotten my way. "I don't know exactly. I can tell you this, that mage needs to be at the Academy. He has amazing gifts that need to be developed and tamed." I thought a moment. "I can also tell you he won't do anything without his brothers. And not one of them will accept the Academy, even if the only other option is death, unless they are sure whoever it is they are protecting will be well taken care of."

Sam let out a long-suffering sigh. "What kind of talent did the shifters show?"

"Not terribly bright," I laughed at the memory, "but pretty nimble. I caught them off guard with my defenseless female act, but I have a feeling if given half the chance, they'd be fierce fighters."

"You do realize there is a problem. Councilor Nesbit has been shrieking for the heads of the highwaymen that attacked his cousin. There is no way he would agree to leniency."

I smiled sweetly. "Of course he has. And he has every right to ask for the maximum punishment when or if those highwaymen are caught. However, I have no evidence these three, very young boys, could be those highwaymen. No loot has been confiscated, and nothing was stolen from my person. As the arresting agent, the only charges I can file against them are for attempted theft, resisting arrest, and assault on a Blade. As the Blade in question, I am open to more productive forms of rehabilitation for these three misguided youngsters."

I think everyone on the floor could hear the thud of Sam's forehead hitting his palms. He sat there like that for a minute, his elbows on the desk, his face hidden in his hands. When he looked up, his face was resigned.

"I suppose that is the testimony you will give before the tribunal if one is convened?"

I nodded solemnly. "Absolutely."

He let out a loud sigh and leaned back in his chair. "Okay. I'll take care of it. I'll go down myself and talk to them. It shouldn't be too hard to get dispensation to use entry into the Academy as an alternative to a tribunal and punishment. If this mage is as powerful as you say, then it won't be hard to show that he would be an asset. And we can always use even moderately powered shifters."

I grinned. "Thanks Sam!"

"Don't thank me yet. They have to actually agree to it. I just pray their "gang" isn't a whole town full of thugs!"

I laughed at his exaggerated grimace. "I'm pretty sure it's not. And I have faith you can make them see the wisdom of making the right choice." I got up and headed for the door. "Now, I'm off for a hot bath and bed."

"Not so fast. I didn't call you in for your report. I have an assignment for you."

"Now?" I groaned and sagged against the doorframe.

"Yes, now. Right now, as a matter of a fact. I planned to scry you before I smelled you come onto the floor. I got a scry this morning from Sonny down at the city crematorium. It seems there is something wrong with a body that was brought in last night. He needs a necromancer down there. So, I need you to go as escort for the necromancer and officially witness whatever the problem is."

"Wrong?" My curiosity was piqued. "And why call us instead of the City Guard? They would have been the one to take the body in. And why would he need a necromancer? He is one."

"He just said it was something he'd never seen before, and he needed the most powerful necromancer available."

I groaned. "The most powerful?"

"Yes, and Sonny knows Barroes works exclusively with the Blades."

"Why me?" I asked the question, although I was afraid I knew the answer.

"Because Barroes asked for you."

I groaned again. "Shit."

THREE
Fiona

There were three types of people I didn't like—the elite rich, academics, and necromancers. Ian Barroes was all three. To make matters worse, he was the only man I had ever met that could make me feel like my blood would overheat and melt me into a quivering mass just by being in the same room with him. Mother Earth, I hated him!

Maybe hate was too strong. I didn't know him well enough to hate him, but I had a strong dislike. Ian Barroes was the founder and head of the Necromancy Guild as well as a professor at the Academy of Magic and Science. Every necromancer in Nash was required to register with the guild. I had to admit that the guild brought a modicum of accountability to a profession that was riddled with liars and thieves, but I still thought it was too little and way too late for those who'd been swindled by so-called necromancers.

Despite my opinion of necromancers in general and Barroes specifically, they were often employed by the City Guard and Blades to assist with magical investigations. Part of the guild's function was to work as a sort of employment agency for members. An individual or organization could contract with the guild for a job and the guild would then assign a necromancer to the position. The Blades had a standing account with a number of necromancers on call at all times. As the head of the Guild, Barroes generally didn't contract out his skills and when he did, it was exclusively for the Blades. He spent most of his time teaching the History of Necromancy to students at the Academy of Science and Magic.

He was arrogant beyond measure and every time we worked together, we denigrated into arguments and petty squabbles. I couldn't understand why in Hades he insisted on working with me whenever a case that needed his expertise came up. Luckily, that wasn't very often.

I stopped on the second floor of the headquarters' building to make a quick visit to the baths. I didn't have time to go home and change out of my muddy clothes, so the best I could do was wipe some of the grime off my face.

The entire floor was enveloped in soap-scented steam. The morning rush on the baths was over. The washroom was empty save an attendant trying to clean up, and a couple of cadets who were rushing to get dressed and to classes they were clearly already late for. I smiled to myself as the two girls ran past me, sliding on the damp floor on their way out. I'd been in their shoes a time or two when I was a cadet.

I caught a glimpse of myself in the steamed-up mirror as I made my way over to a washbasin. My foul mood came crashing back and ratcheted up a few knots. I looked like an unwashed mountain rat! Mud was caked on my clothes and smeared on my arms, neck, and face. And were those sticks in my hair? I reached up and picked one out. Yep, mud and sticks.

"I have a tub available in the stall at the end of the row. Would you like oil or soap bubbles in the water?"

I turned to see a small woman in a light gray bath attendant uniform looking at me expectantly. "Actually, I don't have time to bathe, and I don't have any clothes. I just need to get some of this muck off me."

A dismayed look crossed the woman's face as she turned and walked away. I nearly laughed out loud. Obviously, the woman thought I was a lost cause and wanted no part of it.

I turned my attention back to the mirror and resumed picking sticks out of my mess of hair. The band I'd had it pulled back in had obviously come untied during my fight with the gang and now the raven-black locks were in a massive tangle around my shoulders.

"Here you go, dear." The woman's voice startled me. I looked down and found that the attendant had brought a huge stack of cloth rags and soap. "You start on your hair," the woman said, handing me a comb.

"Thank you," I said and did as I was told. As I picked out the knots, wincing, the attendant pumped water into the washbasin. She deftly dipped a rag in and lathered it up with soap. She held it out to me and pointed to a small chair she'd brought over.

"Sit," she said, taking the comb.

I sat and began wiping the muck from my face and arms as the woman finished smoothing out my hair and pulled it back with a length of ribbon she'd pulled out of the pocket of her white apron. When she was through, she took another rag and scraped as much mud off my clothes as she could.

Within five minutes, I was as presentable as possible. I thanked the woman and left her two bucks. The woman smiled and blushed. Two bucks was a pretty large tip, especially since the Blades paid attendants well and one usually did not tip them as you did in a public bathhouse. However, the woman had been kind, helpful, and probably deserved more because I doubt I could have cleaned myself up as quickly or as well alone.

I was hoping to be able to go straight home after my visit to the morgue, so I didn't bother to get Mal. I didn't have anywhere to stable him at home, so he lived at the Blade stables. That had never been much of a problem because I lived barely a block away from Headquarters.

The sun was starting to brighten and burn off the morning fog, and the streets were crowded with people on bicycles or riding in hired rickshaws. Horses, mules, and oxen were too expensive to use for pleasure transportation and were mostly used for hauling wagons full of goods.

While convenient and faster than walking long distances in the city, the small two- or four-seater carriages pulled by a bicycle rider did not go very fast. Magic-powered rickshaws and buggies were faster, but there were few magic-powered rickshaws for hire. Most drivers owned their rickshaws and lived off the earnings; not many could afford the expensive mechanism that used water and charged crystals to power the rickshaw.

If they could save up enough to buy the water engine, the weekly cost of recharging the crystals would make it too expensive to operate. The small magic-powered buggies on the roads were owned by those rich enough to afford the upkeep. Larger, magic-powered surreys and carriages were much rarer, as the water engines in them were powered by several large crystals, thus making them much more expensive. The few large carriages on the road were owned by the elite class who could both afford the vehicles and employ a driver.

The morgue was only four blocks away. In the morning crush, I could walk it faster than a rickshaw would be able to navigate the traffic, but first I had to get across the street. Though there were stop signs at a few of the major intersections, the closest one was three blocks away in the wrong direction. So, I waited for the right moment and dashed into the street. I reached the other side just in time to avoid getting plowed down by a team of oxen pulling a cart full of crates.

I reached the morgue a few minutes later and rushed in, hoping I'd beat Ian. As I expected, my luck for the day hadn't gotten any better. He was standing in the waiting area, looking coolly impatient.

"Good morning, Miss Moon. It's so good of you to finally join us." His tone was cool and formal. His lips formed a smirk as he looked me up and down, taking in my disheveled appearance.

Of course, he was perfectly groomed. His chestnut hair just touched his ears and the collar of the light tan shirt that peeked out from under his dark brown leather vest. Even the leather boots his perfectly creased khaki pants were tucked into were spotlessly free of dirt and grime, despite the fact that the streets were still muddy from the night's rain.

Damn the man. He had his perfectly shaped nose so high in the air I wondered how he didn't drown when it rained. He was probably afraid I'd get dirt on his spotless and perfectly creased person.

"For shit's sake, Barroes, do we have to go through this every single time we work together? Call me Fiona, or Agent Moon, if you prefer. Don't wrinkle your damned nose at me. Some of us actually have to work for a living. Sometimes, that means getting a little dirty. Can we just go in and see what the hell is going on so I can go home and change?"

The smirk widened into a full-on grin, and he gave me a mocking, sweeping bow. "After you, milady," he said, gesturing towards the door to the back room.

I huffed and barely resisted the urge to punch him in the jaw as I swept by him.

The morgue attendant, Sonny, was sitting at a desk in the far corner of the room when we came in. He immediately got up and rushed over to us. "Agent Moon, Master Barroes, thank you for coming."

I smiled at him. I liked Sonny. He was sweet, kind, and chose to use his power in a job that served others. He was a necromancer, all the morgue attendants were. It made their jobs easier and made it easier for Guards. Under normal circumstances, an outside necromancer wasn't called in when a City Guard or Blade needed to question a spirit attached to a recently deceased body. Though every working necromancer in the city was required to be registered with the guild, the morgue attendants worked directly for the city. Necromancers from the guild were only called in for investigations where there wasn't a body at the morgue or there might be spirit "witnesses" to a crime.

This didn't seem to be either of those situations, so I couldn't understand why Sonny, normally very competent, felt like he needed outside help. Not only that, but I felt the distinct energy of nervousness.

"Hi, Sonny," I said as calmly and soothingly as I could manage. "What is the problem?"

"Last night, a young woman was attacked in an alley. She was able to get away from her attacker by kicking him in the chest. He was dead when the Guard brought him in. But there is a problem with the body."

"What is the problem?" asked Ian.

"Well, sir," Sonny fumbled, "I think you should examine it yourself and see."

Ian raised an eyebrow, but said, "Ok. Let's see the body."

Sonny led us to a long table at the back of the room.

FOUR
Ian

It could be successfully argued that no one in the city-state of Nash, and perhaps the entirety of Appalachia, knew more about Necromancy than Professor Ian Barroes, or Master Barroes, as was his title as the head of Nash City Necromancer's Guild. He came from a long family line of necromancers who believed strongly in recording and passing down their history and knowledge.

He had been actively practicing since he was three years old. His mother had seen the rare strength of his power, even at a young age, and had told his father. From that moment on, Ian had been put through rigorous tests to confirm his power, and he had been thrown into the family business by his sixth birthday.

Having a rich family opened many doors to him, including the closed doors of the City-State Private Archives and Library. As a boy, he spent many hours there and in his family's extensive private library, hiding from his father, and learning and reading everything related to Necromancy and other forms of magic he could get his hands on. When he was old enough, the family money enabled him to enter the Academy of Magic and Science. He was among the first civilIans to be accepted into the college. Up until then, only City Guard and Black Blade Cadets had been formally educated in history, science, and magic. Still today, only cadets and students that entered into a service contract with one of the local guilds received free education, and few families could afford the tuition.

The mages who had measured his power upon entry to the college had been amazed. Even today, anyone who knew anything about Necromancy would argue that Ian was the most powerful necromancer they had ever encountered. And even they had no idea of the true scope of his powers.

Unfortunately, his skills were not helping him now, which is why he was confused. Confusion was not something he had ever dealt with before, and he didn't like it.

Ian was a man of practicality. He didn't consider it conceited to know one's own power and abilities. It was how one knew their limits. In the past, he had never reached a limit in regards to Necromancy that he couldn't push past. His experiences had been vast, and he'd learned from each one. Yet, never, in his entire life, had he ever seen anything such as this. He wracked his brain, but nothing he had ever read or seen came even close. He could find no practical explanation. But he knew that was wrong. There was a practical explanation for everything.

Facts. He had to start with the known facts. He stared at the body, trying to piece together what he knew.

The Blade had said the body was less than twenty-four-hours old. But that couldn't be. The body was dry and shriveled, as if it had been dead for months, or even years. Yet there was no decomposition, no rotting flesh to support that theory. But the most intriguing and perplexing complication was the lack of energy around the body.

Every living thing was made of energy. Even objects most would say were not living, like rocks, vibrated with energy. That energy didn't die or cease to exist. In living beings, specifically humans, the energy that made up their essence stayed strong even after the body died. It could stay connected to the body for up to a year. After that, it began to lesson and float free as what most people called ghosts. Eventually, that energy would be absorbed back into the energy of other living beings, but it took centuries for that to happen.

Necromancers had the ability to see and communicate with that energy. The longer the body had been dead, the more powerful a necromancer had to be to communicate with the energy. Any untrained mage with level-one necromantic powers would be able to communicate with a twenty-four-hour dead spirit.

Ian's power level was the highest ever recorded for a necromancer. He could communicate with spirits whose bodies had died several centuries before. He opened his senses and let his power flow full force. About a dozen translucent images of varying strengths appeared around him. Spirits that were strong enough, and wished to, usually took the form of the body they had inhabited. Newly dead spirits who still clung to their physical form always appeared as a ghostly form of their living body. The morgue was filled with the energy of spirits still attached to bodies and a few unattached, weaker spirits. But none of them belonged to this body. Not even any of the older spirits here had once belonged to this body. The problem was that there was no energy surrounding this body, no spirit to be called.

Ian pulled in his power and closed his senses until every spirit had vanished from his sight. This was useless and getting him nowhere.

"Miss..."

"Agent. You may call me Agent Moon or Fiona, no Miss," she answered curtly.

"Yes, yes," Ian said absently. He knew she hated being called "Miss," and he loved irritating her. The barb had been automatic, but while he loved the way her eyes flashed when she was annoyed and usually enjoyed making them do so, he had no time to deal with Miss Cranky Pants right now. "Fiona. You are certain this is the body involved in the attack?"

She bristled. "As certain as I can be. I wasn't at the scene, and I got here at the same time as you."

"You there, Sonny." He called his attention to the morgue attendant who was standing on the other side of the room, pretending not to be paying attention to them. When the young man walked over to them, Ian asked, "You are certain this is the body that was brought in last night? The one that attacked a young girl?"

The Morgue necromancer stammered, "Yes, sir. I'm sure. It is the only body that has been brought in this week."

Before Ian could ask him another question, Fiona broke in.

"This is the damned body. What is this? Just call the spirit or whatever it is you do, ask him why he attacked the girl, and then tell me so I can go. I've got things to do."

"Miss..." He stopped himself at her sharp look. He'd purposefully intended to bait her, but thought better of it. She looked as if she would throw him through the nearest window if he finished that phrase.

"Fiona," he corrected. He carefully measured his tone as he explained,

"As you can see, this body does not look as if it was alive just last night. Furthermore, I cannot speak to the spirit attached to this body because there is not one."

"Maybe you just aren't strong enough."

He forced himself to stay calm. "I can assure you, I am. If the spirit associated with this body were within a hundred miles of here and less than a thousand years old, I could call it here."

The look on her face told him the seriousness of the situation was starting to dawn on her.

"You are telling me there is no way this body attacked a girl last night?"

"No. I am telling you I cannot contact energy connected with this body. Without further evidence, I can't make any conclusions. I need to speak with the girl."

She turned to Sonny. "What did you find when you examined the body?"

Sonny looked nervously from Ian to Fiona and back to Ian. She had put the man in a difficult position. Technically, he didn't work for Ian, and as an official city employee, he did not rely on getting work from the Guild. However, most necromancers wouldn't like to be asked to contradict the head of the Guild. He was the founder and leader for a reason, after all. However, as a Blade, Fiona would be considered as the ranking official in this circumstance and refusing to answer would make her cranky. Waiting until her head was turned away from him, Ian gave a slight, nearly imperceptible nod for the man to answer.

Sonny took a deep breath. "It is exactly as Master Barroes said."

The man didn't seem to notice Fiona's eye roll when he'd used the formal title, but Ian did. Though the "Master" moniker could be used for any mage with Master-level powers, it was reserved for Ian within the Guild. He had never insisted on its use, didn't really like it for that matter, but to point that out would be to hurt the feelings of those who used it not as a sign of supremacy, but as a sign of respect.

Sonny made his way over to stand next to the body. "This body was brought in late last night. I knew something was wrong the moment I looked at it. It certainly does not look like a fresh, hours-dead body. It doesn't have any decomposition either. Except for being dry and brittle, it is completely intact. So, I began trying to contact the spirit of the man the body belonged to. But, like Master Barroes said, there is no spirit."

Fiona's frown deepened. "No spirit at all? Is that even possible?"

The morgue attendant looked Fiona straight in the eye. "Agent Moon, a few hours ago, I would have told you it was not possible. That is why I called Agent Sam and asked for Master Barroes. I have been training as necromancer since I was sixteen years old. My powers are moderate, but I have a good understanding of Necromancy. I've been working at this job for ten years. I have never seen a body completely void of energy, and I didn't think it was possible. I hoped maybe it was just a very weak spirit that only a Master could contact.

"Unfortunately, Sonny, I haven't seen anything quite like this either. I would like to talk to the girl about what she saw. Maybe that can help us get to the bottom of this." Ian glared pointedly at Fiona.

Wordlessly, Fiona turned away, pulling out a porta-scry as she walked into the next room. He could hear muffled voices as she spoke to someone, and then silence. She stepped back to the doorway.

"Let's go," she snapped. Turning, she began to walk briskly through the building. "I have the address to where the girl works."

Ian watched the swing of Fiona's hips as she walked with a purposeful stride out the door and to the edge of the street to flag down a rickshaw.

"Fiona," he called to her as he started down the street in the opposite direction. "Would you like a ride?" Stalking towards him wordlessly, she eyed the white stretch surrey with undisguised disdain. She brushed his hand aside when he offered to help her up into the carriage.

The leather pants tightened across the lovely curve of her ass quite nicely as she grasped the sides and hefted herself up onto the back seat. Ian couldn't help but smile as he vaulted up alongside her.

She called the address out to the driver with a curl of her lip.

"I take it you dislike my surrey?" Ian asked.

"I think it is not an appropriate vehicle to be driving around on Blade business. I never took you for such a show off, Barroes."

"Tut, tut. If I must call you Fiona, you are going to have to learn my first name too." Ian chuckled.

Fiona huffed and crossed her arms across her chest. Ian laughed again. He saw no need to tell her he'd brought the surrey in to work today because he was lending it and the driver to a colleague who was attending a ball with his lady this evening, with the intention to propose afterward.

She probably wouldn't believe him anyway. Fiona Moon had taken an immediate and complete dislike of him the moment they had met. It didn't seem there was anything he could do to disabuse her of the poor view she had of him. It was too bad because he was determined to have her, willing and wanting, in his bed.

The thought of Fiona, her dark hair spread across his pillow, her pale skin flushed with need, sent heat shooting through him and pooling in the vicinity of his button-fly.

"We're here." Fiona's voice broke him out of his erotic fantasy.

FIVE
Fiona

*T*HE SURREY PULLED TO A STOP IN A NARROW COBBLESTONE ROAD BETWEEN Fourth and Fifth Avenue, a street away from the main strip of the Old City shopping district.

Residents from New Nashville, travelers from the Outer Zones, and from the smaller villages of Nash usually preferred to shop in the large, public market and rarely crossed the river into the heart of Nash City. The residents of the city, however, liked to be able to get goods and services close by. Another plus was most shops in the shopping district had hours that catered to vampire clients—the public market did not.

This road and block of buildings were new, in Nash City terms. They were all post-Cataclysm, only about a hundred years old, and built after the large building that had once been there was demolished. Pinky said it was a large theater where people listened to music, but it was destroyed during the Dark Days. Walled in and protected from the outside wars and natural disasters, the citizens of Nash had to make use of every bit of space they could. Large, public buildings that could not easily be repurposed into housing or to meet other needs were demolished by mages or vampires, so new buildings could be built in their place.

This particular block of buildings was mainly shops and businesses.

There were seamstresses, laundresses, a bathhouse, a cloth shop and, the one we were looking for, a crystal shop.

I located it quickly. The lettering barely visible on the grimy windows said Fegley's Crystals. I knew the shop and the area well, as I lived on the next street and the Blade Headquarters was only a few blocks over. Though it wasn't where I normally bought crystals, I knew the Blades had an account with the shop.

I didn't wait on Ian. Instead, I climbed over him, trying to ignore the warmth that spread through me when my hand brushed his knee, and jumped out of the surrey. The quicker we got this over with, the quicker I could get home and away from this man.

I knew it was irrational to have such a violent reaction to him. *But, damn.* He was so damned arrogant—being driven around town by a hired servant! He probably didn't even pay the man enough to take care of his family. That was how the rich stayed rich, off the backs of the poor and struggling. Ian probably hadn't done a real day's work in his life. He hadn't had to. He'd grown up rich in a family of necromancers and con artists that got rich by cheating people.

So what if he'd founded the Necromancer's Guild? It didn't matter that many of the necromancers registered with the guild worked with the City Guard to solve crimes. At its heart, it was just a guild of thieves and cheats, and Ian Barroes was the head thief.

I shook my head to clear it and focused on the job at hand. As I drew closer to the door, I noticed loud voices coming from inside the crystal shop. I swung open the grimy door and entered the dimly lit crystal shop amid a swirl of emotional energy. I didn't even have to focus my power to feel the anger and despair flying off the young girl standing in the middle of the room.

"But you can't fire me! My family needs the money!" she shouted at the squat, bald man behind the counter.

"You should have thought about that before you closed the shop up three hours early and sent customers away," the man said in a nasal voice.

I disliked the man instantly.

"But, you know why I did! You gave me permission," the girl replied indignantly.

The man rubbed round, wire-rimmed spectacles with a cloth, and then placed them on the tip of his nose.

"I recall giving you permission to close early so you could go take the Mage-Level test. I don't see any results before me, so you obviously lied."

The man huffed out a breath and leaned forward, planting his hands on the counter that stood between him and the girl.

"The only reason I let you leave early is because I thought you would finally become of some use to me. You and that mother of yours keep touting how powerful you are. I kept you around all these years, figuring when you got old enough to put to work as a Charger, you'd finally be worth having around. I've paid you way more than you are worth for more than three years, waiting for you to make me a little money. How do I get repaid? You lose me more than three hours' worth of income, you worthless twit. You lied about going to take your test. Now you expect me to keep you here another six months while you wait for your tests, knowing I can't have you charging crystals until you have passed a mage-level test. You are nothing but a liar. I can find another worthless, slum-row kid to work for half of what I pay you."

The girl, dressed in brown hemp pants that were clean, but worn, and a hemp tunic that was similar in color to the dried mud in my hair, turned the color of a radish and took a deep breath.

"More than I'm worth?" the girl shrieked. "Five bucks a week is more than I'm worth? You pompous…"

"Uhmmm." Ian cleared his throat behind me, interrupting the girl, causing the two arguers to turn and stare at them in shock. It was then that I saw the tears running down the girl's cheeks. Something in my heart pinched.

The bald man's face transformed instantly from nasty condescension to an ingratiating smile. "Good folks. Welcome to Fegley's Crystals. How may I help you this fine day?"

I held up my arm, showing my tattoo, my tone brisk and official. "I'm Fiona Moon with the Black Blade Guard. I need to speak with Miss Millie Linton."

The man hissed at the girl. "I knew you were trouble! I can only imagine what wickedness you've been up to that has the Blades looking for you." He turned to me, his smile accommodating, and pointed to the girl. "That's her."

I ignored him. "Are you Millie?" I asked the girl.

"Yes," the girl answered timidly. "Am I in trouble for that man last night?"

I didn't want to discuss it in front of this man—I knew the type. Anything said in his presence would be spread through the community in less than an hour.

"Can you come speak with me outside?"

The girl nodded and moved toward me, but Ian moved from behind me and stopped her.

"Just a moment, Miss Linton. I have some business first." He turned to the man behind the counter. "You are Mr. Fegley?"

"I am." Fegley eyed Ian suspiciously. "And you are?"

"I am Ian Barroes," Ian said simply.

Recognition flashed across Fegley's face, and he gave a slight bow.

"Master Necromancer. Welcome to my store. How may I be of service?"

I rolled my eyes at the title.

"Well, I have just a couple of questions. This girl works for you?"

"No, sir." The old man shook his head emphatically. "Well, she did, but I fired her this morn."

"I see," Ian replied, his tone neutral. "But she had worked for you for a while?"

"Yes sir. About two years. She came to work for me when she turned of legal work age. Fourteen."

"She isn't your apprentice? She doesn't have a contract to work with you and take over your shop when you become infirm?"

The man looked appalled. "Apprentice a no-good from slum-row? No sir! I have a nephew who will apprentice to take my shop. He'll be turning fourteen next week and will begin then."

I was amazed with Ian's ability to get this man to talk, even if I had no idea why he wanted him to. Though, the little bit about the nephew gave a little insight into Millie's newly unemployed state. A shop this size couldn't afford a worker and an apprentice. Fegley had obviously been counting on putting Millie to work charging crystals to bring in more money, but I doubt he'd planned to pay her much, if any, more than he had been.

"I see." Ian's tone was still quite neutral. "If you will excuse me a moment."

He turned from the man to what seemed like an empty space. I felt a slight disruption of energy as Ian focused his power.

"Good morning to you, madam. You had something you wished me to know?" he said to the air. He stood silently for several minutes, occasionally nodding or saying, "Hmmm."

Finally, he said, "Thank you so much for letting me know. I will make sure things are taken care of. I bid you a wonderful day, Madame."

He turned back to the shopkeeper. "Mr. Fegley, did you know that spirits are attracted to energy? And that crystal shops, with all of their charged, and even uncharged, crystals, are full of magical energy, and that makes them a haven for spirits?"

"Umm, no, I did not know that," Fegley stammered.

Ian's smile was a bit feral, but his tone was still neutral and professional. "It's true. You have several spirits that have taken up residence here. One of those, a very pleasant lady, has taken it upon herself to tell me a bit about your shop. Now, enough with that. On to the business I need to attend to. I believe the Necromancer's Guild has a standing account with you?"

"Oh, yes sir." His greedy smile was back. "I have an order I am currently working to fulfill, as a matter of fact."

"Cancel it."

"Umm, excuse me?" Fegley asked nervously.

Ian's tone dropped from cool to chilly. "I said cancel it. I will have official paperwork and any pending payments sent over this afternoon, but you can, as of this moment, consider the account canceled. I should also inform you that your shop will officially be added to the list of shops and merchants which all registered necromancers are discouraged from doing business with."

Fegley's florid complexion went so white I thought he might pass out. "I, I, You..." He spluttered and slammed his hand on the wood countertop. "You can't do that."

Ian calmly planted his hands on the counter and leaned forward, much like Fegley had earlier during his tirade at Millie. His voice was low and deadly. "I assure you, Mr. Fegley, I certainly can. I cannot stop the Black Blade Guard, The Senate, the Healer's Guild, the Charger's Guild, or the City Guard from procuring their crystals from your shop. However, I can let their procurement agents know the tactics you use in your shop. I'm sure they will be as horrified as I am that you have taken advantage of a poor girl who needs to help her family by forcing her to work six days a week, fourteen hours a day, for a measly five bucks. When she should have been working less than half that and earning at least twenty times that. I should also remind you that fourteen is the legal age to start an apprenticeship, but a non-apprenticed employee must be sixteen years or older."

Fegley opened his mouth as if to speak, but Ian held a hand up, effectively cutting off all protest.

"Don't try pleading ignorance. You told me yourself you knew how old the girl was. If your abuse of the child labor law doesn't appall them, I'm sure they will be disturbed by the fact that you weed out the most inferior and cracked crystals to put into to your weekly bulk orders, like those for the organizations I named. You can be assured they will all be informed. The City Guard will also be informed that black-market smugglers often deliver crates to your back door. I'm sure they will be interested in inspecting your stock to identify where some of your higher-end crystals originate. Good day, Mr. Fegley."

Fegley went from pale white to beet red. He sputtered, but no coherent words came out.

Ian turned to Millie and me. The girl's tears had dried up, and I was staring at him with shock and amazement. "Now, ladies, I believe we have some business ourselves?" He made a dramatic sweeping, bowing gesture towards the door.

I saw the corners of Millie's mouth quirk into a half smile as she quietly exited the shop, not even looking back at Fegley. I shot Ian a quick, quizzical look as I followed the girl out the door, but his face was completely blank.

I knew from the look on Fegley's face that everything Ian had said was true, so I knew there had obviously been a spirit there speaking to him. I didn't know why it was my immediate reaction to believe a necromancer was making things up. I had worked with so many during my years as a Blade and had never found fault with the information provided by any of them, even Ian. Especially Ian. His reputation was beyond reproach. But there was still that little part of me that always jumped to disbelief. The lies of one so-called necromancer had jaded me. I didn't know how to get beyond it.

Out on the street, Ian led us to his surrey. He spoke something in the driver's ear I couldn't hear, and the driver climbed down from his seat, walked down the block, and disappeared inside a small cafe. Ian motioned to the two bench seats in the front of the carriage that faced each other.

Looking a little reluctant, Millie took his hand and let him help her up into the surrey. Like before, I ignored his hand and lifted myself up. I settled on the seat across from Millie with Ian next to me. The street was anything but private, so Ian reached up and let down the cloth curtains on each side of the carriage, keeping any prying eyes out.

He glanced at me. "Can you do a sound ward?"

I shot him a look that questioned his intelligence. Of course I could do a sound ward. Anyone with a modicum of power could do one on a space as small as the surrey. Without responding to him directly, I chanted a basic soundproofing spell.

When I was done, I nodded to him, and then looked at Millie. The poor girl was sitting as stiff as a board on the cushioned seat. She looked scared to death, yet defiant. Her eyes were filled with unshed tears, but she looked like she'd rather die than let them fall. The girl had spirit.

I realized no one had ever answered the girl's earlier question. "Millie, you aren't in trouble. We just have a few questions for you."

She looked skeptical. Her voice shook as she said, "But, the man was dead. I know he was. I saw them take him away in the morgue wagon. I killed him."

"Yes, he was dead." I kept my voice low and soothing. "But you have every right to defend yourself when attacked."

"If I'm not in trouble, why are you here?" Millie said, drawing herself up straighter.

Ian spoke this time, surprising me with how calmly soothing his voice was. "Like Agent Moon said, we have a few questions. I know you had to tell the guards what happened last night, but it would really help if you could go over it again with us."

"Ok, but I don't know what I can tell you that I didn't tell them last night. I was walking along and this man grabbed me. I kicked him, and he fell. Dead." Her voice trembled on the last word.

I opened my mouth to speak, but lost my words when Ian reached over and took Millie by the hand. He rested his elbows on his knees and leaned towards the young girl, his eyes intent on her face. "It's okay, Millie. Take a deep breath. Now, close your eyes. Go back to last night just before the attack. Walk through it slowly and tell us. Where were you? What were you doing? What did you see?"

Opening my senses, I searched for power coming from Ian, but there wasn't any. He wasn't trancing Millie. He was just being kind. And it was working.

Millie began to speak in a soft, distracted tone as if she was concentrating very hard. "I had just closed up the shop. I was in a rush; I needed to get to the public Mage-Level Test. I had a buck to ride the trolley, but the streets were crowded. I was going to miss it, so I cut down the alley. That one." She opened her eyes and pushed back the curtain to point to an opening between buildings that led to the next street.

"Why don't we walk down there? It may help your memory. Do you feel comfortable with that?" I asked.

Millie nodded silently.

"Ok, give me a second." I chanted to remove the soundproofing ward, and then chanted another spell. "Okay, no one but the three of us will be able to hear what any of us say. But we have to work fast; this spell only works for fifteen minutes."

I smiled when Ian raised an impressed eyebrow at me. What, did he think I was an amateur? I was an experienced Blade agent. Secrecy during investigations was imperative. Though it was unlikely anyone had any interest in the current one, you could never be too careful. In a world filled with paranorms with super hearing, as well as unseen spirits, a No-Speak spell in public open spaces was SOP. The only problem was they were dangerous. It was important to be specific with the time on a No-Speak, and to only use them in very short intervals. The last thing anyone wanted was to be caught in a dangerous situation and not be able to scream out for help.

When they reached the alley opening, Millie stopped and looked at Ian. "It was getting dark, and I didn't see anyone in the alley. But I didn't really look. I was in a hurry."

She slowly began to walk down the path between the two brick buildings, Ian and I trailing behind her. She stopped about halfway down the alley. "I think I was about here when I noticed the man. He was standing against the wall near the other end. He started walking towards me."

Ian went to stand next to her. "Concentrate. How did he walk? Did he speak to you? Was there anyone else in or near the alley?"

Millie looked confused by the questions, but complied. "He walked normal. No, wait, I remember now. I thought he walked kind of strange, kind of stiff. He was walking towards me, but I just kept going, then he reached out and grabbed my arm."

She ran up about fifteen feet and stopped. "I was right around here. I remember because I pushed him away and pounded on this door." She indicated a shabby, wooden door that had seen better days. It was obviously a back entrance to one of the shops in the building.

"No one came, and the man grabbed me again. I screamed." She paused, her eyes closed in concentration. "He told me to shut up. He said he was going to make all of my troubles go away. But…but it was weird. His voice was weird. Like it didn't fit his body. I don't know… I can't explain it. It doesn't make sense. I was really scared." She looked at me as if in apology.

"I know. It's ok. What happened next?"

"Well, I'm not very good at magic, at real magic, but I keep a small, charged crystal in my pocket. It was a throwaway, and I can charge it myself," she said quickly, as if they would think she stole it. "Anyway, Mama taught me an easy flash spell. So I put my hand in my pocket and said the spell. The flash of light startled the man, and I was able to pull away. I ran towards the end of the alley."

Not everyone was born with the power to perform magic, and those were sometimes only had specific ones, and might not have the ability to do certain spells. Being a norm, a person with no magic or not enough magic to register on the Mage-Level exams, in a paranorm-dominated world, was both inconvenient and dangerous. So much of the technology today depended on magic. Life was very hard without the power to perform easy spells. And in a world where everyone was stronger and faster than you were, having a little bit of magic to use could mean the difference between life and death. Norms and paranorms alike often carried crystals charged with general magical energy. They enabled the carrier to perform small spells and tasks by touching the crystal and chanting the spell regardless of the person's natural ability to do magic or the type of power they had.

Millie looked defiantly at Ian. "There wasn't anyone else there. I know because I was screaming for help and looking around. There wasn't anyone. I made it to the end, but I tripped here." Walking to the end, she used one foot clad in a ragged boot to point to a hole in the ground just beyond the edge of the alley. She had made it out onto the public sidewalk.

"I fell down, and the man was coming at me. When he reached to grab me, I kicked up as hard as I could. I don't know where I hit him, but I guess his head, because he fell down. And he was dead."

She began to tremble again, but her voice was steady. I had to give it to the girl—she had spunk. It was apparent she thought she was facing a murder charge, despite our assurances, yet she stood strong and told her story without wavering.

"How did you know he was dead?" I asked as I looked around the area. We were now on the street I lived on. The block was made up mostly of bars and restaurants. Even at dusk, the music drifting out would have drowned out the girl's screams. That explained why no one came to help her.

"Because of the way he looked," she said matter-of-factly. "I mean, no one could look like that and be alive. I've never seen a dead body before. I didn't know they would shrivel up like that so fast. It was so weird."

"What do you mean shrivel so fast? How did he look before he fell?" Ian's voice startled us both. He'd been silent for so long, lingering behind us. I had almost forgotten he was there.

"Well, normal, I guess. He was a normal, live person. But then when he fell, after I kicked him, it was weird. Like one minute, his face was normal, then it went all white, spotty, and sucked in. Like all the air and stuff had been sucked out of him. Looked a little like the dried apple chips Mama makes." She paused uncertainly. "Isn't that what happens when someone dies?"

"Not usually," Ian said distractedly. "You are sure there wasn't anyone around?"

Millie's tone was firm and sure. "I'm positive. I didn't see anyone at all until after I kicked him. This street wasn't as busy. There were a few people walking, but they were on the opposite side of the street."

Ian checked his pocket watch. "Well, I think our fifteen minutes is just about up. Thank you for your time, Millie. You've helped a lot."

"Really, that's it? I'm not in trouble, and I can go?" Her face brightened.

"You aren't in trouble. But, before you go, I need to know a couple of more things," I said.

"Okay," she cautiously said.

"Is it true you are a charger?"

"Well, I haven't had an official Mage-Level test. But, those are my powers. I've been working part time with a charger to learn. She says I'm good." Her face fell as if remembering her situation. "But it doesn't matter. There isn't another public test for six months."

I took a small tablet of hemp-paper and a short, charcoal pencil out of a small pocket in my vest. After I wrote on the paper, I offered it to Millie.

"Take this to Maurice at the Academy Testing Center. He arranges the Mage-Level tests for the Blades. He will be able to get you into the next test, which should be in the next couple of days."

Millie stared at the paper, but she didn't take it.

"This isn't charity," I said. "You were the victim of a crime, and you have helped us today. This is the least I can do for you." I shook the paper a bit, and Millie took it.

I scribbled a message on another page, tore it out, and handed it to

Millie. "After you get your results, take them and that note to Leesa Parks. Her office is on the first floor of the Blades building. The Blades employ their own chargers, and Leesa is the head of the department. This isn't charity either. If your results are good enough, she should be able to find a position for you. You'll have to work hard."

Millie's face broke into a wide grin. "I will, I swear. Thank you, Miss Moon."

I winced. I had no objections to my last name. As a matter of fact, it was exactly what I wanted it to be. But Miss Moon sounded like a schoolmarm. I disliked it when anyone used it. "Call me Fiona. Do you need a ride home?"

"No. I don't mind walking as long as it's daytime. Thank you, Fiona!" She started back down the alley and stopped.

"Mr. Barroes, are you really going to cancel your account with Mr. Fegley? And tell the Guard about him?" she asked quietly.

Ian's face was impassive. "I am. Does that bother you?"

Millie chewed her lip. "No. He was mean, and he didn't pay me much. But, I didn't have much choice. My family needed the money. He only fired me because his nephew can legally become his apprentice now. He didn't care one bit that losing my job would hurt us. And he always called me such bad names."

Then, to my surprise, Millie ran over to him and threw her arms around his neck. "Thank you!"

Ian stared at me over the girl's head, looking dumbstruck. He obviously didn't have much experience with emotional teenage girls. I laughed and made a hugging motion with my arms. I nearly laughed out loud when Ian mimicked the motions, stiffly patting Millie on the back.

After a long moment, Millie backed away, her face flushed. "Thank you both. I didn't know how I was gonna tell Mama and Papa I was fired. But knowing I can take my test and knowing Mr. Fegley will get what's coming to him will make it easier." Then she turned and ran down the street.

As soon as she was out of earshot, I let the pent-up laughter fly. Ian still looked a little shocked.

"What are you laughing at?" he asked indignantly.

"You! Big bad Master Necromancer scared of a grateful little girl!" I hooted.

"I was not afraid. She just caught me off guard. Now, can we please get on with this? I have a class in less than an hour."

I forced myself to stop laughing and compose myself. "Okay. What do you think this was?"

"I'm still not sure." If he did have an idea, his face gave nothing away.

"Well, I have an idea. It sounds like a necromancer messing around."

His face remained impassive, but his voice held a sharp edge when he said, "This was not a necromancer."

I had my doubts, but I wasn't up to arguing with him. I was exhausted and still encrusted with dried mud. I wanted to get home. Besides, I'd only been dispatched to witness the questioning and give a report to Sam. This was not officially my case. "Fine. Good day to you, Ian."

"Don't you want a ride back to the Blade building?" Ian asked. We were still standing in the alley way opposite from where we came in.

"No need. I'll scry Sam with my report." I waved my hand at the street behind me. "I'm not far from home."

"Ahh, yes. You live above a bar. I'd almost forgotten," Ian said.

Almost forgotten? How did he know in the first place? No matter. "Well, Pinky likes to call it a pub, but yes, I do. I've been up for about twenty-three hours, so if you don't mind, I'm going to head there now."

"Of course." His voice was stiff and formal again. "Good day, Fiona."

"Good day," I said again. I turned and headed down the street, completely aware he watched me until I disappeared from his line of sight.

SIX
Fiona

*P*INKY OFTEN TOLD ME THAT IN TWO CENTURIES, WITH ALL THAT HAD CHANGED in the world, Broadway was much the same as it had been before the Cataclysm. Back then, it had been a row of mostly bars and restaurants with live entertainment and a few shops mingled in. Now there were a few restaurants, shops, and bars that catered to paranorms, most specifically vampires. Most of the buildings that had more than one floor also housed apartments, or in the case of most of the bars, had become inns to accommodate travelers. To me, Broadway was home.

I don't remember a time when I didn't live over Pinky's Pub, though there was one. There had been a small, yellow house with a white fence covered with flowers and a vegetable garden. Or so my mother had told me. She had met my father, a first generation mage, at the Academy of Magic and Science. My father came from a wealthy norm family from New Nashville. My mother had grown up the daughter of mages in the magic district of Nash City. The District, with its dirty old buildings converted into apartments, was considered only barely a step above the Slums.

They were teamed up for a martial arts class and, according to my mother, it was love at first punch. She never said who punched who, but

I always figured she'd done the punching. They were inseparable. My mother had gotten into the Academy because both of her parents were City Guards. It was her dream to be a Guard, and maybe a Blade. My father's family paid for his place at the Academy, but he applied for Guard training shortly after meeting my mother.

They married after graduating the Academy. To the dismay of my father's family, they applied for the City Guard together and were accepted. To please my paternal grandparents, they bought the little yellow house in New Nashville to be near them. My mother quit the Guard when she got pregnant with me.

My mother's eyes always grew sad and her tone wistful whenever she told me about that time. For a while, we were a family in the little yellow house. Then, just before my second birthday, my father didn't come home for dinner. He and his partner had been tracking a smuggling ring and walked into a trap. They were dead before they even knew the warehouse was rigged with explosives. It always seemed a little strange to me that in a world with magic, my father was killed by the most mundane of methods.

His family blamed my mother for his death. They said he never would have joined the Guard if it hadn't been for her. I think she agreed with them. She couldn't stand the little yellow house without my father, so she bundled me up and went to the one place she knew she would always be welcome.

Throughout generations of my mother's family, Eric "Pinky" Pinkerton had been a constant. I sometimes wondered how sad it must be for him to see the people he loved die every few decades and yet he stayed eternally young. Most vampires move around a lot or avoid bonding with non-vampires for that very reason. Yet Pinky had been a member of my family as much as if he'd been born into it.

Pinky had taken us in, letting my mother rent the top floor of the pub building. He even helped with me when she joined the Blades.

I never saw my grandparents again until my mother died, and they tried to make me come live with them. I didn't cooperate. After a while, they got tired of chasing me down at Pinky's and dragging me back to the big house in New Nashville. Whatever the reason, they gave up trying to control me after three weeks and let me go back to Pinky, who gladly took me in. Of course, they never, not even once, contributed financially to my raising after that.

Pulling myself out of the thoughts of the past, I paid attention to the street as I strolled down the block towards home and bed. I let the sounds and smells, not all of them pleasant, sink into my skin. The enticing aroma of fresh-baked sweet bread wafted out of the bakery across from Pinky's pub, and my growling stomach reminded me I hadn't eaten a bite since early the evening before. Stopping in, I bought three sweet rolls. I ate one of the sticky buns as I crossed the street. There were a few people milling about in and out of shops and the few inns, but for the most part, it was pretty quiet.

Pinky's Pub was located in one of only three four-story buildings on the block. The pub catered mainly to vampires. Unlike many of the bars on Broadway, the pub closed an hour before dawn and didn't open until two hours after dusk. There had been a time when Pinky had kept the pub open twenty-four hours a day for any vampires who chose to risk the sunlight exposure to get to a dark, friendly place for a drink. But, when my sisters and I came along, he'd changed the hours so he had time to spend with us. Though we were all grown up now, Pinky found he had a love of quite alone time, so he kept the nighttime-only hours.

Since it was almost midday, the front doors were locked and barred from the inside. Knocking wouldn't get me in because of the soundproof spells that kept the upper floors quite enough to sleep on. Besides, the only people home would be Pinky and Anya, and they both worked at the pub all night. So, I walked to the end of the block and up the alley to the back entrance instead. The security ward on the back door was keyed to my energy signature, so I didn't have to use a key to get in. Anyone outside of the family who tried to enter would get a nasty shock and be thrown back about fifteen feet, which would slam them into the building behind us. If they were stupid enough to try it a second time, it would kill them.

Like most of the buildings up and down Broadway, the pub was narrow in width, but over half a block in length. The first half of the building was four-stories high and made of brick, but the back half was only two stories and constructed of concrete blocks and wood. Though not even Pinky had been here back when it was built, it was obvious the back half had been added on several decades after the main building.

The building was quiet as I crept through the back rooms of the pub to the back staircase. I paused on the second-floor landing to look out the window. River wasn't in her massive rooftop garden, or at least I couldn't see her. She could be in the jungle-like grove of potted fruit trees or inside the greenhouse, but at this time of day, she was most likely at the public market selling her produce. That meant, with Pinky asleep in his third-floor apartment and with Anya asleep in her bedroom, I'd have the washroom to myself.

Like most older buildings in Nash City, we had the bare minimum of plumbing. It had only been about fifty years or so since water delivery had been restored to most of the city via hand pumps. Flushing toilets were a luxury the older generation hadn't had. Some buildings, mostly those in the slums, still didn't have them. Hot running water was still elusive, though I knew from my history classes back at the Academy that once every home and most buildings had cold and hot running water and every home had a bathtub. These days, hot water that flowed from the pump required a crystal-powered heater and a second set of pipes running throughout the home. Only the very rich had hot water.

There were public bathhouses spread throughout the city where attendants were employed to heat water on coal or magic-powered heaters and kept the tubs filled. Normally, I would use the Blade bathhouse or stop at the one down the street, but I was too tired. Luckily, though it wasn't as relaxing and convenient as a bathhouse, Pinky had rigged us a small washroom in the apartment years ago with a steel tub and a small heater. The heater had been expensive, but necessary. While warming water was a basic household spell, it took more power than most mages could expend at once to heat enough for bathing. We couldn't immerse ourselves in a tub full of warm, scented water like we could at a bathhouse, but we could wash our hair and keep generally clean.

I put on a kettle of water and scryed Sam with my report on the morning's activities while it was heating. I washed my hair with the first pot of water while heating a second to bathe with. Then I braided my clean, wet hair and stepped into the tub to wash the dirt and grime from my body. Once I was clean and mud free, I wrapped a towel around me and went to my room, collapsing on the bed, too tired to worry about clothes, and was asleep within minutes.

SEVEN
Fiona

WHEN I WOKE, MY ROOM WAS LIT ONLY BY THE MOONLIGHT AND HAZE OF crystal-lights from the street below that streamed through the spaces where the blanket I used as a window covering didn't quite meet the windowpane. Groggily, I mumbled a spot illumination spell so I could see the hands on the windup clock on the bedside table. It was a little after eight o'clock, about an hour after the last evening bell. The citywide bells rang several times a day to announce the approach of dawn, dusk, and their full arrival, and midday and midnight.

Groaning, I threw the light blanket off and pushed up to sit on the edge of the bed. I'd actually slept a full eight hours. Of course, now I would be awake the rest of the night, and I had to report for duty early in the morning. Although I'd scryed Sam and gave a verbal report, I would have to type up a formal one on today's activities with Ian as well. I would also have to put my name in queue for another mission.

I touched the crystal-lamp next to the clock, and the room filled with a soft, bluish light. Different lamp crystals gave off a different color cast. I preferred blue. The room was small enough that the few furnishings—a narrow bed, a bedside table, a dresser with a mirror, and one wooden chair—filled it to capacity.

A series of hooks on one wall kept my cloak, belts, and other clothing items neat and orderly when they weren't flung across the chair or bedposts or, more often than not, scattered across the small expanse of floor like the mud-caked garments I'd worn the night before. I got up and made my way to the dresser. Shuffling my feet to make a path through the clothes, I realized I had been wrong. My dirty clothes were not on the floor at all.

Oh, Mother Earth, bless River! My little sister had come in and gathered up my clothes to be taken to the laundress. I knew it had been River. She was ever mothering Anya and me, and while we both pretended not to like it, I secretly treasured my sister's mother-hen ways.

I grabbed a housedress from a hook on the wall and pulled it over my head. The blend of hemp and cotton was soft and cool against my skin, flowing to just below my knees. It had once belonged to my mother, and the emerald color had long since faded to a soft, pale green from years of wear and wash.

The moment I opened the bedroom door, the mouthwatering scent of cooking vegetables and the soft sounds of female conversation wafted in.

Before my mother and I came to live here, Pinky's had also been an inn. All three upper floors had been separated into several small rooms with a larger main sitting room. My mother took out two walls to create a larger main area and leave three rooms. Pinky had continued to rent out the rooms in the lower floors. When my mother died, he had moved from his small rooms on the second floor into the apartment to take care of me, and then River and Anya when they came. Although he had needed the extra money, he'd eventually stopped renting out the rooms on the other floors, claiming it wasn't safe for the three of us. Now that we were all grown up, he still refused to rent out rooms, though he'd moved down to the third floor years ago to give us our privacy.

I quietly moved down the hallway and found my sisters in the main area of our apartment. Anya was sitting at the large, wooden table nestled in one side of the room with a bowl of what looked and smelled like River's tasty vegetable stew and a huge hunk of bread. She was alternately shoveling food in her mouth and chatting with River, who was standing at the counter washing dishes in a large, metal tub.

For a moment, I stood at the edge of the hallway and watched them. No one who looked at the three of us side by side would be able to say we were sisters with our drastically different appearances. In a way, they would be right, but they would also be dead wrong.

I was born Fiona Malaina Hernandez, daughter of Fredrick Hernandez and Malaina Murphy Hernandez. A few months after my mother's death when I was eight, I was fishing, illegally, just outside of the city walls, when I found River. The city walls surrounded the entire city and cross the Cumberland River with metal-grid gates. During the day, the gates are opened to allow merchants and trade ships in and out of the city. There are regular Guard Patrols, but a small child on a homemade raft who knows the patrols can easily slip in and out of the gates unnoticed. It was my favorite pastime as a child, and the fishing near the gates was always good. That day, I had snuck through the gates as usual and lounged on the bank in the shadow of the wall, my body and fishing line hidden from prying eyes by tall grass and trees.

The area had once been a part of the city, but long ago been reclaimed by Mother Earth. It was peaceful and the perfect hideout for a sad kid. As I lay in the grass snacking on cold cornbread, I heard a strange sound that sounded like a cat mewling. Ever the adventurer, I went to investigate. At the juncture where the river and wall met, floating debris like leaves and tree limbs gathered along the banks. That day, a small canoe had gotten trapped along with the other debris near the riverbank. I didn't see anyone inside, so thinking it had drifted loose from its mooring somewhere up river and was fair game to claim, I waded out to it. Grabbing the bow, I pulled it over to the bank, congratulating myself on my new canoe.

I was shocked, and more than a little horrified, when I found the canoe wasn't empty. There was a small, sleeping girl curled in the bottom of the boat. She had a mass of white hair and looked around three years old. There was a message inscribed in the bottom of the boat with charcoal. "Keep this child safe and take her to where she needs to be."

Even at my young age, I knew those words weren't a message to whoever found the girl, but a spell. Words had power, and whoever did it wanted to make sure it was strong and stuck around. As I stood there staring, the little girl woke up and stared back at me with the bluest eyes I'd ever seen. She didn't cry or look scared. She just smiled, crawled out of the boat, and into my arms. I didn't know who this little girl was or where she came from, but in that instant, she became mine.

I took her home to Pinky. His suggestion that we take her to the city orphanage resulted in a tantrum from me, while the little girl hung on to my leg. After ten minutes of my tears, Pinky couldn't take it anymore and agreed to keep her. Though we learned she could talk, she didn't know her name and couldn't tell us where she came from. After several name suggestions, we decided on River.

A little over a year later, River woke up one morning and insisted we go to the Public Market that day. Pinky had balked. He was a vampire after all. Going out in the daytime meant wearing dark glasses and a cloak to protect his eyes and skin. Contrary to the myths popular in the Tech Age, vampires did not burst into flames in sunlight. They were, however, extremely sensitive and their skin would sunburn and blister after just minutes of exposure. Their eyes were also very sensitive to light. Most vampires avoided going out between dawn and sunset.

But, River had been adamant, and we had learned that if she dug her heels in about something, we were wise to listen. Though we didn't know her exact age, we guessed she was around four by that time, and she had already proven herself a seer. At her age, she couldn't articulate to us how she sometimes knew things—she just did. It had started soon after we got her. One day, she got very upset when I was about to go downstairs and insisted I stay away from the stairs. None of us understood why she was so upset until Pinky leaned against the rail. The rail was old and had become loose, and Pinky fell three stories. Luckily, being a vampire, his broken leg and ribs had healed within a few hours. If it had been me that fell, I would have died. From that moment on, if she became upset and said to do or not to do something, Pinky and I listened.

So, that morning, Pinky had donned his daytime protective gear, and we had gone out to the market. But instead of the market itself, River had led us to the lots outside the market where traveling merchants and gypsy caravans camped. She led us right into the center of one caravan. We were getting strange looks, and Pinky was in the process of apologizing for our rudeness in coming into their personal space when we heard a scream. We rounded a wagon to find a young girl a couple of years younger than me with a tangled mass of dark red hair on her hands and knees, a spilled stew pot near her and an older woman standing over her holding a horsewhip. I screamed as loud as the girl when the woman brought the whip down hard across her back.

The next few minutes passed in a flurry, but they were burned in my mind forever. Before I'd even seen him move, Pinky had the whip in his hand and the woman on her knees. Beneath the hood of his black cloak, his normally pale blue eyes glowed with a brilliance as bright as any crystal-lamp I'd ever seen. He held his hand over the woman, but he did not touch her. The woman opened her mouth to speak, but no words came out. He spoke softly to the girl, asking her a series of questions.

She was Anya, she was seven years old, the woman was her mother, and she was being beaten because she'd dropped the stew. Yes, she'd been beaten before, almost every day, because she had been born a norm among a family of mages. The gypsy clan used their powers to make money, both legally and illegally. Because she had no powers, she couldn't contribute; therefore, she was less than worthless to them.

Then Pinky had asked one more question and her answer had been, no, she didn't want to stay there. And so, our family of three became four in that instant. Using the mental powers I hadn't known he'd possessed, Pinky told the woman she had sent the girl away, and she and her clan needed to leave within the hour because a patrol of City Guards who knew of their illegal activities would be there soon. He told her that for their safety, she would forget about the girl and the clan would never return to Nash.

As far as I knew, they left that day and never returned. I never saw Pinky that angry or use his power of persuasion again. I hoped I never did.

Though we had all started out life in very different ways, the four of us became a family. Pinky, the immortal vampire who was over two centuries old but didn't even look twenty-one—the age he'd been when he'd been turned—and three little girls. Anya, River, and I officially became sisters one night when I was fourteen and getting ready to enter the Academy to join City Guard, as the four of us sat in the rooftop garden that River had started growing shortly after she came to live with us. She had a knack for growing things and in a few years, she was already growing almost all of our food. We lounged under the moonlight before Pinky went down to the pub to work, like we did most nights.

Anya had been more nervous about me going to the Academy than I was. She was afraid I'd leave and never come back. I remember Pinky gathering us all up, River on his lap and Anya and I on either side of him, and holding us tight. "My girls, everything in life changes except one thing."

"The moon?" River had asked in her sweet little voice.

Pinky kissed the tip of her nose and laughed. "Well, that too. But, I'm talking about family. Blood doesn't make family, and time and distance doesn't break it. Like the moon, family will always be there, even when it's too dark to see it. Keep strong and it will light your way home, wherever you are."

After one long moment, I declared, "We are sisters and that will never change, like the moon. We are the moon sisters." My sisters tearily agreed with me, and that was who we became. Fiona, Anya, and River Moon. The Moon sisters.

Anya saw me standing in the shadows of the hallway. "Hey, sleepyhead, come join us before I have to go down to work."

River turned, her usual smile brightening her heart-shaped face. "Oh, hi! I have some stew warming for you. You must have been exhausted. I didn't leave for the market until almost midday and you still weren't home."

She'd said all this as she bustled around, filling a bowl with stew, cutting a hunk of bread, and pouring a cup of mint tea. She placed the food and drink in front of me as I sat down. I would have told her I could get it myself, but it would have hurt her feelings.

She sat down with only a cup of tea and talked with us as Anya and I ate. I knew from experience that she had likely eaten her dinner hours ago. Our eating and sleeping schedules hadn't synced since the three of us were kids.

River woke at or before dawn and went to bed a few hours after dusk. She tended her garden and sold the produce, herbs, and tea blends she made at the Public Market. Anya worked in the pub, which meant being up all night. She never went to bed before dawn and woke sometime in the early evening. My schedule was unpredictable. Depending on the case I was working on, I would come home for sleep and a meal whenever I had the chance. Sometimes, I was gone on assignment for days or weeks at a time. We had learned just to flow around each other and spend time together whenever we got the chance.

It had been a couple of days since we had all been together at a meal time, so we took turns telling about what had been happening in our lives. River described the new seeds she'd bought from a traveler from the far south across the Mississippi Sea and how her tomato plants were thriving.

Anya talked about how things were going in the pub. It had apparently been a bad week. Anya and Pinky were two peas in a pod most days, but there were two subjects where they butted heads: renting out rooms and Anya's love life. We'd all tried to talk him into renting rooms for extra money, but Anya, her mind always on making the pub better and bringing in more profit, mentioned it to him at least once a month. That was usually when Pinky would ask her if she was ever going to get serious with a man.

Pinky, the king of stringless sexual affairs, had little use for monogamy or serious relationships, only using the tactic to get her off his back. He had no real interest in marrying her off, but it set Anya off. Of course, then she'd ask him if he was trying to get rid of her, and softhearted Pinky would cave. There would be hugging and no more talk of room renting or serious dating for another month or so. They manipulated each other perfectly.

I told them as much as I could about my night and morning. Of course, it wasn't that much, because of confidentiality rules, but it was enough. The moment I mentioned Ian Barroes' name, my sisters both raised eyebrows at me.

"He asked for you again?" River asked quietly. She was too polite to put into words what the sly smile on her face said.

Anya had no such compunction. "You two have been dancing around for four or five years now. When are you just going to finally jump his bones and get it over with already?"

While River rarely dated or expressed sexual interest in anyone, Anya and I had a similar philosophy on sex and relationships. Neither of us was interested in a long-term relationship—we were happy with our lives at they were. However, we weren't prudes. We were grown women with healthy sexual appetites, which we indulged when and with whom we pleased. We did, however, each have our own personal set of rules that governed our choices for sexual partners.

"He's a colleague," I said, knowing I couldn't say I didn't want to sleep with Ian. That would be a lie, and the Moon sisters didn't lie to each other.

Anya let out a bark of laughter. "Really? And you've never slept with someone you work with? What about Rangel? Isn't he a City Guard? Oh, and what was that Blade's name...?"

"Yeah, yeah," I broke in. "I get your point—no need to start making a list. But it's different with Barroes. I don't think I even like him."

"You don't think?" One of Anya's perfectly shaped eyebrows rose.

"I don't. I don't like him."

"And what's wrong with him besides the fact that he is a fabulously rich necromancer with a great ass?" Anya asked as she took her dishes to the washtub.

"Well, I don't suppose there is a problem with the great ass. But you said the rest yourself," I said indignantly.

"You can't keep hating those who are rich just because we grew up poor. I know you resent the fact that your grandparents never helped Pinky financially and refused to turn your father's inheritance over to you. But that was them, not Ian or any other rich person. I know how much we struggled and how much of the burden you took on yourself to help Pinky take care of us, but you can't hold any of that against Ian." River's voice was soft and calming, yet firm.

I reached over and patted her hand. "I know, little sister. You're right. And I don't dislike him just because he is rich. Though, the fact that his family made their money by using magic to circumvent the law and take advantage of people does not help matters. And before you say that is his family, not him, remember, he is a necromancer."

"He is. But is he not the founder of the Necromancer's Guild? Did he not try to make up for his family's past crimes by creating a governing organization that holds necromancers to higher standards and has eliminated charlatans like the one your mother went to?"

If it had been anyone else, I would have winced at the mention of my mother and likely gotten pissed. But not with River. She meant no disrespect and would never have mentioned it if she didn't feel it was important. That made me a little nervous.

"All of what you say is true, but I'm still not sure about him. Tell me, little sister, why are you? Why are you so adamant that I like Ian Barroes?"

"I'm not. Or, I don't think I am. I haven't had a vision of you two making babies or something, so you can get that terrified look off your face!" She giggled. "I just have a feeling that there is more to Ian than meets the eye, and you would be cheating yourself out of knowing what it is if you don't loosen up and give him a chance."

Anya snickered. "Personally, I think there is a lot under his clothes that doesn't meet the eye, and you'd be cheating yourself out of seeing it all if you don't loosen up and give him a chance."

I couldn't help laughing. I don't know about what River said, but I had a suspicion that Anya was right. Under those clothes, that uptight man probably had a glorious body.

Anya let out a long sigh. "It has been fun, sisters, but I better get downstairs before Pinky comes looking for me."

"Yes, and I need to get to bed. Dawn comes early. What are you going to do with your night, Fee? Do you have an assignment?"

"I'm off until tomorrow. I'm not tired enough to sleep. Maybe I'll go downstairs and help out," I said.

"We have plenty of help tonight, but come down anyway. You can enjoy your night off. Night, Rivs. See you in the morning," Anya called as she raced down the stairs.

"She's right, you know," River said softly as she dunked a rag into soapy water. "You do need to relax and have some fun. Although I'd like to see you meditating a little more, having a drink and conversation with friends will do you almost as much good."

I watched my sister flit around, wiping down the large, wooden table and countertops. Her hair, so pale it was almost white, was pulled back into a loose braid that reached the middle of her back. She looked younger than her nineteen years. She wore a long, loose-fitting dress that was so faded from washings that I couldn't be sure of its original color, but I thought it might have been yellow. It was patched in several areas, and a spot above the elbow was wearing quite thin. It should have been thrown out years ago, but I knew better than to say so to River. Though the three of us had been working and bringing in income to the family for a while now and we could afford simple necessities and a few luxuries, River didn't think new clothes for her were a necessity.

Though she was the youngest, River was truly the mother of us all, even Pinky.

I suppose we all took care of each other in our own ways. I'd always felt it was my duty to provide for my sisters and protect them. I'd done that by getting admitted to the Academy for Guard training two years earlier than I should have been eligible and by talking Sam into admitting both of my sisters to the Academy when they were old enough, even though we couldn't pay like the rich families.

Anya was a skilled enough fighter to be a Guard, even a Blade, but could never be either even though it was her deepest desire. She was a norm. Born without the ability to manipulate magical energy, she didn't have shifter genes, and of course, she wasn't a vampire. That meant that she was useless in law enforcement. With her training, she could have worked in an administrative position, but that wasn't my sister's style. Instead, after graduating, she did what she'd always intended to do, she worked in the pub, taking some of the burden off Pinky and helping provide for us all.

River, too, had gone to the Academy. She had no desire to work in law, but she had a love of learning that amazed me. So she went through the magic and science courses, refusing to take any combat training, instead focusing on Healer training. She excelled and had a position at the hospital waiting for her when she graduated a year ago. But within a month, we all knew it wasn't for her. I think she only stayed as long as she did because she didn't want to disappoint us.

River had a gentle, caring soul. It didn't take long for us to see that being around sickness, death, and suffering all day took a toll on her we couldn't have foreseen. Her empathy kept her worried and up at night, wondering about her patients. Her already pale skin became sallow, and the circles under her eyes were so dark they looked like bruises. Once bright and cheerful, she hardly smiled anymore, the sadness and solemnity of her job weighing heavily on her. She looked almost relieved when we all sat her down and told her we felt like she should find another job.

So, she went back to doing what she loved—tending her rooftop gardens, tending house, and bringing smiles and laughter to all she met. Now she sold her produce and the herbal concoctions she made up at the public market. She was happy and healthy and did everything in her power to keep us that way as well.

"I promise I'll spend half an hour meditating before bed." I took the cup and plate River had in her hand. "Now, off to bed with you. I'll finish cleaning up. No, don't argue. Go on."

To my surprise, River actually obeyed. "Good night, Fee," she said, kissing me on the cheek before padding off to her room.

I finished up the dishes and, using a rope of energy, floated the dishpan out the window to the rooftop garden for River to use for her plants. Then I went to my room to change into something more appropriate to wear downstairs to the pub.

EIGHT

Fiona

I *SUCKED IN THE STALE AROMAS OF MEAD, ALE, WHISKEY, MOONSHINE, JOINT SMOKE,* and body odor. When I thought about it, it sounded disgusting, but it smelled like home, warmth, and safety to me.

The pub was as much my home as the apartment upstairs. Pinky had tried to limit our time downstairs when we were very young, but I used to sneak down at night and sit on the landing in the exact spot I stood now, listening to the buzz of conversation and music. I often fell asleep there and woke up in my own bed. I'd get a mild admonishment from Pinky with the promise that if I did it again, he'd leave me to sleep on the cold floor all night. Of course, I never listened, and he always carried me up to bed.

As we got older, he would let us come down for a few hours and even let Anya and I help behind the bar. River preferred to hang out in the kitchen where Pinky brewed and fermented his own mead.

There were a few nights a week when it was packed wall to wall with the young mage crowd, but for the most part, the atmosphere was more subdued and the regular crowd much older, even if most of them didn't look it. The pub was primarily a vampire hangout, but not like most of the bars in the city. Pinky's had a reputation as a good place to have a drink and conversation in a subdued atmosphere. Of course, calm was a relative term.

On a night when there was a crowd of rowdy young mages on weekend break from the Academy and out for a good time, someone not used to the city would not call the pub subdued. But when compared to many of the vampire clubs where human blood was on the menu and sex on the dance floor was a normal activity, even on the most rowdy night, Pinky's was downright calm.

Pinky's, though called a pub, didn't serve food of any type. That included blood. Nor was the consumption of blood allowed within the building. Of course, human blood wasn't really considered food. Vampires, humans infected with the Nosophoros-V virus, or N-V for short, couldn't get substantial nutrition from vegetables or cooked meats. Though most vampires I knew ate regular foods as well, they also had to consume raw blood to get ample nutrition. Contrary to the myths and horror stories of old, the blood didn't have to be human. The blood of animals was more to their taste and provided them with the nutrition they needed.

There were those who had a taste for human blood, not for the nutritional value, but the other properties it held. For a vampire, human blood wasn't food. It was a drug. Because of N-V's effect on the body, getting intoxicated by drinking alcohol or smoking a joint was hard for most vampires. Their metabolism was such that it took a lot to alter their perception. Human blood did that for them with just a few sips.

There was a time when Pinky had served blood, but when he took in three little girls, he changed the pub's policies quickly. Only animal blood was legal to serve in any restaurant or bar, but any bar or club that allowed the consumption of blood also had to deal with the suckers that came along with it. There were non-vamps, both mage and norms, who offered themselves up to vampires to have the blood sucked directly from their veins. Some did it for money, but others did it only for the high they got from the combination of blood loss and the agents in vampire saliva that brought on a euphoric feeling. Suckers were junkies, addicted to getting bitten.

Super strength and low inhibitions are a natural side effect of N-V, but human blood tended to magnify those effects while also clouding the mind. Add non-vamps with lowered inhibitions that would do anything to get sucked on, and you could get a rough scene going. Pinky didn't think it was safe to have that sort of crowd just a couple of floors below us.

Instead, the pub catered to older vampires who craved something a little more peaceful—a taste of a time before vampires were allowed to give into their every whim in public. Though they would be comfortable in any norm or mage bar, they preferred Pinky's because, except for my sisters, me, and the young kids on the weekends, most of the regulars were centuries old. While most of them didn't look past thirty, they often sat around talking about old times that took place hundreds of years ago.

Tonight, the pub was busy but not crowded. There were around thirty people, most of whom I recognized, scattered about the main room, sitting at the bar, chatting at tables, or dancing to the songs being crooned out by the single guitar playing singer on the corner stage. I couldn't see the back room from where I stood, but I would bet there were five or six men sitting around a large table playing cards.

Pinky was at one end of the bar, pouring drinks and chatting with customers. His wide grin was infectious. I wasn't sure what profession he had before the Cataclysm—he didn't talk much about his past—but whatever it was, it couldn't have been as perfect a fit for him as being a barkeep. With his friendly blue eyes and effervescent personality, he put people at ease and invited conversation. There was a bright, full-of-life quality to him that seemed to breathe life into the most somber room.

His shaggy brown hair, three-day-old beard growth, and lanky build added to his laughing blue eyes gave him an approachable sexiness that drew people to him like moths to flames. Though he'd seen as many bad days as anyone else who ventured into the bar, he had a perpetual air of youth, vitality, and openness about him. He made even the straightest of men question which team they played for, which was lucky since he was flexible on the subject himself.

Few people knew the strength and determination hidden behind the smiles. Though he looked like he'd just hit manhood, he was the only father my sisters and I had ever known. When it came to the safety and happiness of any of his girls, as he called us, the soft openness could be replaced with a hard ruthlessness within seconds that few could imagine.

As I watched him serve drinks and flirt with customers, a man walked in, stepped up to the bar, and waved to catch Pinky's attention. The man's back was to me but there was something about his broad-shouldered build, mannerisms, and immaculate khaki pants that gave me a good idea of who he was. Pinky leaned across the bar towards the man, listened for a moment, and then leaned back, his eyes darting around the room. Within seconds, he found what he was looking for and with a grin, pointed up at me. My stomach clenched as Ian turned and fixed his gaze on me.

What in Hades was he doing here? To my knowledge, Ian Barroes had never set foot in Pinky's Pub before. I would lay bets that with his uptight attitude, he'd never set foot in any bar before. But he wasn't in just any bar—he was in my bar. My home. And he was, very apparently, looking for me.

I glanced down at my clothes to make sure I looked okay. My outfit wasn't too different from what I wore for work. I wore leather pants and a vest, but the vest was new. I wore a black tank top underneath. I'd also left my weapons belt upstairs and borrowed a pair of Anya's spiky-heeled boots instead of my clunky, mud-caked combat boots. Freed of its normal braid, my hair fell around my shoulders in a mass of ebony waves.

I suddenly felt like a complete idiot. I wasn't some lovesick girl, and he wasn't my next conquest. He was probably there to discuss something work related—something too sensitive to talk about on the scry. Yes, that was it. This was a business call. Yet, a small part of me couldn't help but be glad I'd done as Anya had said and dressed appropriately for the bar.

I took a deep breath and headed down the stairs to see why Ian Barroes had invaded my home territory.

NINE
Fiona

By the time I made it down, Ian was seated on a stool sipping an ale Pinky had poured for him. A glass of strawberry mead sat in front of the stool next to him. I had no reason to ask if it was mine… Pinky knew what I liked.

"I thought you were one of those early to bed, early to rise people," I said, nodding at the clock above the bar that indicated it was nearly midnight. Early morning in vampire or barkeep hours, but Ian was neither. As far as I knew, he kept very early hours, both with the guild and his Academy classes.

"I usually am, but tonight, I can't seem to get to sleep," he said, sipping his ale.

"Is it the case this morning? Have you found out anything new?" I asked, hoping he would say yes. Not so much because of the case, because I had made my report to Sam and I was no longer on it. But Ian might not know that. So I was hoping he had found something out and came to talk to me because he thought I was the case agent in charge. The alternative was too uncomfortable to think about.

"As I told you this morning, I can't explain the lack of spirit around that body. I sent my report over to Sam. There is nothing more I can do.

It's for the investigators to figure out at this point." He kept sipping his ale as he talked. He didn't even turn to look at me. I swear it was as if the man knew exactly how to irritate me and did so on purpose.

"I see. Then why are you here?" I asked, my voice clipped.

"I told you, I couldn't sleep and wanted a drink."

Although I knew it was unethical, I opened my senses for just a moment. I felt no intense emotion at all coming off him. He was cool, calm, and telling the truth. I shut down my power to prevent the strong emotions from the other bar patrons from disturbing me. Trying to read emotions in a crowded room was like having a headache in a crowd of screaming people and trying to pick out one voice from the masses.

He might appear to be cool, calm, and collected, but I didn't buy it. I had no doubt he was skilled at keeping his emotions under control, even when lying. He had come here for a reason, and I was going to find out what that was, one way or another.

"So, you decided to come out hours after your normal bedtime, to a bar more than a mile from where you live, passing, what, fifteen or sixteen bars and restaurants on the way?" I didn't even try to hide the skepticism in my voice.

"Maybe I heard Pinky brews the best ale in the city-state and wanted to try it for myself." He smiled just enough to give him a look of innocence that most women would fall for. Most, but not me.

"He does, but I don't buy it, Barroes. Not when I'm sure if you had been that curious, you would have had one of your servants buy you some at the market. River sells it by the pint in her booth, which I figure you already know. Try something else."

This time, he unleashed his full grin as he turned to me, leaning with one elbow on the bar. Holy Mother Earth, how had I ever thought this man boring? He had charm in spades when he wanted to. Damn it!

"Well, then, maybe I wanted to buy you a drink," he said, smoothly gesturing towards the glass of mead in my hand.

"Buy me a drink? In my own bar? Really, Barroes? That's what you are going with?" I tried for as much sarcasm as I could muster to hide the way heat had just shot through my body at his words. So the unthinkable really was true. He was here just to see me.

Crap!

The grin faded slightly and his eyes darkened. "Dance with me."

It wasn't a question, but a soft demand.

"What?" Damn! Why did my voice sound so weak and bewildered?

"Don't look so scared. It's just a dance." His voice held amused arrogance.

But it wasn't just a dance. I knew that as certain as I knew my own name, and I knew he knew it too. I'd spent years resisting the magnetic force inside me that dragged me towards Ian. I didn't like him as a person, but I yearned for him as a woman. I'd denied the attraction, forcing myself to stay clear of him. He was not the type of man I wanted in my life, though at that moment, I couldn't remember exactly why. If I took his hand, it wouldn't be just a dance. If I went into his arms, I wouldn't be able to keep that distance anymore. I knew myself well enough to know that once I felt his arms around me, it wouldn't be enough.

When I didn't answer, only stood there looking at his hand like it would bite me, he lowered it and leaned against the bar. "My fair Fiona, why are you scared of me?"

"I'm not scared," I lied.

"Okay, then why do you hate me?" He asked the question casually, conversationally, as if he were asking the time of day.

"I don't hate you, Ian." It wasn't a lie. I didn't hate him. Although I tried to tell myself I did. Even just this morning I had thought how much I hated him. But that had been the lie. "But, I don't like you."

His lips twitched. "Why?"

"You are an arrogant, snobbish, boring, stuffy elitist." Most of it was honestly how I felt. Except the boring part. He was a bookish academic, a professor, so of course he was boring. Yet, whenever I was within ten feet of him, I felt anything but bored. It was as if the air around him was charged in a way to excite me, and only me, to the very core.

The damn man actually had the nerve to laugh. Laugh! It was a rich, throaty sound I had never heard before. He was always so serious; I didn't even know he knew how to laugh. Though admittedly, our contact had always been of a professional nature, and there wasn't much reason to laugh when standing over a dead body.

"What is so fucking funny?" I asked, not even attempting to hide my annoyance.

"I didn't realize you knew me well enough to have such a precise opinion of me," he said, wiping his eyes as if wiping away tears.

It hadn't been that damned funny, yet he had a point. We'd worked together many times over the past five or six years. I knew how he worked, I knew his reputation, and I knew basic facts about him. I knew what any coworker would know, but most of my knowledge about his life and history was secondhand from other agents.

"Okay, I concede that I don't know you well enough to have a personal opinion of you," I said, neutrally.

"And every time I've given you the opportunity to know me outside of work, you have refused."

It was true. It was not unusual for a team of Blades, Guards, and necromancers working a case together to have a meal or drinks together. Getting to know the people you worked with made it easier to trust the person at your back in a tense situation and promoted interagency relations. I often spent time outside of work with the men and women I worked with, yet any time Ian had been included in the group, I had come up with an excuse to skip out. I had also refused his personal offers of drink or meals or anything that would cause us to be alone while not working a case.

I wanted to tell myself it was because he was a necromancer, but I knew it would be a lie. I worked with other necromancers, and while I wasn't close, personal friends with any of them, I did my best to put my prejudices aside and did not avoid social situations where they were concerned. But, then, I didn't have the overwhelming urge to strip naked and jump any other necromancer every time they were within fifteen feet of me.

"You should at least give me the chance to earn such a low opinion," he continued, his eyes brimming with challenge.

It was a trap, and I knew it. I knew with every fiber of my being that he felt the sexual tension between us as sharply as I did. He knew if we danced, it wouldn't just be a dance. It would be the beginning of something hot and complicated.

I was the last person to run away from hot. Hot sex was the spice of life. But complicated had never been my style. I liked to know what was happening and what would happen next in a relationship. I couldn't possibly see how getting involved with Ian wouldn't be complicated. The worst part was I had no idea how it would end. My affairs usually had clear beginnings and rules for clear endings. Complicated usually meant a bad ending.

I could say something flippant, turn, and leave him standing here alone and avoid the situation for a while longer. I had been avoiding it for more than five years—I could keep doing it. But avoiding was getting so tiresome. And it was the coward's way out. I wasn't a coward.

Hoping my eyes didn't give away the tremble in my belly, I made my voice as aloof as possible. "Ok, fine. Let's dance."

I didn't take his hand. Instead, I put my glass on the bar, turned, and walked to the dance floor. When I found a clear spot, I turned to see he was still lazily leaning against the bar watching me. I tapped my foot impatiently and gave him my best, *well, let's get on with it* glare.

He grinned, drained the last of his ale from his glass before putting it on the bar, and then casually walked over to me. *Ugh! The nerve of the man.* Intellectually, I knew he was playing games with me. Oh, I had no doubt he actually wanted to dance with me, maybe even wanted me. But he was being as infuriatingly arrogant and insufferable as possible. Even more so than normal. I was sure he was doing it to see how much I would take. To gauge whether or not I was truly attracted to him.

I should teach him a lesson by turning on my heel and prancing off the dance floor leaving him there alone and looking like a fool. That was exactly what I should do. But I didn't. I knew I was letting him win. But I was tired of fighting it. My brain wanted to throttle him, but my body wanted to press against him. My body won the fight.

When he reached me, I took his outstretched hand and went to him, as grudgingly as I could manage. The moment his skin touched mine, all of my defiance melted, and my legs nearly did too. He pulled me to him, but I put up a token resistance, trying to keep a little space between us.

"Chicken," he purred in my ear as he tugged me closer. He smelled like old books laced with ale and a male spiciness unique to him. It was intoxicating. I gave up and let him fold me into him, my arms going around his neck as his hands firmly grasped my waist. We began to move gently to the music, Ian in the lead. We danced like that, staring into each other's eyes without speaking, for several moments. It felt almost as if it were a dare to see who looked away first. I was determined it wouldn't be me.

His eyes were dark, expressionless, and his face still held the same cocky, self-assured expression as before. My body tingled every place it touched his, but I couldn't tell what he was thinking or feeling, if anything at all. Just as I was about to open my senses again, he smiled a very sexy, almost naughty smile. My stomach lurched.

"See, dancing with me isn't so bad, is it?" His voice was low, smooth, and sexy.

I didn't respond, but he didn't seem to expect me too. He reached up, pushing a strand of hair out of my face and behind my ear, then used his finger to trace my earlobe and down my neck. Heat curled in my belly and shot through me in sharp bolts of lightning.

"You are so fucking beautiful!" It came out of him in a harsh rush, almost as if he hadn't meant to say it out loud, and from the look on his face, he hadn't.

It was my turn to flash a smug, knowing smile. I knew it! He felt the sexual pull just as surely as I did. And, he was just as thrown by it. I got a sick sense of satisfaction out of the knowledge. It also turned me on. As infuriatingly sexy as his arrogant act was, knowing he was actually a bit unsure and nervous was even more so.

I slid my hands up his neck and curled my fingers into his thick hair. He responded by looping his arm around my waist and pulling tight, so that we were plastered together from chest to hip. His other hand wrapped around the back of my neck and pulled my head to him. It was slow and deliberate, as if he was purposefully building the tension in me, in both of us. Just when I thought I could take no more, his lips touched mine.

Fire erupted inside me so intense and hot I was sure he could feel it too. His lips were warm and firm. I stuck out the tip of my tongue and ran it along his bottom lip, shivering from the pure pleasure of it. Fuck, he tasted so damned good.

Ian took this as a sign and deepened the kiss. His tongue invaded my mouth, licking at me with long, firm strokes. I returned the treatment fiercely.

This isn't a good idea. This isn't a good idea. The mantra beat weakly in the back of my mind, but for the life of me, I couldn't remember why it was a bad idea. I couldn't bring myself to care either. All I could think about was his scent, his heat, and how they surrounded me. The way his touch set me on fire. I wanted more. I needed more. Very much more. I had enough clarity to know I couldn't have him right there on the dance floor, but I wanted him. I wanted him so much. I would have him, too. I couldn't take him upstairs to my apartment where River was sleeping. But even though we didn't use the second floor rooms as an Inn anymore, a few were kept clean and stocked with linens.

Part of me wanted to tug him upstairs right that minute and have my way with him, but there was still one rational brain cell working. Having sex with Ian could complicate matters more than I was ready for. I'd had no-strings relationships with co-workers before, and it had never been a problem. But, I wasn't sure it would be the same with him.

I needed to know what he was feeling right now. I knew he wanted me. I pressed my hip into the hot, hard proof just to prove my point. He moaned against my mouth and tightened his grip on me. Oh, sweet fuck! I was almost lost. I clung to that last dreg of sanity for a moment longer. I couldn't read his thoughts, but feelings could betray thoughts pretty well. I needed to know he was as lost as I was, and I needed to make sure he wasn't feeling anything messy and complicated.

I opened my powers up just a little and the hot, raw patterns of sexual desire mixed with pure male satisfaction pounded against my senses. I had never opened my senses before when I was this sexually aroused. It was more intoxicating than I ever could have imagined. I pressed my hip into him again and felt a fresh wave of lust flow off him and wash over me. Oh, yeah, this was going to be fun. I wanted him, he wanted me, and we would have each other. Now. Consequences be damned.

I fought for enough control to push away long enough to suggest we go upstairs, but that meant pulling away from his heat and I didn't want to. He was so hot. I was so ...

Cold. One moment I was on fire, then a sudden, icy cold clamped around me. I had been bathed by my own arousal and the waves of energy coming off Ian, and then suddenly, there was no energy. I opened my senses as wide as they would go, but there was nothing. It was a complete lack of energy surrounding me. My hands dropped from Ian's neck, and I staggered back out of his grasp. My stomach lurched.

"Fiona. Fiona, what's wrong?" I could hear the growing concern in Ian's voice, but I couldn't respond. I could see Ian, Pinky, and all the other people in the bar, but the air around me was completely and totally devoid of energy as if they were dead. No, not dead, because their spirits would be there. There would be energy from the stone in the walls, the wood in the bar and chairs. But there was nothing. It was as if nothing existed. I was in a void, a vacuum.

Then, as suddenly as it had left, all the energy popped back into place. With my senses wide open like they were, the emotional energy of every living thing in the bar slammed into me all at once, sending me stumbling forward. If Ian hadn't reached out and caught me, I would have been on my knees. As it was, I grasped at his arms and clung to him for support while I quickly shut down my senses.

"Fiona, damn it, answer me. Are you okay? What's going on?" Concern and fear were thick in his voice.

"I'm fine. I'm fine." I tried to make my voice as normal as possible as I brushed back his hands and stood on my own. "I..."

What? What was I supposed to tell him? I couldn't tell him the truth. No one outside my family knew about my ability to read emotional energy, and this was not the time or place to tell him, even if I trusted him with the secret. Which I didn't.

"I'm just tired. I haven't slept much in the past couple of days, and I think I got a little overheated out there."

At least he had the decency to try to hide his smug grin. "You should probably go up and get some rest. We can continue where we left off some other time when you are well rested and up to the task." He stopped trying to hide the grin and let it fly full force.

I pointedly ignored the last part of his statement, even though my still quaky insides threatened to burst into flame again. I shot him my best don't-fucking-argue-with-me look and said, "What I really need is another drink."

For a moment, he looked like he wanted to protest but then thought better of it. He lightly took my elbow and led me back to the bar. Normally, I would have protested being led like a child, but I was still shaky on my feet and the extra support was welcome.

When we got to the bar, Pinky reached across and grabbed my hand. "Are you okay, Fee? What do you need?"

I smiled into his kind eyes. I didn't want him to worry, and there was nothing I could tell him in public. I shot him an, I'll-tell-you-later look and hoped he got it. "I'm fine. Could use another glass of that mead though."

To my relief, he seemed to get the message and didn't argue with my order. Within moments, I had a fresh glass in my hand. I turned to Ian, who was still glaring at me in concern.

I was just about to tell him again that I was fine, and possibly get a little pissy about it, when something by the door caught my eye. The crowd parted to let a tall, lethal-looking man walk in. He was around 6'4 and broad shouldered with dark brown, shoulder-length hair and about three days' worth of beard growth. As if the black leather pants, ankle-length leather duster, and shaded glasses in the middle of the night didn't make the vampire look scary enough, the huge, curved sword at his hip did the trick.

Forgetting my dizziness, I took off at a dead run towards him and jumped. He caught me effortlessly and pulled me into a hug. "How are you, Tiny Fee?" he asked affectionately, with a slight hint of an accent he hadn't lost after more than five hundred years.

I hugged him hard around the neck and laughed. "Jarrett, I am not tiny. Quit calling me that. And let me down, you big lug!"

He grinned. "You are tiny to me."

"A building is tiny to you, you monster," I quipped. But damn, the man was sexy. He was tall, but his frame was lean and muscular. Even without the super-vampire strength, he would be a force to be reckoned with in a fight. If he weren't my best friend, outside of my family, I probably would have slept with him long ago. Many times in fact.

"What are you doing here? I didn't know you were in Nash," I asked. I was also surprised to see him in Pinky's. Jarrett rarely made it into Nash, and I didn't think he'd ever come to Pinky's before. Pinky's was my home and even though he was one of my best friends, Jarrett was, like Ian, a part of my work life, and I usually tried to keep the two separate.

"I just flew in today," he said.

"Oh, yeah. I saw an airship docking this morning. I had no idea you were on it."

"Yeah, no one did. Trying to keep my whereabouts a little hush-hush," he said, unnecessarily. Jarrett always tried to keep his whereabouts a mystery. His job demanded a low profile. Well, as low a profile as a huge, super-sexy vamp could have.

"So, how long you here for?" I asked.

"A couple of weeks, actually. I'm waiting on an informant to show up. Wanted to get a little down time in before the meet." He pulled his dark glasses off and winked at me.

Wanted, like hell. Being a Blade, especially a field agent, didn't exactly come with regular office hours. When you were in the field, as Jarrett was most of the time, you were on the job non-stop. As a result, field agents had to take a certain number of mandatory leave days a year. Most Blades looked forward to the time off. Jarrett wasn't most Blades. He lived and breathed his job, and he had to be forced to take leave time. But either way, it was cool for me. We'd get to hang out a bit without being worried someone was going to try to kill us. It would be a first.

"Oh, but I'm here because Sam sent you a message," he continued. "He said to tell you he got the reports from you and Barroes and sent them on to the Guard. The case is back in the Guard's hands, and you can take a few days off."

"Well, looks like we are both on leave." I grinned.

"Since I'm here and neither of us has anywhere to be tomorrow, can I buy you a drink? Or is your boyfriend over there going to try to slit my throat?" he asked, looking over my head.

"He's not my boy…" I trailed off as I turned and saw the murderous expression on Ian's face. "Oh, hell. Come on before he kills us both."

I pulled Jarrett over. "Ian, this is my friend Jarrett Campbell." I put emphasis on the word friend, not knowing exactly why. My relationship with Jarrett was none of Ian's damned business. "Jarrett, this is Ian Barroes."

"The head of the Nash Necromancer's Guild," Jarrett supplied. "I've heard a lot about you. Great to meet you." He reached out a hand, which Ian grudgingly shook. "Look," he continued. "If you guys are in the middle of something, I can head down to the end of the bar and chat up that cute redhead."

Obviously realizing Jarrett was no threat to him, Ian's expression softened. "No, it's okay. It's obvious you two have some catching up to do and frankly, it's way past my bedtime. I'm going to head out. It was nice meeting you." He gave Jarrett an absent wave and headed towards the door. As he passed me, he stopped and leaned in as close as he could get without touching me. His breath was warm on my ear as he said, "We will finish our earlier, um, conversation another time."

Chills of anticipation shot through me as he straightened and walked away.

Once Ian was gone, Jarrett said, "That looked pretty damned intense. You want to talk about it?"

"Not even a fucking little." I chugged the rest of my mead.

Jarrett laughed.

"I haven't seen you around these parts in a couple of months. You been in the wild and scary south?" I changed the subject not so subtly.

Jarrett laughed. "Actually, no. I've been in No Man's Land."

"Fuck! Detroit? I'm glad to see you're still alive." I said it with a laugh, but we both knew I wasn't joking.

Jarrett was the best of the best. The Blades were the most powerful, toughest paranorms in the world, at least the ones on the right side of the law. Jarrett was a part of an elite team of Blades called the Kukri, named after the curved, machete-like blades they all carried. The Kukri was made up of the toughest, hardest, and most powerful of the Black Blade Guard. But there was more to it than power. If that were all it took, I would have been a Kukri long ago. The Blades that were a part of the elite team had a certain lethalness about them. The Kukri weren't normal Blades. They were spies and assassins. They did the dirtiest, most dangerous jobs, and took no prisoners. If you were bad enough to have a Kukri sent after you,

you'd soon be dead. With the Kukri, there were no second chances.

As badass as Kukri were, even they rarely ventured into the No Man's Land of Detroit. According to the history books, Detroit had been a thriving metropolis several times the size of Old Nashville on the banks of a lake the size of a small inlet sea back in the Tech Age. In addition to the ravages of the Cataclysm, it had, like most of the major metropolitan areas of the Americas, been bombed during the Religion War that erupted at the start of the Cataclysm and, like all of the big cities, famine and disease ran rampant.

While Nash, parts of Atlanta, and some other small towns and cities had been at least partially saved by paranorms coming out of the hiding they had been in for millennia, showing their powers and using them to save themselves, norms, and as much of their society as possible, Detroit experienced the polar opposite. Radiation and chemical poisoning from bombs and industrial plants made many areas unlivable by all but vampires and some mages. Any norms that didn't flee the city when the Cataclysm began were killed either by the effects of the bombs or by the invading vampires and mages.

They took over, rioting, killing, and pillaging. The city was now overrun with the most dangerous thugs and criminals the world had to offer. The Paranorm Council took a hands-off approach to Detroit and only rarely sent agents in to follow a criminal, and usually only if they suspected the criminal had plans to recruit a crew for future crimes in a Paranorm Council Allied city-state. The magnitude of those future crimes would have to be pretty bad. If Jarrett had been sent in to Detroit, then someone awful had been on the loose.

"So, is there a big bad coming down the line I need to be prepared for? Or did you get your guy?" I asked, only half joking. Normally, a Kukri always got his guy, but when you went into a viper's nest like Detroit, you had to play your cards a little differently. Sometimes just getting in and out alive with a little more info than you had when you went in could be considered a major win.

"No worries, Fee. I got the guy I was sent in after." His face was expressionless, but something in his eyes told me he hadn't told me the whole truth. It also told me not to pry. If he needed to talk, he would in his own time.

He drained his glass and said, "But enough about work. Let me buy you a whiskey, and you can tell me all about that hot redhead."

I followed his gaze and couldn't hold back the peal of laughter.

"That's my sister."

One eyebrow shot up. "I see. Does that mean you'll kick my ass if I hit on her?"

I laughed. "No. But I can't guarantee she won't."

"Hmm." He grinned. "A challenge! I love to be challenged."

I just laughed. I could have told him about Anya's rule about never dating, or even fucking, vampires, but I didn't see any need. Anya was a big girl and if she didn't want his attention, she'd tell him so. While I knew he thought of sex and conquests in much the same way as Anya, I knew I could trust him to back off if she said no. And if he didn't, I put my money on my sister, even if he was a badass Kukri.

I settled onto the bar stool next to Jarrett, took the glass of whiskey, and drained it in a single gulp. It burned going down, and then a warmth spread through my body, pushing out the coldness that had invaded after leaving Ian's arms.

Slamming the glass on the bar, I said, "Buy me another one and I might even put in a good word for you with my sister."

He did. Then another and another. We spent the rest of the night drinking, laughing, and reminiscing over old times, and I did my damndest not to think about what had happened out on the dance floor. Not about the weird energy disappearance and not about Ian and what it had felt like to be in his arms.

TEN

He watched her as she laughed with the tall vampire, sliding into his divine sight one more time. The way the energy ebbed and flowed around her, the way her aura pulsed with every color of the rainbow, made his mouth water. She was magnificent. He'd known it the moment he'd walked into the dingy little bar earlier and saw her drinking with the other one, the necromancer. He'd been using his second sight then, too, hunting out someone worthy enough to be his next meal. Then he'd just thought she was a magnificent meal waiting to be devoured. He hadn't realized she was the one he'd been looking for. The one that would change everything.

He'd hoped the necromancer would leave, and he could buy her a drink. Perhaps lure her outside where they had some privacy. He'd sat at a table in the corner and watched, but the necromancer never left. He'd just been ready to give up the juicy prize and find another worthy soul when the beauty began to dance with him. He couldn't resist the urge to get a little closer. She was so full of energy that it lured him. In this state, in this body, he couldn't feel the energy, but he couldn't resist the urge to take a closer look at her pulsing aura.

So he asked some stray woman to dance and pushed her across the dance floor to be near the beauty. Now he was so glad he had. He'd just slipped into his second sight when her aura began to pulse wildly. The energy in the room began vibrating towards her. Her aura flared so bright it blinded him for a moment, so that he stumbled and nearly knocked his dance partner into the other couple.

He got too close. Her aura blinked out, and she'd stumbled. He could tell she hadn't known what happened and he retreated quickly, so that she wouldn't figure it out.

He'd been stunned. She wasn't just a quick and yummy meal. She was everything he'd been looking for but hadn't been sure existed.

He wanted her, and he would have her. But it was clear the vampire wasn't going anywhere soon. This body was starting to tire. He'd have to leave it soon, and he needed new energy. He'd been deprived last night by that horrible little thing, not just of her essence, but also of a perfectly usable body. He'd find her again, and when he did, he'd devour her in the most painful way possible. Because of the little brat, he couldn't afford to wait around to try to get the beauty alone. He needed sustenance soon.

Slipping back into regular sight, he left the bar to follow a group of girls who he heard talking about going to another bar down the block. He was sure that with this body, he could lure one of them away from the group. They all had low- to mid-level powers, but that was okay. He could make do with substandard nourishment for a little while longer.

He'd find the beauty again, soon, and she would be his. Forever. She wouldn't just nourish his body for a day or two. She would transform him. She would make him a God.

ELEVEN
Ian

*I*AN CLOSED THE BOOK WITH A DULL THUD AND LEANED BACK IN HIS CHAIR, rubbing his tired eyes. Nothing. It had been three days, and he still had no explanation for the dried and withered spiritless corpse in the morgue. Although the case had officially reverted to the jurisdiction of the City Guard and they had not asked for his help, Ian had not been able to let it go, neither had Sam Harrison. Ian had scryed Sam with the details of Millie Linton's interview the moment he'd arrived back at his office. He knew Fiona suspected a necromancer had done this foul deed, as did Sam, and at first, so had Ian himself.

He had never seen or heard of anything like it. He'd promised Sam he would do some research and see if he could find out what could have caused the spirit to leave the body so completely. He'd immediately scryed the caretaker of the family compound in the mountains and had him round up every text on Necromancy in the library. It had taken the man almost an entire day to round up the nearly one hundred texts and another day and a half for the wagon driver he hired to bring them into the city.

Four hundred years ago, the Barroes family had been little more than a traveling band of con artists. Back then, the paranorm society had been a secret hiding in plain sight. They lived in the norm world, following the rules of norm society as well as the rules of the Paranorm Council. The Barroes family was an old paranorm family with a history of producing children with necromantic powers. Back then, most necromancers lived on the edge of both the paranorm and norm legal systems, and the Barroes clan had been no different. As a matter of fact, they had celebrated it. Children with necromantic powers were taught from an early age how to use the information they could glean from the dead to con and bilk unsuspecting people, norms and paranorms alike.

They had lived on the road, traveling from city to town, executing con jobs and moving on when norm or paranorm authorities started catching on. Until, that was, sometime in the mid-1800s when a Barroes girl, Ian's several times Great Aunt Matilda, had been born with the power of foresight. It wasn't an uncommon power in the Barroes clan, especially among the girls, but Matilda had been different. Her powers had been extremely strong and accurate. For years, the family used her visions to make more and more money. Then, when she was in her thirties, she began to have terrifying visions. She saw death and destruction hundreds of years into the future. The end of civilization.

The girl's father, having witnessed several of her visions come to fruition, took what she saw very seriously. The family found a place deep in the mountains of Tennessee. For the next two hundred years, using Matilda's detailed journals, the following generations had built up their wealth and turned the mountain home into a compound, a fortress really. The underground bunkers held food and supplies. They had horded everyday items that had cost pennies back then, but after the Cataclysm, they could be traded and sold for a hundred times their original worth. They had become rich off the combination of Matilda's visions and their necromantic powers, and had emerged from the Cataclysm almost unscathed and even richer than they had been before.

The library had been one of the things they had horded. In order to make sure the Barroes family, for they'd had no interest in sharing their wealth and knowledge with the rest of society, was well educated in the dark and ignorant times after the Cataclysm, they had amassed an impressive library full of books on history, science, and math. They'd also made it a point to get a copy of every book on magic, especially Necromancy, they could put their hands on. Not the silly books put out by norms that had no idea of the real existence of paranorms or magic, but the secret, underground texts.

There were hundreds in the family library. Ian had spent as much time as possible in the library bunker when he'd been a child. He'd loved learning. When he had left the family compound for good to live in Nash, his father had forbidden him to bring any books. In the years since his father's death, he'd brought many of the books to his home in Nash and had even donated some to the city archival library for the use of Academy students. He used some of the historical texts on Necromancy in his classes, but he had left most of them at the compound. Now they were all here, and he'd spent all day yesterday and all of this morning going through them.

He glanced at the ticking clock on the wall as he sipped the cup of tea Mrs. Gary had brought in a few minutes earlier, along with a plate of bread and cheese and a steaming bowl of vegetable soup. It was midday. He'd been reading through books since dawn. He'd read and reread dozens of tomes on the history and scientific theory of Necromancy and was no closer to knowing what had separated that man's spirit from his body than he had been three days ago. The only thing he knew for sure was this was in no way related to Necromancy. There was definitely magic involved, and someone very powerful. But it wasn't Necromancy, so it wasn't his business.

He looked at the pile of books again. Since he had them here now, he'd lend them to the city archives so they could be copied and added to the library. But that could wait. First, he'd eat his lunch and maybe find Fiona. He hadn't seen her since the night they'd danced at Pinky's. His body tensed and began to harden at the memory of her in his arms and that kiss... Could he call it a kiss? It had been more like a mutual devouring.

He had always known if he ever got her in his arms that the connection would be powerful, but the reality of it had been far beyond his dreams. He hadn't meant to kiss her. Hadn't even meant to dance with her.

He'd spent the entire evening going through magical history books from the City Archives and had, of course, come up with nothing. He'd been wide-awake, restless, and thinking about Fiona. Since seeing her that morning, he had barely been able to concentrate on anything else. It was like that every time he worked with her. For days afterwards, all he could think about was what it would be like to touch her sun-kissed skin and taste her full, pink lips. He imagined her dark hair spread across his pillow. It was beginning to get out of hand. That night he'd been fed up. Enough was enough. It was time for him to take matters into his own hands. Time to man up and start on the road to making those imaginings a reality.

Before he could think better of it, he'd found himself in Pinky's ordering a drink and asking about Fiona. He hadn't intended to do more than have a drink and say hi. He wanted her to see him outside of the work environment, start seeing him as a man instead of just a necromancer. He'd also figured that showing up on her home turf would shake her up a little. She was so steady, so unflappable. He needed to catch her off her guard, and he figured invading her home territory would be just the way to do it.

But then she'd been there next to him, and she'd been so beautiful and so pissed off. He hadn't been able to resist pushing her a bit. Nothing risked, nothing gained. So he'd asked her to dance. He hadn't been sure he'd be able to get her to agree, but she had, finally. It was just supposed to be a dance. One dance to shake her up a little. To show her his intentions—to prove that he would be back for more. But it had been so much more than he had expected. The moment their skin touched the world had ceased to exist for him. A conflagration had erupted inside him that threatened to burn them both to cinders. He knew, from the look in her eyes, she had felt it too.

She'd been so incredibly beautiful, so intensely warm in his arms, that he had not been able to resist the pull to taste her. And when he had, he'd been lost, completely and utterly lost. If she hadn't stumbled, he would have had her even if he'd had to find a dark corner to do the deed, and from the intensity in her kiss and the gyrations of her body against his, he'd known she wouldn't have objected.

But then she'd stumbled and gone pale. It had scared the life out of him, but she'd sworn she was okay. He didn't believe for a moment she'd just been tired. Something strange had happened to her, he knew it. He'd felt her using her magic, felt the pull of energy towards her, and then it had abruptly stopped. He'd let it go because she seemed to recover quickly, and he hadn't wanted to push too hard. He would have eased back into the subject, but then that damned good-looking vampire had shown up.

As he'd watched her wrap her curvy body around the huge man, a white-hot fury of jealousy he hadn't thought himself capable of flooded his senses. He'd always thought himself an intelligent, civilized man who used his brain first and his brawn second. But for a moment, a long moment, there had been nothing he'd wanted to do more than punch

Jarrett Campbell in the throat.

Bzzzz. A soft buzzing and a pulsing, blue light pulled him out of his thoughts. Someone was scrying him. He turned to the large, flat crystal attached to the wall next to his desk and touched it to activate it. Instantly, the light faded, and Sam Harrison's face appeared in the crystal.

"Hello, Sam," he said jovially. He liked Sam. Most Blades were punch-first-think-later types. Sam wasn't. He was well educated and articulate. He was one of the few people Ian liked talking to.

"Ian." Sam's tone was a bit brusque. "Sorry to be abrupt, but I need to know if you found out anything about that body in those books of yours. And don't tell me you haven't looked because I know better. Jurisdiction wouldn't mean crap to you if there was a possibility of a necromancer being involved."

Oh, how well Sam knew him. He smiled wryly. "I've read every book I have and some from the City Archives. Twice. Nothing. I can find no explanation."

"Damn," Sam spat out. "I was hoping you might have some sort of lead." Sam's face was creased with worry. Not a usual look for him.

Ian asked, "Did another body turn up?"

"No, not exactly. But as of this morning, this is an official Blades' case and I need you on it."

"If Necromancy isn't involved and there aren't any bodies, is there anything I can really do?" Ian asked. Not because he was unwilling to help, he just didn't know how he possibly could.

"Oh, I'm pretty sure there are bodies, lots of them. We just haven't found them," Sam said, running a hand over his face tiredly.

"A lot of bodies? Shit, Sam. What's going on?" There was never a shortage of work for the necromancers that worked with the Blades, but that was because they could glean information from spirits on all types of cases. Actual murder, while rampant in the unprotected Outer Zones—the wild territory between the safety of the walls of the various cities, towns, and communes—was very rare inside the walls of Nash City. A lot of potential bodies could only mean murder.

"I can't really explain it all right now. Can you get down here?"

"I'll be there in half an hour." He swiped his hand across the scry, and Sam's image disappeared. Grabbing a hunk of bread and cheese from the plate, he headed for the door.

Sam looked up from a thick stack of papers as Ian walked into his office in the Blade Headquarters less than twenty minutes later. "Ian, thanks for getting here so quickly. Have a seat." He gestured to a well-used wooden chair across from his desk.

Ian took in Sam's tired and haggard appearance, his rumpled clothes, and the papers strewn across his desk. His friend's abrupt and urgent request for him to get here had made him wonder what had happened. Everything he observed since he stepped on to the thirtieth floor was evidence that it was something major. "What's going on Sam? It's a madhouse out there," he said, jerking his head at the general chaos of agents and office personnel rushing around in the outer offices.

"It's been that way since about three this morning, and I'm afraid it isn't going to get much better anytime soon." He leaned back tiredly in his chair.

"Okay, I was supposed to be off the rest of the week but I get an urgent message to get my ass in your office ASAP, so I'm here. Looks like all hell has broken loose. What's up…?" Fiona stopped short in the doorway. "Oh, sorry, I can come back."

Sam waved her in. "I was waiting on you to get started. We'll discuss later why, when you live a block away and Ian is more than a mile away and I called you twenty minutes before him, it took you longer to get here."

Fiona let out a loud sigh, rolled her eyes, and plopped into the chair next to Ian. "I had a late night; I was on leave you know. Plus, it takes a while to look this fabulous."

Ian's eyes scanned her body, taking in her appearance. She wore a multi-pocketed leather vest over a loose, blue tunic. Her leather pants were tucked into black combat boots that were worn, but cleaner than they had been three days before. Her thick, black hair was pulled back into a haphazard braid. The only thing about her outfit that could have taken more than three minutes to throw on was the myriad of blades he knew she had stuck in her boots and the thick, leather utility belt that was slung low over her hips.

Nonetheless, she did look fabulous. The leather pants clung to her firm, rounded thighs beneath the hem of her tunic and the snug vest did nothing to take away from the lush curve of her breasts. Her clothes were like any other Blades', utilitarIan, tough, and ready for action, yet on her, they added to, rather than detracted from, her raw, sexual beauty. Ian felt himself hardening involuntarily, a craving for her that never really went away starting to grow into an intense hunger. He fought for control, sliding his gaze back to Sam in order to dampen his lust and get his brain back on track.

"So, Sam, what has happened?" He hoped his voice didn't sound as strangled as he felt.

Sam raised one eyebrow at Ian. He'd obviously seen Ian's reaction to Fiona but after a moment, he must have decided to dismiss it in light of other, more important, issues. He picked up two files from his desk and tossed one to each of them. "For starters, we have identified your dead body in the morgue."

Ian and Fiona spoke at the same time.

"What do you mean "our" dead body?"

"Who is he? How did you ID him?"

Sam shot them a hard glare. "Give me a minute to go over the details, would you? There are quite a lot of them. First, Fiona," he said her name pointedly. "*Your* dead body because this just became an official Blades' case, and you two have landed the lead positions. I'll go into the whys on that in a minute." He held up a hand as Fiona opened her mouth. "Don't interrupt me."

He continued, quickly, before either could respond. "Let me start at the beginning. Yesterday afternoon a transcriber in the typing pool at the City Guard headquarters noticed a disturbing trend. He found three women and two men, all mages, that were reported missing in an eight-week period. Their profiles are in the files I gave you. They all lived in different districts around Nash City and New Nashville. That is why no one caught it before now."

Ian leaned forward, resting his elbows on his knees. "If they lived in different districts, how are they connected and what does it have to do with the body?"

Sam sighed. "Well, as the transcriber pointed out to his supervisor, each and every one of them were last seen in or around businesses on Broadway. This morning around three, the med-mages finally identified the body in the morgue. His name is Abel Evans, and he was twenty-four years old when he went missing a little over five weeks ago. He was the third name on the transcriber's list."

Fiona sat up and slid to the edge of her chair. "So our attempted kidnapper went into hiding and kidnapped four people before he was stopped by a sixteen-year-old girl?"

"Wouldn't it be nice if it were that cut and dry? But then you wouldn't be sitting in my office annoying me, I would have gotten a good night's sleep, and all those agents out there wouldn't be pulling double shifts." Sam shot Fiona a tired, exasperated look.

"It's a plausible theory," Ian said, not sure why he felt the need to defend Fiona, especially after she shot him a look that clearly told him she could take care of herself and he should shut the fuck up.

"Agents covered that first thing this morning. When questioned about the dates of the two previous kidnappings, his mother gave him solid alibis. She hadn't yet been informed of his body and had been told by the agents they were investigating the possibility that someone tried to harm him on those dates. Unless other evidence is found, we are going with the theory that there is someone else behind the kidnappings, though we aren't ruling out that he was involved. He could have had a partner."

Fiona looked thoughtful. After a moment, she asked, "What have the med-mages said about his body? Could he have had a disease of some sort? Perhaps he wasn't trying to hurt Millie, but was sick and trying to get help and scared her?"

"Nothing so far. There were no bodily fluids at all, so it is making analysis slow going, but so far, they've found no toxins and no contagions." He rubbed a hand over his face. "Frankly, we still have no clue on that front. As strange as it is, it is actually our secondary concern right now. The disappearances officially became a Blades' case when his body was identified, and I currently have agents scouring the last six months' worth of Guards' cases to see if there are any other cases that fit the trend."

Ian flipped the file in his hand closed. "I can visit the residences and places of work of the victims. Even if they haven't died and returned, there may be spirits that know something that can help."

"That is exactly what I want you to do. Together. We aren't sure what we are messing with so I can't be sure you wouldn't be in danger alone. But, we have a more pressing matter. Another young girl was reported missing yesterday," Sam said.

"You think it is related? Does it fit the pattern?" Fiona said.

"She was last seen three nights ago just outside of Pinky's Pub," Sam said, his tone measured.

"I was down in the pub three nights ago," Fiona said. Her face was an unreadable mask, but Ian detected a slight tension in her voice.

"We both were," Ian added. "I didn't notice anything unusual." Other than Fiona's reaction to their kiss, but he didn't feel Sam needed to know anything about that.

"That doesn't surprise me. According to the investigation reports by the Guards, other than the attempted abduction of Millie Linton four nights ago, there were no public disturbances involving the victims. Considering the dark alley Miss Linton was in, if she hadn't succeeded in getting into the open, there might not have been any trace of her either," Sam said, getting out of his chair to walk around and sit on the corner of his desk closest to Fiona.

"Now, Fiona, you should know at least two of the missing women were in Pinky's Pub at some point the nights they disappeared," he continued, his voice low and calm, as if breaking unsettling news to a child. Ian understood, immediately, why. Fiona wasn't known for her levelheaded thinking, and though he didn't know her nearly as well as he wanted, he knew her well enough to know that she would be very protective of her family.

Fiona's hands gripped the edge of the chair so tight her knuckles turned white, but when she spoke, her voice was low and carefully moderated. "Pinky had nothing to do with these disappearances."

"I know," Sam said quickly. "No one thinks otherwise. If I did, you wouldn't be in my office getting the rundown on the case. But both he and Anya will have to be questioned. River also, since she lives in the building. It's standard procedure. I've already sent two agents."

"I want to be there." She started to stand, but a light touch from Sam on her shoulder made her sit back down. Ian marveled at their relationship. He imagined that if he had touched her, he would have ended up with a couple of broken fingers.

Sam's voice was low, but stern. "No. I need you here. There is something more important for you to do than babysit your family through routine questioning. But, I did have Jarrett tag along with the agents. He isn't officially on the job, but he was in the office this morning, at loose ends, and I knew you'd feel better knowing he was there with them."

Ian could see some of the tension that had held her stiff and straight in the chair ease out. Her posture softened visibly, and she sunk back into the chair. But she didn't relax completely. Her stony gaze was fixed on Sam. "Okay, but don't think this is over. You ambushed me with this. I know you were just trying to make things easier for the other agents by making sure I was out of the way first, but I don't like it and we will discuss it later."

"Fair enough," Sam replied, seemingly unconcerned.

With that little exchange over, Ian decided it was time to inject himself back into the conversation. "I know enough about procedure to know that since Fiona lives in the building, she shouldn't be on this case. As a matter of fact, since we were both in the pub the night the most-recent victim went missing, neither of us should be on this case. Even assuming you have checked our alibis for the nights the others disappeared—am I right in assuming you checked case files on Fiona, and that the moment I set foot in this building, you sent agents to my building to question the guards about my whereabouts the nights in question?"

"Yes, on both. Just to avoid any appearance of impropriety," Sam replied, obviously not surprised or offended by the question.

"Okay," Ian continued. "So, assuming we are cleared of any possible suspicion, we are still potential witnesses. That makes it highly irregular to have either of us anywhere near the case, much less in charge. Not to belittle the importance of several missing people, but that doesn't seem big enough to flout procedure when there are many well-qualified Blade agents and Guild-certified necromancers that can take charge. What makes this case special?"

Sam returned to his desk chair, sat down, and handed each of them another file folder. "Farah Purcell, the young woman reported missing most recently, is the daughter of Granger Purcell. Not only is he a Norm senator, but he is slated to be the next Norm Chancellor at the end of the year."

In the chair next to him, Fiona let out an audible groan and slammed her palm into her forehead. Ian was too professional to indulge in such a display of emotion, but inside, he mentally copied her. This was, indeed, a complicated case.

"As soon as the pattern of disappearances was discovered by the Guards, there was an audit of most recent cases. Of course the senator's daughter was already a high priority for them, but when they saw her disappearance fit the pattern, the commander informed the Chief Magistrate of the City Guard, who sent the info over to us to become a part of our case. As is her duty, Magistrate Collins then took it to the chancellors, waking them up. From what the magistrate told me, it took them all of three minutes to scry me to make the Purcell case top priority."

"I'm surprised a missing senator's daughter hadn't already been made a Blades' case," Ian said, matter-of-factly.

Sam let out a short snort. "Nan Collins has ambitions beyond Chief Magistrate of the City Guard. She aspires to run for one of the Mage senate seats in the next term election. The Purcell case would have been one hell of a feather in her cap. I'm sure that is why she kept the case under her jurisdiction."

Fiona laughed derisively. "And I'm betting the second she saw it was likely related to the strange dead body case, she handed it over gladly. The thing about career-making cases is that they can break them too. No one wants to be stuck with a case so bizarre that they have no hopes of solving it. So goody for us, we get to take charge of the weird, unsolvable case."

"I've never seen an unsolvable crime, just those that took more effort and time to solve than others," Ian said, his tone and manner much more haughty and self-assured than he felt. He was just as unenthusiastic about being on this case as Fiona. Despite the fact that he was looking forward to the time heading up a case together would force them to spend together, there was something strange about this case that gave him a bad feeling. Of course, though he had a contract with the Blades as a consultant, he was under no obligation to take this or any case. He could walk away and not look back. But Fiona couldn't. She was a Blade and took what was assigned to her. Ian's gut feeling was that something very dangerous was lurking in the shadows of this mystery. Something more dangerous than even tough-as-nails Fiona could handle alone. So, really, he had no choice but to work the case.

"Never seen an unsolvable crime?" Fiona's tone was mocking. "Since when are you a Blade or Guard? You are a glorified teacher who consults on the odd case every once in a while. Suddenly, you think you are an expert on crime solving?"

Ian drew himself up straighter in his chair and turned towards her. This time as he spoke, he didn't have to pretend confidence. *How dare she mock him?* Her attitude was beyond bearing sometimes. "I will have you know, I have been consulting with the Blades and the Guards since I was sixteen and started in the Academy. Which would have made you, what, about nine years old?"

"Oh, were you a late bloomer? I started the Academy at fourteen," she said sweetly.

Ian was about to respond when the sound of something heavy hitting the desk interrupted them.

"Children!" Sam thundered, his voice booming through the office. Ian pulled his gaze away from Fiona to see Sam standing, bent over his desk with his hands bracing him as if he was ready to vault over it. "That is enough. While I normally find your constant bickering amusing and the entire agency has bets on how long it will take you two to climb into the sack, today my patience is wearing too thin to deal with your pent-up sexual tension. I have lost track of how many hours it has been since I last slept, and I have spent the morning getting scrys from every senator in the city-state, getting raked over the coals about not solving Farah Purcell's disappearance fast enough and allowing a serial kidnapper to run loose in the streets. It doesn't seem to matter that the Purcell case just fell on my desk a few hours ago and it is the City Guards' job, not the Blades', to protect the citizens from dangers in the streets. In addition, hours that could have been better spent trying to find all the missing people, I have instead spent trying to convince the senators not to go public with this, create a panic in the streets, and alert the kidnappers we are on to them. So, as you can see, I'm in a bad mood, and I need you to work together with some sort of professionalism. I don't care if that means you have to beat each other bloody in a back alley or find a room and fuck like bunnies. Whatever it is, work it out on your own time. I need you focused!"

TWELVE
Ian

*I*AN SNAPPED HIS MOUTH SHUT AND LISTENED TO SAM'S TIRADE IN COMPLETE silence. Even if he'd wanted to respond, he couldn't have. As much as he hated being chastised like an errant kid, he had to admit that Sam was right, on all accounts. He had acted childishly. He could excuse himself by noting that Fiona provoked him, but that would be both pointless and childish. Fiona always agitated him. It was what she did. It was as if it were a second career for her, irritating him to the ends of his sanity.

Just because she provoked him did not mean he had to respond. He was an educated man with better sense and decorum than that. Though, admittedly, both seemed to disappear every time he was in the same room as Fiona Moon. On one hand, he was sure that Sam's assessment of the situation was right on. He'd also been right about how to solve the problem. Ian and Fiona would never be able to get their professional relationship on an even keel until they sorted out the attraction between them. They would sort it out, Ian was determined on that front, but it would have to wait. In the meantime, he needed to try to keep his common sense about him.

"You are right, Sam," he said, and then turned to look at Fiona. "I apologize for acting like a juvenile."

Fiona didn't respond except to glare at him so hard he was sure that if she had telekinetic powers, his heart would have exploded.

"Fiona!" There was a low growl in Sam's voice.

Sam was calm and rational so much of the time that it was easy for Ian to forget he was a shifter, that beneath the easygoing exterior lay the instincts and soul of an animal. The growl in his voice when he said Fiona's name brought that reality home to Ian. Even though he trusted Sam completely, his human reaction to an animal's growl was to go on alert, and even a little initial fear. That was normal and the type of reaction Ian would expect to have. What he didn't expect was the overwhelming protectiveness for Fiona that erupted in him. The rumble in Sam's throat had been nothing more than a gentle warning, yet it had been directed at Fiona and some deep, primal instinct flared inside Ian. It was all he could do to fight the urge to jump up and stand between them.

Fiona, however, did not seem the least bit fazed by Sam's display of alpha power, nor did she seem to notice Ian's reaction, though the tiny twitch in the corner of Sam's mouth told Ian the were-jaguar had noticed.

Fiona slowly turned her icy, dagger-shooting gaze from Ian to Sam. "Don't growl at me. I'll mind my manners. Now, missing people, dead bodies, where do you want us to start?"

Sam shook his head as if defeated and sat back down. "There is a list of addresses in the files I gave you. Go check out the homes and work places of each of the victims."

"We should probably check out the places each of them were last seen, and walk the streets and alleys nearby. Spirits often linger in an area if they experienced a traumatic death, or return to the last place they were before the trauma," Ian interjected.

"Okay, but go to the Purcell's first. The family is there now, and they are expecting the two of you. The lead Guard Detective on this case is also there now. He is to be kept in the loop. While we have full jurisdiction, we are affording the Guards every professional courtesy, so play nice." Sam said the last with a pointed stare at Fiona.

"I always play nice," she said, her icy tone from a few minutes earlier gone and replaced by her usual casual insolence. "But it doesn't seem like going around, looking for spirits, is going to get us far. We should be doing something a little more proactive. And don't get your undies in a knot, Barroes. I'm not saying we shouldn't do that. I'm just saying that unless they are already dead, we won't get much. We should be trying to do something to stop the guy before they get dead."

"Okay, Miss Moon. What do you suggest we do?" He had to bite the inside of his cheek to keep from laughing at the death stare she aimed at him for calling her "Miss Moon". Perhaps it was a tad childish, and he had just promised to act with a little more decorum, but he couldn't resist baiting her a little.

To her credit, she didn't take the bait. "The second male victim should be high on our priority list." She glanced down at the file in her hand, and then back up. "If Abel Evans was the offender, and the disappearance of Farah Purcell is related, then he had to have a partner. While it is possible it is a woman, it isn't likely. The other missing man, York Reeder, would be the most likely place to start looking."

"That's a lot of ifs," Sam said. "But you are right. I'll have a full profile on Reeder worked up. Go by his house and workplace, but I'll send agents out to do interviews of all his friends and family."

"If neither of the two missing men are involved, then this case is going to be a lot harder to crack," Ian said. "With both men and women missing, my first instinct is to look in the direction of a blood slavery ring. But the victims are all mages, some with very high levels of power. Vamp slave runners don't usually target mages that have any significant level of power. Norms and low level mages are easier to control."

"Agreed," Sam said as he jotted something down on a notepad. "I'll have an agent on the Anti-Slaver Task Force ask around and see if there are any new blood-slavers in town, but I agree with you, Ian, the likelihood of that is pretty low."

"What about anti-mage or anti-paranorm groups? I know the Guard keeps a tight handle on that sort of thing in the city, but they run rampant in the Outer Zones. Could be a new cell moved in and set up shop?" Fiona suggested.

"Already on top of it. The Guard has the full Anti-Hate Task Force out rousting every known hate monger in the city. They are looking at anti-norm groups as well, as this could be an attempt to breed discord," Sam told them.

Ian nodded. "Could be. Doesn't quite feel right, though. It has been done so quietly. It seems like if hate groups were involved, it would have been a little more public. But, it's foolish to try to give logic to people who think in terms of hate. Looks like until we have more evidence, everything that can be done is being done. Now we just have to get out there and find some evidence."

"Not quite everything. I was actually thinking of something we can do that is a bit more proactive," Fiona said.

Ian shifted in his chair. "Such as?" he asked, not sure he really wanted to know.

"Well, we know at least four people have gone missing in eight weeks, six if the two missing men aren't the offenders. There could be any number of unreported victims. This means whoever is responsible is hunting at least every two weeks, but most likely more often. Farah Purcell went missing three days ago, which was just one day after Millie was attacked. If it is slavers, they may have some sort of quota to fill. I say put a little bait out."

Ian had been right. He hadn't wanted to know. Fiona's idea made sense, putting some undercover Blades out in the streets in area the victims had been last seen was the fastest way to find the offender, but if he knew her, she wanted to be the bait.

"I'll put together a couple of teams to patrol the streets and bars. We'll have one mage on each team as bait, and vampire or shifter backup for each since all the missing are mages. I'll also have a few extra vamps and shifters milling around. It will likely be a mix of Guard and Blades to get enough manpower. I assume you will pitch a fit if I don't put you on one of the teams?" he said the last with a pointed look in Fiona's direction.

Fiona grinned. "Ahh, you know me so well. And I want Jarrett as my backup, if you can authorize pulling him off leave for this case, Sam."

"I can authorize it, and I don't think he will mind putting his leave on hold."

Ian stiffened. He didn't like the pang of irrational jealousy the man's name invoked, but it was there, nonetheless. "I will be there too. We are partners, after all," he said, before he could think twice about it.

Fiona rolled her eyes, but Sam was the one to voice the obvious objection. "You would be a potential target. You can't watch her back if you are a target. I agree you should be close by though."

"We can use Pinky's as a staging area," Fiona offered. "Barroes can help us coordinate from there."

"Fine," Sam said. "I'll get it all set up. I'll scry with the details. You two get out to the Purcell house and see what you can find out. Then grab a couple of hours sleep. It's going to be a long night."

Ian and Fiona rose to leave the office, but Sam stopped them. "Oh, Fiona, you were right about those three boys you brought in."

"I usually am right, but I never tire of hearing you say it, Sam," she said, saucily. "So, not a gang?"

Sam laughed. "No, not a gang. They were taking care of four other orphans. We found a girl about the same age as the boys, along with a boy a few years younger, and two toddlers at an abandoned cabin a couple of miles from where you encountered them. They have been brought in and are being housed in one of the empty Blade apartments until a better situation can be figured out. The agent that picked them up said they were pretty ragtag and skinny, but the first thing the older girl did was ask for a job."

Fiona thought a minute. "Let me know if she can't find one, or if they don't have somewhere to go when they can't stay here anymore."

Sam smiled. "Don't worry. They will be fine. I think they are considering her for a maid position in the barracks and apartments, which would qualify her for a worker's apartment."

"And you got the tribunal waved for the boys?"

"Yes, with the stipulation that they spend two years at the Academy of Science and Magic. The boys agreed as long as we agreed to make sure the other four were taken care of. At the end of the two years, the boys will take the same test as other paranorm students, and if they pass, they'll have the option of entering the Guard, or the Blades, if they are extremely exceptional." Sam winked at Fiona as he said the last sentence.

Ian was completely lost in this conversation, as he had no idea who they were talking about. But he did know what Sam was referring to about exceptional students. The Academy had a two-year regular program. All students took the same basic courses the first two years. At the end of two years, all students took a test that had both intellectual and physical components. Students who passed it with marks above a certain level could enter City Guard training.

Those students then moved to the City Guard barracks for another year of training, which was mostly physical. After two to four years of service, City Guard soldiers who showed exemplary intelligence and skill could take a test to apply for either City Guard detective training or Blade training. Most took the test every two years, but few qualified. If they qualified for Blade training, they would move to the Blade Training Facilities, housed in the Blade Headquarters building, and go through two years of intense training that also included more classes at the Academy.

Very rarely, a student showed an exceptional level of intellect, power, and physical skill after their first two years at the Academy and was offered the chance to skip City Guard training and service and go right into Blade training. Though there had been a few to qualify after only two years of Guard service, Fiona had been the only student in the last twenty years to score so high on her Academy finals that she went directly into Blade Training. What made her case even more exceptional was the fact that she'd started the Academy two years earlier than was normal, no doubt due to her power level and a little string pulling by Sam. She had only been eighteen years old when she'd went through her graduation ceremony and became a Blade six years ago.

"Yeah, well, not everyone can be spectacular. It can be quite exhausting," she said, twirling the end of her braid around her finger.

Sam laughed. "Yeah, well, get your spectacular ass out of here and solve this case for me, so I can get some rest!"

Fiona turned and walked out of the office. On the other side of the threshold, she stopped and turned, "Well, come on, Barroes. We don't have time for your dilly-dallying." Then she turned and strode down the hall.

Without looking at Sam, who was undoubtedly doing his best not to laugh, Ian followed. Though he knew the other man had not truly been assessing Fiona's body parts, as he followed her, Ian couldn't help but agree with Sam. Fiona Moon had one spectacular ass.

THIRTEEN
Fiona

*A*FTER LEAVING SAM'S OFFICE, I WALKED QUICKLY TO THE LIFT AND WAITED FOR Ian to join me. I wasn't as annoyed at being pulled in to work a case as I acted. I was actually a bit relieved. I hated mandatory leave time. Although I enjoyed spending time with my family, more than a day off and I became cranky. I hated having nothing to do. I tried to make myself useful around the pub, but I got in the way more oft than not. The only thing that kept me from being bored to tears had been spending the evenings reminiscing and drinking with Jarrett. But sitting around getting drunk and whining over old times wasn't really either of our styles and somewhere near dawn this morning, we had decided we would take a trip out into the Outer Zone tonight to see if we could get a little action.

Thankfully, Sam had scryed this morning, and although I had a bit of an ale-induced headache, I was glad to be doing something productive, even if I wasn't happy about the circumstances.

I don't know what drove Jarrett to go skulking around the Blade offices this morning after I stumbled drunkenly to bed, but I was grateful he had. It didn't matter that I understood why Sam had sent agents to question my family after I left, I still didn't like it one bit. At least I knew Jarrett would watch out for them and not let anything they said be misconstrued. I also knew his presence would at least put Pinky and Anya more at ease. River had only met him once, last night, so I wasn't sure if it would make a difference or not for her.

I had the feeling that once he awoke this evening, Jarrett would be thanking me for suggesting Sam pull him off leave to be on the stakeout detail. The poor guy would have gone crazy with two weeks of leave time and nothing to do but sit around and think. Hardly ever a good thing for vampires, or Blades. Never a good thing for Kukri.

I tapped my foot as Ian strolled up the hall at a slow, leisurely pace. It was as if the man's favorite pastime was infuriating me. Okay, so maybe I deserved it for that dilly-dallying remark, but I'd be damned if I'd let him win. Reaching up, I grabbed the gate handle. The instant he stepped inside the lift, I slammed the gate down, barely missing his foot.

I pressed the crystal into the hole for the first floor and leaned back against the wall, arms crossed over my chest as the lift slowly descended.

"Bought a horse yet?" I asked, snidely.

"No, and I doubt I will. But I know my rickshaw won't do very well on the road out to New Nashville, so I will borrow a horse from the stables, like I usually do," he said, way too reasonably.

"Fine," I said, a little irritated that he robbed me of the chance to make a dig about the impracticality of his vehicles.

The lift came to a shuddering stop and Ian lifted the gate before I could reach for it, irritating me just a little more, though I couldn't say why. "I have a stop to make before I go to the stables."

I turned and walked across the main entrance area and into the maze of halls and offices that made up the first floor of the Black Blade Guard Headquarters. While all the agent offices were on upper floors that were accessible only to authorized personnel, departments that dealt with the public or the Blades Training Academy on a regular basis kept offices or reception areas on the main floor.

I expected Ian to go on down to the stables to get his horse, but I felt him behind me when I reached the door I was looking for. Ignoring his presence, I knocked twice before opening the door and stepping in, Ian on my heels.

The office was a large room filled with three worktables covered with crystals of varying shapes and sizes. A woman with short, silver-white hair and kind, gray eyes sat at a desk in the corner, peering at a crystal through a magnifying glass.

"Hey, Leesa," I said, cheerily.

She looked up from her work. "Fiona! Oh, I'm so glad you stopped by. I wanted to thank you for sending over Millie."

She stood and came around the desk, stopping when she noticed Ian. My gut twisted with a sharp pang of emotion I refused to name jealousy as her gray eyes slid over him in obvious appreciation.

"Hello," she purred, obviously not concerned with the fact that she was old enough to be his mother.

I waved my hand absently at him. "Leesa, this is Ian Barroes. Ian, Leesa Parks."

"Ahh, yes. The celebrated head of the Blade chargers. I've heard many wonderful things about you. Very nice to meet you," he said, pouring on the charm as he extended his hand to the blushing woman.

"So, Millie came by already?" I said, breaking up the exchange between the two.

Leesa dropped Ian's hand, which I think she'd held just a bit too long, and looked at me. "Oh, yes. She is here now, actually. She is with Drew in the store room, learning how to log the inventory."

"Oh. I was actually coming by to tell you about her. I knew there would be a test coming up, but I didn't think she would get her results back so fast."

"She came by three days ago, I think right after speaking to you. She doesn't take her mage-level test until tomorrow. But, since you sent her over and she was so eager to show me her skills, I gave her a mini-test of my own." Leesa walked back to her desk and sat on the corner. "Millie is very talented, Fiona. Though her actual skill is low, due to sub-standard training, she has a natural affinity for working energy into crystals, one that I haven't seen in a long time. I have a feeling her power level is going to be off the charts."

I couldn't help but smile. I was genuinely happy to hear Millie was doing well. "That is great. So, she is working here?"

"With the raw talent she has, she should have been apprenticed two years ago. But there is nothing we can do about that now. She will be apprenticing here, at least until her test results are back. I am going to try to talk her into applying to the Academy. If her scores are what I think they will be, there won't be a problem getting her schooling paid for through the Charger's Guild, if she agrees to a two-year work service contract when she graduates."

"That's great," I told her, sincerely. "When I sent her to you, I thought you might be able to help her find a job or apprenticeship. I never imagined you'd put her to work here. Thank you. I hope it works out."

"No need to thank me. I'm glad you sent her. Like I said, she is very talented and very eager to work. I think the arrangement will benefit us all, and I'll do what I can to help her get on a path to reach her full potential," Leesa said.

"If you have any problems, let me know, and I'll see what I can do to help," I said, turning towards the door to go.

"Will do," Leesa told me in a matter-of-fact tone. Then she turned to Ian and her tone was flirty again. "You stop by any time."

Ian gave her a charming, awe-shucks grin that I wanted to slap off his face, but thankfully stayed silent as we walked out the door.

Irritated, I started back down the hall, Ian on my heels. The problem was I wasn't so much mad at him as I was aggravated at myself. I was not jealous of anyone, ever. I didn't like it. I doubly didn't like feeling this way about Ian Barroes. There was nothing between us. But that wasn't true—there had been a kiss. And oh, what a kiss.

Just as my brain started turning to mush and sliding down memory lane to think about what it had been like to have Ian's arms around me, his mouth on mine, a loud squeal sounded, jerking me back to reality. I turned and saw Millie Linton coming down an adjoining hallway at a fast clip. I was genuinely glad to see the girl, and not just because she saved me from my own musings.

"Mr. Barroes and Miss, um, sorry, Fiona! I'm so glad to see you," she said when she arrived in front of us, slightly out of breath. "I wasn't sure I'd ever get to see either of you again, and I really wanted to thank you."

"I'm glad to see you, too, Millie. But, you don't have anything to thank us for," I told her.

"Oh, yes, I do! Because of you, I'm going to be able to take my test tomorrow, and I have an apprenticeship here at the Black Blades Headquarters. I'm apprentice to the head charger, and I'm making three times as much as crabby old Mr. Fegley paid me."

When she stopped to take a breath, Ian said, "That's wonderful, Millie. But you earned this job on your own. From what I understand, you are a very talented young woman."

Millie's face flooded with bright red, and she stared at Ian with hero worship in her eyes. I wondered if he knew just how much those few simple words probably meant to the young girl. When I saw the red creeping up his own neck, I realized he did.

Ian said something to Millie and she responded, but I didn't hear what they were saying. I was too intent on watching them. The way she giggled and he smiled at her in an indulgent, big brotherly way. She was chattering away and he looked at her intently, obviously listening to every word. He may not have known how to deal with her exuberant hug a few days ago, but it was apparent he had no problem chatting with an excited teen girl. He even looked like he was enjoying the conversation.

I suppose it shouldn't have surprised me, considering the man had chosen to be a professor at the Academy when he could be doing any number of other things with his money and power. I had always thought it was because he liked feeling superior to everyone else. That he liked knowing more than others, doling out the information as it suited him, and making those who didn't measure up to his intellectual standards feel inferior. But, what if that wasn't the case at all? Perhaps he enjoyed being around kids, and maybe, just maybe, he was a professor because he wanted to help them gain the knowledge they needed to pull themselves out of the ruts society had put them into.

A pang of something I couldn't quite name slammed into my gut. For the first time, I looked at Ian and didn't see a necromancer or a stuffy academic, but a man who seemed to truly care about people. But just because he was nice to one young girl didn't mean anything. Did it? No, I decided, as I pulled myself together. Being nice to one kid, especially one as sweet as Millie, didn't make him a saint, but maybe he wasn't quite as inhuman as I thought.

"That would be so awesome!" Millie squealed, pulling me out of my thoughts. "Agent Fiona, do you teach at the Academy, too?"

"Um, I'm sorry. My mind wandered for a moment. What was that?"

"That's okay," Millie said, unperturbed. "You probably have an important case on your mind. I was just asking if you teach at the Academy, too. Mr. Barroes said that if I were to go to the Academy, I would take some of his classes."

"No, I don't teach, but it is great that you are thinking about attending," I told her.

"Well, I don't know if I will be able to. Maybe if my test scores are high enough, and I can get a work contract with the Chargers' Guild."

"I bet none of that will be a problem for you. Will you keep me informed? Leesa knows how to contact me."

"Oh, yes, I will. But, I better get back now. I have some crystals to polish, and I've been away too long already." She darted down the hall before either Ian or I could reply.

Ian laughed, "I wonder, Fiona, did you have that kind of exuberance when you were her age? Or were you born moody?"

No way was I going to take that obvious bait. Ignoring him, I strode down the hall toward the stables.

I glanced at over at Ian. He stared straight ahead as his horse navigated the winding road.

His obvious jealousy when I'd suggested Jarrett join the team both galled and amused me. Jarrett was the last man Ian needed to be jealous of. There was nothing between us but a deep friendship forged by saving each other's lives. I checked myself. No, Ian had no reason to be jealous of Jarrett because he had no right to be jealous of anyone. He might act as if one kiss meant he owned me, but he was sadly mistaken.

So was Sam. I couldn't deny my sexual attraction to Ian, but it wasn't on the level Sam seemed to think. If hadn't been for the fact that he'd been right about us being unprofessional by bickering, and the fact that I started it, I would have told him so. There was nothing between Ian and me. One kiss. That was all. It meant nothing. The man was idiotic, arrogant, sexy, delicious… My thoughts veered off track as my mind went back three nights ago and the memory of his lips on mine came slamming back. My blood warmed, and my skin tingled.

I shook my head. "No." I wasn't dealing with this right now. I had a job to do.

"No, what?" Ian asked.

Crap! Had I said that out loud? I scrambled to come up with something. *Come on, Fiona, think!*

"Oh, um, nothing. I was talking to Mal," I said quickly.

Mal snorted and shook his head, as if to let Ian know I was lying.

Stop that, I told him mentally. *Behave and I'll bring you some of River's carrots tonight.*

He snorted one more time, and then quieted.

"Sorry, he tends to get cranky when he has been stuck in the stables for a few days," I said in effort to cover.

Ian grinned. "You two have a unique relationship."

"We're partners," I said, knowing Ian had not been referring to the fact that Mal and I could communicate, but rather to the manner in which we did. While it took a mage with some level of animus power to communicate with most animals, horses and dogs were very open to communication with humans. Even the lowest-level mages, and even many norms, could talk to them if they made the effort to try. Not many did.

"It seems like it's a bit more than that. I've never seen anyone who didn't have animus powers interact with their horse quite as much as you do," Ian said.

Mal snorted.

I laughed. "I suppose our relationship is a little unique. Mal is a pretty special."

"He's powerful. What? Why are you so shocked?"

Mal, was indeed, powerful. He had a very strong shield that could deflect both magic and physical objects. If I were riding him, or touching him in any way when he activated the shield, it covered me as well. He could also, in very short bursts, run at unimaginable speeds. Both abilities had gotten us out of quite a few tight spots in the past.

"It's just that most people who don't work with animals, have pets, or have animus powers don't realize that a lot of animals can use magic in some way," I said, trying not to sound as shocked as I apparently looked.

"Well, I do happen to be a professor at the Academy of Science and Magic," he said, flashing his most charming grin.

"Yes, a professor of Necromancy," I shot back, with perhaps a little disdain as I said the last word that I couldn't seem to hold in.

The grin disappeared, and his voice was much cooler. "One of these days, Fiona, you are going to realize there is much more to me than being a necromancer. I do teach a class on the history of magic, which it happens, is a particular interest of mine. My greatest joy as a child was reading. I was lucky enough to have many books at my disposal, but they were mostly volumes of old, Paranorm Council approved texts on the history and various types of magic and dated back before the Cataclysm. It became a hobby of sorts for me."

I wasn't sure why, but I instantly felt ashamed of myself. Though I could have made a crack about his rich, privileged upbringing when most kids weren't even taught to read, but it would have been unfair and a little hypocritical. It was true that children from poor families didn't get tutors hired for them. And though there were many day schools where families grouped together to pay a teacher for their children, the poorest of families couldn't afford even that.

My family had been one of those. However, my sisters and I had been lucky in our own way. While city officials and Academy students had access to the City Archives and parts of the library, the library was actually privately owned. Before the Cataclysm, Carly Corsini, a vampire, had worked the evening shift at the city's public library. When the city government shut down and riots began in the streets, she and her husband boarded up the library and lived inside to protect the books. Thanks to them, a lot of history had been saved from loss. When the Reconstruction began, they took formal ownership under the homesteading laws that were passed by the senate.

Pinky was friends with the Corsinis, as he was with many of the vampires that had lived in Nash City through the Cataclysm. Carly helped Pinky teach us to read, and Anya, River, and I had been able spend as much time as we wanted in the library. While I hadn't loved it as much as River, I had spent many a winter day in the fiction room reading fantastical tales about life before the Cataclysm. I had been so fascinated because I'd never quite known what was made up and what might have been true to life at the time.

"I'm sorry, Ian. I..." I searched for what else to say. He was right—I'd been unfair to him in assuming his entire life and being was, and always had been, consumed by being a necromancer.

Luckily, we went around a bend in the road right then and New Nashville was spread out before us. I was saved from having to continue.

"The Purcells live on Hollow Lane, which is the second left off the main street," Ian said, obviously dismissing my feeble attempt at an apology.

It didn't matter how many times I came here, New Nashville always seemed like a foreign land to me. Although the town was walled, you couldn't actually see the walls. Once you went through the southwestern city gate out of Nash City, you were technically in New Nashville, but a forest of trees a quarter of a mile wide grew between the outer wooden walls and the town itself. A narrow lane winded through the young forest and opened up onto the small town, situated on the edge of a large lake. The area had been a part of the city before the Cataclysm and there had been homes, buildings, roads, and other structures. But this area was not shielded during the Cataclysm as Nash City had been. Many of the buildings were now underwater, in what was now Hollow Lake, and the rest were destroyed in the Cataclysm or during the Reconstruction, when the entire area had been cleaned out, trees planted, and a community with new buildings was planned and built.

Every home and building in the town was constructed of wood and stone and was less than fifty years old. New Nashville was, as far as I knew, the only completely new town in Appalachia that had been built from the ground up in the last two hundred years. The other small towns and farming communes dotted across the countryside sprang up in or around the ruins of old towns and communities. What buildings could be salvaged and repurposed were. Those towns and communes had come into existence out of need. New Nashville had been planned more as a luxury, as a place for rich mages and norms to live. And that was exactly who lived in New Nashville. Though Nash City was the official capital of the city-state and the senate was housed there, most of the senators and many City Guards lived in New Nashville. The buildings were all one or two stories and only housed a single business or family. It had always seemed an extravagant waste of space and materials to me.

We rode the next few yards in silence, and then turned the horses onto Hollow Lane. I knew this road well, though I hadn't been here since I was a child. As we passed the third house on the road, I let my gaze shift to take in the large, two-story house my grandparents called home. It was neat and well kept, sitting several yards back off the road surrounded by flower and vegetable gardens that were, no doubt, tended by servants. A well-kept rock driveway circled around the house to a barely visible stable that undoubtedly housed more than one horse. There likely was at least one crystal-powered surrey despite my grandparents' abhorrence for magic. The ability to afford a magic-powered vehicle was a mark of status among norms and paranorms alike. My grandparents were the type to take advantage of all the conveniences provided by modern magic innovations, while still looking down their nose at those who could do magic.

"Do you think that is the kidnapper's lair?" Ian's strong, slightly amused voice broke into my thoughts.

"What?" I said, a little discombobulated.

"You were scowling at that house with such ferocity I thought maybe you had reason to believe it housed our kidnapper, or perhaps a hoard of thieves." He didn't even seem to try to keep the humor out of his voice. "Do you know who lives there?"

"No. Some random rich people, I assume," I lied. "According to the address, the Purcell house is the next one on the left." I nudged Mal with my heel so he quickened his pace and got ahead of Ian.

The Purcell home was a large two-level with stone siding. A wide, covered porch wrapped around the entire first floor. The front yard was a maze of neatly tended flowerbeds. Once again, the waste of space struck me as extravagant. Flowers were great, but the space would have been put to better use for growing vegetables, herbs, or even fruit trees. I couldn't wrap my mind around the idea of appearance being more important than function.

We tied the horses to the porch rail at the front of the house and mounted the stone steps. The heavy, wooden door swung open before we crossed the porch, and a man with close-cropped pale blond hair and blue eyes appeared. He wasn't especially tall at a couple of inches under six feet, but he was broad and muscular. The fabric of his gray City Guard uniform seemed barely able to contain him.

Inside, I groaned long and loud, cursing Sam for not warning me, but outside, I kept my face blank as we crossed the porch.

"Fee! They told me the Blades were sending one of their top agents to talk to the Purcells. I should have guessed it would be you." He grinned wide, his blue eyes twinkling.

"Hello, Rangel," I said, purposefully using his last name, as was professional custom. My short-lived relationship last year with Marcus Rangel had been purely based on sex, which had been fabulous. It had ended after a couple of months when I left on a long-term assignment. For a while, we still got together when we were both alone and in need of recreation, but we hadn't done that in over six months. Things had never been tense or awkward between us, and we'd worked together several times since ending our trysts. Yet, today, for the first time, I felt uncomfortable.

If Rangel noticed my coldness, he didn't let on. He extended his hand to Ian. "Barroes, great to see you. I thought you retired from crime work."

I felt Ian's assessing gaze on me for an instant before he turned his full attention to Rangel and took the proffered hand. "For the most part I have, but I help out when Fee needs me."

What? I hadn't asked for his help—it had been the other way around. When Sam had called him to go down to the morgue, he had requested me as his Blade liaison. And how dare he call me "Fee"? That arrogant jerk!

My mind was racing fast, coming up with a hundred different ways to tell him off. I almost missed the twitch at the side of his mouth. He was baiting me. Damn the man. I shot him my best death glare, which only made his mouth twitch even more.

Rangel seemed oblivious to our byplay. "I'm glad you are here. We need all the help we can get."

"You are the GI in charge?" Ian asked, his tone neutral.

"Yep, though now that the Blades have taken over, I'm just here for extra help."

Oh, just my luck. The tiny bit of hope I had been hanging on to that Rangel was just one of the Guards stationed at the Purcell home for protection fizzled and died. If he was the Guard Inspector in charge of this case, it meant we would be dealing with him every day until Farah Purcell was found. From the glint in Ian's eyes, he had caught on to my discomfort and would revel in torturing me with it. We needed to find the Purcell girl, fast. Both for her safety and my sanity.

FOURTEEN
Fiona

The Purcell home was immaculate with crisp, white plaster walls and gleaming wood floors. Ian and I followed Rangel down a long hallway past closed doors and into a large room decorated in light yellows and greens.

Two young girls, around eighteen or nineteen, sat on a cherry wood sofa covered in cream fabric woven with delicate pink and yellow flowers. The girls were holding hands and talking in hushed tones to a woman sitting in an armchair that matched the sofa. A tall, thin man with hair that was more gray than brown was standing at the window looking out, a drink in his hand.

When we walked in, the ladies stopped talking and turned to look at us. The woman stood up, smoothed her pristine skirt, and walked over to us. The man turned, but stayed where he was. His expression clearly stated that he would not move until he was sure we were worth his time and effort.

"Mr. and Mrs. Purcell, this is Agent Fiona Moon of the Black Blade Guard and Master Necromancer Ian Barroes." Rangel made the introductions with practiced smoothness. "They are taking the lead on your daughter's case."

"If you are taking the lead, shouldn't you be out looking for our daughter? She certainly isn't here in our sitting room," Mr. Purcell said from his spot by the window.

"Mr. Purcell, I understand your concern. I assure you that every available agent in the Black Blade Guard, as well as every City Guard Officer, are working to find your daughter," I said, much more diplomatically than I felt. "Master Barroes and I just need a few minutes of your time."

Suddenly, Mrs. Purcell let out a gasp. "Master Necromancer? Are you saying you think our Farah is dead?" She wailed, a little belatedly.

Behind her, the two girls whimpered a bit.

Before I could say anything, Ian cut in, "No, ma'am, we do not think that at all. As you know, all living beings are made up of energy. We leave bits of energy everywhere we go, especially in places of strong emotion or where we are particularly comfortable. I am trained to connect with energy left behind, which may give me clues to help look for Farah."

Mrs. Purcell relaxed perceptibly at Ian's smooth, soothing tone as he gave her the standard, approved party line given by all necromancers during crime investigations. It wasn't a lie, exactly, just a crafty way of not telling the whole truth.

All beings were made up of energy, and they did leave behind residual energy everywhere they went. Also, necromancers were trained to connect with energy left behind in certain locations. However, that was where the truth got murky. The energy necromancers could "connect" with was the energy of people who have died.

But it doesn't seem too smart to tell people, "Um, yeah, there are ghosts everywhere, and sometimes, they see things and know things no one else may see or know." People just didn't seem to take well to the idea that there could be ghosts watching their every move. And, understandably, if they knew, they would not be happy about necromancers going through their house, talking to the ghosts there that could tell all of their dirty little secrets. So, the Necromancer's Guild had a patent explanation they told that didn't lie, but didn't tell the truth.

"So you are here to poke around Farah's room?" Mr. Purcell asked, finally walking over to us.

"We would like to look around Farah's room, yes," I said, softly. "But we would also like to speak to you and Mrs. Purcell about the last time you saw Farah. We would also like to talk to Shani Lin and Maria Reece." I nodded towards the two girls who still sat huddled on the sofa. It only seemed logical the two girls were the friends Farah had been with the night she disappeared since, according to her file, she didn't have any siblings.

"Whatever you need, Master Barroes. Maria, Shani, why don't you two go wait for the agents on the back porch," Mrs. Purcell said.

"I'll go with you." Rangel smiled at the young women and ushered them out of the room.

"Fine," grumbled Mr. Purcell, settling into a large armchair.

Mrs. Purcell sat next to him, perching on the edge of the sofa. "Please, have a seat," she said, graciously.

Ian smiled and settled into the armchair opposite Mr. Purcell, leaving me to sit on the other end of the sofa. "Thank you. This won't take long," he said.

"I hope not. I am due at the senate house for a meeting with the chancellors," Mr. Purcell said impatiently.

How nice it was of him to remind us of his importance. The man was really starting to chafe my nerves. The man's daughter had been missing for three days, and he was acting as if we were wasting his time. I wanted to give him a piece of my mind. Ian obviously sensed my mood because he gave me a quelling glance. I tipped my head at him, almost imperceptibly, but he got the message and took the lead.

"I understand you have gone over all of this at least twice before, but it will help Agent Moon and me to hear your accounts directly from you. It is also common for details that may have slipped your mind to come back to you the more you retell the story," he said, his tone soft and professional, effectively taking the bluster out of Mr. Purcell.

Though I had groused earlier that Ian wasn't a crime investigator, he certainly had the spiel down. He had been working with the Blades long enough to learn the tricks of the trade. He also had a way of handling people without them knowing they had been handled.

I opened the file folder I had grabbed out of Mal's saddlebag before we came in. Skimming the report inside, I looked up, directly into Mr. Purcell's eyes. "Farah was only reported missing yesterday, but according to the report, she was last seen three days ago. Is it normal for your daughter to be away for a few days at a time without leaving word as to where she is?"

I had carefully schooled my tone to be professional and neutral, but I still expected Mr. Purcell to take offense at the question. I couldn't have been more wrong. While Mr. Purcell did show strong emotion, it wasn't outrage on his daughter's behalf.

"As a matter of fact, Agent," he blustered, obviously finding it too bothersome to remember my name. "It is exactly the kind of thing she does. She is likely holed up in some slum with some paranorm trash and will come straggling in when she runs out of bucks."

It took everything I had to keep from pulling the man up by his ears and showing him what paranorm trash could do. But, of course, that would probably not go over too well back at headquarters. Damned rules. Instead, I made due with screaming at the idiot in my head. *If I had a father like you, I'd stay gone for days at a time, too.*

I glanced at Ian and saw by the tightening of his jaw he was trying hard to hold on to his ever-present control. His voice was measured as he said, "If that is true, Mr. Purcell, then why did you report her missing?"

"I didn't," Mr. Purcell snapped.

Nervously, Mrs. Purcell leaned forward a bit more on her perch on the edge of the sofa and turned to face us. "I reported her missing."

The woman was so distressed that she was shaking, but I couldn't tell if it was because she was concerned about her daughter or scared of her husband. I opened my senses just a bit. There was definite fear blasting off her, but when she leaned over and placed her hand on her husband's knee, a wave of comfort washed over her. I closed down my magic.

"Mrs. Purcell, if your daughter is often gone, what made this time different?" I asked, making my voice as calming as possible.

"Oh, Granger exaggerates a bit. He and Farah have been having a hard time understanding each other lately." She patted his knee and surprisingly, he didn't protest her admonishment. He just covered her hand with his as she continued. "Farah is the first of either of our families to be a magic user. Though we have been assured by testing that her power levels are quite low, the differences are there. It is perfectly normal for her to want to hang out with other people who are like her."

Assured her power levels are low? She said it as if being a mage was some sort of disease and power level was the indicator of how seriously infected the person was. I felt a pang of sympathy for Farah Purcell. Despite the trouble it would cause, I suddenly hoped Farah had decided to run away. If that was the case and I found her, there was no way I would drag her back to such a house, nor would I let anyone else do it.

Oblivious to the horror I couldn't keep from showing in my face, Mrs. Purcell went on. "The reason it took me so long to realize she was missing was because she told me she was spending the weekend with Shani and Maria. When she wasn't home yesterday morning, I scryed them both and they told me they hadn't seen her. I immediately went to the City Guard office here in New Nashville and reported her missing."

Tears welled in her eyes and her voice shook. "She might be a little wild, but it's only to be expected of a girl of nineteen, especially one who is different from all of her friends and family. She always lets me know where she will be, even if she doesn't tell her father." She said the word "different" in a whisper, as if it were something to be hidden away, because who knew what the neighbors would think if they knew.

I now understood Mr. Purcell's obvious dislike of us being in his home. Ian and I both, along with all of the City Guard officers and Blade agents were "paranorm trash". Having us traipse through his home, touching his belongings, must be grating on every nerve in his body. I made a mental note to drag my hands along the walls as we went out.

"Mrs. Purcell, do you know the names of any of Farah's paranorm friends?" I asked. The girl might just be holed up somewhere in Nash with friends, not realizing or caring that her parents may be worried. With the attitude they had shown me so far, she might think they wouldn't care if she disappeared. Unfortunately, knowing the way Farah's parents felt about her paranorm abilities opened more angles to explore instead of narrowing things down. There was a very good possibility that the girl had just ran away.

Mrs. Purcell sniffled. "I don't think she has any, exactly. When she goes out, she always goes with Shani and Maria. The girls like to go into Nash City to the bars and shops frequented by other mages."

"Are Shani Lin and Maria Reece mages as well?" Ian asked.

"Of course not," Mr. Purcell said, shortly.

Mrs. Purcell squeezed his hand and added, "Shani and Maria have been Farah's best friends since childhood. They have been very supportive of Farah since the emergence of her, um, abilities. They always go with her into the city. "

Three would be a safe number, during the day at least. At night, in the heart of Old Nash, three teenage girls, especially two norms and one low-level mage, would not be safe. It was foolish, or perhaps just ignorant, of Mrs. Purcell to condone such trips. Perhaps she thought Fiona could take care of herself.

"What nature are Farah's powers? Has she studied with a mage-teacher to learn to master them?" I knew she was not enrolled at the Academy of Science and Magic, but perhaps she had a private tutor. That was common among rich families.

Mr. Purcell answered, "Farah is a telekinetic, but she can do little more than open and shut doors. She was seventeen when we realized her magic levels were high enough to register her as a mage, and she threw tantrums until we registered her at the Academy. Unfortunately, Farah has very little focus. She had fantasies of being some high-powered mage, but she was the weakest of her classmates. You see, among her friends around here, Farah is a novelty, the popular girl who is special because she can toss a ball across the road without touching it. At the academy, she was nothing special at all. In fact, compared to her classmates, she was a bit of a joke. Perhaps if she'd put in the work, she could have done well, but she barely lasted a month before throwing another tantrum to come home. Since then, she only uses her powers to show off for Shani and Maria."

The more Mr. Purcell opened his mouth, the more I disliked him. Figuring we knew everything they could tell us at that point, and not wanting to be in the same room with them any longer, I thanked the Purcells for their time and asked if we could see Farah's room before we spoke with her friends.

Mrs. Purcell led us up stairs and left us at the door to her daughter's room, telling us to call her if we needed anything. I heard heavy footsteps in the downstairs hall and the front door slam just before we stepped into Farah's room. Mr. Purcell was off to his meeting at the senate house.

Farah's room was bigger than my apartment's living and kitchen areas put together. The walls were covered in soft pink floral wallpaper and all the fabric in the room was of various shades of pink. The polished wood floor was covered with a large, woven rug in a soft pink and white chevron design. The room was immaculate. The large bed was neatly made with a fuchsia coverlet, a neat row of rag dolls arranged across the pillows. On the cherry vanity, several hairbrushes and combs were laid out in a neat row next to a cluster of glass bottles and vials that held various oils, lotions, and a basket with sundry hair clips. I opened the myriad of small drawers in the vanity and found hair clips, ribbons, jewelry, and other girly toiletries.

Farah Purcell was only a few years younger than River, but this room looked more like the room of a girl of nine or ten. When my sisters and I were in our late teens, our room had been a disaster of clothes and junk knick-knacks we bought at the public market covering every horizontal surface. Here, there was no dust or dirt, and nothing seemed out of place even a centimeter. The few knick-knacks and books were neatly arranged on the top of the large dresser.

I halfheartedly opened and closed the drawers of the dresser. All I found were neatly folded handkerchiefs, undergarments, and nightclothes. The closet held rows of expensive-looking clothes and shoes, but nothing else. The small writing desk in the corner was completely bare of anything but a jar of pencils. I hadn't really expected to find anything since the entire place had been searched by the City Guard already and anything that might hold a clue, including Farah's school notebooks, had been taken to Headquarters to be examined.

I was really just trying to look and feel busy, not useless while Ian did his thing. I never quite knew what to do with myself as a necromancer did his or her work. Once the spirits were summoned and the questioning began, I would interact a little, asking questions as needed, but the start of the process was a solitary practice that could take a little time. When there wasn't a body to interact with, the necromancer summoned as many spirits in the vicinity as possible, then would speak to them for a moment to weed out those who might know something and were willing to cooperate. In my years of working with necromancers, I've learned that though there were spirits everywhere, most of them did not pay attention to living humans. Most of the older spirits who had been passed for more than a few decades faded to the point that they didn't even see the living anymore, unless summoned by a necromancer. Only the strongest, or most stubborn, of spirits hung on to life and watched the living. Those spirits were often cranky. While a necromancer could summon such a spirit, coaxing them to cooperate was quite a different matter.

When I ran out of drawers and closets to look in, I turned to watch Ian. He stood in the middle of the room, his arms bent at the elbows and extended in front and slightly to either side of his body, palms up.

Every necromancer had a different way of summoning, but Ian always used this posture. I had asked him once why he stood that way, and he told me it was his way of bestowing respect on the passed spirits. He held his body open to them, showing he had nothing to hide and that he was asking for, not demanding, assistance. Whatever the reasoning, it worked. Ian had a higher success rate at getting helpful information than any other necromancer I had worked with.

I was careful to stay close to the wall, away from him, knowing he preferred privacy for this part. As I watched Ian look at people I couldn't see, speaking in low, hushed tones, inclining his head, clearly listening to something I couldn't hear. After a few moments, he relaxed his pose, dropping his hands to his sides, turning his head towards me, and motioning for me to come over.

I approached, careful to stand slightly behind and to the side opposite from where his body was turned. According to Ian, the spirits hated it when someone stood in the middle of them. I couldn't blame them; the idea didn't sound too good to me either.

"Fiona, I'm speaking with Hailey. She has agreed to answer a few questions. She has already told me a little. Hailey was with us as we spoke with the Purcells. She told me Farah's mother dotes on her, spoils her, but forbids her to speak of magic, especially around Mr. Purcell," Ian said to me, turning his head back in the direction of the invisible Hailey.

"Hailey," I said, keeping my gaze low in order to keep from staring past the spirit. "Have you ever heard Farah talk about a boyfriend? Do you think she would have run away?"

Ian didn't have to repeat my question. Even though I couldn't see or hear Hailey, she was completely aware of me. After a moment of careful listening, Ian turned back to me. "She doubts Farah would run away. Her father drowns her in gifts and money, even though he barely speaks to her. According to Hailey, Farah is spoiled and too attached to the luxury her father's money and status affords her. As for a boyfriend, no. But Hailey has heard Farah and her friends talk about boys and men they have had sex with quite often."

He turned his head back in the other direction for a moment, and then back to me. "It seems Farah goes out with her friends almost every night, and almost every night, she is quite disheveled when she gets in. Hailey says she has seen people look like that before, and it usually means they are addicted to drugs."

I took in the information and nodded. "Hailey, do you know if you saw Farah the last time she was home? Before she went out?" I worded the question carefully, because ghosts didn't have a good sense of time.

It took several minutes before Ian spoke. "Hailey likes to spend time around Farah, she reminds her of her little sister, so she is with her most of the time she is home. She was with Farah the last time she was here. Nothing seemed any different than any other night."

"Thank you, Hailey," I said.

Ian inclined his head, and then spoke again. "Hailey asked me to ask you to please find Farah. She really is a good girl, and it is very lonely here without her."

My heart lurched. I didn't know how long Hailey had been dead, and it would be rude to ask, but it was obvious she was clinging to the living world so fiercely that she couldn't even interact with the other spirits in the area. What an incredibly lonely existence.

When I spoke, my voice was rough with emotion. "I will do everything in my power, Hailey. I promise. Thank you for talking with me. It was an honor to meet you."

"Yes, thank you, Hailey." Ian said, and then we left the room.

When we were in the hall, I quietly asked, "No sign of Farah's spirit?"

"No, not at all. I don't think she has passed, though it is still possible. Under normal circumstances, a spirit stays with the body for a few days, and in any circumstances, this house may not be where her spirit would choose to bounce back. It doesn't seem to be a place of much comfort for her."

"True enough," I replied. "Okay, let's go talk to those girls, though I'm not sure they will be much more help."

It was getting late, so Ian and I split the girls up and questioned them separately. Ian's contract with the Blades made it legal for him to question suspects and witnesses as long as he had a Blade agent or Guard officer present, so he and Rangel took Maria Reece to the front porch while I stayed on the back porch with Shani Lin.

I stood in front of her while she sat on a porch swing, rocking back and forth and fidgeting nervously.

"We were at this bar, Pinky's something, but there was no action so we decided to head over to the Blue Vein." The girl sniffed.

When she said the name of the bar they went to after Pinky's, my eyes immediately went to the girl's arms. Sure enough, there were several small scars on her wrist. The other arm had similar scars on the wrist and inner elbow. They were tiny and innocuous enough if you didn't know what you were looking at, but I did. The Blue Vein was a notorious sucker hangout. It seemed Farah and her friends liked to get high by having their blood sucked. I wondered if it was a passing fad for them, if the scars I could see were all they had, or if they had started out getting bitten in places that weren't easily seen and had progressed to not caring if the scars were visible. If that were the case, it wouldn't be long before the girls were completely absorbed by the sucker culture.

Shani noticed my eyes on her wrist and pulled her hand behind her back. "It's not what you think. We aren't addicts. We just like to have a little fun, get a little high on the weekends."

That may be true, but the fact that the girls routinely frequented sucker bars added another possible layer to the case. Farah's disappearance might not be related to the others at all, or there could be a possibility they hadn't yet looked at in the other cases.

"Miss Lin, did you know there are slave traders who look for strong, young women like you and your friends to sell to rogue vamps in the Outer Zones?" I asked, my voice unemotional.

She blanched, and the tears started again. "Are... are you saying that is what happened to Farah?"

I sighed. "No, I am not. We don't know what happened to Miss Purcell, but we will follow every lead. What I am saying is that every time you and your friends go into a sucker bar, you are putting yourself at risk. Every time you allow an addict vampire to bite you and suck your blood, you are putting yourself in danger. All it would take is for you to let the wrong vamp bite you. All they'd have to do is suck a little too much, just enough to make you pass out. You could wake up far from Nash as a slave. Then you would have no control over who bit you or how much they took. You would be lucky if you weren't killed by them taking too much. Though, if you ended up sold as chattel to someone in No Man's Land, you'd be luckier if they did kill you quickly."

Her eyes were wide now, and she was trembling so hard it was a wonder I couldn't hear her teeth chattering. I felt a little guilty at terrifying her, but only a little. If she were scared, maybe she would think twice before letting an addict vamp bite her again. I might have been a little too brutal with the truth, but I hadn't lied. The danger was very real.

I put my hand on her shoulder and tried to sound a little nicer. "Look, there is nothing to indicate that is what happened to Farah. I can promise you we will do everything we can to find her. But, you do need to know the real danger you and your friends put yourselves in. Getting high just isn't worth the risk of what could happen. Just be careful and think it through, please."

She sniffed and wiped the tears streaming down her face with the back of her hand. "I... okay. I'll think about it. I swear."

I had no doubt she would think about what I'd told her and would stay out of the bars for a night or two, but I had no idea if it would have any lasting impact. I nodded at her. "Okay, let's continue. You were headed over to the Blue Vein."

"Oh, yes. The street was crowded, and there was a line to get into the bar. We were just about to the front of the line when Farah said she saw a hottie that had been looking at her in the last bar, Pinky's. She said he waved her over, and she was going to talk to him. She said if she didn't catch up to us by the time we left, to just go on home and she'd see us in the morning."

"Did you see who she was talking about?" I asked.

"Of course not. She knew I would have tried to snake her if she pointed him out," Shani said with a teary laugh.

"What?" I was thoroughly confused.

"It's a game. We get points for every hottie we go home with, or out back, or wherever, if you know what I mean."

I did know what she meant, and it made me a little sick at my stomach, but I stayed quiet and let her continue.

"We get extra points if it is a paranorm of any race, double points if it is a shifter, since they are so rare in the city. We also get double points if we snake a guy out from under some other girl, triple if it's one of us. Farah is ahead of both Maria and I, but a triple score would have put me way in the lead, so there is no way she would have pointed him out to either of us. I think he might have been blond though. Farah likes blonds. What? It's just a little harmless fun," she said, obviously seeing the horror on my face.

Harmless fun? These girls were completely oblivious to the danger they were putting themselves into. It was one thing for adults to engage in consensual sex, but these girls were playing games with their lives. My hopes of ever finding Farah alive plummeted. The girls engaged in so much risky behavior that anything could have happened to Farah. It was pure luck the other two weren't alongside her wherever she was. I bit my tongue to keep from laying into the girl. It wasn't my place to lecture her. Besides, I doubted it would help. I'd seen out-of-control kids before, but I'd never heard of something like the game the girls played.

"Okay, Shani, I think that's it. Thanks for talking to me. Please let the Blades know immediately if Farah gets in touch with you, okay?" I said, ready to end this conversation.

"Okay." She got up and started to go inside, but stopped when she reached the door. "Do you think our game is the reason Farah is missing? Do you think the hottie did something bad to her?"

I sighed. "I truly don't know. But what you girls do, letting vamps bite you, going off with strange men, you must know it isn't safe. I know that must be a part of the thrill, the danger. But danger isn't fun; it is, for lack of a better word, dangerous. I think you know that. What happened to Farah may have nothing to do with the way you three party, but the odds are that if you don't stop, one day, I'll be standing in your parents' home, asking them when they last saw you."

I tried to keep my tone sympathetic, though I knew my words were brutal. To my great surprise, Shani didn't burst into tears again. Her face was sober and tear streaked as she nodded at me, then she opened the door and disappeared inside.

I stood there for several minutes, giving her time to retreat and giving myself time to compose myself. My job was never pretty, but what I'd heard here today just made me heartsick. I took a few deep breaths, and then headed back through the house to find Ian. I was ready to go home, it had been a long day, and we had a long night ahead of us.

FIFTEEN
Fiona

I STARED AT THE SPIKE-HEELED EXCUSE FOR BOOTS, AND MY FEET STARTED ACHING at the thought of putting them on. I was so exhausted all I wanted to do was crawl back in between the sheets of my snug little bed, pull the quilt up over my head, and sleep for a week. As I flipped over, my head landed on my soft, down-filled pillow, and I seriously debated doing just that.

For the past four days, I'd spent the mornings and afternoons investigating with Ian, and then, after a few hours of sleep in the evenings, patrolling the bars and other nightspots of Broadway all night. Despite all the time we'd spent, we still weren't any closer to finding any of the missing mages, including Farah Purcell.

Over the last three days, Ian and I had visited the homes and work places of every missing person that fit the pattern, spoken to all of their families, and visited the places they were last seen. So far, not a single lead had turned up.

We couldn't find anything that linked any of the victims. As far as we could tell, none of them knew each other, or had mutual friends or acquaintances. They all had very different jobs, friends, personalities, and lifestyles. They did all have two things in common, but even those commonalities were varied. First, they all were last seen either at an establishment on Broadway or on their way to somewhere on Broadway, but some of them never met up with their parties, so we have no idea if they even made it to Broadway. Second, they were all mages, but their levels of power ranged from just barely enough to register as a mage to a level seven on the ten-scale.

After our visit to the Purcell's home, Ian and I weren't sure if Farah's disappearance was related to the others. There was a very good chance she had just run away. She did have good reason to want to stay away from her family. However, considering the extremely risky behavior she and her friends engaged in on a regular basis, any number of terrible things could have happened to her. It could just be a coincidence that it happened in the same area and timeframe as the other victims. But, I didn't think so. Something told me that whoever took the other missing mages and tried to take Millie Linton had Farah Purcell.

With that thought in my head reminding me why I needed to get up and get dressed, I pulled my aching body into a sitting position and grabbed the boots. I slid my foot in, the supple leather sliding up my leg and over my knee. I tightened the laces that held the wide strip of leather together from the tip of my toe to my lower thigh and tied them tightly. Luckily, the brown leather contraptions also had a thick piece of leather resembling a belt attached to the top that wrapped around the lower part of my thigh and fastened with a heavy, metal buckle. I suspected the belt was for fashion purposes as much as to keep the boot from falling off.

The boots weren't mine. I had never seen the point in wearing shoes that made me four inches taller than my already considerable height, were precarious to walk on, and impossible to run in. After all, my job involved a lot of running. Though, I had to admit, the boots would make a handy weapon when kicking someone in the head. Unfortunately, I'd never be able to balance on just one of the thin, little heels.

I borrowed the boots and the other shoes, as well as some of the clothes I'd worn over the past few nights, from Anya. Her clothes, even those she worked in, were a little more appropriate for "party girl" cover than my own. I was supposed to look sexy and approachable, but according to Anya, Pinky, and to my dismay, Sam, my clothes were less "come hither, big boy," and more "touch me and I'll fuck you up."

I stood up to look at tonight's get-up in my wall mirror. The outfit I wore was one that Anya had made herself. It was a fluttery concoction of four wide ruffles made out of a pale lavender, thin, semi-transparent fabric cut at an angle so that the back reached down to the back of my knee but the front just skimmed the middle of my thigh. The ruffles layered over each other so that only a few inches on the bottom was actually see-through.

The top was a lavender brocade half-corset that ended at least two inches above my belly button and laced up in the back with a matching lavender ribbon. The effect of it all together was actually quite flattering, even if it wasn't my usual style. I think I would have even liked the outfit if the boots had a more practical heel.

Brushing my hair, I let it fall in soft waves around my shoulders. I preferred having it braided or at least tied back, hating when it blew in my face. It was also more practical, but I couldn't deny that leaving it loose made me look softer, more approachable. Deciding I looked presentable enough, I tucked a small, throwing dagger in the top of each of the thigh-high boots. The bulk of the belt and buckle hid them from prying eyes, despite the snug fit of the thin leather against my skin. I would have felt more comfortable with my hanbo, or even my large dagger at my hip, but weapons didn't project the friendly and cuddly attitude I was going for.

The wardrobe choices for the patrols had been made based on what many of the missing women had been wearing the nights they disappeared. Several of them, like Farah, had been out partying, either with friends or alone. After the first night when I'd showed up in what I would normally wear down to Pinky's, Anya had been quickly enlisted by Sam to usher me upstairs and make me look a little more feminine. Since then, Anya had made all clothing decisions and approved my look before each night's op.

I took one more look in the mirror, decided it was as good as it was going to get, and went out into the living room to get my inspection.

"Wow," Anya said, letting out a loud wolf whistle. "Ian's brain is going to explode when he gets a load of you in that outfit."

"The point of this get-up isn't to make Ian's brain explode; it is to make me look sexy enough to have the kidnapper approach me," I said, though if Ian had a meltdown, it would be a happy coincidence. It had actually been quite fun seeing his reaction to the skimpy outfits Anya had provided for me over the past few nights.

He never made a verbal comment, as we were always surrounded by people during our evening briefings and then were separated the rest of the night, but I saw the way his eyes darkened and he swallowed hard every time he saw me in a new outfit. Surprisingly, he hadn't said anything during the day to me either. Though we had been working alone together over the past few days, he had been completely professional, except once.

Unbidden, the memory of the day we got the case popped into my head. After we left the Purcell home, we rode back to Nash City while discussing everything we learned from the Purcells and Farah's two friends. Our earlier baiting of each other was forgotten as we debated the different possibilities of what may have happened to Farah. When we arrived at Blade Headquarters, we took care of the horses, and then walked out together, making plans about what we would do the next day. But as we took the stairs to the main floor, Ian grabbed my arm, pushed me gently against the wall, and leaned in to me, one hand on the wall on either side of my head, our bodies separated by mere centimeters.

"You know," he said, softly, his breath fluttering warmly against my cheek. "Sam was right. We do have something between us we need to work out."

My body screamed, "Yes, our clothes are between us. We definitely need to work on that." But my brain was a little more sensible. Well, not much. I suddenly didn't want to fight the attraction anymore; my only objection was that this wasn't the time or place to explore the sexual heat between us.

"Ian, I..." He cut of my words by laying his index finger against my mouth.

"Shhh. Just listen." He slid his finger along my cheek and down my throat, his hand resting on the curve of my neck and shoulder. "We have to focus on this case, but when it is over, we will work it out. No more running away, for either of us. But, until then, a little something to tide us over."

Before I could say anything, he slid his fingers to the back of my neck, leaned into me, and lowered his lips to mine. My objections to our location faded away as every cell in my body focused on the feel of him against me, the taste of him on my lips. My arms went around him, pulling him closer, my hands sliding over the taut muscles of his back.

The kiss wasn't frenzied and fierce like the one we'd shared on the dance floor at Pinky's; it was slow, sensual, and brain-meltingly intense. His lips moved over mine, leisurely, tauntingly. I pressed harder against him, pushing for more, but he held back, setting his own pace. His tongue traced the outline of my lips thoroughly, as if mapping them as he tasted. When I opened my mouth to give him access, he sucked my bottom lip into his. Heat pooled in my abdomen and slowly sank lower.

My whole body went limp and I let out soft moan as he pulled away, his teeth pulling and grazing my lip as he let it go. He pressed his forehead to mine and whispered, "I'll see you tonight."

Then he pulled completely way from me and he was gone, taking the stairs up to the next floor before I even had the energy to open my eyes. I sagged against the wall for quite a while, until my knees solidified enough for my legs to work.

Despite my training, I hadn't reacted when he grabbed me. There were so many things I could have done, so many ways I could have kept him from cornering me, yet I had done nothing. I would use the excuse that I was surprised and startled, but I'm trained to always be on guard, to anticipate everything, and to think and react quickly when in danger. The only explanation I could come up with over the countless times I'd thought about it over the past few days was that I had instinctively known I wasn't in danger, so there had been no reason to break Ian's wrist or body slam him into the concrete floor.

That kiss had been the singular most sensual moment of my entire life, and it had lasted all of half a minute. I had a hell of a time getting rest that evening before our first night of stakeouts with that little interlude playing repeatedly in my mind. True to his word, except for the lust in his eyes when he saw me in the barely there outfit Anya made me change into, Ian had been one hundred percent professional that night, and every night since. Even though we spent our days together, alone much of the time, our focus had been on working, and he hadn't even baited me once. I missed it a little, and seeing his reactions to the outfits Anya cooked up had become something I looked forward to each night.

"Earth to Fiona." Anya waved a hand in front of my face.

"Huh? What?"

"I was explaining, for the hundredth time this week, that you don't need any extra help in the sexy department; my clothes just make you look a little less intimidating. But, of course, you were zoned out again. That seems to happen every time Ian's name gets mentioned, big sister. What's going on with you two?" Anya asked.

"Nothing," I said. She didn't buy it. "Don't look at me like that. There isn't anything going on, at least not right now. But when this case is over, well, I'm not sure then."

Anya grinned. "Oh? What happened to change your mind since last week? After that kiss he laid on you on the dance floor downstairs, you were impossible to live with and insisted it was a fluke. That there would never be anything between you two."

"I protested too much, did I?" I asked, wincing a bit.

"Only a little." She laughed. "So, what happened?"

"He kissed me again, and I changed my mind," I said, shrugging as if it were no big deal.

"Ooh, do tell!"

I was trying to figure out how to extricate myself from the conversation when she turned her head and I noticed a dark purple smudge along her hairline just over her ear. Looking closer, I realized the top of her ear was the same dark shade.

"You've been fighting again," I accused, my voice slightly smug at having found a way to avoid answering her question and turn the tables on her at the same time. I let out a small hoot of laughter at the horrified look of guilt on her face. "You know, if you want to keep from getting found out, you might want to get River to make you some heavier makeup."

"This is the best she has; I must have missed a spot." She ran over to the mirror on the wall near the door and tossed her head around, looking for the telltale bruise.

"Over your left ear. No, your other left. You know, Pinky is going to kill you when he finds out," I told her.

She rubbed some tinted cream along her hairline and over the top of her ear. The bruise faded away as if it had never been there. "He's not going to find out. Unless you tell him." The last was accompanied by a pointed glare.

"Down girl, you know I'm not going to rat you out. But you know he always finds out," I said, grinning at her.

"I know. Damn. I just don't get it. He doesn't give you any grief when you come home with bruises."

"Oh, he does, just maybe not as much as you. But there are some differences, you know. For one, fighting is a part of my job. I'm not cruising the docks and back alleys for street fights."

She flashed a grin at me. "You could technically call it a job for me, since I made two hundred bucks off today's bets."

My forehead met my palm with an audible smack. "Crap, Anya, do I even want to know how you managed to bring in that much in one afternoon?"

"Probably not. Sit so I can do your makeup."

I did as I was told, but leveled an expectant glare on her as she began rubbing cream into my face. "Tell me anyway."

"Oh, sheesh. It was no big deal. There was a fight down at the docks.

They were all sailors, new around here. They got taken in by the tiny little girl that wanted in on the action. Got me good odds. I cleaned out four of them without a mark on me. The last guy just got a few lucky shots in. Wouldn't have gotten those if he hadn't been juiced up."

She was brushing shimmery mineral powder over my eyelids so I couldn't facepalm. I settled for a heavy sigh. Juicers were the opposite of suckers. Instead of letting vamps sink their fangs into them, juicers got their high by drinking shifter blood. When ingested, components in Were blood caused increased hormone and adrenaline production, which gave the user a temporary boost in speed and strength. Juicing also caused aggression, rage, and loss of control.

"Damn it, Anya, you are going to get yourself killed," I told her, my words coming out muffled and distorted because she was rubbing some concoction of River's on my lips to make them fuller and redder.

"Be still, unless you want to look like a hornet stung you repeatedly in the face. Don't worry. I'm a better fighter than any of those guys. Hell, I'm a better fighter than you, and you come home from every mission with no problem."

On one point, she was completely right. She was a better fighter than I was. But I had advantages she didn't have. My skill, or rather luck, at always coming out of fights alive relied as much on my magic as it did my fighting abilities. More, sometimes. I also usually had a partner, or Mal, watching my back. Even so, there had been a few times that I'd barely made it out alive. If Anya had ever seen me right after some of those fights, she'd be on Pinky's side when he got on his kicks and tried to get me to quit the Blades. But she never had, and if I could help it, she never would see me that hurt.

Mages usually healed a little faster than norms, but the nature of my power, the fact that I could pull energy into my body before dispelling it, seemed to make me heal much faster than any mage I knew, except those with self-healing powers. I couldn't heal vampire fast, but if I were conscious enough to pull in a little energy, it would take just a matter of hours to get rid of cuts and bruises, and only a couple of days to mend broken bones.

Anya had no such advantages, but reminding her of that fact would do nothing but piss her off. Being a norm was a sore spot with my sister. It kept her from the one thing she wanted most. A norm couldn't be a Blade. She could work for the Blades or the City Guard as an analyst or in the typing pool, or some other menial desk job that would drive her crazy.

No matter how good a fighter she was, and she was likely the best in Nash, she could never do fieldwork.

As if reading my mind, she said, "Don't feel sorry for me. And don't worry about me either. I carry packets of River's potions with me."

"There are injuries her potions and brews can't protect you from, or heal. If you don't think about yourself, think about how River will feel if something happens to you that is beyond her power."

Anya leaned back and inspected her handy work on my face. "Okay, you're done. And, if something does happen to me, it won't be River's fault."

"Yeah, but you won't be around to tell her that, now will you?" It was playing dirty, I knew, but I had no doubt that if the argument had been reversed, Anya would have played the River card herself, and it would have worked as well as it did now. We may both be a little reckless with our own lives, but we would do anything to protect River, even from ourselves.

"Okay, okay. I get it. I'll stop fighting," she said as I helped her put away the tubs of makeup goo.

I laughed. "That's a lie."

She grinned. "Okay, I'll pick the little ones and stay away from juicers."

"Good enough. Now come on, you've dolled me up enough, and we both have jobs to get too."

SIXTEEN
Fiona

ANYA WENT DOWN THE FRONT STAIRS, DIRECTLY INTO THE BAR, WHILE I TOOK the back stairs into the small room off the kitchen that acted as the base of operations for our nightly patrols. There were four teams of four people, each consisting of a "mark" and three backups. Based on the profile of the missing mages, which was pretty much all over the place, there was one male and three female marks, including myself, dressed in various modes of attire.

We had no idea why only mages were targeted, but it was safe to assume the bad guy had some sort of aura power. It was dangerous to have mages on the backup teams, but we were so short on manpower, and Sam didn't want to hire mercenaries.

Although the "Vanishing of Farah Purcell" was headline news in the city newspaper, the fact that the Blades were aware of a rash of disappearances had been carefully kept from the public. While hiring freelancers through the Mercenaries Guild was standard practice for the Blades when more manpower was needed, Mercs were notorious for their love of storytelling. They were not bound by the same laws of confidentiality as City Guard and Blade agents.

That meant the entire operation was a little more dangerous than an average stakeout. To be safe, each backup team had at least one vampire or shifter member and mages were paired in twos. Which is how Ian came to be on my backup team along with Rangel and Jarrett.

We didn't want to call attention to ourselves by congregating sixteen Blades in one place, so the teams checked in with Sam in the back room at staggered intervals before heading to the section they were patrolling. Since my team was based around Pinky's, we were the last to check in. As I reached the back hall, another team left the operations room and headed out the door. I nodded at them, wished them good luck, and then went in to find Sam, Rangel, Jarrett, and Ian already there, sitting around the small table in the center of the room.

I stood in the doorway for a few minutes, listening to Ian brief Sam on the day's investigation. It didn't take long. We had spent the afternoon speaking to friends and family of the other missing man, York Reeder. Despite hours spent going through his home and work, we hadn't found out anything particularly helpful.

Magically speaking, he was pretty unremarkable. Though he was a Level Six Mage, he had no ability to work magic without a charged crystal. The leveling system for mages was quite simple and scientific. Norms used ten-fifteen percent of their brain function. The ability to use more brain function gave an individual the ability to access the energy of the universe and manipulate it in different ways. In order to even register as a mage, brain activity had to be at 25%, which was level one. From there, the scale was broken into fifteen levels, up to 100%. No one knew exactly why different powers manifested, or why they could manifest differently in each individual mage, but it was speculated that it depended upon the areas of the brain that were active and the level of activity in each.

Reeder's powers were mental in nature. He was a Word Caller. I didn't like that term. It was a mystical and nonsensical name given to mages who had the ability to write perfect spells. Though almost anyone could use words to focus energy and do simple magic, Word Callers created words of power to do intricate and complicated spell work with highly accurate results. Of course, the worker of the spell still needed to have the ability to work energy either naturally or with a charged crystal.

Reeder worked in a spell shop near the river. According to his boss, he was a good worker, always on time, had a high accuracy rate, and was talkative and jovial with clients. His personal life was much the same. He was friendly, outgoing, and had a lot of friends. He and his husband of twelve years lived in a small apartment in the Magic District, not far from

Broadway.

The night he disappeared, York was supposed to meet his husband, Gray, and a group of friends for dinner at a tavern on Broadway, just a block away from Pinky's. He never made it. York had been last seen at the far end of Broadway, closest to the river, by a friend he had stopped to chat with before continuing on his way.

Nothing indicated that the friend or York's husband had anything to do with his disappearance. In fact, Gray Reeder's grief and worry for his missing husband had been quite real. There was also no evidence that York Reeder had ever met Abel Evans, the man that had died trying to abduct Millie.

I waited until Ian had finished summing up our day before I stepped inside the room and made a show of twirling around to show off my outfit. Making a joke of it made me feel a bit less like a freak, yet I couldn't help the smug satisfaction I felt when I saw Ian's eyes go wide and dark with lust. It was even a little flattering to see Rangel's mouth drop open just a bit.

Jarrett let out a wolf howl of appreciation. "Mmm, mmm, you look good enough to eat," he drawled, coming towards me as if to grab me.

"Oh, no you don't! You'll muss me up. Down boy!" I said as sternly as I could through my laughter.

He skulked back to his chair, his head hung low, as if chastened, but when he raised his head, his face was split in a grin. Ian's, on the other hand, was pinched up in a scowl. Jarrett looked over at him and winked, and I knew his lusty animal show had been put on just for Ian's benefit. It wasn't the first time over the past few nights that he'd playfully flirted with me in front of Ian. He had obviously picked up on the necromancer's jealousy and found it as entertaining as I did.

"If you two are done playing, could we please get to work?" Sam's tone was disapproving, but he couldn't hide his grin.

"Okay, so, anything new?" I asked, taking my place at the table.

"Unfortunately not, and that is a big problem," Sam replied.

"Every hour we go with no leads, the less likely we are to find Farah Purcell," Jarrett said.

Sam nodded. "Yes, but it's more than that. I spent my afternoon in a closed session with senate. They feel we have taken up too much of the city's resources by having every available Guard searching for a girl that could very well be a runaway."

"What? Are you kidding me? Her father is on the senate." Rage boiled in my stomach.

"I know," Sam replied, his voice calm and measured, as usual. "It seems he is spearheading the drive to pull the Guards off the case. He thinks his daughter has run away or is staying away to embarrass him."

I opened my mouth to speak, but Ian beat me to it.

"From what I gathered, her very existence is an embarrassment to him," he spat in disgust.

Sam nodded gravely. "Be that as it may, the senate has given us two days to come up with something or the entire City Guard will be pulled off the case." He looked at Rangel. "That includes you."

"But you don't answer to the senate," Jarrett said.

"No, but we are already shorthanded. Losing the use of the City Guard's people, as well as their resources, will severely limit what we can do. Even you, Jarrett, will have to go back to your regular duties when your informant gets to town. Your case takes priority."

"But what about all the other missing mages?" I asked, incredulous.

"That is what bought us two more nights." Sam leaned back in his chair. "If we haven't made some sort of progress by the end of tomorrow night's stakeout, we lose most of our manpower. And, realistically, I'm not sure how feasible it is to keep dedicating so much of the Blade's resources to a dead-end case either. There are other crimes going cold because we are dedicating everyone we can to finding these missing mages. I'm starting to have my doubts we will be able to, unless someone else goes missing and more evidence is left."

"I don't think we are going to have to wait until tomorrow night. I have a strange feeling something is going to happen tonight," Rangel chimed in.

Everyone at the table turned to look at him.

"What makes you say that?" asked Ian.

"It's just a feeling. I get them sometimes," Rangel replied, almost sheepishly.

"But you're not clairvoyant," I said. Though our dating had been casual, we'd been friends for quite a while. I was certain I would know if he had psychic-type powers.

"No, I don't have visions. My only real power is teleporting, but my mother was a seer, as was both her mother and father. I seem to have inherited it a bit in the form of strong intuition. It's what makes me good at my job. I don't hear voices or get visions, just strong feelings that something is wrong, or I should turn left instead of right, or knowing for sure someone is guilty of a crime. Of course, a feeling can't be used as evidence in a tribunal, but it helps me know I'm on the right track. And, it has saved my hide a time or two."

"So, what is your feeling about tonight?" Sam asked, taking him at his word.

"It isn't anything specific. I just feel like we are going to get a break in the case. I've felt like that since I woke up this afternoon."

"Okay, you heard the man. Be extra vigilant tonight. Keep your emergency crystal handy, and backup, keep eyes on your mark at all times," Sam said. Everyone at the table nodded, almost automatically. "I mean it," he continued, his voice hard. "Fiona, if anything happens, you push energy through that crystal and let us know. Whoever this guy is, he's taken down mages almost as powerful as you are. And you guys keep her in your sights." He turned his gaze on the three men. "You know we can't trust her not to go off on her own, and that crystal will only let us know she is in trouble, not where she is."

I opened my mouth to protest, but shut it when I realized he was right. I couldn't be trusted not to run smack dab into danger if I saw an opening. The fact that I knew that about myself was good, right? The first step to change was acknowledging you had a problem. Except I didn't really see it as a problem since it usually got me results.

I opened my mouth again, this time to say something witty, and then shut it again as I saw the looks on the faces of the four men surrounding me. They were all grave faced and nodding.

"Don't worry, Sam. We have her back," Jarrett said.

"Yes, we do," Ian said, a little more emphasis on the word "we" than necessary. Rangel was smart enough to keep his mouth shut, but he nodded along with the others.

"Oh, for crying out loud!" I exclaimed, disgusted. "Just because I look like some delicate princess in this get-up doesn't make me one. I can kick every single one of your asses. Well, maybe not yours, Jarrett, you have that unfair vampire advantage, but I swear, I'll get in some good licks before you take me down."

Every single one of them burst out laughing. Every damned one.

"Ugh, can we get to work now?" I said over their laughter, letting annoyance drip from my voice.

"Go, go. And be careful, all of you." Sam ushered us out the door.

Once in the back hall, we split up as had become our normal routine. Ian and Rangel had come in the back door and went back out now. They would circle down two blocks, wander in and out of a few of the bars along the way, before coming in to Pinky's. Jarrett, who had come in the front door of the pub earlier, had a drink, and then came to the back, would go back into the main part of the bar for another drink.

Because Farah Purcell had been last seen in Pinky's the night I had been there with first Ian, then Jarrett, we had to take into account that the kidnapper had seen me with one or both of them. For that reason, I went back upstairs and through the hall to the front stairs, which I took down into the pub, just as I normally would do. I went to the bar, ordered a drink, and sat in my usual seat at the end of the bar where it crooked around, so I could sit slightly sideways with my back to the wall and see the entire room.

Jarrett moved down and we talked for a few minutes until he finished his drink, which like mine was nothing more than colored water. Then he left the pub to stroll along the street outside and take up a watchful spot where he could see the entrance to Pinky's as well as a good portion of the street.

After Jarrett left, I continued to drink and chat with Pinky, Anya, and other bar patrons. For all intents and purposes, except for my frou-frou clothes and watered-down drinks, I acted just as I normally would. I started dancing with some of the men in the bar, including both Ian and Rangel, who had come in and sat together at a table near the window, looking for all the world like a couple of chums out for a few drinks.

It was after my dance with Rangel, when I went back to the bar for another drink, that I started feeling eyes on the back of my neck. I turned, expecting someone to be right behind me, but no one was there. Someone was watching me; I could feel it in my bones. And it wasn't my team. I didn't get intuitive feelings like Rangel, but there was little inherent magic in everyone that helped sense danger, and that was what I was feeling right then.

I casually sat and leaned back in my seat, discreetly scanning the room. I didn't see anyone or anything out of the ordinary, but I hadn't thought I would. I glanced up at the clock. I'd been out front in Pinky's a little more than an hour. It seemed like as good a time as any to head out onto the street and start my nightly foray through the other bars close by. I knew, instinctively, that whoever was watching me would not approach me in Pinky's. It just wasn't crowded enough, and I was too in my element.

I drained my drink, called over my shoulder to Pinky that I was going to go find some fun and not to wait up for me, and then went out the front doors.

Once out on the street, I stumbled a bit and leaned up against the building as if to get my bearings. The feeling of being watched intensified. My gaze swept the crowded street. There were a lot of familiar faces in the partiers that passed by. I had seen most of them over the past few nights, but no one seemed to be paying particular attention to me, so I started walking toward the Blue Vein.

I only made it a few steps before I got goose bumps across the back of my neck. Before I could help myself, I broke the number-one rule of casual surveillance; I turned quickly, making it obvious I was looking for someone. As I whipped around, I caught a glimpse of what I thought was a familiar face, but not anyone I'd seen on the streets or in the bars over the past few nights. I couldn't be sure. I had only seen them for a moment before someone had passed between us and they were gone. But if I had seen who I thought I had, there was no doubt it was the person that was following me. I needed to get somewhere less crowded to be sure.

I turned and resumed my course, knowing someone, other than my backup team, was following me. In front of me, there was a sudden commotion and raised voices as a group of four men came out of a bar, followed by another group of three. From the looks of them, they were all vampires and by the words flying back and forth between the two groups, they were itching for a fight. I sped up my pace and got past them before the first punch was thrown.

The commotion behind me got louder, and the crowd on the sidewalk started gravitating towards the brawl, which moved to the middle of the street. I looked back to see that, in just a few seconds, the crowd around the fighters had grown to encompass the sidewalks on both sides of the street. I couldn't see Jarrett, Ian, or Rangel. They must have been caught up in the growing crowd. Neither could I see anyone that might be following me.

I glanced around to get my bearings. I was about two blocks away from Pinky's. To my right, there was a dark narrow path between two buildings. To give my pursuer, and hopefully my backup team, time to get through the crowd and catch up to me, I stepped into the alley entrance, careful to stay in a moderately lit area, and leaned against the building.

There was a skittering in the dark behind me, and I cringed. I hated rats, and the boots I had on were too thin for me to feel comfortable standing in a rat-infested alley. I opened my senses and pulled in a little power in anticipation of a fight, or having to fry some rats, and hoped

132

someone came along soon.

I didn't have to wait long. A figure moved into the alley and leaned against the building next to me, blocking the way out. His shoulder was against the building and he was facing me, the light casting a shadow across his face.

"It's kind of dangerous for a lady like you to be out here alone." The hoarse, raspy voice wasn't familiar.

I moved back and towards the middle of the alley and, as I hoped, he shifted his stance and turned just enough to let me see his very familiar face in the full light. Perhaps if I hadn't spent an hour looking at various artwork depicting those large eyes and full lips, I wouldn't have recognized him. But Gray Reeder was a talented artist, magically talented, in fact. His lead and charcoal sketches were as detailed as the old photographs I'd seen in the books at the Archives. And his favorite subject was his husband. Their tiny apartment was filled with sketches and paintings of York Reeder.

"Oh, I can take care of myself," I said, forcing my voice into a soft, sultry lilt and giving him a coy smile. I didn't want to break cover just yet.

"I'm sure you can," he said. "But you did look a little lonely here. Can I keep you company or were you waiting on someone?"

There was something off about his voice. The flat, raspy quality didn't fit the thin man in front of me, and it seemed a bit disjointed from his mouth movements. As I looked closer, I realized, though I was absolutely sure this was York Reeder, he barely resembled the laughing, exuberant man in the pictures. His skin was sallow and sagging, and his eyes were dull and lifeless. Something was terribly wrong.

I glanced towards the street, but I still had no backup. Turning my attention back to Reeder, I made my voice as flirtatious as possible. "What if I told you I was waiting for you?"

"I would say it was fortuitous because you are exactly what I've been waiting for, for a very long time."

Though the voice's flat, uninflected tone hadn't changed, something about that statement made a cold ball of dread form in my stomach. I pasted the coquettish smile in place.

"Ooh, that sounds exciting," I said, moving across the alley to lean seductively against the far building wall, putting as much space between us as possible. I fingered the small, amethyst crystal hanging around my neck, pushing a little power through it, giving my team the signal to move in.

"It is," said Reeder, moving slowly towards me.

He was only about a foot away from me when his hand began moving towards me. I forced myself to stay in my role as party girl, hoping the cavalry would arrive soon. As his arm swung around, light glinted off something metallic in his hand.

Instinctively my arm shot up to block him in an effort to knock the needle out of his hand, but his other arm snaked up my back and his hand was wrapped around my hair. He gave it a sharp tug, forcing my head back so hard I had to bend at the knees to keep from falling.

"Don't worry, my love, this won't hurt for long," the cold, monotone voice crooned. His hand came at my neck, almost as if in slow motion.

"Maybe not, but this will." I pulled up my right leg and slammed the sharp heel of Anya's boot down into his instep.

Surprisingly, he didn't squeal in pain, but it was enough to knock him slightly off balance. I took advantage of that and forced my elbow into his solar plexus. That knocked him back and the needle syringe went flying as he hit the ground several feet away.

"Oh, you like to play rough, do you?" The voice was a near growl now, sounding even more far away than before. "I can give you rough."

"I bet you say that to all the girls," I crooned.

I opened my senses to pull in energy and blast him back, but I was met with a dark coldness that made my stomach lurch. I shut my senses down, instantly. It was the exact same feeling that had come over me the night I had been dancing with Ian. The night Farah had gone missing. My head swam, and the world tilted. I staggered, and then I fell to my knees, gravel scraping my bare skin. I gasped for air, struggling not to empty the contents of my stomach.

What the hell was happening here? I took a deep breath, forcing myself to focus.

Reeder lunged at me, but he moved stiffly, almost as if it were an effort to control his body. I had just enough time to stagger to my feet and move to the side before he slammed into me. Instead of hitting me full force, he clipped me on the shoulder, knocking me aside as he slammed into the wall of the building behind me.

I moved in behind him and pinned him to the wall, my knee in his back. "It's over, Reeder."

The man began to laugh, which sounded eerie, disturbing, and sent chills up my spine.

I was about to ask him what was so funny when I heard my name being called from the direction of the street.

"In here," I called back, but it came out a hoarse whisper, and the world spun again. I leaned into Reeder, supporting my weight on his back until the world righted again. Taking another deep breath, I shouted again, this time my voice ringing out in the empty alley. "Here."

A moment later, a broad figure strode into the alley.

"Rangel! It's about damn time," I said, glancing behind him. "Where are Ian and Jarrett?"

"Still stuck in the crowd. I teleported out, but it took me a few minutes to find you. Sorry."

"No problem. Can you help me with chuckles here?" I said, jerking Reeder's arms behind his back so Rangel could cuff him.

We flipped him around to face us.

"York Reeder," Rangel said, his tone authoritative. "You are bound by law under my authority as a Guard of the City-State of Nash."

Oh, no, he didn't just try to take over my apprehension! "And, my authority as an Agent of the Black Blade Guard under the jurisdiction of the Paranorm Council of Elders." My tone and the look I shot him dared him to protest. Perhaps this wasn't the time or place to get into a pissing match, but this was officially a Blades' case and I had dominion here.

Apparently neither of our statements or our bickering had any effect on Reeder, who continued with that creepy laugh.

"What is so funny?" I asked, at the end of my patience.

He stopped laughing abruptly. "Silly girl, York Reeder isn't here anymore. This body belongs to me now."

A shiver of anxiety ran through me at his words. Who the hell was this guy and why couldn't I access my magic around him? Had he been in Pinky's that night? Or was I losing my power and it had nothing to do with him at all? I shook my head slightly and forced myself to focus.

"Oh, just who are you then?" I asked, trying to sound flippant.

"You may call me Bokor." The monotone voice actually managed to sound superior.

"Well, then, Bokor, you are bound by law…"

The laughter started again, cutting me off.

"You silly, silly child. You think you can bind the likes of me? That your laws apply to me? You have no idea what you are dealing with."

"Really? Then, please, do tell us," Rangel bit out.

"Oh, you'll find out in time," Bokor said, ominously, his eyes focused on me. "You will know my grace and my power when I devour you."

What the hell? Devoured me? Before I could ask him what he meant by that, York Reeder's already vacant eyes went gray and cloudy. His body went slack, and then stiff, his skin becoming dry and brittle, and within seconds, the very much alive man was dead and his dry corpse slumped forward on to me.

I heard a shriek and realized it came from me. I looked up, saw Rangel's horrified face, and knew it had to mirror mine. My stomach clenched and my knees buckled. I was able to register Ian running towards me and calling my name just before everything went gray, and then black.

SEVENTEEN
Fiona

"I CAN'T BELIEVE I FUCKING FAINTED," I SAID, LEANING ON THE TABLE WITH BOTH elbows, my face buried in my hands. I was talking more to myself than the room at large.

But River heard me as she set a mug of hot honey and lavender down in front of me. She ran her hand over my hair. "You had a pretty big shock, so it's to be expected. How are you feeling now?"

"I'm fine," I snapped, immediately regretting it. I looked up and grabbed her hand, pressing it to my cheek for a moment before releasing it. "I'm sorry, Rivs. I'm fine, really. Please don't fuss."

"Sure, whatever you say. Drink your tea," she ordered, smiling indulgently, then moved around set a mug in front of Rangel, who looked as pale and freaked out as I felt. "You too." River was an equal opportunity mother hen.

After I passed out (fainting was just too weak and puny a word, and I was not weak and puny) Ian had carried me back to Pinky's. Apparently, River had dreamed of meeting Ian at the back door with my unconscious body. She'd woken up and went downstairs. Having learned long ago to take River's dreams or visions seriously, everyone had sprung into action. So by the time we arrived, Pinky and Anya were already clearing the pub out and closing down early. Ian had reluctantly given me over to River's care, and he and Sam had went back to the alley. A few minutes later, Rangel and Jarrett had come in.

That had been over an hour ago, and now we were in the cleared out bar waiting for Sam and Ian to come back from the morgue. Pinky and Anya were busying themselves by doing the other bar closing duties. River was helping them by wiping down tables and fussing over Rangel and me. Jarrett sat silently by the door, watching out the front window, his body tense and on guard.

I sipped the hot tea River had given me, letting the warm, sweet taste wash away the lingering nausea. My mind raced, trying to make sense of what had happened, what I'd seen. But it didn't make sense, not any of it. Before I could think about it too much, Ian and Sam came in. Their faces looked as grim as I felt.

They joined us at the table and, after River and Anya delivered drinks all around, Sam said, "I sent the other teams home to get some rest. I also gave them all the day off tomorrow. There is no use in continuing our nightly patrols with Reeder dead. As a matter of fact, except for a small team to try to trace his tracks in hopes of finding some of the missing women, I might as well call off the whole team. I'm afraid that with a dead suspect and no new leads, we may never find them."

"York Reeder was not the kidnapper," I said, with utter confidence.

"You think there is another accomplice?"

"No. I think Reeder was a victim, not a kidnapper. That might have been Reeder's body in that ally, but whoever, or whatever, that spoke to me was not York Reeder." I filled them in on everything that had happened from the moment I glanced at Reeder on the street until everything went black.

Next to me, Rangel nodded. "I agree with Fiona. I don't know what the hell that was, but it wasn't Reeder. There was something far away and detached about the voice, and the words and mouth movement just didn't sync up. Someone or something was controlling that body. And the way he died, it was like... Well, like nothing I'd ever seen. One moment he was breathing and alive, although kind of sickly colored, and the next, he was a dried-up corpse."

"Someone controlling the body? Did you see anyone else in the vicinity?" Sam asked.

"No, but it was dark and my attention was on not getting killed," I told him.

"I got to the alley entrance in time to hear him talking, and there was no one else in that ally or anywhere within line of site of Reeder. If there had been, I would have seen them, or scented them," Jarrett said.

Sam mulled that over for a moment. "Ian, is there any way a necromancer can control a body like that?"

"No. That is not what necromancers do. I got to the alley in time to hear the tail end of his speech and see the body collapse. That is nothing I've ever seen or heard of. I can't explain it, except to say that whatever powers were used, they were not Necromantic."

I wasn't convinced. "Someone, either alive or dead, was controlling that man. Is it possible he was possessed by a spirit?"

"No. Two life energies, or spirits, cannot possess the same body, and a spirit cannot jump into a dead body and control it," Ian informed the room at large in his stuffy-professor voice. As I opened my mouth, he continued, "And no, to my knowledge, it is not possible for any necromancer to force a spirit into a dead body and control it in that manner. Besides, there was no spirit to control."

There was something about the way he said "in that manner" that caught my attention, but I decided to ignore it, for now. "So the body was like the other one?"

"Identical," Ian said. "I have yet to find any explanation for it in any of the books and research materials I have. Of course, that doesn't mean such incidents have never happened before. It just means the information was lost during the Cataclysm. That isn't uncommon, especially for very rare phenomena that may have only been recorded in one particular place."

"So, on that note, we are no further than we were a week ago," Sam said, with a weary sigh. "Let's concentrate on what little new information we have. What exactly did he say to you, Fiona?"

I recited the words again, suppressing a shiver of dread and fear at the last part.

"Devour you? What the hell does that mean?" Everyone turned to look at Pinky. I'd almost forgotten my family was still in the room. Under normal circumstances, it would have been a breach of protocol, but since Sam didn't mind, neither did I. Besides, Pinky's was their home and livelihood, and this person had been here at least twice, and could come back. They deserved to know what was going on.

"I don't know, but I don't care," I lied, my voice full of false bravado. "I'm not going to give him a chance."

"Wait, did you say his name was Bokor?" Anya asked. She had finished cleaning up and was sitting at the bar sipping a drink.

"Yes, why? Have you heard that name before?"

"Yes, I think I have." Her expression was thoughtful, as if trying to conjure a memory. "But it wasn't a name, it was a title."

"A title? Like a job or position in the community?" Ian asked.

"Community, I suppose," she said slowly. "Back when I lived with the gypsies, we often met other clans and sometimes camped and traveled with them. Some of the clans from the lost Creole Coast practiced a religion called Voodoo. I liked to listen to the clan elders tell about their myths and practices. Each clan seemed to have their own take, their own customs and myths, even their own names for their religious leaders. There were a couple of clans I remember that called their priests Bokor."

"I've heard of Voodoo," Ian said. "I've ran across it in my research before because it was a religion based on magic. But I don't know much about it. I will have to do some more research."

"I've heard of Voodoo, too," Jarrett said. "I don't know anything about it, really, except that it was widely practiced in LouisIana and Haiti. Seems like there were a lot of different versions of it."

I had no idea where those locations were, but I assumed they were part of the lands that had been lost to the sea in the Cataclysm.

"That makes sense," Ian said, thoughtfully. "Most religions had many variations in their myths and practices, even back when information was widely available. I imagine that after two hundred years of verbally handed down customs, they are quite different. I suppose the place to start would be knowing the basics. I'll hit the archives first thing tomorrow."

"I'll help you," I told him. Though the prospect of spending hours surrounded by dusty tomes reading dry, boring magic research books was abhorrent to me, I knew two sets of eyes would be better than one. Besides, I had to do something, and at this point, researched seemed to be the only thing there was that could be done.

"I might be able to help, too," River said from her spot at the bar. "I know a Voodoo priestess."

"You know a Voodoo priestess?"

"Could she be the kidnapper?"

"How do you know a Voodoo priestess?"

The questions came out all at one time in such a jumble it was impossible to tell who had asked what. But my sister was unfazed by the clamor. She just smiled, and then answered the questions one by one.

"One of the gypsy clans that comes to the market worships Voodoo. Their priestess is a dear friend. No, I do not believe she could be in any way responsible for the disappearances or deaths. Her title is not Bokor; it is Mambo."

"Can you get her to talk to us?" I asked, knowing River never would have brought it up in front of everyone if she didn't.

"I think so; she is very sweet. But I'll only introduce you if you promise not to go in there treating her like a suspect. She is a good, kind-hearted old woman," River said, an edge of steel in her sweet voice.

Ian spoke up before I could. "Do not worry, River. If you believe her to be good, then I do too. We will treat her with the utmost respect."

River nodded. "Okay, then you guys can meet me at the market any time tomorrow afternoon. I'll see her when I go in to set up in the morning and talk to her then."

Once the next day's meet up was settled, River went upstairs to go back to bed since she had to get up in just a few hours to be at the market at dawn. After we had gone over the entire night in detail one more time, to catch any details that might have been missed, we all decided to call it a night.

"I'm going to head back to the office and get my report done to turn in to the senate tomorrow. At this point, we might as well stand down the City Guard and send them back to their normal duties. Fiona and Ian, I expect a full report tomorrow night on whatever you manage to dig up. But for now, you guys go get some sleep," Sam said.

"I'll scry you with a report tomorrow," Ian told him. Then he turned to Pinky. "I'm a little concerned about your safety. This bad guy is nothing I've ever seen before, and he now has his sights set on Fiona. I know you keep this place warded and you and Fiona can take care of yourselves, but I'd like to offer up a couple of my guards."

"I've never had any problem protecting my girls, but I agree with you, Ian. This is an unknown and having a little backup would be fine by me," Pinky said, in that easy way he had.

"No need to wake anyone up, Barroes. I can stay until dawn, a little later if I can borrow an umbrella to get back to Headquarters," Jarrett said.

"I tell you what, Jarrett. If you are willing, you can stay here for the duration. Even though I haven't rented out rooms in nearly twenty years, I still have several rooms with soft, comfortable beds and vampire-safe windows. Anya can make you one up, and you can bunk here. If that is acceptable," Pinky said.

"Sounds good," Jarrett agreed.

Sam stepped in. "Good. I'll send a Blade to escort River to the market and guard her while she is there if you can send your guys over to watch the Pub while Pinky and Jarrett get some sleep tomorrow."

I stood back, watching the four men make decisions without even consulting me. Opening my mouth to protest, I shut it without uttering a word. They were right. Because of me, my sisters were in danger and they did need extra protection. So if it made them feel like big, masculine men to arrange for guards without consulting Anya or me, despite the fact that we could kick the crap out of all of them, that was fine with me.

"I'll see you in the morning," I told Ian. I kissed Pinky on the cheek, wished everyone else good night, and retreated upstairs. I needed some time alone to process the night's happenings. I was also looking forward to a little more rest than I had gotten over the past week.

Two hours later, I was still awake and pacing in the tiny space between my bed and dresser. Despite having the window open, the air was too hot and thick; it felt as if I were breathing through River's pea soup. My stomach churned and my skin crawled with nervous energy. I looked over at my bed. There was no way I could lay down feeling like this. I needed to get out. I needed some fresh air. I needed to walk, no run, off some of this energy.

When I came up, I had changed out of Anya's outfit into a thin, cotton tank top and shorts. I pulled on and laced up my comfortable old boots, my feet welcoming the way the soft leather and sole shaped around them. So much better than my earlier footwear. I quickly plaited my hair into a crooked, haphazard braid and tied it with a length of twine.

I slipped out of my room. The apartment was quiet. River was likely asleep already, and Anya was probably still down in the bar. I went out into the hall and stood at the top of the front stairs. I could hear voices, a male and female. I paused. If it were Pinky, he'd be able to hear me and would never let me go out alone after what had gone down tonight. Damn vampire hearing.

I took a moment to mutter a sound-deafening spell that would cover me until I got outside. I took a couple of tentative, normal steps. When no one reacted, I hurried down the hall and down the back stairs. I paused at the back door, my ears alert. The voices from the bar were soft, in easy conversation, though I could now hear that the male voice talking to Anya wasn't Pinky. It was Jarrett. I froze for a moment, listening and wondering if something had happened. Then I realized he and Anya were having the same problem with going to sleep as I was, though for entirely different reasons. While my schedule was as flexible as they come, Jarrett was a vampire, so he mostly worked at night and Anya worked in a vampire bar. Two in the morning was barely midafternoon for them.

I relaxed. Nothing was out of place and from the easy flow of their conversation, they hadn't heard me. Without another thought for them, I slipped out the back door. In the alley, I breathed the cool night air deep into my lungs and started running. I ran through the city, avoiding major streets that would be full of nighttime workers, shoppers, and partiers.

Having a little residual energy after a magical fight was normal for me. Under normal circumstances, and for most mages, a mage worked magic by using concentration and energy to manipulate the energy of the universe in one way or another. I had always worked magic differently, by pulling it into my body then dispelling it in different patterns to do what I need. This used up my own energy as well, but my battle magic worked very differently. Pulling energy into my body, and then dispelling it to create short bursts of energy as a weapon doesn't normally use up my own energy. Instead, a little bit of the energy lingers. Mixed with the adrenaline that starts pumping during a battle, I am always a bit edgy afterwards.

Usually, a run would dispel the energy enough for me to sleep, but it didn't seem to be working tonight. But then, my nervous energy had nothing to do with magical battle. I hadn't been able to pull any energy tonight.

My boots pounded the ground as I ran as hard as I could, winding my way through the back streets of the city. I tried to concentrate on my breathing and the movement of my body, but it was no use.

I had seen a lot of death in the years since I graduated from the Academy. A lot of senseless, wasteful death. I had even dealt some of it out in the course of my duties as a Blade. Death was always senseless and wasteful, even when the person deserved to die for their crimes. I'd killed criminals, and I'd held their victims in my arms as the life seeped from them. Yet tonight, something had been different. Probably because the man, the completely innocent man whose body had been used, hadn't been sick or injured. He'd been full of life, if a bit pale and stiff moving, one moment, and then the life energy had gone out of him, leaving his body dry and slumping against me.

The worst part was the sadness and hope I had seen in York Reeder's husband's face and radiating off him in waves earlier today. Gray Reeder had been holding on to faith that he would see his husband again. But he wouldn't. That hope and the life-loving exuberance I had seen in the paintings of York had been wiped from his life forever, and I felt responsible. Had there been anything I could have done?

Probably not. York Reeder had no control over his body, if his consciousness had even been in there. Perhaps it hadn't been in his body for days or weeks. I had to accept that there had been nothing I could have done. There was no way I could have saved York Reeder. But that was worse than taking the blame. It made me feel powerless. And I hated that more than anything in the world.

I'd been running for nearly an hour, but my skin was still jumping and I hadn't even started to tire. I needed something more than a run to help me dispel the energy surging through me. As the thought occurred to me, I stopped running and looked around to see where I was. I recognized the area immediately. I stood a few steps from the riverfront entrance to the Necromancer's Guild headquarters building. Though I'd started running in the opposite direction and taken the long way around via back alleys and little used roads, I had unconsciously headed straight for where I wanted to be.

The wards that had protected the city from the destructive storms had not been able to prevent the swelling of the Cumberland River. Whole streets and buildings had sunk deep into the mud and yards, and even miles, in places beyond the city walls, had been lost to the river. During the reconstruction a hundred years ago, most of the buildings that sunk and were half covered in water were torn down and a barrier wall and walkway had been constructed along the new borders of the river.

The building was a squat four-story that took up half a block, dated back to a decade or two before the Cataclysm. It was situated on the riverfront, just a few yards from the water, though when it was built it had likely been three or four blocks away. A guard stood just inside the glass door. The room behind him was lit with blue-tinted crystal lamps that cast a shadow over his face, so I couldn't tell if he saw me or not.

When he stepped away, I gathered he must not have seen me standing there watching the building, or he would have stayed by the door. I stood another moment trying to decide whether to go up knock. Of course, it was stupid. Undoubtedly, Ian was asleep already. And even if he wasn't, what did I think I was doing? Was I ready for what would happen if I went up there? Ian had promised we would visit the topic of the sexual tension between us after this case was over. I shivered at the memory of that knee-melting kiss. Perhaps it was just best to wait until then, until I could think more clearly.

Did I really want to think clearly? Did I really want to wait any longer? Forget my need to push tonight out of my mind; the clear, undeniable truth was that I wanted Ian Barroes so bad that I could taste it. We had been dancing around each other with sniping and baiting for years. I was getting tired, I wanted to give in, despite the pure fear that coursed through my blood at the thought of doing so. I wasn't afraid of Ian, but of myself. Of the feelings being with Ian would open up.

I stood there for several minutes silently arguing with myself and was no closer to a decision when the matter was taken out of my hands. The glass door of the building swung open, and the guard strode across the street to me. "Agent Moon, Master Barroes asks that you join him upstairs for a drink."

EIGHTEEN
Ian

A KNOCK SOUNDED ON HIS PRIVATE APARTMENT DOOR. HE SET THE TWO GLASSES of wine he'd just poured on a low table in the center of the sitting area and settled back onto the cushioned sofa. "Come in," he called.

The heavy door swung open and Danielson, the night guard on duty, stepped in, followed by Fiona.

She came fully into the room, maneuvering around Danielson, and stood wordlessly in the doorway. The flickering light from the fire in the hearth and the two crystal lamps he'd activated, one on his desk on the other side of the room, and the other in the corner of the sitting area, offered enough light for him to see the damp spots on her shirt and the glistening sweat on her skin. Her hair was a mass of loose tendrils that had worked out of her crooked braid and floated around her head like a chaotic halo. Her appearance was as disheveled and unkempt as he'd ever seen, yet, at this moment, she was as beautiful to him as ever.

He cleared his throat to make sure the lust that had flooded his body didn't show up in his voice, and said, "Thank you, Danielson. That will be all for the evening."

Danielson didn't blink. He clipped out a brisk, "Yes, sir," and left the room quickly, shutting the door behind him.

"You have very efficient people," Fiona said, nodding her head towards the door. "Does he wake you in the middle of the night every time a strange woman stands across the street for more than two minutes?"

Ian let out a bark of laughter. "Hardly. Actually, I was already awake. Couldn't sleep."

"Seems to be going around," she said, noncommittally.

When she didn't continue, Ian went on. "After a bit of tossing and turning, I got up to have a drink and watch the boats on the river. It helps me relax. I was at the window and saw you running alongside of the river. When you stopped just outside my doorway, it seemed polite to ask you in for a drink. I thought you might need one as much as I do." He gestured towards the glasses on the table.

Fiona shrugged. "I am a bit thirsty."

She crossed the room, sat in an upholstered armchair opposite the sofa, picked up one of the glasses, and took a tentative sip of the dark liquid. "Mmm," she moaned, and then took another sip. "You got this from Pinky." It wasn't a question.

"Yes, I did, actually. He gave it to me tonight before I left." He took a sip, his first, and let the fruity taste roll over his tongue. "Wow, that is strong."

Fiona laughed. "I would say so. It's his special Blackberry wine. It has a higher alcohol content than any other wine he makes, almost as high as whiskey. But it has a sweeter, fuller flavor. He makes only a few bottles a year and lets it age for several years before it's ready to drink. He doesn't sell it or serve it in the bar. He keeps it for special occasions and friends."

Ian took another, larger drink. "It's delicious. I can see why he saves it. He handed both Rangel and me a bottle as we left. I figured it was a thank you for having your back tonight."

"Either that or he figured you guys would need something a little stronger than normal after what went down tonight. I'm sure Jarrett is back at the bar, being treated to some of Pinky's finest whiskey."

"No doubt. Why aren't you there imbibing with him?" He let out a chuckle at her raised eyebrows. "Not that I'm not happy to share my wine with you, I just figured you would have already belted back a stiff drink or two."

She sighed, settling back in the chair with her wine. "Too restless."

"I imagine that is normal for you, considering the way you pull energy." Ian drained his glass.

"It happens. Running usually helps," Fiona replied. Then, as what he said sunk in, she sat up straighter, sliding to the edge of the chair. "Wait. What do you mean, with the way I pull energy?"

"You are a succubus," Ian said, matter-of-factly.

"I'm a what? What do you know about how I pull power?" Fiona asked, her tone becoming higher pitched with every word.

"Calm down, Fiona. I've known you work your special brand of magic by pulling energy into your body since the first time I worked with you. I don't blame you for keeping it close to the vest, though."

Fiona eyed him suspiciously, but her voice was calmer when she spoke. "What makes you think I work magic differently than anyone else?"

"Clever ploy to get the information you want without actually admitting to anything. You might want to go into politics; you'd make a great magistrate, or even better, senator." He laughed at Fiona's glare. "Okay, I'll play the game. I'm a necromancer. By definition, I see energy. Most necromancers only see life energy that has passed out of a body. It's common for a mage to have a minor ability or two or three, in addition to their main power. I happen to be able to see currants of energy. It's a minor power, and I can only see when large amounts of energy are being worked. Though I can usually feel the shift in energy when someone is about to perform magic very close by, with the exception of spell and crystal work."

"Currents of energy? Like auras?" Fiona relaxed back into her chair, obviously intrigued.

Ian grinned. "No, auras are usually colored and denote specific types of energy. I only see pulses of white, a bit like the energy streams that you produce when you focus your energy with your hanbo, only not quite so rope like, and I have to focus my own magic to see it. But, I think you know that already."

"Oh, so since you have told me something about yourself, now I'm supposed to spill all my secrets." Her tone was flippant, but her eyes took on that suspicious look again.

Ian silently debated how much he should tease and bait her. Considering what she'd been through tonight, probably not much at all. But he had her here, in his apartment, and they were sitting and chatting, and that felt amazing. He didn't want it to end. He knew if he pushed enough, he could get her talking, possibly even sharing some of her secrets, or what she thought were secrets. Then they'd be having an actual conversation. He couldn't let an opportunity like that slip by.

"No," he told her. "I don't expect you to tell me anything. How about I tell you?"

Fiona's lips tightened. He could tell she was desperately trying to hide a smile. "Okay, then. Enlighten me."

"Okay, then. I don't know the exact nature of your secondary ability, but I believe you can see energy patterns that tell you when someone is lying."

Her face was impassive, her tone measured, giving away nothing. "What makes you say that?"

He had her. Any moment, she'd actually be contributing to the conversation. "You have an uncanny ability to tell when people are telling the truth. And, I've felt you pull energy during interrogations. It was simple deduction."

"You are close, but not entirely accurate." She paused for several minutes, but when Ian didn't say anything, she seemed to make a decision. "I can see the energy waves of emotions. Unlike what you see, they aren't bright, but more of a smoky gray. I can tell what they are by the patterns. It took me a long time to figure them out, but by my late teens, I was an old pro."

Ian leaned over the table, picked up the bottle of wine, and offered it to her. Wordlessly, she held out her glass and let him refill it. Once he'd replenished his own drink, he sat back and thought a moment. "And you kept it a secret both because it was handy and because you thought it was unusual?"

Fiona took another long drink of her wine. "I was a hellion child raised by a vampire that slept all day. No matter what Pinky did to keep me inside, I found ways around it and around any babysitter he hired. Before my sisters came along, I spent my days roaming the streets. A kid that is good at finding hiding places can hear and learn a lot. Among the things I picked up was that having a very unusual power was not a good thing. I heard stories about people's family and friends taken away by Science-Mages to be studied, or to be forced to work for the city-state in some way, whether they wanted to or not. At the time, I was too young to realize the stories came from the very old, and those practices were no longer legal in Nash. But, by the time I got old enough to realize that, I was also old enough to know that illegal didn't mean it couldn't or wouldn't happen."

"Your ability to detect emotions isn't that rare, but you wouldn't know that unless you took advanced magical studies at the Academy," Ian told her.

She let out a hoot of laughter. "No way. I barely made it through the two primary courses required of all mage agents. I learned the basic spell work needed in law enforcement, and I even bungle those upon occasion. My ability, my main ability, using energy as an offensive and defensive weapon, is more instinctive than intellectual. Training as a fighter helped me hone those skills more than any books or magical practice."

Ian nodded. "I can understand that. You wouldn't have learned about succubus powers in a primary course, either."

"What the crap is a succubus?" Fiona asked, thoroughly curious now.

"In ancient times, succubi were believed to be demons that fed off the sexual energy of men. Hey. Stop." He ducked as the two pillows he kept in the armchair Fiona was sitting in whizzed past his head.

"You just called me a soul-sucking demon. You're lucky I haven't finished my wine yet or I'd be throwing this glass."

"Sex-sucking, not soul-sucking," he said, and threw one of the pillows back, smacking her in the knee and eliciting a giggle out of her. A jolt of awareness zinged through him. Had he actually just made Miss Sourpuss Fiona laugh? Probably just the wine.

"Oh, well, that makes a huge difference. Carry on."

Ian laughed. "Well, we now know that succubi aren't demons; there are no such things. Succubi are actually mages, female mages if you want to be technical, that work magic by pulling energy into their bodies before expelling it. The types of energy they work with can be different, so I imagine there are some that pull sexual energy. How they work it is different, as well."

"So, not all succubi have battle magic?" she asked.

"No. A succubus doesn't really denote a type of power as much as a unique way of working the power. Succubi are rare, but not unheard of. Like I said before, for hundreds of years, even in the magical community, succubi were touted as demons. Even in modern times, it makes people nervous."

"Don't worry; I don't plan to start telling my secrets. I'm still a little freaked out that you figured it all out. I'm guessing that you've kept your mouth shut this long, I can trust you to keep doing so." She smiled at him, making his heart jump.

"Mum's the word."

"I can't believe I told you my deepest, darkest secrets. You now know almost as much about me as my family does," she said as she leaned forward and refilled her glass and then his a third time, emptying the wine bottle.

Not likely. He could study her for a hundred years and still not know everything there was to know about her, and still not get bored of trying to learn. He took the full glass from her and leaned back. "Oh, I doubt that. There is more to you than you would like people to see. But would that really be that bad, me knowing more about you? Despite your preconceived notions of me, which I don't completely understand, I'm not such a bad guy. You would know that if you let yourself get to know me a little."

"Okay, then, I'll bite." A slow, mischievous grin spread across her full, kissable lips, and she leaned back again, this time crossing her legs so that the expanse of bare thigh below her shorts' hem caught his eye. "You know two secrets about me, but you only told me one about you. Tell me something about Ian Barroes that isn't common knowledge."

"Okay, then, let's see." Ian tapped his finger to his mouth while he thought. There was so much he could tell her that she likely didn't know about him. As a prominent member of the Nash City society and the head of one of the largest guilds in the city-state, there was a lot of public speculation about his life, not to mention the fact that the Barroes family was quite notorious. But very little of what the public knew about his life was accurate, and it was his guess that Fiona, in her ongoing quest to keep distance between them, hadn't ever bothered to dig deeper than public opinion and rumor.

So, almost anything he told her would be new to her, but something told him he needed to choose his next words carefully. He finally had her engaged in a conversation—had her full, undivided attention. He could be light and flippant, or go the way of heavy innuendo. After all, it was the middle of the night, they were on their third glass of wine, his bed was just a few feet away, and his body had been on high alert since she'd walked through the door. He knew, deep down, she wanted him as much as he wanted her, yet she'd never admit it. He didn't think that, if put his cards on the table, or the bed, so to speak, she would turn him down. But something told him that wasn't the way to go. Not yet. She had very real reservations about getting involved with him. Whatever he said next, while it may not get her into his bed tonight, needed to break down some of the walls she'd built between them based on what she thought he was.

It only took seconds for all of that to race through his mind and for him to come to a decision. "Most of my wealth comes from my family," he said, matter-of-factly.

A shadow passed over her face. "That's not exactly news," she clipped out.

"Perhaps not. It is popular misconception that my money comes from my father's family." He couldn't help the rush of satisfaction that went through him at the raw curiosity that came into her eyes. Yes, this had been the right topic.

"Oh?" she asked, not quite aloofly.

"There is no debating the fact that the majority of the Barroes' family wealth was accrued through manipulation, if not downright cheating. It is also no secret that I inherited a large amount from Father, including the family compound. A part of my inheritance is set aside to upkeep the compound so that my aunts, uncles, and cousins have somewhere to live. Their own coffers have dwindled since the enactment of the Necromancy laws, and it is seen as my family duty to care for them," he told her.

"You don't seem to see it that way. Yet, you do it anyway. Why?" Fiona's tone and quizzical expression told him she was genuinely interested in knowing.

"Cheating and manipulating using their necromantic and clairvoyant powers was a way of life going back generations, centuries even. The fact is that using those powers is what got the Barroes family through the Cataclysm. Doesn't make it right, just makes it fact. As much as I hold my father accountable for his own actions, I also know that it was how he was raised. There was no love lost between us. He made a lot of people's lives hell with his lies and cheating, and taught me, forced me, to do the same from the moment he realized I had power and just how strong I was.

"When I was sixteen, there were charges against my family for fraud, theft, grave robbing, and smuggling. My father forced me to confess and take the rap. Sam Harrison offered me a deal. The deal was go to the Academy and work freelance with the Blades, or go to a work farm for ten years. I took the Academy. From that point, my father considered me a traitor to the family. He never spoke to me again." Ian watched Fiona's face carefully for signs of pity or sympathy; he wanted neither and saw neither. What he saw was a slow dawning of understanding.

"That sucks," she said.

Ian grinned. "Yes, that is one way to put it. When my father died, I used a large portion of my inheritance to establish the Necromancer's Guild as a way to give back to the community and to stop not just my family, but others as well. But, in doing so, I decimated their way of life. I have a couple of cousins that have taken on legal Necromancy work and have even registered with the guild, but for the most part, I'm considered the ruination of the Barroes family. So, I have an overseer that is in charge of the inheritance and is using it for the upkeep of the Barroes compound, and out of my own sense of familial duty, my cousins and their families have lifelong rights to live there, and I live miles away in the city."

"I can't believe I'm about to say this, but, here goes. I was wrong to judge you by your family's reputation. It doesn't mean I'm pro-necromancer," she said hastily. "But, I do concede that you've done a lot to make up for some of the bad seeds."

Had he heard right? Had Fiona Moon just admitted to being wrong? He tried his best to make his tone nonchalant, but his heart was singing out. He'd just scored a minor victory. "I suppose that if that is as good as I can get, I'll take it. A mage cannot control what powers they are born with, only how they choose to use them."

"I will grant you that," Fiona conceded. Then she swept her arm around to indicate the large studio apartment. "So, tell me, what pays for all of this luxury if not your inheritance from your father. Granted, this apartment is much smaller than what I would have thought, but it is comfortably furnished and you do own the entire building."

"Along with a couple of others, several factories, and few farming compounds outside of the city," Ian replied, a grin tilting his lips. "I do, like most people, have two sides to my family tree. Both my mother's father and grandfather were inventors. Very successful inventors."

Fiona let out a low whistle. "Wow, I didn't know you were so well endowed." She laughed. "So, what did they invent?"

Ian tried to focus on her question and not on the extreme rise in blood pressure, among other things, her innuendo had incited. He forced himself to breathe and answered her question. "Quite a few things, actually. They both worked a lot with Mateo Corsini."

"I know Carly's husband is an inventor and invented the printing press that is used by the newspapers and bookmakers. Your grandfathers helped with that?" Fiona asked, not even trying to hide her interest and curiosity.

"Among other things. Great-Grandpap was on the first senate council with both of the Corsinis back at the very beginning of the reconstruction. Though books are still expensive now, they are available. Back then, the only books that existed were in the private libraries of those families that had been able to hoard a few and keep them safe. That included the Corsinis. The City Archive Library was their home. They still live there now, in an apartment, but at the time, the entire building was their private home. It had been a public library before the Cataclysm, and the Corsinis lived there to protect the books from vandalism and to keep as much knowledge of the previous society intact as they could. They kept it private, not to keep the knowledge from the general public, but to preserve it until it could be reproduced."

"Yeah, I do know that much. I spent a lot of time at the library as a kid. Carly is the closest thing to an aunt that Anya, River and I have. She tried to keep us out of trouble during the day while Pinky slept," she told him.

"Ah, yet another thing I didn't know about you, my mysterious Miss Moon." He laughed and ducked to avoid the pillow she threw at him. "Okay, so no need to give you a history lesson. My great-grandfather and grandfather worked with Matt on several projects to help reconstruct some of the technological conveniences of the pre-Cataclysm era using crystal technology and renewable resources, including processes for making ink out of hemp and flax seed oils, paper making, the printing press, and other manufacturing machines."

Fiona looked skeptical. "That's great, but it doesn't seem like you would get rich off that. Especially not since the Corsinis aren't that rich."

Ian laughed. "They do okay. But no, it was one of my grandfather's individual inventions that built the empire. His only lone invention, actually. He spent almost his entire life on it."

Fiona rolled her eyes. "The suspense is killing me. So tell me already."

A silent debate on the prudence of this topic was sliding through Ian's head. He had to tell her now, but he hated the thought of losing the progress they had made so far. Oh well, nothing ventured, nothing gained. "My grandfather was Russell Hughes, the inventor of the…"

Fiona cut him off with a laugh, "The crystal- and water-powered engine for magic-motorized vehicles. I'll be damned! Well, that explains a lot."

Not the reaction he'd expected, but he wasn't complaining. "Like what?"

"Well…" She giggled, actually giggled. "For one, why you have so many magic vehicles."

"I only have a two-seater rickshaw and a surrey," he said defensively.

"Which is more than normal people—who don't even have one rickshaw. I thought it was because you were pretentious and all along, you just own the company. Hell, if I owned the engine company, I'd probably have a magic vehicle of every color." She let out another hoot of laughter.

Okay, her laughter was getting a little annoying, yet infectious. "I thought you disapproved of magic vehicles on principal."

She took a deep breath and quit laughing, but was still smiling when she said, "No, I think magic motors are a great invention. Especially when they are put into freight carriages. Rickshaws and surreys are not practical for travel anywhere but inside the city, but they are great for that. My biggest problem is that they cost so damned much. Oh, and the snotty people who drive around in the surreys as if they are better than anyone who can't afford the damned things."

"I can agree with you on the cost. They are expensive to manufacture, and the factory is only capable of producing a couple of engines a week. I have science mages researching and working on the problem, but with the cost of some of the raw materials, a large price drop and increased availability is just not in the foreseeable future. And, unfortunately, there isn't anything I can do about snotty people," he said, flashing his most-charming grin.

"Damn it, Barroes, I don't like this a bit," she said. Her words had a serious edge, but her tone still light and joking.

"What?" he asked, a little confused.

She flashed a bright, shining smile at him. "I might actually have to start liking you."

"Oh, the horror," he mocked. Oh, yes, progress had been made. It might not be tonight, but he was definitely one step closer to having her in his bed.

Fiona lifted her glass for a drink and stopped short when she realized it was empty. "Crap," she said, her eyes flitting from the glass to the empty wine bottle, then his empty glass and back to the bottle. "Who drank all the wine?"

"I think we did." Ian laughed.

"Figures," she said, flippantly. "I'd ask if you had a bottle of something else, but it probably wouldn't be attractive if I had to crawl two miles home on my hands and knees."

A vision of Fiona on her hands and knees flashed into his brain.

Before he could think of a coherent response, she asked, "Where's your bathroom?"

NINETEEN
Ian

*I*N ADDITION TO THE FRONT DOOR THAT LED TO THE HALL AND THE REST OF THE building, there were only two doors in the apartment. Both doors, one that led to the bathroom and one that led to a large, walk-in closet where Ian kept his clothes and various items, were against the far wall. The rest of the apartment that took half of the top floor of the building was an open space that was split into distinct areas with the strategic placement of furniture and rugs. The center of the room, against the wall opposite the door, was the sitting area, a grouping of a sofa and two chairs, all upholstered with a soft brown fabric, and grouped around a low, wooden table in front of a stone-lined fireplace. Next to the sitting area was an eating area with a small, round table. The sitting and eating areas separated Ian's home office area with his desk, a comfortable chair in the corner, and several bookcases occupying the end with the large windows that overlooked the river. His sleeping area, which consisted of a large feather bed on a wooden frame flanked by two wood tables, was next to the bathroom and closet.

Ian pointed out the bathroom door to Fiona and watched her sashay across to it. Her stride was smooth and graceful with no stumbling to indicate she was impaired by the three glasses of extremely strong wine she'd consumed. Once she disappeared behind the door, he stood and took the empty bottle and wineglasses to the counter behind the dining table so that his housekeeper, Mrs. Gary, would be able to find them in the morning.

He shook his head as if he could shake loose the memory of the way Fiona's thin shorts clung to her rounded ass. "Take it easy, Barroes," he mumbled to himself low enough that only he could hear.

Glancing at the mantle clock, he saw they had been talking for nearly two hours. He considered the fact that Fiona Moon had been in his apartment for that long and wasn't yet in his bed a tragedy. He would have to be happy that they had been in the same room together, alone for two hours, and hadn't argued or strangled each other. That was actually amazing progress.

He poured himself a glass of water from a pitcher on the counter and was resigning himself to the fact that the only way he'd sleep tonight was if he dipped himself in a tub full of cold water after Fiona left, when she opened the door and exited the bathroom.

"Wow, that's a huge bathroom," she said. "I was a little disappointed by your apartment when I first came in."

Ian furrowed his eyebrows. "What did you expect?"

She laughed, "I don't know. More, I guess. I mean, it's decorated nice enough, but I really expected something larger."

"I don't really need any more space. This is actually more than I really need… to be completely honest." He waved his arm to indicate the large, open expanse.

"I suppose it's enough for one person, but I still expected something a bit larger, and I guess more lavish. But, that bathroom, wow! I could put my bed in there and still have plenty of room. And hot and cold running water in the sink basin and the tub. Now, that's living." She laughed heartily.

Heat zinged through Ian. He'd heard her laugh before, but it was a rare treat, and this was different. She was usually laughing at him, often cynically, but this was a relaxed, joyous laugh full of humor. And it was sexy as hell.

He couldn't help but laugh with her. "There are a few perks to being rich, I suppose." She was so beautiful when she smiled. He almost said as much, but stopped himself. Better to leave that to another time. Instead, he said, "I know you are a big, bad Blade and can take care of yourself, and I'm risking your wrath by saying this, but in light of the earlier events of the evening, I don't think you should walk home alone. You probably shouldn't have been out by yourself earlier. Let me take you home in my rickshaw. Or, I can have Danielson drive you."

He braced himself for the oncoming storm of temper, but it never came. Instead, Fiona just leaned back against the wall between the bathroom and closet doors, one foot against the wall so that her knee jutted out.

"Normally, that would piss me off, but I actually agree with you. Wow, I've never seen a jaw drop open so fast. Close your mouth, Ian. I can be reasonable. Sometimes. Until we know more about what's-his-name, everyone in that alley tonight should be careful and not be out alone. I just needed air tonight and acted on impulse," she said, mouth quirking up at one corner.

"You acted impulsively?" he quipped.

She laughed. "I know. Hard to believe, isn't it? But I don't want you or your guard to drive me home. I have a better idea, actually." Her grin faded away, and her expression took on a sensual quality. "Instead of going home, how about I stay here with you tonight... and then I can take a hot bath in that gorgeous tub in the morning?"

The moment the word "stay" passed her lips, Ian started moving. He was across the room in fewer strides than it had ever taken him before, and she had barely finished uttering the word "morning" when his lips came down on hers.

He pushed her against the wall, nudging her leg to the side so that he nestled against her, their bodies touching from hip to shoulder. The kiss was hot and intense. She tasted like blackberry wine and that unique Fiona flavor that had haunted him since their first kiss on the dance floor.

He forced himself to pull his head back, give them both a moment to catch their breath. Framing her face with his hands, he gazed down at her. She was flushed, her lips pink and swollen. Her eyes were glazed with heated passion. So damned beautiful.

"Should I be concerned that you only want me for my hot water and bathtub?" he asked, breathless.

Her sexy grin melted him into a puddle. "Oh, I wouldn't say that's all I want you for," she said, running her hands over his back.

He bent down to taste the curve of her neck into her shoulder. It was hot, sweet, and her shivery moan made his blood boil. He pressed his hips into her, feeling the heat of her body through their clothes. He wanted her so fucking much. But he needed to make one thing very clear, first.

"Fiona, if you stay tonight, it's not just a one-night stand. This isn't like your other no-strings flings," he said, nipping at her shoulder.

"Mmm, whatever you say," she half moaned, slipping both of her hands under his shirt to caress the bare skin of his back.

It took every ounce of Ian's strength to pull himself back, but he did it. Reaching around, he grasped her wrists and pulled them away from his body, pinning them against the wall on either side of her head. He inched his body back enough that they weren't touching anymore, but he was still close enough to feel the heat radiating off her body.

"I'm serious, Fiona. Before we go any further, things need to be clear between us. I'm not interested in just having sex with you. I know all about your aversion to relationships and complications, but that is exactly what I want from you. I won't be like any of your past flings, a few good fucks, and then an amiable adios. I think there is something between us, could be something, more than sex. I want to explore that. If you aren't willing, you need to go." He let go of her wrists and then did the hardest thing he'd ever done in his life. He stepped back and away from her, out of her path to the door.

For a long moment, they were still, their heavy breathing the only thing breaking the silence in the room. Fiona pushed away from the wall and Ian's heart plummeted, then skipped a beat when she went to stand next to the bed. Turning, she looked at him, her gaze steady.

"I knew what I was getting into when I walked into the building tonight." She laughed nervously. "Well, maybe I don't know exactly; this is uncharted territory for me. I'm not ready to make any long-term promises, but I'm willing to be open and see where it goes. And don't give me that look. I'm not so drunk that I don't know what I'm doing or that I will regret it in the morning."

Ian watched, his heart pounding in his ears, as she peeled her clothing off, piece by piece. As the shorts hit the floor, he realized her feet were already bare. She must have taken her shoes off in the bathroom. While he'd been resigning himself to a cold bath, she'd been preparing for something quite different. The woman amazed him.

He had planned to wait until this case was over, and then go about convincing her they were meant to be together. He'd planned on a slow, methodical seduction. He should have known better. Fiona was a force of nature. She rarely did the expected and never fit her life to someone else's schedule.

The last bit of cloth fell and he stood there, dry mouthed, taking in every inch of her smooth, silky skin, from the curve of her shoulder, down to the heavy fullness of her lush breasts, over her belly to the curve of her hip, down to her creamy thighs and the ebony curls that rested between them.

He wanted to move, to reach out and touch her, to press his body into hers, but he couldn't move his feet. He stood there, rooted to the spot, frozen despite the hot lava flowing through his veins. Obviously aware of the effect she was having on him, she shot him a sexy, seductive smile—no, it was a smirk, a sexy, seductive, self-satisfied smirk—then slowly crawled into the center of his bed. She carefully, almost demurely, arranged herself on the bed so that she was sitting on one hip, resting her weight on one outstretched arm. Her legs, modestly closed, were stretched out to the side and bent slightly at the knee so they hooked behind her a bit.

"Are you going to stand there and stare all night?" she asked, a mischievous glint in her eyes.

"Not staring," Ian replied, his voice hoarse, "just admiring the view. You look like a goddess sitting upon a cloud surveying her domain."

Her seductive smile took on a triumphant air. "I am a goddess. And I command you to worship me."

His brain sputtered, trying to come up with a witty retort, but since all the blood had rushed south, he was coming up blank. Just this once, he decided, he would do her bidding without argument or complaint. Yes, worshiping Fiona Moon was something he had no objections to what so ever.

He stripped his shirt off as he moved, crossing the expanse of floor separating them and kneeling on the bed beside her in two fluid motions. Staring into her eyes, he wordlessly began roaming her body with his hands. He started with light touches to either side her temple with just the tips of his index fingers. Then he traced lazy circles down her cheeks, and down her throat to her shoulders. He gazed into her eyes while he touched, watching the humor slide away, replaced by hot, smoldering desire that he knew matched his own. Still, he took his time, letting just his fingertips slide over her smooth skin, down her arms, then back up again, over her collarbone.

The gasp she let out when his fingers grazed the underside of her breast sent fire through his veins, and he almost lost control. He sucked in his breath and forced himself to focus. As much as he wanted to just push her back and bury himself in her, he wanted more to make this moment memorable, for them both. He'd waited so long to have her here, naked and trembling in his bed, and now that she was, he was going to take full advantage.

Still, he wasn't sure how much more of this teasing he could take. He lingered for a moment more on her breasts, tracing hearts and flowers up over her chest, then back up her neck. She opened her mouth as if to say something, but he silenced her by placing his fingers over her lips.

Leaning in, he reached behind her and pulled her braid around so that he could see the end. Pulling the string holding the strands together off, he tossed it aside. He began running his fingers through the braid, slowly pulling it apart, careful not to pull or tangle her hair. Once it was all loose around her shoulders, he pressed her backwards. He hovered over her, using one hand to hold her as he lowered her to a supine position. He dropped her hair, letting it flow over the pillow like a dark cloud.

"Perfect. More beautiful than I imagined," he whispered against her lips, and then captured them in a deep, probing kiss that he didn't break until they were both breathless.

"You imagined this? Me in your bed?" she asked as she gasped in air.

"Oh, yes. In great detail." He sucked her bottom lip into his mouth, tugged gently with his teeth, and then let go. "Every day since the day I met you."

Her arms tightened around him, pulling him closer as her body arched up against him. "Show me what else you imagined," she purred.

He wordlessly lowered his mouth to the hollow of her throat and, as before, began doing as she had commanded. He trailed his mouth down her body, alternately licking, sucking, and gently nipping as he tasted every inch of her soft, silky skin. She tasted like warm, honeyed vanilla and something deeper, spicier, something uniquely Fiona. She moaned and clutched him tighter as he sampled each of her breasts in turn, spending time on each nipple, licking and sucking them into hard little peaks before continuing down.

"Ian..." She gasped as he dipped his tongue into her navel. "I want you. Now." Her breathing was ragged, and the words came out clipped.

He smiled against the smooth skin of her belly. "Not yet," he said as he continued to lick and kiss across her body in a zigzag pattern.

If he had his way, he would have Fiona in his bed like this every minute of every day until the end of time, or at least every night for the rest of his life. And he would do everything in his power to make that happen, but there were no guarantees in life. But it was just as likely that she would walk away from him the second they were both sated. Just in case, he fully intended to draw this moment out, to give them both every ounce of pleasure possible.

He went slowly, making sure his lips and tongue touched every bit of exposed skin, working his way down until he reached the apex of her thighs. He changed course to kiss down her hip. Fiona whimpered in protest, thrust her hands into his hair, and tried to move his mouth back to the original course. He resisted and continued to use his tongue to trace the curve of her hip and thigh.

"Ian. Please. Now."

"Shhh. I'm worshiping you," he murmured lazily against the silky skin of her inner thigh.

Her only reply was a strangled, wordless cry as his mouth covered her and his tongue found her center. As he enjoyed her, he reveled in her moans and writhing until she tensed, cried out, and came in a fury of shudders and whimpers.

Hot desire mixed with self-satisfaction washed through him, nearly breaking his tenuous control. He couldn't wait anymore; he needed to be deep inside her. Now.

Sliding back up her body, he barely took the time to push his pants past his hips. He paused, holding himself above her, poised at her entrance. He stared down at her, wanting to take in every emotion that crossed her face as he slid slowly into her, but Fiona took the moment out of his control. She bucked her hips up, simultaneously wrapping her long, muscular legs around his hips, pulling him down. Watching Fiona's expression became a moot point. Sensation exploded within him, blinding him for a moment, as he slid deep into her hot, silken depths in one swift, smooth motion. They gasped out their pleasure and shock in unison. Her body pulsed and clutched around him, and her nails dug into his back. Ian nearly shattered.

By some miraculous feat of strength and self-control, he held on, holding her close and still while her body got used to the intrusion, and he pulled himself together enough to be able to move without exploding.

"Oh, baby, what a fit. Are you okay?" he whispered, his mouth right at her ear.

"Fuck, Ian, you are a bit more than I was expecting. But yes, I'm wonderful," she gasped out, her death grip on his back loosening just a bit.

"Good, me too." He kissed her earlobe. "I don't think I can be still much longer. Are you ready for this?"

Her reply was a deep, guttural moan. "Oh, hell yeah."

Then there were no more words. Ian started rocking into her, slowly and gently at first, a little more as her body softened and opened to him. Soon, he was thrusting into her in long, deep strokes, and she was moving with him, her hips moving up to meet his.

The world melted away and there was nothing, no existence in the universe, but the two of them. A void surrounded them and Ian could see, hear, feel, taste, nothing but the woman beneath him. He drove into her, heat and tension throbbing through his body. Each moan and shudder from her doused fuel on the fire within him. Just when he didn't think he could take any more, she arched and tensed beneath him, her cries echoing in his ears as her body tightened and convulsed around his. Inside Ian, something hot and fiery broke apart; shards of lava rocketing through him and the universe shattered and fell away in tiny pieces, dropping him into oblivion.

He had no idea how long it took the world to start resolving around them, the shattered pieces gluing back together to form a coherent reality where he could see, hear, breathe. When he finally started coming back to himself, he rolled onto his back, taking Fiona with him. He pulled and manipulated until their legs were entwined and she lay half on him in the crook of his arm, her head resting on his chest.

They lay like that for a long while in silence, catching their breath, while he ran his hand lazily up and down her back.

"So, I take it you are one of those girly-men who likes to cuddle and be touchy-feely after sex," Fiona said, breaking the comfortable silence.

Ian barely had enough energy to laugh. "Yes, as a matter of fact, I am."

"Okay," she said, sleepily. "I can live with that."

Ian chuckled and just pulled her tighter. Within a few minutes, her breathing slowed, indicating she'd fallen asleep. Ian kissed the top of her head and let himself drift off, too.

TWENTY
Bokor

PAIN RADIATED THROUGHOUT HIS BODY AS HE SLOWLY FOUGHT HIS WAY TO consciousness. When his essence bounced back into his corporeal body from far away, it was always painful and it took him hours to wake afterward. He usually vacated the shells he wore when they were only a few feet away. But he'd been forced to leave bodies behind miles from his own not once but twice in the past week. Not only did it hurt, but he'd also lost two perfectly usable avatars and now he had none. No way to walk amongst the unclean to find beings worthy to nourish him and his flock. He would have to rely on his minions to find a shell worthy to be his next avatar.

Rage filled him. "Amos!" he roared, his voice echoing through the hall, eliciting whimpers of fear from the occupied cages that lined the walls.

His most trusted and loyal disciple was at Bokor's feet, pressing his forehead to the floor within seconds. "My Lord, how may I serve?"

"You may rise," Bokor magnanimously told him. As his right-hand man, Amos was afforded the privilege to stand in his presence. "You were behind my throne, waiting upon my call. I take that to mean Irwin has returned?"

"Yes, My Lord. He returned almost an hour ago," Amos replied.

"Bring him," the order thundered through the hall, bringing on more whimpers. "And bring me whichever one of those mewling animals is making all that noise."

"Yes, Master," Amos bowed and backed away, turning his back only when he was out of Bokor's direct line of sight.

A few minutes later, a tall, thin man in a tattered, gray robe that signified his place in Bokor's flock entered the hall. His eyes firmly on the ground, he picked his way along the littered floor and dropped to his knees in front of the raised platform that held Bokor's throne. He immediately raised his arms above his head and bowed down, pressing his head to the cold floor. "My Lord, I am here as you command."

Amos followed, shoving a crying female to the ground next to Irwin. "Hush up and keep your eyes down, cow," he hissed in a low voice, and then backed up to stand in his place next to the throne.

Bokor ignored the whining animal and focused on his disciple. "Up, Irwin."

Irwin raised his head, pulling his back straight but remained on his knees, his eyes carefully trained on the floor just in front of him. He knew "up" did not mean stand, as only Amos stood in the presence of their master.

"Amos tells me you arrived back from the hunting mission an hour ago. Am I to take that to mean you witnessed the scene in the alley?" Bokor queried, his voice measured.

"No, Master. I saw you go into the alley. I waited and watched from my post as ordered, but you never exited the alley. A while later, it was roped off by Blade agents and I mingled with the crowd that formed at the edge. I saw your abandoned avatar being loaded onto the back of a wagon."

"Were you seen?" Bokor demanded.

"No, My Lord. I saw the necromancer and vampire enter the alley, but they didn't see me. I was at my post using my disguise just as you ordered." Irwin's voice quavered with growing fear.

"And when you were peering into the alley? No one saw you then?" Bokor inquired.

Irwin trembled, but kept his gaze lowered. "No, Sire. Even if they had, I would have been unremarkable and no different from the masses. As soon as I saw your avatar was dead, I hurried back here to let Amos and the others know you would be returning."

"It seems the authorities have caught on to my little game and were lying in wait for me," Bokor muttered, speaking more to himself rather than to his audience.

The woman, the one with the brilliant aura, the one destined to be his queen, the one that would help him rise above his earthly limits into Godhood, she was an agent for the Black Blade Guard. That would make things a little more difficult. Excitement hummed through him. Life had become quite humdrum lately, and he loved a challenge. There was much to do, for before the new moon rose, she would be his and he would be a God. But first things first.

"Irwin," Bokor said, turning his full attention to the kneeling man. "You were also with me on the hunt the last time I had to leave my avatar before returning it home?"

"Yes, My Lord." The man's voice shook. "I was on the street and recognized the moment you left the body and returned here immediately."

"Ah, yes, I thought so. Don't worry, my son. You did well, both times, in returning home as soon as you had visual confirmation that I had returned to my own corporeal form."

The disciple let out an audible sigh of relief and his shoulders relaxed. "Thank you, My Lord."

Irwin was one of Bokor's most loyal followers and trusted minions. He had always done as ordered. He, like the rest of the flock, worshiped Bokor as a God, as well they should. Bokor provided for them and taught them right from wrong as any God would. However, only Bokor knew he was not quite a God yet. But he soon would be. Unfortunately, Irwin could stand in the way of that. The man had been at the scene of both of the recent incidents. Irwin mingled among the non-believers every day as he earned money to help provide for the flock. Bokor could not take the chance of someone seeing him and remembering his face as one that had been at both places. Despite the man's usefulness, he was too great a risk now. It was time to reward him for his service.

Bokor slipped into his divine sight and peered at the man's pale aura. Irwin, like all of Bokor's trusted minions, was a norm. Some of his followers were mages. In the past, there had been many. But they were given the ultimate reward much sooner. Those with no magic provided little nourishment, and their shells could not be used as avatars. They were best used as beasts of burden to perform menial tasks that were necessary, but beneath Bokor. There had been a time, when he was just beginning to realize his potential, that he fed on such lowly creatures as a matter of course. But no more. Mages were his preferred nourishment now. They provided the energy and power he craved. Yet, upon occasion, it was necessary to feed upon one of the unworthy, be it for reward or punishment.

"Irwin, you have been a perfect example of piety and obedience," he decreed, his voice taking on an air of grave importance. "Your name will be honored and revered. You will be remembered as a great man who served his God, as well as his people, in life and nourished their bodies and spirits with his own."

Irwin's head snapped up as he forgot to keep his gaze down. His eyes went wide with fear and awe as they met Bokor's, and his mouth opened, but no words came out.

Bokor focused on the energy surging and pulsing within Irwin. He opened his senses and began pulling the disciple's life essence towards him, into his own body. Bokor felt his own aura pulse and his power surge slightly as he absorbed the man's energy. All too soon, the flow of energy stopped and Irwin's body fell limply to the floor.

The whimpering girl on the floor let out a scream, pulling Bokor's attention to her. Her aura was much stronger than Irwin's and pulsed with color. She wasn't endowed with great power, but enough to slake the hunger that Irwin's energy had awakened. Without preamble, he sucked her energy, watching the colorful strands of light as they pulsed towards him, then mingled with his own, making his aura burn brighter, hotter. As his hunger abated, he realized her aura had dimmed to a barely visible smoke-colored haze. He immediately stopped the flow of energy, tamped down his power, and slipped back into regular sight.

The girl was no longer crying, instead lying still in a crumpled heap. She was still alive, her breath shallow but steady. Beneath the dirty, greasy blonde hair and dirty clothes, he recognized the girl he'd taken last week. He'd fed off her a couple of times and after a day of rest, he'd be able to feed again, possibly twice more before completely depleting her and giving her over to nourish his flock.

"Amos, take her back to the cages." Bokor waved in the direction of the girl.

"Yes, Master," replied Amos as he hooked his arms under the girl's and dragged her away.

Bokor eyed the corpse of his former minion. Though the bodies of the mages he took as avatars became dry and brittle after his spirit left them, when he pulled a soul out of a body and into his own, the leftover shell was still quite fresh and usable. Once the soul nourished his body, he gave the flesh over to his followers to nourish theirs.

"Have that shell taken to the village cooks. The flock shall feast tomorrow," he ordered when Amos returned to him.

Amos clapped his hands twice, and two guards that were stationed outside the hall's entrance hustled in. Amos relayed Bokor's orders. The two men picked up the body and hurried away.

"Irwin had family?" Bokor queried.

"Yes, My Lord. A wife and two children," Amos answered.

"Let them, as well as the whole flock, know that Irwin was a pious man and he has given himself up to nourish their bodies as well as their Lord. He is to be honored and revered. Make sure his family is well cared for in the coming months."

"Yes, My Lord," Amos answered automatically, used to such requests.

Bokor settled back into his throne with a groan. The energy he'd just absorbed was starting to wash away the aches in his body, but he would need some rest before he would be back at top form. Not that it mattered. He was now stuck in his corporeal form until another suitable avatar was found.

"Amos, summon the Circle."

"Yes, My Lord." Amos bowed and hurried out to do as he was ordered, without hesitation. That was why he was Bokor's most trusted minion. His loyalty and obedience was beyond reproach. He asked no questions and offered no protests, despite the late hour and the fact that the disciples of the Circle would need to rise in a few hours to begin their day's work.

The Circle was the ten most loyal servants Bokor had. They were his top, most-trusted minions. But there were only nine now that Irwin was gone. He would have to hold a ceremony to add the next member soon. The Circle was trusted with the welfare of the flock. They, and only they, were allowed to venture beyond the village into the land of the unclean to work and earn money. They were also his hunters, accompanying his avatar when he hunted for those worthy enough to become nourishment or future avatars.

Within half an hour, nine gray-robed figures shuffled into the great hall and took their places on their knees before the throne.

"My sons, I have two very important tasks for you," Bokor announced without preamble. "My avatar has been lost, and I need a new one so that I may walk among the unclean. I know I usually choose the hosts before you take them, but I must rely upon you to choose a male mage for me.

Bring me one, and I will arrange a hunt to replenish our stocks."

"Yes, My Lord," nine voices rang out in perfect sync.

"The second task is a bit more delicate. Tonight's hunt was thwarted by two law officials who got in the way. I want to know everything there is to know about them both. The first is a male Nash City Guard, named Rangel. I assume that is his last name. The second is a Black Blade Guard named Fiona Moon. I will leave you to decide the best way to get information, but I expect you to be discreet and absolutely no harm is to come to Agent Moon. I have plans for her, but it is not time yet."

"Yes, My Lord."

"Split the tasks up, along with your regular work, and be careful not to draw attention to yourselves. I would like a full report in two days. Now, go get a few more hours rest before you start your day." He held out his hand, dismissing them. One by one, they rose, approached him, with eyes downcast, brushed the back of his hand with their lips, bowed, and left the room.

When they had all left, Bokor dismissed Amos and leaned back into his throne for some much-needed rest.

TWENTY-ONE
Fiona

I STRETCHED LANGUIDLY, LIKE A CAT WAKING WELL RESTED AND CONTENTED FROM an afternoon nap. I might have even purred. Despite the slight soreness in my muscles and between my legs, I did, surprisingly, feel well rested and contented. My brain was a bit fuzzy, so not sure why I felt so good, but I instinctively reached to the other side of the bed and found it empty.

That was when I came fully awake. I was in Ian's bed, and I felt warm and glowy inside and out because of the delicious things we had done here, not once but three times last night. But Ian wasn't here. I rolled on my back and waited for relief at his absence to hit me. It didn't. Neither did the expected regret, need to rush out, or reluctance to see him again. I waited another moment. Nope. Nothing. What I actually felt was disappointment that he wasn't there to kiss me, or something else, good morning.

Oh, crap. What the hell was happening to me? One night with Ian had turned me into a complete mush ball. For a moment, I wondered if I had been bespelled. I quickly dismissed the idea. Ian might be a lot of things, but he wasn't the kind of creepy perv that cast infatuation spells. Besides, he knew if he did that, once it wore off, I'd kill him, or worse.

I was going to have to face the facts. If there was any kind of bedazzlement going on, it was the natural kind. Ugh! That was worse than being magicked. A spell would wear off in a day or two, and I could blame any ridiculous thoughts or behaviors on it. But, nope, I was laying here, feeling giddy and grinning like an idiot and I had no-freaking-body to blame but myself. Or, Ian. Yes, I'd blame Ian. Damn him for being so... so... Ian!

I grabbed the pillow next to me and buried my face into it, as if I could hide from reality for a few more minutes. Then, I took in a breath and was assailed by Ian's scent. Warmth flooded my body from the tips of my hair to the tips of my toes, but was highly concentrated in the center between the two points. "Arggh!" I halfheartedly screamed into the pillow. I sucked in another whiff of sexy necromancer, making my toes curl with want, and tossed the pillow aside.

Doing my best not to think about the feel of Ian's skin next to mine, I looked around the apartment for a clock or something to tell me what time it was. The sun coming in through the tall, pane-less windows spaced evenly across two walls and washing the entire apartment with a bright and cheery glow indicated late morning or early afternoon. In the daylight, the room looked larger and more spacious than it had the night before. Though, in all fairness, my focus had been pretty tight on Ian. We could have been in the public market stadium surrounded by onlookers and I never would have noticed.

Finally, I saw the small clock on the table next to the bed. It was just past ten in the morning, which meant I'd gotten even less sleep than I had thought, considering it had been dawn the last time Ian and I had drifted off. Yet, I felt pretty good. I wondered how Ian was feeling; he'd obviously woken before me.

Where was Ian, anyway? I did another sweep of the apartment, no Ian. The door to the bathroom was open, and though I couldn't see in, I could tell it was empty. He better not had gone to the market without me. I shook the thought out of my head. No, he wouldn't do that. I was just about to get out of the bed and look for my clothes, then Ian, when the apartment door began to slowly, quietly swing open.

I sat up, quickly grabbed the sheet that lay over me, and clutched it to my breasts, suddenly overcome with a ridiculous shyness. *Oh, get it together, Moon!* I chided myself silently. I was acting like a teenager with her first crush, all giggly and silly. It was ironic, because even when I had been a silly teenager, I hadn't acted this way over boys, or sex.

Pinky had a frank, no-nonsense style of parenting. When Anya and I hit puberty, he had explained sex, the feelings it could induce, the repercussions, and how to be responsible, both physically and emotionally. He'd done the same with River, of course, but, as was the usual happening with younger siblings, Anya and I had already filled her in. I understood my body's physical needs and had never gotten those mixed up with my emotional needs. I hadn't even thought I had emotional needs, at least not pertaining to men and a sexual relationship. Not until now. Not until Ian. Now I felt all squishy and tied up in knots inside and, something I had never been about my body, a little bashful. That was complete lunacy, especially after the way I'd presented myself to him naked on his bed last night. I took a deep breath, willing away the tremors in my belly, and dropped the sheet.

But the person that came in the door wasn't Ian. I gasped and grabbed the sheet again, tugging it around me as tight as possible as a small, silver-haired woman entered the room carrying a large bundle of something.

"Oh, Agent Moon, you are awake. How did you sleep, dear?" the older woman asked.

"Um, fine, thank you. Please, call me Fiona," I said, a bit feebly. I had no idea who this woman was, but I was meeting her while completely naked and in a bed not my own. I figured we'd already hit first-name status.

"Fiona, such a pretty name," she said, moving over to the table near the middle of the room and depositing her bundle. "I'm Helena Gary, Master Ian's housekeeper. You can call me Helena, but I'll tell you now, Ian only calls me Mrs. Gary. Sometimes, that boy is too proper for his own good." Her smile was so motherly that it made me warm inside.

I laughed. "Tell me about it."

Mrs. Gary walked over to the counter behind the table and clicked on a crystal-powered hot plate, filled a teapot with water from a pitcher, and set it on the burner. "Well, I was just going to bring those up for you and leave them, but since you are awake, how about if I go ahead and run you a hot bath? Master Ian said you'd like to try out the tub."

"A bath would be lovely, but I'm sure I can manage it on my own," I said.

"Nonsense. I'll run the bath while you have yourself some tea and wake up. And don't argue with me, I kind of like fussing over a female once in a while. Between Master Ian, the guards, and my husband, I'm surrounded by men all the time. Here, you can wear this for now." She picked the bundle back up and tossed me a flannel robe as she bustled past me into the bathroom.

Despite her completely unruffled demeanor at finding me in her boss's bed, her words seemed to indicate that Ian didn't often have women over. At least not any that had hung out long enough to meet his housekeeper. That sent an absurd thrill of pleasure through me.

I put on the robe and padded over to the counter with the teapot. There were mugs, several glass canisters of tea leaves, a jar of honey, and a steeper all ready. I loaded the mesh steeper ball with a generous amount from a canister labeled "nettle and mint," put the ball in a cup, and poured the hot water over it. Stirring in a spoonful of honey, I took my mug and followed Mrs. Gary into the bathroom.

Water was flowing out of two spigots in the wall into the huge, marble tub. "That is some tub," I said.

"Yes, I think it and the one like it in my apartment are some of the only things Master Ian brought from his family's compound. Besides books, of course."

"You live in this building?" I asked.

"Oh yes, on the floor below. There are rooms for traveling necromancers that come into the city to register or find work and a couple of the single security guards live here as well," Mrs. Gary answered.

I sipped my tea and watched her in silence for a moment while she unbundled the items she had brought in with her. She was about four inches shorter than I was, with an average build, with just a little of the softness that comes with age, which I assessed to be somewhere in the early to mid-sixties. Her face was round and only slightly creased. She had big, brown eyes that were warm and welcoming. She wore a dress of thin, blue paisley material that ended halfway down her calf and doeskin moccasins. Her long, silver hair was pulled back in a braid that reached halfway down her back and tied with a ribbon that matched the blue of her dress.

She turned to me, holding three bottles of colored liquid. "What bath oil scent would you like? I have lilac, lavender, and rose." I must have made a face because she quickly said, "These are from my own collection. Ian doesn't keep an assortment of female toiletries in his bathroom."

"Wow, am I that transparent?" I asked, not sure I wanted to know the answer.

The older woman laughed. "Well, you don't exactly wear your heart in your eyes, but I'm an old woman. I've learned to see things others can't, even in themselves."

I didn't know how to respond, so I just said. "The lavender would be lovely. Thank you."

She poured the oil in the tub and a beautiful lavender perfume rose in the steam, scenting the entire bathroom in just a few seconds. Then she turned and gestured to the stack of clothes on the counter. "I took your clothes down to wash; I'll have them sent over tomorrow. There are towels and clothes there for you. I think the clothes should fit just fine, but if not, let me know and I'll find something else."

"You have clothes that will fit me? I'm afraid I'm a bit taller than you." And a bit more endowed in the chest area, but I didn't see the need in adding that part.

She laughed, "Oh, dear, you would look quite funny in my clothes! No. We have a storehouse with clothes and boots of all sizes. You would be surprised at how many necromancers from far away villages show up in rags. Despite the progress Master Ian has made with the Guild here in Nash, in the outlying villages, especially those not a part of the city-state, and communities in the Outer Zones, necromancers are called frauds and treated shabbily."

"Really?" I asked, with genuine curiosity.

The tub was over half full of water so she turned it off. "That is hot, so you will want to let it cool a few minutes." Then she settled onto the edge of the tub to answer my question. "The years during the Cataclysm, and afterwards, were hard on people, and those who used their powers, no matter what they were, made it even harder. Unfortunately, Master Barroes' ancestors were not the only ones that used their abilities, or pretended to have abilities, to cheat people. There are many places where necromancers have to hide their abilities in order to keep from being harmed. There are communities in the South, across the sea where all magic users are looked upon suspiciously and necromancers are stoned or burned, just for being born with the ability."

I didn't know any of this. I wanted to ask questions, but she was really warming up to the subject, so I just leaned back against the counter and listened.

"There isn't a month that goes by that we don't have some bedraggled, poor soul, sometimes whole families, come straggling in, looking to get registered and hoping for work. Many sell anything they can to get passage across the sea just because they heard of the Guild. As far as I know, it is the only Necromancers Guild in any of the Allied cities."

"And you take them all in?" I asked, a little stunned.

"Master Ian does. We keep of clothes, blankets, necessities, and toys for the children. Like I told you before, there are rooms on the third floor for visitors. They stay here while the Guild finds them work. That is also why we have security staff around the clock. It helps them feel safe, something some of them have never had. Many are sent to necromancer-friendly villages, and Master Ian has started networking with other Allied city-states in hopes that other Guilds will be set up. Not everyone who comes is a necromancer, and even those that are, we may not be able to find work for them in that field, but we take in anyone who asks and we help them all find work." Her smile was wide and full of pride. It was obvious the older woman thought a lot of Ian.

"That is amazing," I said. And, I meant it. I spent a lot of years hating necromancers, but not even I would want to see someone stoned to death or starving just because of the power they possessed. Besides, I didn't hate all necromancers. The guys that worked down at the morgue used their powers in a good, productive way, and I liked them. You couldn't persecute someone just because of the abilities they were born with. It wasn't what they had; it was what they did with it.

"There is more to the Guild, and to Ian, that meets the eye," Mrs. Gary said.

"Yeah," I replied. "I'm beginning to see that."

She smiled. "Well, I'll leave you to your bath."

"Okay. Thank you." She started to leave the room, but I called her back. "Oh, Mrs. Gary, wait. Where is Ian?"

"He is down in his office doing a bit of work. The new semester at the Academy starts in a week or so, and I think he wants to have his lesson plans all made up in case he has to have someone substitute for him. He works so hard. I'm sure he'll be back upstairs by the time you are done."

"Enjoy your bath," she said and disappeared, closing the bathroom door behind her.

I disrobed and slipped into the hot water. The feel of it sluicing around me was delicious. It soothed the aches and soreness from last night's fight with Bokor and the later, more sensual battle with Ian. I leaned back in the tub, letting the scented oil soak into my body, and thought about what Mrs. Gary had just told me. There was definitely more to Ian Barroes than met the eye. The warm, fuzzy ball that had been in the pit of my belly since I woke up doubled in size.

TWENTY-TWO

Fiona

THE PUBLIC MARKET WAS SITUATED ON THE BANK OF THE RIVER OPPOSITE FROM the living and business districts of Nash City, yet still inside the old, original city wall. The market stadium was a huge, oval building with rooms and hallways that circled the outside, but the main part of the building was open to the sky. The walls were a series of concrete steps. According to my City History professor at the Academy, the building had been built as a place to where sporting competitions had taken place. During the Cataclysm, despite its open roof, it had been used as shelter for hundreds of refugees. Mages had used shield spells to keep rain and weather out of the building, much like the larger shield spells that had been used to cover everything within the city walls and protect the buildings and inhabitants from the harsh storms of the Cataclysm. Today, a smaller, weaker shield powered by crystals and charged regularly by mages employed by the city kept rain out so that the market could be open rain or shine.

On any random day, there were dozens of vendors and merchants from Nash or nearby villages selling their wares at the market. The regular merchants had permanent spots separated into small shop areas by sheets of cloth hung over ropes strung on poles. Their merchandise was spread out on wooden tables or strung up along the cloth walls on ropes. A steady stream of customers from Old Nash City and New Nashville browsed, picking out fresh vegetables, soap, and other daily necessities.

The first week of every month, market week, was quite another story. Hundreds of merchants from all over the Appalachlan Peninsula, as well traders from across the Mississippi Sea that came in on trading barges crowd the market to sell their wares and buy goods to take back to their communities. Farmers and crafters from Mountain communities pulled their full wagons right up into the market and sold their merchandise right out of the back. Others carted their wares up onto the steep steps of the walls to set up their tables. Tables, carts, and bins laden with dried fruit, hemp cloth, beeswax candles, carved, wooden children's toys, and other staples and goodies vied for space. Shoppers from all over Nash crowded the narrow walkways, browsing the stalls for goods that weren't available in the local areas.

The lots around the outside of the market were just as crowded and busy during Market Week. Near the market building there two rows of lean-tos and shacks that housed blacksmiths, metal smiths, tanners, and other tradesmen that found it convenient to have their businesses close to the market. Merchants and shoppers who couldn't afford a room at an inn for the duration of their stay pulled their own wagons up and pitched tents and built cook fires. Around the far edges of the market lot, Gypsy clans circled their wagon homes.

It was mid-week so the Market Week crowd was in full swing. We arrived shortly after noon. The odor of grilled meats and vegetables and fried sweet cakes from the food vendor stalls and vegetable stew and corn cakes from campfires permeated the air. I had only had time for one more cup of tea before Ian and I had left, and my stomach was quite empty. My mouth watered at the smells.

"Everything smells so good," I said as I led the way through the throng to River's stall. "I'm starving."

Ian smiled apologetically. "Yes, I know. I am too. I'm sorry I didn't let Mrs. Gary fix us something to eat. It just would have taken too long, and she tends to make a feast when she cooks. It could have been another hour or two before we got out of there."

"A feast sounds good right about now, but I completely understand. We have too much to do to sit around getting fussed over by your housekeeper. But I reserve the right for a future date," I said, and barely controlled the urge to slap my hand over my mouth. Had I really just implied there would be future opportunities for me to be at Ian's apartment? Yes, I had. And I had done so very casually, as if it were no big deal.

One night of sex and I was already talking as if Ian and I were in some sort of long-term relationship. Despite his words last night about wanting more than a quick fling, I had no idea what he really wanted, and we hadn't had time for a conversation this morning. When I had emerged from the bathroom after my bath, dressed in the khaki pants, light green shirt, and brown canvas vest Mrs. Gary had brought up, Ian and the housekeeper were both in the apartment. Ian was at his desk, making notes, and Mrs. Gary was bustling around, cleaning and trying to get Ian to let her bring a tray of food up. Ian explained that we had to leave rather quickly, and reluctantly, she had relented and went to clean the bathroom. Her presence in the apartment, as I sat on the sofa and put on my boots, kept the conversation between us to platitudes on the weather.

On the drive to the market in Ian's rickshaw, the conversation had been about the case and what we hoped to find out from the Gypsy. All mentions of the night before were about the events in the alley and the pub. Neither of us brought up the reason we were riding together from his apartment with me garbed in his clothes. Nor did we discuss the several sweaty hours we'd spent together in his bed or what they would mean for us. That was fine with me; I didn't really want to have that talk yet. While I was completely in the dark about what Ian wanted, I had even less idea what I wanted.

Maybe the din of the crowd around us had drowned me out and Ian hadn't heard what I'd said. No such luck. Reaching out, he grabbed my hand, stopping me in my path, pulling so that I turned towards him. He tugged one more time so that I was right up against him. One arm snaked around my waist, pulling me close, and the other slid up to the nape of my neck. I shuddered, the memory of his mouth and hands on me slamming into me. He lowered his mouth to my ear and said, "You can count on it." Then brushed a quick, hot kiss against my parted lips and released me.

I stood there, breathless and stunned for a moment. He'd just kissed me in the middle of the public market. Belatedly, I thought I should punch him in the throat for such an offense, but my bones were all melty and it just seemed like too much effort. I opened my mouth to protest. I wasn't sure what I was going to say, something about not liking public displays of affection, but before I could catch my breath and find my voice, he grabbed my hand again and was pulling me through the crowd.

"Here, I can't give you a feast right now, but I can feed you," he said, stopping in front of a food stall. I instantly forgave the kiss and decided he could do it again in front of the whole city-state if he wanted to if I got to have something to eat.

We ordered grilled cornbread fritters filled with little bits of lamb, roasted vegetables, and goat cheese. The vendor wrapped them in newspaper and drizzled the tops with honey before handing them to us. I took mine and dug in immediately as we continued on our way to find River. It was warm and tasty.

I must have been making noises reminiscent of last night because Ian said, "Damn it, Fiona. I'm doing my best to be professional today, but if you keep making those noises like that, I will be forced to drag you off somewhere private and really make you moan—this case, the Blades, and missing mages be damned."

For a moment, I was stunned enough to stop eating. Then I looked over at him and the expression on his face was so comically pained, I couldn't help but laugh.

"Oh, think that is funny do you?" A wicked grin spread across his face.

"A little," I said, licking honey off my finger. His eyes went wide and for a moment, I thought about teasing him a bit more, seeing how far I could push him. But, from the heated look in his eyes, I had no doubt he would follow through on his threat, consequences be damned. As much as I wanted to be somewhere spending the rest of the day having hot, animal sex with Ian, the people damned by the consequences wouldn't be us. They would be the innocent women that were still missing. "But, you are right. Work comes first, so I'll try to contain my glee while I eat. It will be hard; this is damned good. But I'll do it to save your sanity. I do, however, reserve the right to take you up on that moaning offer in the future." This time, I knew exactly what I was saying.

His eyes went so dark with desire that for a moment, I thought he was going to make good on his threat and drag me off somewhere. Instead, he just reached for my hand, put it to his mouth, and slowly licked a bit of honey I'd missed off my pinky finger. "Oh, you can definitely count on that."

He dropped my hand, and I shoved another bite of fritter into my mouth to keep from moaning. "Come on," I said, around the fritter, not caring at that point that it was unmannerly and completely unsexy. That actually worked for me at the moment. "River's stall is right over there." I pointed and started walking. Ian took another bite of his own fritter, laughing quietly, and followed.

River had a large stall on the main floor of the market stadium that backed up to and included three steps of the wall. The colorful cloth-walled stall was filled with bins of both fresh and dried vegetables and fruits. A table along one side held small bins of dried herbs. Another table held small, cloth pouches and clay pots of herbal mixes, teas, and medical remedies, each carefully labeled with contents and instructions for use. Shoppers crowded her stall, and a short line was formed to the side for those who were waiting to get in.

I was always amazed with how productive my little sister made her tiny, rooftop garden. Imagine what she could do with a whole farm, or even as the head of a farming compound or commune. I shook the idea from my head. As much as I wanted my sister to be happy and successful, River had dismissed the idea of taking such a job every time any of the family had spoken of the idea. But, in truth, neither Anya nor I mentioned it very often and Pinky never did. The thought of River going off where we couldn't watch over her was more than we could stand. Though she was a grown woman, she would always be that little lost baby to me. If I were completely honest, I would have to admit both Anya and I loved the care and attention River doted on us. If she were to move away, we couldn't watch over her, but more, she wouldn't be there to take care of us.

"Oh, hello!" River saw us and came over, her cheery face split in a grin and her blonde hair flashing in the sun. "I wasn't sure when to expect you, but I told Miss Leona we would be stopping by today, so she is expecting us."

"Do you need to wait until your customers are gone?" Ian asked, eyeing the crowd at River's booth.

"Nah. Bonnie can handle them, just give me a second," she said and walked over to say something to the young girl that helped her out during market week. Bonnie was twelve, lived in a hemp farming compound, and traveled in every month with the farmers and merchants. She wasn't officially of legal work age, but helping River for the week gave her something to do. River paid her the same wage an adult would make so that she could help her family and still have a little spending money of her own.

We watched silently as River flitted around, greeting customers, before rejoining us, followed by the guard Sam had sent to watch over her. "Okay. We can go now." We followed her out of the market building to the tent-crowded lot. "Miss Leona's wagon is right over there, the one with blue flowers painted on the side." She pointed to a group of brightly colored wagons about fifty yards away from the entrance.

The three of us headed in the direction of the wagons, but River pulled on my arm so that we could walk a little bit behind Ian, motioning to her guard to walk behind us a bit.

"Spill it, sister!" she whispered as soon as Ian was out of earshot in the bustling crowd.

"Spill what? I don't know what you are talking about." I whispered the lie smoothly.

"Ha!" She laughed. "Maybe we should start with where you were when I went into your room this morning to ask you if you wanted to come to the market with me to talk to Miss Leona before the crowds showed up?"

When I kept walking along silently, she continued. "Or maybe you can tell me why, when I touched your bedpost, I got a vision of you asleep in a bed covered in... was that real linen?"

I snapped my head around. "You saw that?" I said through clenched teeth. "River!" I sputtered, trying to keep my voice low.

"I wasn't trying! You know I can't control it!" Her voice was indignant. "So, I know you weren't at home. I know those clothes you have on don't belong to you. And, I only know of one person you know that is rich enough to afford real linen bed sheets." She cut her eyes towards Ian.

"So, spill it, sister! I want details!" she said.

Exasperated and unwilling to discuss the subject at all, much less in the middle of a public market just a few feet from Ian, I clenched my teeth and said, "There is nothing to tell. It was just a thing. One night. It's nothing." I said it, but I didn't even believe it myself. I knew it was more than that. Our little exchange a few minutes ago had proved that. But I didn't know exactly what it was, so I wasn't ready to discuss it with my sisters yet. Especially not right at this moment.

River didn't look convinced. "Okay, I won't push. Just remember one thing, sister of mine. I usually only see things that are going to make a huge impact in our lives."

She dropped her hand from my arm and quickened her pace to lead the procession to the gypsy camp. I didn't have time to process what River had said before we reached the camp and were standing in front of a red wagon with blue flowers painted on the side. I put it out of my mind and focused on the task at hand.

The wagon was more like a small home on wooden wagon wheels, complete with a door brightly painted blue and a small window on one side with a matching blue window box that held growing herbs. The area in front of wagon looked homey and inviting with various small chairs and tables circling a small, stone-ringed fire. Hooked, wrought-iron bars held an ancient-looking cast iron soup pot and an even older-looking water kettle over the smoldering fire.

"Miss Leona?" River called.

"I'm here, child. Give me a moment to get my old bones moving," a surprisingly strong voice called out from inside the wagon.

"Take your time, Miss Leona," River called back.

A few minutes later, the door swung open and a woman emerged, carrying a wood tray with a ceramic teapot and four mugs. From River's description, I had expected a doddering old lady, but Miss Leona was far from that. She stood straight and tall, and her skin was a smooth mahogany. The only lines in her face were around her eyes and lips. It was impossible to tell her age. While she looked to be anywhere from forty to sixty, her eyes held a wisdom that said perhaps she was quite a bit older than that.

A vampire, perhaps? I had my answer when she stepped onto the first step and into the full sunlight without blinking or flinching. Vampires had varying degrees of allergic responses to sunlight, but there was always some sort of reaction, most especially eye sensitivity. Even Jarrett, who had the highest tolerance to sunlight of any vampire I had ever met, wore a hat or hooded cloak to keep the sun out of his eyes, and always wore long sleeves. Miss Leona wore a short-sleeved tunic the color of fresh-churned butter tucked into faded denim pants and covered with a brown leather vest, but no hat or eye gear. So, not a vampire.

Ian strode over and stood at the base of the steps, "May I help you with that, Madame?"

"Well, aren't you a sweet one? Sure. Here, set it there on the table by the fire." She handed him the tray, then descended the stairs and crossed over to us where we stood. She greeted River with a kiss on the cheek.

"Miss Leona, these are the people I was telling you about this morning, my sister, Agent Fiona Moon and her partner, Ian Barroes."

"Very nice to meet you all. I was just about to have some raspberry leaf and stevia tea. Will you join me?" she asked, graciously.

"Oh, not me," River said. "I need to get back to Bonnie. It's too busy today to leave her alone for too long." She waved goodbye and headed back to the market stadium, her guard following silently behind.

"Please, have a seat," Miss Leona said, gesturing to the assortment of chairs around the fire. Then she grabbed a thick towel off a stool near the fire and used it to grasp the handle of the kettle and pour water into the teapot. After replacing it, she sat down, and Ian and I sat in chairs facing her. "Now, what do I owe the pleasure of a visit from an agent of the Black Blade Guard and the Head of the Necromancer's Guild?"

"You know who I am?" Ian said, taking the mug of tea she poured and offered to him.

"Of course I do, Master Necromancer," she answered, handing me my own mug of tea, then settling back in her chair. "I am the Mambo of my tribe—that gives me the responsibility of knowing the laws of the lands we visit, especially those that pertain to any of the tribe. There is a necromancer amongst us, and we spend a lot of time in Nash City. Though, as a gypsy, she is exempt from the registration law, I see to it that she is informed of and adheres to all the rules put forth by your guild."

"I see," Ian said with a smile. "I have no doubt you do."

"Mambo—that is a religious title?" I asked.

The older woman's dark brown eyes were wary. "In some tribes, yes. In ours, it is both a religious and legal position. I am the head of our tribe, though I answer to a council of elders, just like your own senate."

"I see. It is actually the religious part of your job that we are here to ask you about," I said.

The wariness in her expression morphed into pure fear, but her voice was clear and steady, though a bit tight. "Agent Moon, it has been two months since my tribe has visited Nash City. Have the laws governing religious freedoms changed?"

Ian answered before I could. "No, Madame. We aren't here to accuse or harm you or anyone in your tribe. We just need some information, and River thought you might be able to help us."

She didn't look convinced.

"You know River would never have agreed to introduce us to you if we had any ill intentions," I added.

She relaxed a little, but not completely. I wasn't sure what to say to put her at ease. If she were nervous or upset, she'd be less likely to give us the information we needed. While I was trained to talk to all sorts of hostile and scared witnesses and victims, this was a fear I had never quite faced. Luckily, Ian came to the rescue.

"Please, forgive me if I overstep by asking, Madame, but were you perchance alive during the Religious wars?" he asked, his voice the same soft and soothing tone he'd used with Millie.

The tension started to flow from her, and then left completely when she looked at me and burst into laughter. I must have looked as baffled as I felt. There was no way she could have been alive during wars that took place over two hundred years ago during the beginning of the Cataclysm.

"Oh, goodness, child, don't looks so perplexed. I'm a hundred and ninety-two years old. I'm a dhampir; my father is a vampire." She laughed.

The aged wisdom in her eyes made a lot more sense now. Dhampirs were children born of human mothers and vampire fathers. They were rare, but not unheard of. Usually the N-V virus rendered both females and males infertile, but like with every other disease, it could affect some individuals differently. A small percentage of male vamps could father children for several years after their initial infection. An even smaller number of those never became infertile. Dhampirs did not have to take their nourishment from blood and most didn't have the same allergy to sunlight. They didn't live as long as their vampire parents, but they did age slowly and usually lived to be three to four hundred years old.

Miss Leona focused her attention on Ian, her body completely relaxed now. "You are very observant, Master Necromancer. I am a Cataclysm Child. Few of us, the children born during the first decade of the Cataclysm, survived past infancy. I credit my parentage for my survival. Dhampirs are heartier, even as infants, than normal children are. I was too young to remember the wars, but I remember quite clearly the time after. The time forbidding practice of any religion, even quietly in your own home. It was a horrible, bloody time, and even now, across the sea, there are still regions where such laws exist. Our tribe once traveled far and wide, but we've come to like Appalachia, and this land has become our home. Very few villages in Appalachia allow religious persecution. We steer clear of them and have lived in peace for many decades. Unfortunately, nightmares take longer to go away. I am sorry, Agent Moon, Master Barroes, that I leapt to conclusions so quickly."

Now I understood her reaction, and I didn't blame her. The anti-religion laws had been banished in Nash long before I was born, but I had taken the required history course at the Academy, and Pinky had told us stories.

During the Cataclysm, the religion wars broke out because people believed the weather and natural disasters of the Cataclysm were happening because their deity was angry because of other religions, science, and "godlessness." People started killing each other in the name of their God, determined to put an end to other religions, non-believers, and thusly the Cataclysm. Soon, all across Appalachia, anti-religion laws were implemented to stop bloodshed, but had ended up creating more. People were dragged from their homes for possessing religious paraphernalia and put on work gangs or in extreme cases, put to death. The anti-religion laws lasted much less time than the religion wars. As the Cataclysm ended and weather patterns shifted so that freak storms were less frequent, travel between communities was easier, and the Council of Elders started working with the city-states to rebuild and become allies, the anti-religion laws were redacted and laws that were more lenient were put into place. Now every citizen had the freedom to choose or not choose to follow a religion as they saw fit. The only prohibition was on publicly trying to convert others or requiring people in a community to confess to a particular belief. By Nash law, religion was a personal choice that could neither be taken from nor forced on any person.

"I am sorry you had to go through such a time," I told her, sincerely. "I also apologize for not wording our reason for being here a little more clearly."

"Nonsense. No apologies are necessary. I'm just getting a bit doddering in my old age. Now, how may I help the two of you?"

"Have you ever heard the name Bokor?" Ian asked.

"It's not a name, but a title. A Bokor is a type of Voodoo Priest. But I think you already know that." Her look was sharp.

I smiled. "We weren't completely sure. We are investigating a rash of disappearances and possible murders. Last night, I encountered a suspect and before he got away, he told me to call him Bokor. We thought it was a name, but someone who grew up in a gypsy tribe recognized it. She said her tribe had sometimes camped with a tribe that practiced the Voodoo religion, and she had heard the title there in relation to their Holy Man."

She nodded. "And when you heard the term Voodoo, River said she knew someone who practiced the religion, and so here you are."

"Yes," Ian agreed. "But neither you nor anyone from your tribe is under any sort of suspicion. We know your tribe only just arrived in the city, and so none of you could possibly be responsible."

This seemed to appease the older woman. "Okay. Proceed with your questions."

"This person we are chasing, we believe he is a man, is a very bad guy. He has kidnapped numerous mages, and he has powers that we have never seen before. He told me to address him as Bokor, so the name, the title must mean something significant to him. This likely means he either practices or is familiar with the Voodoo religion. Is there anything you can tell us that might help us track him down?" I asked.

"I'm not sure that I can help you track him down, I don't know any Bokor, at least none I've met in the last fifteen or twenty years. But I can tell you this, if your bad guy is calling himself Bokor, I have no doubt that he truly is as bad as you say. Bokor are priests and leaders, like myself, but the religion they worship, the magic they practice, is not the same. Voodoo takes many forms and goes by many names, Voodoo or Vodoun just to name two, and even those can be practiced in many different ways. Bokor and their followers practice dark and evil magic in the name of their religion," she told us.

"Magic is neither good nor evil, dark nor light. Magic is the use of energy to perform functions," Ian replied dryly, in that know-everything academic tone that drove me crazy.

"Such a learned definition, Master Necromancer. It is true, magic is nothing more than a tool, but the use of that tool is colored by the intentions of the wielder," the old woman crooned, a sly smile playing on her thin lips.

Ian tilted his head, eyes down slightly in a gesture of deference. "I concede your point, Madame. Are you saying Bokor and their followers are inherently evil? That their magic is dark because their souls are?"

"That is not what I'm saying and you well know it. I'm too old and tired to play such games. You don't believe in pure evil any more than you believe in our deities. Nor do you believe in souls, at least not as beings of good or evil."

"That is true. What some religions call souls are simply spirits, the life energy and consciousness that remains even after their body is dead," Ian said, obviously enjoying the debate. "I don't believe, but you do. And, I am assuming, other practitioners of the faith believe that as well. So, do you believe that Bokor and their followers are evil?"

The gypsy sipped her tea before replying. "There are only a few tribes left that I know of that worship any variation of Voodoo or Vodoun. Fewer still that follow a Bokor. The few Bokor that I have come across tend to worship deities that have darker teachings than most."

"Dark teachings?" I asked, intrigued. The concept of religion had always fascinated me.

While superstition and religion seemed to be a little more common among gypsy tribes and small mountain communities, in Nash and Atlanta, it was almost unheard of. It didn't mean no one believed in higher powers, it just meant they kept that belief to themselves. My mother had not had any religious beliefs, and Pinky had taught us that no one could ever know all the mysteries of the universe and to respect all ways of life.

"The Goddess my tribe worships is one of light and love. Our traditions include humility, love, and charity to all. Not all Gods and Goddesses are the same. Some are deities of war, strife, or mischief," Miss Leona continued.

Our Bokor definitely wasn't of the love and light variety. "Do you know which deities Bokor and their followers worship?"

The gypsy woman's smile was indulgent. "Child, there are as many deities as there are stars in the sky. No two gypsy clans worship the same religion, or the same God, in the same way."

"I can understand that. I imagine that two hundred years of nomadic life has turned each clan into its own micro-culture," Ian said.

"Another learned observation. But, yes, Master Necromancer, you are correct. The ways of the gypsy tribes are an amalgamation of traditions handed down for two centuries. We don't all originate from the lost lands, or even from Appalachia. There are tribes that started out as groups of families surviving the Cataclysm and wars together by traveling from place to place in order to find fairer weather, food, shelter, and safety. By the time the weather began to subside and the wars no longer had anyone to fight them, no one was left that remembered what it was like to have a permanent home. Freedom is the only culture shared by Gypsy clans."

"You must have amazing stories of your travels," I said, deciding I liked this woman very much.

"That I do, child. You should come with your sister to visit me sometime, and I will tell you some of them." Her smile was so genuine I couldn't help but return it.

She rose, signaling the audience was ending. Ian and I followed suit. "Miss Fiona, Master Ian, I am sorry I could not help you more. I could tell you the lore of my clan for hours, but I can promise you that none from my tribe has done these terrible things," she said as she walked back to her wagon.

Strangely, I believed her, and from the expression on his face, so did Ian.

"Madame, you have been more helpful than you think. With what you were able to provide, our search through the City Archives will be much easier."

Her eyes went wide with wonder. "You have books about Voodoo and the Gods from before the Cataclysm?"

"Perhaps not whole books, as I believe even then it was not widely practiced. But I am sure there is some information. I do remember running across references during past research," Ian answered, obviously missing the eagerness in the woman's expression.

"Perhaps when I come back, we will both have tales," I said, delighting in the way her face lit up. She was obviously very curious to learn about the pre-Cataclysm practices of her religion. "You can tell me about your travels, and I can tell you what I learn about pre-Cataclysm Voodoo."

"That would be perfect. You and that sweet River are welcome at my fire any time. You as well, Master Necromancer," she said, then without another word, she turned and went back into the wagon. The door swung shut after her, effectively dismissing us.

TWENTY-THREE
Fiona

"Nothing in that one," I said, slamming shut the dusty tome and added it to one of the piles stacked haphazardly around the table. "You should be more careful with those books. They are more than two hundred years old. Great care has been taken to preserve them," Ian said in that annoyingly superior tone of his.

I shot him a dirty look, which he missed because he was busy making notes. "What have you found so far?"

He scribbled a couple of more words, and then looked up. "Not much. Most of the references to Voodoo I found were fictional, even those that were supposedly factual. The people of the last century before the Cataclysm had vivid imaginations and little regard for scientific fact. The theories 20th and 21st century norms had about magic and paranormal beings amazes me. Most of the pre-Cataclysm magical books I've studied were council-approved texts that were not for the mainstream norm public. I find these very interesting. I will have to do more research into the fiction and myths of the pre-Cataclysm age."

I rolled my eyes. "Okay, Professor, wipe off the drool. I'm sure it is all very interesting and you can spend countless hours with it later. Right now, fiction doesn't really do us a lot of good."

Ian leveled his penetrating gaze on me. "That is not entirely accurate. In the 20th and 21st centuries, and for centuries before that, the mainstream norm society held all magical and paranormal phenomena to be myth and fiction. In the 16th century, the Paranorm Council created official channels for sharing information among the paranorm community. However, books and information did leak out. That information was treated as fiction by society as a whole. So, if you know what you are looking for, you can find facts among the early fiction."

"Ugh!" I let my head fall to the table with a thud. A sharp pain shot through my forehead, yet it was less painful than listening to Ian prattle on about ancient history. "Please spare me the history lesson. We've been at this for hours, I'm bored, my eyes are crossed from so much reading, and I'm starving. Did you find anything we can use?"

Apparently unconcerned by my outburst, Ian continued, "Not yet, or at least I don't think so. We should probably combine notes, see what we have so far, and try to figure out where to go from here."

Lifting my head, I shoved my notebook towards him, and then stood. "Can we get some food first? And fresh air? The smell of old books and dust is starting to get to me."

"I thought you spent a lot of time here at the library when you were a kid," Ian said.

"I did, and I didn't care for the dusty books then either. Carly usually let me take my books out into the enclosed garden to do my school work."

"That must have been nice. When I was growing up, books were not allowed out of the library rooms of the compound, much less outside into the open air," Ian said.

"Then you probably know how I feel right now. I need air and food. Aren't you hungry? The only things we have eaten today were those fritters at the market. We came straight here after talking to Miss Leona and that was more than six hours ago," I whined, not caring a bit that I sounded like a petulant child.

Ian looked up at me, a wicked gleam in his eyes. "I scryed Mrs. Gary about an hour ago when you went to look for more books. There will be a pot of her venison stew waiting when we get back to my place. No fussing tonight, as I told her to leave the pot on the warmer and go on and relax, but her stew is delicious. Join me?"

It was a good thing I was sitting down because my knees went to jelly as I realized venison stew was not all that would be on the menu if I went back with him. I didn't hesitate for a second, though I told myself it was because my mouth was watering for that stew. "What are we waiting for then? Leave the books; we'll put them back tomorrow. Let's go get me some food!"

As I suspected, and secretly hoped, food wasn't the only thing on the agenda. It wasn't even the first thing on the agenda. The entire ride back to his apartment in the rickshaw, I was trying to decide how to make my move. Should I be subtle or just crawl in the middle of his bed, naked, like I did last night? Turned out that I didn't have to make a move at all.

The moment we entered his apartment, Ian grabbed me and pulled me to him, pushing me against the door as it closed. We melded together in a flurry of hot mouths and hands. I went from a little hot and bothered to full-on, fuck-me-now lust mode in about five seconds. I could feel the length of him hard against my thigh. As I pressed against it, I was rewarded with a moan. "Fiona, damn, I want you right this second."

Heat soared through me. "You have me, take me," I urged.

He unbuttoned my pants and started sliding them down. I thought he was going to do just that. My vision went a little blurry at the prospect of up-against-the-wall sex with Ian.

But after they were just a little way down my hips, he stopped tugging on my pants. I was disappointed until one hand slid down between my legs. Automatically spreading them, I gave him better access as one long finger slipped inside of me. "Oh. Oh, Ian," I gasped as he positioned his hand so that his thumb rested against the throbbing nub of my clit, and he slowly began to move his finger in and out.

My body thrummed and my hands shook as I fumbled with the buttons on his pants. I wanted, no needed, to touch him, to return some of the pleasure he was giving me. I finally got the buttons apart and his pants down enough that he sprang free, half erect. Immediately wrapping my hand around him, I savored the way it began to lengthen and harden at my touch. I began to slowly stroke him, matching the rhythm of his hand between my legs. But, then, he inserted a second finger and though I still grasped him, I lost all ability to do anything with it.

My entire world was focused—the pleasure starting between my thighs and pushing out in shards of flame through my entire body. I shamelessly rode his hand until the tiny shards converged into ball of fire that consumed me. My orgasm broke over me in a white-hot wave.

My body went limp and if it hadn't been for Ian's hand, I would have slid down the wall. I rested my forehead against his shoulder, trying to catch my breath.

As I slowly came back to myself, I realized I still held him in my hand, and he remained hard as granite. I began to move my hand, wanting to bring him to his knees like he had done to me. But he gently took my hand away. "Let's go to the bed," he gruffly said.

I followed him to the bed, and we quickly divested ourselves of our clothes. But instead of pulling me to him, Ian said in a soft, but firm voice, "I want you on the bed like last night, but with your legs spread, waiting for me."

Tiny shivers of anticipation raced through me. This was a different side of Ian, and I liked it. I did as he ordered. With my legs spread, I felt exposed and nervous, but so turned on, I thought I'd vibrate right off the bed.

Ian crawled on the bed. Starting at my ankle, he dropped light kisses all the way up my leg, past my knee, across my thigh, and stopped at the apex of my thighs. He rose up so that he hovered over me, on his knees between my parted legs. "I want to watch you as you come," he said, gripping my hips and pulling them up so that my bottom was several inches off the bed. He placed himself at my entrance and then plunged inside. I gasped and bucked against him. Once he was seated deep inside, he moved his arms so that he was gripping my hips with my legs over his arms. "Put your legs on my shoulders."

It took a minute for his words to penetrate my pleasure-fogged brain, but when they did, I complied. I wanted to say something, but I was too busy moaning as every movement shifted him inside me and brought a new round of bliss. Once he had me the way he wanted, he started moving. The pace he set was immediately fast and deep. I cried out a string of intelligible words as he took the heel of one hand and placed it firmly against the top of my mound. With each thrust, his hand pushed against my sensitive nub and sent spasms of liquid heat rushing through my body.

"Cup your breasts," he told me. "Play with them."

Oh. Oh. Wow, this was so different from anything I'd ever expected from Ian, and I loved it.

I did as he said, and loved the way his face flushed as he watched. He was so beautiful and brain-meltingly sexy over me like that. His muscles were tight and tense beneath his skin. His skin was slick, and I ached to reach out and touch him, but I kept my hands where he'd told me to put them.

"Pinch your nipples." His command came out in a gruff whisper. He was close to the edge of his breaking point, I knew. I wanted to send him over, but in the position we were in, all I could do was take the pleasure he gave, and not give any myself.

So, I did as I was told, and twin spikes of electricity jolted through me from my nipples down to the center of my pleasure between my thighs. Everything exploded, white sparks falling around me. I threw my head back and screamed as I bucked against Ian, my inner muscles clenching around him as my orgasm rocked me. From somewhere far off, I heard Ian let out a guttural roar as he shoved into me, his own body shaking. Then he fell forward and to the side, rolling and taking me with him, keeping our bodies joined.

We were both gasping for breath and shuddering.

"That. That was... Wow," I said.

"I know. Wow."

"Really wow."

"Yes. I don't...wow," he said, pulling me tighter.

And at that point, I decided to shut up because my brain was so muddled that if I kept talking, the next thing that came out of my mouth would be a confession telling him that had been the best orgasm of my life. True or not, it wasn't something he needed to know, not yet.

TWENTY-FOUR
Ian

FIONA PULLED AWAY FROM HIM, AND HE ADMIRED THE CURVE OF HER THIGHS AND sway of her hips as she walked to the bathroom to retrieve the robe she'd worn earlier in the day.

She flashed him a grin as she settled down at the food-laden table. "I'm not bringing you dinner in bed. And I can't guarantee that there will be anything left if you lay over there too long. This stew smells delicious."

Ian rose, grabbed his own robe, and joined her at the table. Mrs. Gary had provided venison stew, rolls, butter, honey, and a plate of sliced fruits and vegetables. There was a pitcher of lemonade to wash it all down. "Well, I promised a feast, and Mrs. Gary delivered." He laughed.

"This is amazing. Do you eat like this all the time?" Fiona asked, munching on a cucumber slice as she dished hot venison stew into her bowl.

"Yes and no. Mrs. Gary, or the cook on Mrs. Gary's instruction, prepares three meals a day and afternoon snacks. The food is always delicious. But usually, except for tea and a snack, I eat down in the cafeteria with everyone else. As Mrs. Gary says, just because I own the place doesn't mean I'm any better than anyone else that works here."

Fiona laughed. "She makes you eat downstairs, doesn't she?"

"Yep," Ian said, sheepishly.

"She seems like a wonderful woman, and she definitely cares about you. Has she worked for you a long time?"

"All of my life. Mrs. Gary was my nanny when I was a kid and the housekeeper at the main house in the compound when I was older. She and her husband came to live here and work for me when my father died. She's like a mother to me."

"So, why did you get to eat up here tonight?"

Ian laughed. "It's you. I think she likes you. She probably thinks you are better than the guys that work here, or at least more special."

"Well, I'm not one to argue." Fiona laughed, popping a piece of roll into her mouth.

While they ate, they talked companionably about whatever came up, but steered away from work. But, by the time they had finished, the conversation had rolled back around to the case they were working on.

"I think the key to figuring this out is going to be in finding out what he is doing to the bodies. How is he able speak through them, and then cause them to dehydrate?" Ian said.

"It seems to me that he is somehow controlling or removing their life energy, their spirits, and turning them into zombies. I know you say it's not possible, but it sounds like Necromancy."

"This wasn't done by a necromancer." Ian's voice was tight.

"No?" Fiona's voice was filled with barely veiled sarcasm.

"I realize you are skeptical. You believe in what you can see or feel. That because you cannot see or feel the energy of spirits, you don't believe in them."

"No, that is not true. I'm a mage, Ian. My power lies in feeling energy around me, even energy others cannot feel or manipulate. I believe the energy of the dead remains, and can communicate with mages with certain powers—necromancers.

"What I do not believe is that all who say they are necromancers, actually are. What I don't believe is that those who are necromancers always tell the truth. I think they prey on people who are vulnerable and willing to pay anything for a connection with a dead loved one. I think that practice has been going on for hundreds of years... and it's not likely to stop."

"After all the years you've spent working with me and other necromancers, why do you still have such a poor view of us? I can't think of any case that would cause you to feel that way."

"I hate necromancers because one killed my mother."

She'd said the words calmly, as if she were saying, "The sky is blue." A calm, factual statement. Her face was devoid of emotion.

His mind spun, trying to remember what he knew about Malaina Hernandez and her death. He'd made it his business to know the professional background of any Blade or City Guard he worked with, though his interest in Fiona's history had been a bit more personal. He had full security clearance within the Blades and had read her mother's file long ago. From what he remembered, Malaina had been killed taking down a smuggling and slaving gang. The same gang killed her husband nearly seven years before, only Malaina had managed to take down the ringleaders before she'd died. Ian didn't remember the mention of a necromancer in the files.

"A necromancer killed your mother?" He did his best to keep his voice casual. He wasn't sure how to approach the subject, and was a little surprised she had.

"Well, she wasn't really a necromancer, and she didn't shove the sword through my mother's body, but for all intents and purposes, she killed her. She, and others like her, stole my mother's life long before the blood pumped out onto the ground." Her voice was cold, hard steel.

Though her voice was steady and her face blank, he could see the sorrow of old grief in her eyes. Fiona was not the sharing type, and other than last night in his bed, it was the first time she'd allowed him a glimpse of real emotion. If he pried, she could shut down.

If Ian had a weakness, other than his all-consuming desire for Fiona that had not yet been slaked, it was his unfailing curiosity. His curious nature was what drew him to books and learning. It was even what made him teach, because even as he taught his students, he was constantly learning from them. That natural eagerness to know the unknown paired with his feelings for Fiona created a lethal combination.

He wanted to know everything about her, what made her happy, what made her sad, all the ways to make her gasp and moan. He knew as much about her past as any outsider could, but that was all academic. Facts. Even though he lived his life by facts, he knew that there was so much more to life, more to knowing Fiona. Right now, something about her mother's death, that had nothing to do with the public facts, was upsetting her. His need to know more worked against him, until he had to ask her about it. Though he knew he shouldn't, he couldn't help himself.

"How did a necromancer cause your mother to die?" He wasn't sure how else to put the question, but once it was said, he knew it had been the wrong thing to say.

Her eyes flashed with anger. "Look, Barroes, just because we are sleeping together doesn't mean you get to stick your nose into my life and ask about things that are none of your business."

At least she'd said, "Sleeping together," as if it were going to be an ongoing activity. That was good. But she was wrong about it not being his business. She was his business, even if she wasn't aware of it yet.

"I have to, honorably, disagree with you, Fiona." He put emphasis on her first name to remind her they were on a first-name basis. He knew she'd used his last name to put some emotional distance between them. He wasn't going to let her.

"Ok, Ian, I'll bite. What do you disagree with?" She casually strode across the room to the bed where her clothes were strewn across the floor.

She shrugged off the robe and his mouth went dry at the sight of the bare skin of her back, soft, silky, and begging to be touched. He ached to drag his fingertips from the base of her neck down her spine, over the full swell of her ass and down to the back of her knee. He wondered if she was sensitive there. If he pressed his lips to the indention there, would she moan?

The echo of her moans from an hour before ghosted through his mind. He went hard. He wanted her. Even after barely getting any sleep last night, even after spending an hour making love to her before dinner, and even though they were arguing, he wanted her right now.

He shoved his hands in his pockets to keep from crossing the room and... damn!

She trying to distract him from the topic of discussion and, for a moment, she had been successful. He pulled himself together as she slipped her shirt on, covering most of her nudity. It did nothing to slake his lust, but he was pulling himself back together.

He took a breath, trying to sound as neutral as possible. It wouldn't do for her to know he wanted nothing more than to forget the entire conversation and tumble back into the bed with her for several more hours, or days. "First, I should point out that we are partnered on a case right now, which means we need to trust each other. I'm a necromancer and if you distrust all necromancers, then we have a problem."

She threw him a look over her shoulder as she pulled on the pants. "Okay, I'll give you that. It still isn't your business why I feel the way I do, but I will concede that I have no reason to distrust you, personally."

"It's a start, but not quite good enough." He strode over to her and pulled her around to face him. Though desire was still pulsing through him, now that she was clothed, he felt like he could touch her without losing his mind.

His voice was deeper, huskier than he meant it to be. "I know you are used to no-strings fuck partners, but I'm not one of them. I told you last night that I wanted more than just sex, that I want us to get to know each other, to see what this is between us. That means we are going to have to talk. Eventually, you are going to have to let me past that shield you have erected. Don't give me that look. If you can trust me enough to let me into your body, you should be able to trust me enough to let me into your life just a little."

"It's not that simple." Her voice was quite, almost a whisper.

"I know it's not. And I don't think it should be simple, or easy. But if you can't do it… I told you I want more than just sex from you; I need more than that. But, I can compromise and say maybe right now isn't the time to go into this."

Relief flooded her face, but he went on before she could say anything. "Eventually, you are going to have to trust me enough to tell me why you hate me and my kind."

He let her go, walked back over to the table, and sat down. Nibbling on a roll, he drank some tea while she sat on the end of the bed pulling on her boots.

For a few moments, she was quiet as she laced up the boots. The dark fall of her hair shielded her face from him. He hadn't expected her to say she didn't hate him, and she didn't. Though, he didn't really think she did.

When she had the boots tied, she got up and joined him back at the table, sitting across from him and sipping her tea.

"Okay. Tell me why you are so sure this wasn't done by a necromancer," she said.

"Necromancy is, at its core, about communication. Necromancers communicate with the dead; we don't control them. The idea of necromancers taking control of dead spirits while in their bodies and creating undead creatures that prey on human brains is a fictional creation from the Age of Technology. How, in a time where magic is known to be a scientific fact, such a ridiculous myth can still be given any credence…"

Fiona held up a hand. "Calm down."

Ian took a deep breath. He hadn't realized his voice had been rising as he spoke. When he spoke again, the cool, professional dignity had returned to his voice. "I am perfectly calm. I do apologize, however. I do have a sore spot where this particular subject is concerned. The fact remains—this is not a matter of Necromancy."

Fiona sighed. "So, what you are telling me is zombies don't exist, right?"

"They don't."

"So, how do you explain what happened to me last night? How do you explain the two dried-up, spiritless bodies in the morgue?"

"I can't. I've never seen anything like this." And that concerned him more than he wanted her to know.

He took a deep breath, trying to decide how much to tell her about what he did know. How much could he really trust her? As she'd already made clear, just because they had sex didn't make them confidants, and it didn't mean she trusted him beyond the bed. Why should it mean he could trust her?

It didn't. But he felt like he could. Not because they'd had sex, but because he knew the type of person she was. Perhaps the way to make her trust him was to show her that he trusted her.

He couldn't guarantee she wouldn't hate him or even fear him when she found out, but he knew she would keep his secret. That is, if she heard him out and believed he'd had nothing to do with it. He couldn't be sure of that, but it was a risk he had to take.

He paced across the room, his hands thrust in his pockets and his posture stiff.

"Look, this is the bottom line of what I know. Necromancy is specifically about speaking to spirits and not about putting spirits back into bodies. It is not possible to put a spirit back into its body." He blew out a breath, but he continued quickly before she could speak. "But, it is possible to re-animate a dead body using energy. But, there is no way that is what was happening last night. There is no way the body of the person that attacked you last night had been dead before."

"Really?" she asked skeptically. "And how can you be so sure of that?"

"Because I can re-animate the dead."

And there it was—what he'd feared the most was there in an instant—abject horror on her beautiful face.

"You can re-animate the dead? Since this mess started that is the one thing you have been telling me over and over can't be done. Now you are telling me you can do it." She grabbed the vest he'd lent her and put it on as she stalked towards the door. "You know what? This is all a bit much. You can tell me tomorrow just how you can make the dead walk again."

"Fiona, wait." He started toward her, but stopped short at the stay-back glare she gave him. "Let me explain. You don't have to be afraid of me."

She rolled her eyes, and then strode over to stand toe to toe with him. "Get over yourself, Barroes. I'm not afraid of you." Her voice was deadly calm, but she punctuated each word with a finger poke to his chest. Her point made, she turned and walked back to the door. "I'm going home to get some rest because it has been a long two days. A lot has happened, you know, with a guy turning to a desiccated corpse and falling on me, then sex with you, then hours and hours of reading, then more sex. I'm a wee bit tired and have been, for the past half hour, wavering between wanting to punch you in the face and wanting to kiss you.

"After you dropped your little bombshell and then looked at me like me as if I were going to run screaming, the punch-you-in-the-face urge intensified. Since I might want to have sex with you again in the future, that probably isn't a good idea at this time. So, to keep that from happening, I'm going to go home, get some rest, and try to process the past two days. I suggest you do the same. While you are at it, you might try to give me some credit for being able to understand, and not freak out, about having a power that is odd and a little scary."

Ian stared, dumbfounded. He tried to think of something to say, but by the time he opened his mouth, she had opened the door to leave.

"I'll take a hired rickshaw home. That should be safe enough. I'll see you at the library at eight in the morning," she said, then was gone.

TWENTY-FIVE

Fiona

The next morning, Ian was waiting for me at the library. He was sitting at the same table from the day before, but the pile of already read books from yesterday was cleared away and a fresh stack was waiting. When he heard me approaching, he looked up, searching my face expectantly. I didn't blame him for being a little wary, considering how I stormed out the night before. I'd lain awake a long time trying to come to terms with the past two days. It was a lot to process, especially the part where I'd fallen not just into bed with Ian, but into a relationship. It was a first. The whole "sharing" thing had me spooked.

I crossed to him and before he had time to figure out what I was going to do, I bent down and kissed him. It wasn't a good-morning-how-are-you-nice-to-see-you peck on the cheek. It was a full on I-missed-you-I'm-still-a-little-mad-but-I-want-to-toss-you-down-and-have-my-way-with-you kiss, complete with tongue. We were both a little breathless when I pulled away.

I went around the table and sat directly across from him. "Okay, Master Necromancer, you want to explain to me how it is that you make zombies, you know, even though zombies don't exist and necromancers can't create them?"

Ian, still stunned from the kiss I laid on him, blinked. "I don't create zombies."

Oh, whatever. "Okay, re-animate the dead, whatever it is you do. Explain."

"I can't put spirits into dead bodies. As far as I know, that is not possible. Or at least there has never been a real documented case, not in any of the books I've ever read. And trust me when I tell you, my family has copies of every book or journal on Necromancy written in the last thousand years."

I believed him. Of course even last night I knew whatever it was he could do was nothing like what Bokor did, but I was too pissed off to tell him so. "Okay. So, what can you do?"

"I can use my energy to make the body move. It isn't like using energy to say, move that book." He pointed at a book. "What I do is put small bits of my own energy into the empty body. Then I can control the body, but there are huge limitations. The mobility is somewhat limited, and talking is not possible. I don't put my life energy, my consciousness, into the bodies. I have to keep my focus on what I'm doing, or I lose connection. I have to be close, within a few yards, and have line of sight."

"That is why you were asking all of those questions before. You were checking to see if it was someone with the same power."

"I've never met anyone else that could do what I do. Well, as you can imagine, it's not the kind of power you advertise having. Even though there isn't really any practical application, telling people you can make dead bodies walk around tends to freak them out a bit."

I laughed. "I imagine so. I do have to ask, how do you even know you can do this, and the limitations? I mean, it's not like it is on the mage-level tests."

His eyes got a faraway, sad look as he answered. "Growing up, I had a dog named Ghost. He was my best friend. Ghost was several years old when I was born, so it was no surprise, to anyone but me, when he died of old age. I went out one day to play with him, and he just laid there. I held him, cried, and I begged for him to get up. I sat there willing it so hard, and then he did. He stood up, stumbled a few steps, and then fell again. Still dead. My father had been watching and immediately realized what happened. Of course, his first thought was how this could help him scam a buck. So, that night he started taking me to cemeteries and digging up bodies, or when it was convenient, killing animals for me to practice on. That lasted for a couple of years, until he realized that no matter how strong my powers grew, there was no real profit in it."

That was horrible. My whole body screamed out to go over and pull him into my arms, but I knew it would make him think I pitied him. I didn't. But my heart broke for the little boy he had been. I asked the next question quietly, not sure I wanted to know the answer. "How old were you?"

A shadow crossed his face then was gone, almost if it hadn't been there. "I was seven when Ghost died."

My breath burst from me in an explosion. "That asshole. If your father weren't dead, I swear, Ian, I would gladly make him so."

Ian laughed, actually laughed, at my death threat. "It's good to know you are starting to care about me."

Oh. Crap. "No, I'm not... Well, okay. Maybe just a little." I grinned.

The smile he flashed back made my stomach twist in knots. "So we are okay?"

"We're okay," I agreed.

"Good," he said, sliding a book across the table to me. "Because we have a lot of work to do."

Three hours later, we had another huge searched-through pile of books, notes, and a few handwritten journals that had been found and given to the library. There was a lot of fascinating information, well, Ian thought it was fascinating, but nothing we read seemed to have anything to do with Bokor or what was causing the desiccated bodies.

"I think I've skimmed every magical-medical book in this place and there are no documented cases of anything like those bodies in the morgue. Every med-mage in Nash has examined them, and none of them have a clue," I said, knowing my frustration was showing. I couldn't help it. We were getting nowhere, and I wanted to scream. "I just can't believe there is no explanation. How can we find him and stop what he is doing if we don't even know or understand what it is he is doing or how he is doing it?"

"The universe is infinite," Ian said, his tone calming in that strange way he had. "It is full of things we cannot yet explain, may never be able to fully understand, but that doesn't mean they are mystical or unknowable. It means we have not yet reached the level of knowledge it takes to comprehend the complexities of the universe. Up until two hundred years ago, norm society believed magic and paranormal beings were nothing more than myth and fiction. Those who did believe thought magic was some sort of mystical religion and paranorms were evil demons. I suppose that in some parts of the world, there are still people who believe that sort of drivel."

"There are. In the south, there are cities and villages with religious governments that deny the existence of magic, or worse, believe all paranorms are evil. There have been cases of such zealots going on killing sprees in Allied city-states. There have even been mass murders of entire villages. It doesn't happen much in Appalachia because most of the territory is claimed by either Nash or Atlanta, and our Blades keep a close watch on potential threats. Even in the mountains where most of the villages are autonomous and separate from either city-state, most of the inhabitants are were or vamp clans, so there isn't much problem of that sort," I told him. "As a matter of fact, when Sam first started briefing us, I thought that might be what we were dealing with. But a norm wouldn't be able to pick out a mage on the street, and there were no attacks on norms or other paranorms. Also, other than the man that attacked Millie, there were no bodies, and pro-norm fanatics always leave bodies."

"I can see that. It is possible, if not easy, for a norm to kill a paranorm, especially if the mage doesn't have the ability or knowledge to use their power for self-defense, but it would be next to impossible to hold a mage with any sort of talent for long, unless they kept them drugged," Ian said thoughtfully.

My brain slammed into overdrive. "Drugs! That's it! You are brillIant!" I leaned over the table and smacked my lips hard against his, surprising us both.

"It's great that you are finally recognizing my intelligence, but can you let me know why I'm brillIant at this particular moment?" he said, a hint of laughter in his voice.

"Hang on," I said, waving one hand at him as I fished through the notes I had taken earlier, until I found what I was looking for. "Zombies!" I said, thrusting the paper at him.

"Fiona, I thought we covered this. Zombies don't exist." Ian's voice was full of exasperation.

"Yes, I know. I get it. Would you just read the damned paper?" I said, not really annoyed, because I knew I was right and had finally stumbled on some sort of answer for what was happening. "Necromancers can't create zombies. But according to my research, Voodoo priests can."

While Ian read my notes, I flipped through the book I found the information in. Finding the page, I read over it again to refresh my memory and look for clues I missed.

"According to this, some Voodoo priests created zombies by using drugs that mimicked death. Later, after they "resurrected" the "corpse," they gave the person hallucinogenic drugs, keeping the person in a dreamlike state that allowed the priest to have mind control. This must where the original legend of zombies began," I said. I then read quietly for a few more minutes before gasping. "Wanna guess what the priests who worked with zombies were called?"

A grin spread across Ian's too-handsome face. "Bokor?"

"You win the prize," I said. Ian waggled his eyebrows, and I hurried on before he could ask what the prize was. "I can't believe I didn't catch this when I was reading it before. I guess since I'd already found out Bokor was one of the names priests were called, depending on the sect or whether they were considered good or evil, I didn't really pay attention when the word popped up again."

"It doesn't matter. You see it now," he said. "So, you think Bokor is drugging his victims and mind controlling them."

"It explains why he tried to stick me with a syringe. Drugs also explain how he was able to abduct some very powerful mages with very little struggle. But how does he inhabit their bodies?" I asked.

Ian was quiet, his brows knitted together in thought. Then, as if a switch flipped on, his eyes went bright with dawning realization. "What if you were right all along and Bokor is a necromancer?"

I was confused. "Didn't we just have a huge fight last night where you told me there was no way this was done by a necromancer? You said that necromancers can't reanimate the dead, not in a way that would make it possible for them to talk and interact."

"They can't. But I don't think that is what he is doing. I can put bits of my energy into empty bodies, dead bodies. What if that is what he is doing? What if he is putting his entire consciousness into the bodies?"

A sick, creepy feeling washed over me. "Okay. But you can put your energy into bodies that are empty. The spirits of the people he has used haven't turned up, anywhere. If he is killing them first, why aren't you able to call their spirits to their bodies?"

He stood and started pacing back and forth in front of the table. "I have a theory about that, too. The other night, when I told you that you were a succubus, I told you I knew that because of the way I work with energy."

"I remember," I said slowly, trying to figure out where he was going with this.

"Our power types are related, kind of interconnected. Perhaps he has an advanced form of the power you have. You can pull energy from the world around you and into your body before you release it, which is harmless because everything is made of energy and you don't suck the energy out of any one thing. But, what if he can pull the living energy out of a person and into his own body, but not release it?" He stopped pacing and turned to look at me.

"Oh, crap. That makes sense. The thought of that makes my skin crawl."

"I know," he said. "Mine too. But, it is a plausible theory."

I nodded. "Okay, so you think he is pulling their energy out of them, perhaps leaving just enough to keep the body alive, and then puts his own energy into their still-living bodies?"

Ian came to sit back down. "I do. I think that can explain why the strange mummification happens to the bodies when he pulls his energy out. Something in the transfer leaches out the bodies fluids. Really, I can't explain it. But like I said earlier, there will always be unknowable factors in life."

A cold chill ran through me, curdling my blood. "Ian, he told me he was going to devour me. You are right. He is sucking their life energy into his body, feeding off them. That's heinous."

"I know. We have to put a stop to what he is doing. But I just don't know how. So far, nothing we've come across gives any insight into where he might be holed up," Ian said, his tone exasperated.

"Actually, I have my own theory about that. He's calling himself Bokor, which is a Voodoo priest. He's obviously using Voodoo methods to create zombies. So, whatever his motivation is, it is religious in nature. I think that wherever he is, the building is, or was, a sacred or holy place."

"Okay. But there is only one problem with your theory," Ian said. "Voodoo was primarily practiced in the Lost Lands, and wasn't a mainstream religion before the Cataclysm. It is now practiced by a few bands of gypsies. I doubt if there are any Voodoo holy places in Nash City."

I grinned at him, loving that I had finally caught on to something before he had. "No, I doubt there are. But remember, Miss Leona told us every tribe worships their religions in different ways, that the religions have changed over the years. And, right here in my notes," I tapped the paper, "I noted that early Voodoo was a tribal religion and that it changed over the course of years into many different versions. Some of those versions merged traditions and beliefs from the Catholic religion with the original traditions."

Ian's mouth quirked up into a smile. "Very clever. So you think we should search old Catholic Churches."

"Not just Catholic. People of all religions were displaced when the Lost Lands sank into the sea. It could be very likely that he could consider any, or all, former religious sites holy ground. I'm betting there is a list or a map in the archives of locations that were once churches or held some other religious function. One would have been compiled when the anti-religion laws were in effect."

It was Ian's turn to lean over the table and kiss me. "You are brilllant, Fiona Moon," he said, and then rose. "Well, come on. We have research to do."

TWENTY-SIX

Bokor

"M*y lord...*" Amos hurried across the room, his voice echoing off the chamber walls.

Bokor came awake with a startled gasp. He glared at Amos and boomed with rage, "I told you not to disturb me. I am resting."

"I know, My Lord. I'm sorry to disturb you, but some of the hunters you sent out have returned. They have captured a vessel for you." Amos bowed his head, his tone genuflecting.

Bokor's rage diminished. "Fine, fine. Send them in."

Two empty-handed disciples strode quickly across the hall and dropped to their knees before the throne. Following them were two more disciples, half carrying/ half dragging a large man between them. His head was drooped as if he were unconscious.

When the disciples reached the throne, they dropped their burden and joined their comrades as they knelt and bowed in reverence. The blond, muscular man fell to the dirty floor with a thud and a moan.

"Rise and bring him forward." Bokor motioned towards the man writhing and moaning on the floor.

The four minions rose, heads down. The two in front stepped to the side while the two that had brought the man in grabbed him under his arms and pulled him forward across the dirty floor until he was about five feet away, directly in front of Bokor's throne. Then they pulled him up to his knees and released him. As Bokor expected, he didn't fall forward again, as he would have if he'd been as injured or mentally fogged as he'd played. The man's back straightened and his head rose, revealing alert blue eyes. Without warning, he struck out at the disciple nearest to him, sweeping one large fist to the side, striking him in the stomach and doubling him over. The blond jumped to his feet and turned just in time to catch another disciple across the throat, sending him to the floor gasping.

"Get him! Don't let him get away," Bokor thundered.

But the man wasn't running; he was fighting. A third disciple lunged at him but slid to a heap in the floor when the blond disappeared. Bokor blinked as the blond reappeared behind the fourth minion, wrapping his arm around the man's neck and squeezing.

"Amos!" Bokor howled, but Amos was already placing a long tube to his mouth. There was a hissing sound, and the large man let the minion go as his hand flew to his neck. He stumbled back, pulled out the dart, and glared at it for one long moment before his entire body went limp and he slid to the floor. Around him, the beaten disciples began to get to their feet, coughing and stumbling.

"You fools!" Bokor bellowed. His rage was so intense he was sputtering. "That is the City Guard I sent you to get information on. I did not tell you to bring him to me."

One of the disciples, Bokor was so enraged he could not think of his name, stepped forward. "My Lord, he is a mage and very strong. We knew you wanted information about him, but we also knew he would be a good avatar. We thought you could force him to give you the information you need."

He could. Actually, force wouldn't even enter the situation. It would be easy to find out everything Rangel knew. But that was not the problem. "You idiot. The number-one rule is to be inconspicuous. Do not draw attention, and do not get caught. The authorities have already investigating missing mages. He is a Guard; his disappearance will be noticed. It will be impossible to hunt in the city any longer."

"But My Lord, the information he has..."

"Will be useful. That is the only reason you are still living. Get out of my sight," Bokor hissed. "The rest of you, take him to the women to be cleansed. I will prepare and the ritual will take place as soon as the drug keeping him paralyzed wears off."

The minions hefted the unconscious Rangel and hurried out of the hall. "Amos, send out men to find the other hunters and call them back. I think I will get all the information I need from Rangel. I think it is time to change tactics and accelerate my ascension."

"Understood, My Lord."

"Now, leave me. I need to prepare for the ritual. Give me one hour for my prayers, and then send the women in for the cleansing."

"Yes, My Lord," Amos said and backed away, following the disciples.

Bokor took in a deep breath, trying to dissipate the anger and rage within him. This would put a twist in his plans, but perhaps speeding things up was for the best. In just a few hours, he would know everything City Guard Rangel knew. It would, perhaps, give him an insight into how to bring his Fiona to him. And soon, he would be a God.

He looked up at the serene, stone face high above him. "My Goddess, bless me, your humble servant. Make my body strong, soul pure, and give me the power to defeat my enemies." He bowed his head and continued the prayer that would start the soul-exchange ritual.

TWENTY-SEVEN
Fiona

"I HATE REPORTS," I SAID TO THE EMPTY BAR. PINKY, ANYA, AND JARRETT WERE still asleep upstairs, River was in her garden on the roof, and I sat at a table in the corner doing status reports. Not that I had anything to report.

It had been six days since Ian and I had decided there must be a religious angle to Bokor's motives. In those six days, we had scoured the entire city, searching every building or piece of property that had once held a church or religious school, even if the original building was no longer standing. So far, we had come up empty handed. It had been slow going, though. Two days into the search, the senate approved the complete removal of all City Guard personal from the case, with the exception of Rangel, who was still supposed to be working as a Guard representative. But, the next day Rangel called in sick, and he hadn't been back to work since.

That left Ian and me, with a handful of Blades, to canvas the entire city. But, two days ago, Sam had been forced to pull those Blades back to their own cases. We hadn't had a new lead in almost a week, and the ones we had prior to that were weak, at best. It was all going down the drain fast. Sam had mentioned letting the case go cold and reassigning me, but

I threw a fit. Farah Purcell was still out there. After forty-eight hours, the chance of finding a missing person alive went from slim to almost zero, so I knew it would be a fucking miracle if she were still alive, but I just couldn't give up. Not yet.

I agreed to an afternoon off, though. Well, agreed really meant that Sam and Ian were insisting and I was too tired and burned out to fight with them. So, instead of the two of us traipsing through abandoned buildings, Ian was at his office working on his lesson plans for the start of the semester at the Academy, and I was sitting here, writing status reports on every location we had searched over the past few days.

I had tried to do my paperwork at my desk at the Blade Headquarters, but Sam chased me out, saying something about taking the day off meant not doing work, even paperwork. So, I took my stack of reports and came to the pub. At least here it was quiet and I had unlimited ale. It had the added benefit that everyone would be up soon and I could spend the evening with my family. That, more than a day off, was long overdue.

This was the first time I had been home longer than the time it took me to grab clothes and necessities. I'd spent the last six days working side by side with Ian, and the nights at his apartment and in his bed. We had spent hours talking and getting to know each other on a level that I'd never had with anyone outside of my family, not even Jarrett. And when we weren't talking, we were making love. I had never spent so many nights in a row with the same man. I couldn't believe I still craved him. Even now, just the thought of his touch made my whole body erupt into flames.

During the few hours we'd spent apart over the past week, he'd been constantly on my mind. I wasn't sure what was happening, not for certain, but I thought I might know. I thought I might be falling in love with Ian Barroes. The idea filled me with both a sense of awe and bone-chilling terror.

A rapid tap, tap, tap on the pub's front window drew my attention, pulling me out of my thoughts. I looked up and saw Rangel, backlit by the orange-gold setting sun, leaning close, his face almost pressed against the glass, waving to get my attention. I glanced at the cuckoo clock above the bar and saw it was almost time for Pinky and Anya to come down and start preparing for the evening's business. I said the combination spell, a series of nonsense words Pinky had made up, that released the intruder alarm and sound-deafening spells on the downstairs of the building, and motioned for Rangel to come in.

"I'm glad to see you are feeling better," I said, gathering up my paperwork and shoving it in a leather satchel as he walked across the room and came to sit with me.

"Thanks," he said, his voice scratchy.

Crystal-lamp sconces lined the walls of the pub and when they were all lit, they cast the room with a soft bluish light that gave the perfect dim atmosphere to the bar. But, when I came in earlier, it had been full daylight and I only activated two of the lamps directly over the table I was sitting at. Now, with the early evening glow outside fading fast, it was much dimmer in the pub than normal. It wasn't until Rangel slid into the booth across from me, his face coming into the full light of the crystal lamps that I realized how pale he was. Well, that was to be expected.

But, no, he wasn't pale. His skin had a sickly grayish tinge. Perhaps he was still sick. Or maybe it was just a trick of the lighting. After all, the crystal lamps gave everything a slightly bluish tone. Yet, deep in my stomach, something cold and slimy began to crawl.

I clutched the satchel and began to slide out of the booth. "I'm going to put this away and grab some more ale. How 'bout I bring you a whiskey with a little honey mixed in? Sounds like you're still feeling shitty. That should knock the last of it out of you," I said, trying to keep my tone steady. No need to tip him off to my growing panic. After all, why was I panicking? To be honest, I wasn't completely sure, but something felt wrong.

"That sounds great," he said in that croaky-not-quite-right voice. Then he looked up at me, a broad smile plastered across his face, and I had the undeniable evidence staring right at me. His eyes, Marcus Rangel's beautiful blue eyes, the ones that always had a twinkle in them and had been what attracted me to him, were clouded and vacant. My friend and ex-lover no longer lived behind those eyes.

I forced myself to smile and do the one thing I was trained never to do, turn my back on the enemy, clutching the leather satchel tight in front of me to hide the fact that my hands, along with my entire body, were shaking. Waves of sorrow, rage, and fear washed over me. The man, the monster, we had been hunting, had hunted us back and killed my friend. I had no doubt, after what I had seen in the alley the week before, that Rangel was as good as dead. That thing sitting at the corner table wasn't my friend—it was a dangerous predator. And it was in my home, with my family.

My mind raced as I walked at a normal pace, which seemed slow and torturous to the bar. My hanbo, which I usually carried in a sling across my back when I was on duty, was hanging on a hook in the back room. I glanced at the shelves behind the bar. Damn, a jar of honey was sitting in plain view, so I couldn't use that as an excuse. I tossed the satchel on the bar, nonchalantly, and moved in behind it, chattering inane nonsense about the weather and how we'd missed him while he'd been sick. Anything to keep him distracted.

I bent down, supposedly looking for a glass, but easily finding my real target. Pinky didn't have anything wooden that resembled a staff downstairs, but he did keep a sword under the bar. It wouldn't work as a means to focus my magical energy, and I wasn't as skilled in combat with a heavy sword as I was with my short staff, but it was what I had on hand and it would have to do. I tried to push the fact that I was about to rush at one of my friends, my one-time lover, with a sword with the intention of running him through, out of my mind.

I was about to rise when something brown caught my eye. I reached in, back behind the glasses, and pulled out a long, round piece of wood. A memory flashed through my mind. Pinky had said a chair back had broken and he needed to fix it, but he'd forgotten where he'd put the broken spindle. I'd just found it. I tossed it up a little, testing its weight. It wasn't long or sturdy enough to use as a hand-to-hand combat weapon, but maybe, just maybe, it would be useful in another way. I looked at the splintered end, it looked like oak, and I thought most of the chairs in the bar were made of the same.

Rising up, I used one hand to put a glass on the bar, the other to grasp the spindle. I started to open my senses, and then remembered the last two times I'd done that near Bokor. I didn't want to get hit with nausea just now, so using the slightest bit of power, I opened my senses. Nothing happened. I pulled in more energy, and I was fine. Bokor, in Rangel's body, was at least fifteen feet away. Perhaps proximity had something to do with the energy void he caused. I pushed a tiny bit of energy through the spindle, testing it out. A glass flew off the shelf and hit the floor, shattering.

Bokor looked up, and I shrugged. "I'm such a klutz. Pinky will have my hide for that."

I took in more and more energy until I had a reserve built up, then quickly pulled the spindle from under the bar, aimed, and released the energy surging through me. A white lightning bolt of energy burst out of the end and blew the wooden booth bench into a million tiny, flying splinters. But Bokor wasn't there. One second he was sitting there, and then, just before the stream of energy hit him, he was gone. "Where...?"

My words were cut off when a strong arm closed around my throat, squeezing tightly. "Wow, what a rush." The course, gravely abomination of Rangel's voice sounded in my ear. "It is rare that I find an avatar whose power and body are strong enough for me to use that power once I have become one with them and entered their body. Even more rare to have an avatar with such a fun and useful ability."

I coughed, my hands grasping at his arm, trying to lessen the pressure on my airway. "What do you mean... 'become one'?" The possibilities made bile rise up in my throat.

"Oh, you'll see soon enough, my sweet Fiona," he crooned in my ear. "Now, come quietly and none of your family will get hurt."

"Bullshit," I gasped. "I'm not going anywhere with you."

I held tightly to his arm with both hands and, using my own weight as leverage, threw myself forward so that he flew over my back, across the bar, and into a barstool. Coughing and gasping for air, I grabbed the sword from under the bar, but by the time I was in front of him, he'd pulled one of the broken bar stools legs off and held it out in an en-garde position.

Damn, Pinky was going to be pissed. First the glass, then the bench, and now a stool.

Bokor laughed; it sounded obscene and wrong. "What are you going to do, my sweet girl? Will you cut your friend's heart out? Are you willing to kill your lover to protect your family?"

What? How the fuck did he know that?

"Oh, don't look so surprised, my sweet, luscious Fiona. When I consume a person's energy, they merge with me. Their thoughts, their memories, all of their emotions and knowledge become a part of me. It's a beautiful and spiritual thing."

My hands tightened on the sword. "You aren't Rangel. You've already killed him. I'll gladly run a sword through that body's heart if it means killing you."

He laughed again. "Oh, my dear, you are feisty. No need to bloody that pretty sword. No matter what you do, this body will continue to live until I withdraw from it. And nothing you do to this body will harm me in any way."

Rage filled me and before I knew what I was doing, I swung the sword. He countered with the stool leg and for several minutes we sparred, neither of us making any real connections or hits. Then, as I drew back for another swipe, he grabbed the stool leg in both hands and swung it like a bat, catching me on the side of the head, knocking me backward.

Pain erupted in my head, and then my back as I fell onto a table, which promptly crumpled to the floor, knocking the breath out of me. As if from far away, I heard my name being screamed, and then two large blurs flew from the top of the second-floor stairs, landing on Bokor, taking him to the ground with them.

I scrambled to my feet, shaking my head and rubbing my eyes to clear them. Pinky and Jarrett rose, dragging Bokor up between them. "I'm guessing this isn't our friend anymore," Jarrett said sadly.

"No," was my only reply. To Bokor, I said, "What do you want?"

His leer made my blood run icy. "I told you, my sweet Fiona. I want you. Come with me now and no harm will come to your family."

Pinky growled and yanked harder on the arm he had twisted behind Bokor's back. "You are in no position to bargain or make threats."

"You have no idea what kind of position I am in, Vampire. And, please do keep wrenching that arm. It hurts me so much." That hateful, obscene laughter erupted again.

I lurched forward, pushing the point of the sword against his throat. "Shut up, you asshole. We may not be able to hurt you right now, but I can cut out his vocal chords so you can't speak."

"Oh, my sweet, how quick you are to mutilate the body of someone who loved you. Did you know he could have used his teleportation abilities several different times to escape me, but he stayed to fight because he thought it would make you love him if he captured me and saved the pretty little girls."

My skin went hot. *No, don't listen to him.* "Rangel did love me, as a dear friend. He stayed and fought because he was a brave and honorable person. You cannot sully that. You might as well as leave his body because I don't care if I have to chop it into pieces, you are not getting it."

"Fine, fine. I will go. But I should give you one last chance to walk out of here with me. It will save you a lot of pain and trouble."

"I'm not going anywhere with you," I hissed.

"Oh, my sweet, Fiona." His tone was chiding. "You will. You have no idea of my power. You cannot escape me. I will take you, by force if necessary. But, I think you might come to me quite willingly to get back what you have lost."

"What the hell are you talking about? I haven't lost anything."

"Well, I suppose the proper wording would be what I've taken. But trust me; something you would like to protect isn't where you think it is. And once you realize it, you will come looking for her."

Her? My sisters' faces immediately flashed into my mind. But, Anya and River were safe upstairs, weren't they? Panic exploded in my stomach.

"Who do you have?" I screamed, but that eerie laugh echoed through the pub as every sign of life left Rangel, leaving Pinky and Jarrett holding on to a dry corpse.

Pinky and Jarrett lowered Rangel's body gently to the floor, and I fell to my knees, sobbing. Pinky came to rest next to me, his arm around me. I looked up at him, tears in my eyes.

"Pinky, he kept saying 'it', but then at the last he said 'her'... Anya? Or, River?" I barely had my sisters' names out of my mouth before Pinky was up the stairs and out of sight, using his vampire speed. I looked at Jarrett. "We need to call Sam and Ian."

"I'm on it," he said, pulling a porta-scry case from his pocket.

A few moments later, Pinky descended the stairs flanked by both of my sisters. I ran to them, holding them tight. They were safe. I had no idea who Bokor had taken, but my sisters were here and they were safe and right then, that was all that could matter.

Several minutes later, I was sitting on the stairs, flanked by my sisters, their arms around me, when I heard my name being called. I looked up to see Ian coming through the pub door. I shook my sisters off and ran across the room, flinging myself into his arms. "You are safe," I said to him, in a sob.

"Hey, hey. Isn't that what I'm supposed to say to you?" Ian said, gently, brushing strands of hair away from my damp face. "What happened?"

Before I could answer, Sam and two Blade Agents came barreling into the bar. Pinky pulled two tables together, pushing the wreckage of the other one out of the way. We all sat, and I told everyone what happened.

"Okay, you two," Sam said, nodding at the Blades. "Get a cart in here to get the body over to the morgue and call in the forensic mages. I doubt they will find anything they didn't on the other bodies, but we will try everything we can. Ian and I will head over to Rangel's place and see what we can find out."

"I'm going with you," I said.

"No!" Four male and two female voices rang out in unison. The only two that remained silent were the two Blade Agents that I was unfamiliar with.

"Bullshit!" I spat. I expected such treatment out of Pinky, Ian, and even Sam. All three of them tended to treat me like a delicate flower when they thought they could get away with it. But Jarrett and my sisters? They were always on my side. "I'll be damned if I'm going to stay here with my thumb up my ass while the 'boys' handle it!"

"Agent Moon." Sam's voice was hard. He never, ever, called me Agent Moon. Not even when he was super pissed at me. Intellectually, I knew he wasn't angry with me; he was worried. But that didn't stop the tiny shiver of fear and sorrow that went through me. "You were a target tonight. As was your family. You will remain here in a defensible environment and guard them. That is an order. Are we clear?"

Well crap! I hated it when he pulled rank, even if he was right. "Yes, sir." I nearly choked on the words.

"Jarrett, you've been guarding them this long, I'd like you to stay," he said, back to his normal tone.

"No problem," Jarrett said.

"And feel free to knock her out if you have to," he said, pointing at me. "I don't want her leaving this building until we are back."

Pinky answered Sam. "Don't worry, she won't leave." He gave me a pointed glare.

I looked at Ian. Though I got a look of sympathy, he agreed with the other three. "I know you are big, bad, and can take care of yourself. But this guy is a lunatic. You are a target. Besides, Sam is right. Your skills are best served here, protecting your sisters."

"Fine," I relented. I walked over to him and leaned in to whisper in his ear. "Please be careful; I can't lose you." I blinked back the sting of forming tears. The thought of having to watch him die like Rangel hurt so bad it nearly took my breath away.

And then, not giving a crap that we had an audience, and ignoring the giggles and snickers, I pulled him to me and kissed him hard and thoroughly.

TWENTY-EIGHT
Fiona

I SAT IN THE PUB, WHICH WAS ONCE AGAIN CLOSED DOWN AND LOSING A WHOLE night of business. This time because several chairs and two tables were demolished. Anya, River, Pinky, Jarrett, and I sat at the bar, trying not to discuss the day's events while we waited for Ian and Sam to return from Rangel's apartment. Jarrett was telling a story about his sailing days back before he was a vampire, and I was so entranced in the story of buccaneers that it took me a moment to realize there was a buzzing coming from the top pocket of my vest. I reached in and retrieved my portable-scry case, which was vibrating to let me know someone was trying to contact me. I popped open the case to reveal the flat, polished crystal inside as I stood and walked to the other side of the room for some privacy. It was more from a force of habit than because I didn't want the others to hear what was said. I touched my thumb to it to activate it, and Leesa Parks' face filled the screen.

"Leesa, what's up?" I asked, a bit surprised to see her. I had been expecting Ian or Sam with some news. I was about to tell her it wasn't a good time, when I saw the frantic look on her face. "What's wrong?"

"Fiona, have you seen Millie?"

"No, not since the day I stopped by your office. What's going on?"

Dread crept into my stomach.

"I'm not sure, but Millie is missing."

"Missing?" The dread in my stomach started to envelop my entire body. Bokor had said, *"You are missing something dear, and when you realize what it is, you will come to me to get it back."*

I forced myself to breath and not panic, walking back near the others so they could hear what Leesa said. I did my best to keep my voice and facial features calm, in an effort not to alarm Leesa. "Tell me everything that has happened. Why do you think Millie is missing?" Perhaps there was just some sort of misunderstanding and Millie was safe at home.

"Millie didn't show up for work yesterday. I figured she was sick. It would have been better if she had called, but I know her family doesn't own a scry-crystal, so I wasn't concerned. But then she didn't show up again today. I was starting to get a little worried, but still thought it might be a case of her skipping work to spend time with her friends. That doesn't seem like Millie, but I figured when she came back in, we'd have a talk about responsibility."

"No, that doesn't seem like Millie," I said. Though I had only met the girl a couple of times, she seemed very eager to work and improve her position, and that of her parents, in the world. I couldn't imagine her jeopardizing that for a few hours with friends.

Leesa continued, "But late this afternoon, just as I was getting ready to leave for the day, Millie's mother, Nancy Linton, came into the office, looking for Millie. Her classes start next week and she is working half days now. Millie usually goes home directly after work and when she was more than three hours late, Nancy got worried."

"If she always goes home right after work, why didn't her mother notice she was gone yesterday?" I asked.

"Apparently, Nancy had to work a late shift yesterday and she thought Millie was in bed when she got home. Millie's father always works the late shift and hardly ever sees his daughter. It was late—hours after Millie would have come in to work today, when the Lintons woke up. When I told Nancy that Millie hadn't come into work, I went back to their home with her. We checked Millie's room, and there was a pile of clean clothes on her bed that Nancy said she put there yesterday after doing the washing. That indicated Millie hadn't been home. That was when Nancy told me that a City Guard Inspector came to their apartment yesterday morning just as Millie was getting ready to leave for work. The inspector said he needed to ask a few more questions about the incident a couple of weeks ago and offered her a ride to work. She left with him."

My blood went icy, and I clutched the scry case to keep from dropping it. "Did Mrs. Linton catch the Guard Inspector's name?"

Leesa's eyes crinkled with concern. "It was GI Rangel. But, Fiona, that is why I'm calling you. Something is very wrong here. I'm at the City Guard headquarters right now, and they told me that GI Rangel has been out sick for several days. They told me that anything pertaining to his current case had to go through the Blade Agent in charge, which is you. Fiona, do you know where Millie is?" Her tone wasn't accusing, just concerned and curious.

"No, Leesa, I don't. Until this moment, I had no idea she was missing," I fumbled, trying to decided how much I could tell her, or even how much I should. "Rangel was working with me on the missing mages case. As far as we knew, he had taken a few days off sick. But, about two hours ago, we received information that he may have met with foul play." That was the understatement of the year. "Right now, Rangel is classified as missing. Sam has already dispatched half the Blades to look for him. No one had any idea he had been with Millie when he went missing. I will let Sam know about Millie. Getting her back safe will be the number-one priority."

Leesa's face was ashen. "I get the feeling there is something you aren't telling me. That's okay; I know the confidentiality drill. What do I tell the Lintons?"

I felt sorry for Leesa. She was not a field agent—not an agent at all in any real sense. She worked with crystals, not people. Telling a family their daughter was missing wasn't easy for anyone, but if you were untrained, it would be hell.

"Leesa, I can send a Blade over to fill them in. You don't even have to go back," I told her.

"Thank you, Fiona, but no. I owe it to Millie and to her parents to be there for them until she gets back. I'm a Blade, even if I spend my time in a room full of rocks. I can do this. Tell me what I can tell them."

"Okay," I said, admiring her determination. "You can tell them a shortened version of what I told you. That we just learned that Guard Inspector Rangel was abducted, but we did not know until just now that Millie was with him. Assure them that now that we do, finding her and returning her home safely is our number-one priority. Also, take a City Guard back with you. I will have Sam send two Blades over to replace him in a little while."

"Two? Fiona, are the Lintons in danger?"

"No, I don't think so. This is mostly for their comfort and because it is standard to have someone at the home of an abducted person in the case of ransom."

Leesa saw through my lie immediately and scoffed. "Ransom. Fiona, give it to me straight. The Lintons are dirt poor. They live in a slum apartment smaller than my office. Their rooms are little more than closets. There is no way there will be a ransom demand. I can't give them that line."

"Okay, there won't be a ransom demand. Millie was likely targeted because she thwarted the first attempt, which we think was random. This guy is deranged and unpredictable. It isn't out of the realm of possibility that he would try to hurt her parents just to hurt her more. But don't tell them that. Besides, I feel like they need to know we are working on the case. Their daughter is no less important than the daughter of a senator, ransom demand or not," I said.

"I'm sure they will appreciate that. But two agents?"

"I do realize two agents may seem like overkill, but trust me, it is a necessary precaution. Remember, one of the abducted persons is a very capable mage as well as a City Guard Inspector. I can't go into details, so please don't ask. Just trust me that two agents are necessary." It was unlikely Bokor had been able to abduct another Guard, or a Blade, in the short time since he'd left Rangel's body, but we still didn't know how he managed to insert his spirit into the bodies of the mages, so it was better to be safe. Having two guards was a precaution, just in case Bokor was able to take one of them over. I could just send a were or vamp, and perhaps I would, but even though only mages had gone missing, we had no real evidence Bokor couldn't take over other paranorms.

"Please find her," Leesa said, a tremor in her voice.

"I will Leesa, I swear." And I meant it. I would find her, and I would make the son-of-a-bitch that took her and killed Rangel pay, with his life if possible.

The moment the scry-crystal went blank, I collapsed. I barely registered the activity around me. Pinky rushing from behind the bar with vampire quickness to catch me before I hit the floor, lifting me into a chair Anya pulled out. Jarrett was standing in front of me with his own porta-scry held out as he repeated what Leesa had just told me to whoever was on the other end of the call. I heard Sam's voice, but I didn't catch the words.

"Fiona, are you listening?" Jarrett said, loudly. He leaned down so that his face was right in front of mine, grabbed my shoulders, and shook me lightly. "Do you know Millie Linton's address?"

"Uh, I, no. But it is in the files. Sam should have a copy of my report, but if not, the file is in the top right drawer of my desk," I said, the world slowly coming back into focus.

"Did you catch that?" Jarrett said into the crystal as he straightened and walked across the room. He was too far away now for me to hear his voice but after a few seconds, he snapped his scry case shut, shoved it in his back pocket, and came back to where I sat, my family hovering around me.

"Sam and Ian are at Rangel's apartment right now, still trying to find leads to where Bokor took him, or even how Bokor got a hold of him. Sam is sending two Blades over to the Linton home and will call in the City Guard to help canvas the city," he told me.

"They won't find them. We've been going over the city for days now. I've got to go..." I tried to stand, but Anya was standing behind me. She put both hands on my shoulders and pushed me back down.

"You've got to go nowhere, big sister," she said. "What you've got to do is sit there and get your bearings. You're so upset that you are vibrating. There's a whole battalion of Blades and Guards out looking for that little girl. They'll find her."

"She's right," Jarrett said, crouching in front of me again. "There are plenty of capable agents out there scouring the city. You need to sit tight here. He's after you, Fee. If you are out there in the mix, you will be a target, and a liability. If you were out there, the agents around you would be focusing on protecting you, not finding Millie. Use your head, Moon." His words were firm, harsh even, but his voice was so tender and understanding that it brought the tears I'd been holding back since the moment Leesa had said Millie was missing to the surface. My throat tightened, and I nearly choked.

"But he has her, Jarrett! I should have went with him, and now he has that sweet little girl and I don't know how to find her," I raged, frustration clogging my throat and making the words come out strangled.

"Fee, you couldn't go with him. You know that. He would have killed you, and there is no way you would have been able to save Millie." Jarrett took my hand and squeezed it gently.

He was right. I knew he was right. But every fiber in my being ached with the guilt of knowing that innocent young girl was out there, alone, with a lunatic. I might not have been able to save her if I'd went along with Bokor, but at least she wouldn't be alone.

"You're right. I know that. I just... I need to be alone for a bit, need to gather my thoughts," I said. What I needed to do was get out from under the pitying stares of my family. And, I needed some air.

"Oh, no you don't, young lady. I will put a keep-in spell on every door and window in this joint. You are not going out there. Didn't you hear what Jarrett said? You are this creep's main target," Pinky raged in his most fatherly tone, which could be quite comical coming out of his teenaged visage.

I couldn't help but smile, just a little. He knew me too well. But in truth, I hadn't meant to try to leave, I just needed to escape to somewhere less crowded. "I'm not going to go anywhere, Pinky. I swear. I just need to get some air. I'm going to go up to the garden. I won't sneak out." I held up my little finger and waggled it like I had done as a child. "Pinky-swear."

He smiled at me, grabbing my finger with his own and shaking it once. It was the most solemn promise in our family.

After hugging every member of my family, more for their peace of mind than mine, I climbed the stairs to the roof. Once I reached the mini-jungle River had created with plants and trees, the real weight of everything that had happened hit me hard enough to double me over. I sat on the ground under a potted apple tree and let the tears flow freely. My body shook, my stomach and heart hurt, and I wished, beyond anything else in the world, that Ian were there with me. But he was out working, doing his part to find the fiend that had murdered my friend and kidnapped an innocent girl, and it was selfish of me to wish for him to be there comforting me. So I sat there alone, bawling, hugging myself, and feeling completely miserable and sorry for myself.

I wasn't sure how long I sat there under the stars, surrounded by the exotic fragrances of River's plants and flowers, and engrossed in my thoughts, before Ian came up. An hour, perhaps two. I heard the roof door creak and, without looking, knew that it was Ian. River had already been up once to bring me a blanket and a pot of chamomile tea. She promised not to let anyone bother me until I was ready to come down. Like the pinky-swear, the rooftop sanctuary was sacred in our family. Pinky had always encouraged us to deal with our problems together, as a family. But it was understood that sometimes we needed a little alone time, so Rooftop Sanctuary had been created. Whenever any of us needed some time alone, we just went up to River's garden and shut the door. We were allowed up to four hours of complete alone time. The only person allowed to break Sanctuary was River, and that was because it would break her heart if she couldn't bring food, drink, and love to whichever one of us was hurting, angry, or confused.

I knew Ian wouldn't know, or care, about Sanctuary, and no one downstairs would be able to keep him from coming up to me, if they even dared to try. It was funny how I could be so sure about that after a few days of a relationship, but I did. Nothing would keep him from me tonight, not after everything that had happened today. He would want to comfort me, though I didn't think there was any comfort to be had.

I didn't move as he approached and sat beside me on the blanket I'd spread out across the dirty floor. He didn't touch me, just sat quietly next to me, as if waiting for me to either break the silence or give him a sign that I wanted him there or wanted him to leave. We sat like that, both of us watching the stars, for a long time before I finally spoke.

"Did you find anything useful at Rangel's apartment?" I asked, careful to keep my voice neutral, trying not to fall apart again.

"Unlike every other person that has been taken, it looks like he was taken right from his apartment. It looks like he opened the door to whoever it was, and then there was a struggle. Rangel is... was a big guy. There had to be at least two people. There was food on the counter that had gone bad, so we think he was taken several days ago. Probably the night before he scryed in sick."

"Were there any witnesses?"

"No. No one we talked to tonight heard the struggle. There could be a sound-deafening spell on the apartment; it's not uncommon. But agents will make another round of the building tomorrow to talk to people that weren't home today. I don't hold out much hope. Everyone seemed to know Rangel was City Guard. If anyone had witnessed anything, they would have reported it immediately."

"So, none of "your kind" of witnesses either?" I asked, stealing a glance at him.

He smiled a little at my joke. "None that could tell me anything substantial. Strangely, Rangel had an energy ward on his apartment."

I shrugged. "Not so strange. Rangel's grandmother—or was it mother—one of them was a clairvoyant. Energy wards don't just keep out spirits. They can't stop someone from having visions about you, but they can keep powerful seers from, well, seeing into somewhere you want to keep private. We have one, too."

He let out a small laugh. "I know—I can detect energy wards. I didn't really think it was odd; I just figured you and Pinky were paranoid."

I couldn't help but smile at him, though it hurt my cheeks. "Well, we are."

"Well, now I understand why Rangel had it. But back to your question. There is a very old spirit that lives in the building, and he remembers seeing two men guiding what looked to be a drunk man out of the building. But the spirit was very old and weak. I took a great deal of my own energy to be able to communicate with him. I suspect he died over five hundred years ago. Anyway, he remembers seeing something, but not when. I'm not sure that what he saw was Rangel. When a spirit gets that old and faded, mortal time doesn't really mean much to them anymore."

"So, we are no closer to finding that asshole than we were yesterday?" I spat.

"I'm afraid not. But forensic mages are combing the apartment and all the hallways. If there is any evidence, even a speck, they will find it," he said, and I knew he believed it. I believed it, too. At least I knew the Blades employed the most powerful mages in Appalachia. If there were anything to find, they would find it. But what if there was nothing to find? Even if there were, there was no proof it would be in time to do any good.

"We have to find Millie," I said, finally bringing up what we had both been shying around. "She's completely innocent in this, Ian."

"I know, honey. We'll find her." Finally, he put his arm around me, pulling to me up onto his lap so that he cradled me against his chest, his chin resting on my head.

The moment he touched me, something broke inside me. The tension that had been coiled in my stomach let loose. I didn't cry, I just kind of heaved, my breath coming in gasps as if I had been holding it in for hours. I sank against him, getting as close as I could, as if I just got close enough to him, he could fix everything, make every moment of the past day fade away and put everything to rights. When had this happened? When had he become my everything? My reason for being, for breathing? When had he slipped so far into the fiber of my being that I would never be rid of him?

He wrapped his arms around me, enveloping me in his warmth. "Shhh, baby, I'm here."

"Hold me," I said, sounding a little desperate. "Don't let me go."

"Don't worry; I'm not letting you go. I'm not going anywhere," he said into my hair.

It wasn't true, I knew. Eventually, he would have to let go. I would have to make him. We had jobs to do, and we couldn't do them hiding in a rooftop garden wrapped around each other. But for now, I needed this, needed him, more than I needed to breathe.

I turned my face up to him, our lips collided, and instantly the kiss turned hot and needy. Without pulling away, I turned my body so that I was straddling him. His hands slid around me, cupping my ass and pulling me close. I could feel the hot, hardening length of him pushing against my center, despite the layers of clothes. I pressed down against him, liquid heat welling up inside me.

As our mouths licked and tasted each other, I pushed his suspenders off his shoulders and pulled his shirt out of his pants almost frantically. Ian pulled back, breaking the kiss just long enough to help me pull the shirt over his head. He pulled me back to him, his hands working to free me of my own shirt as my hands roamed his bare torso. The muscles of his back flexed and worked under my hands.

Then, without me realizing how it happened, I was naked from the waist up and our bare skin was pressed together. His chest hair teased my nipples into tight, almost painful, little buds. I clutched at him, wanting to melt into him. "Ian, make love to me, please," I gasped out as he took one nipple into his mouth, grazing it with his teeth.

"No, now. Please, I need you inside me," I pleaded. Need vibrated through my body. I didn't want, or need, preliminaries. I needed him inside me, filling me, pushing out everything else but the feel of him, the feel of the two of us together.

"Shhh, honey. I want to make sure you are ready," he said, his face still pressed against my breast.

I pushed back from him, leaning up enough to unbutton my pants and push them down my hips. Grabbing his hand, I pushed it against the damp curls at the apex of my thighs. "I am ready," I gasped as his finger slipped into my slick, heated depths.

"Fiona." My name came out in a half growl as he pulled me down to him, recapturing my mouth with his, kissing me with the same needy urgency I felt. He maneuvered us until I was lying on the blanket and he was kneeling above me. He broke the kiss again and leaned up to pull my pants off. Then he stood and divested himself of his own boots and pants, kneeling back between my knees.

"Hmm, this ground is a little rough," he said, distractedly. Instead of settling between my legs as I wanted, he lay down beside me. But, before I could protest, he pulled me on top of him. "I don't want you to scrape up your back."

I barely registered the words as I slid across him, my sex finding his, almost instinctively. I rose up over him, and then slowly pushed down, until I had taken him all in. I savored the stretched, utterly full feeling for a moment before I began to rock against him.

"Fiona," Ian gasped again, pulling me down so that he could wrap his arms tight around me. I slid my hands up under his arms, clutching at his shoulders as we moved together. The frantic urgency of a moment before was gone. Now, we rocked together in a slow, steady rhythm, as if we both wanted to draw this moment out, make it last as long as possible. At least, that was what I wanted.

I wanted that moment to last forever. I wanted his arms around me, my body wrapped around his, the two of us joined with our bodies and our energies melding together. I wanted that for eternity.

But, nothing lasted forever. We rocked together like that, for a long time, the heat and tension building, until every fiber of my being cried out for release. I pushed up until I was over him again. Leaning back, I braced my hands on his thighs and began to move, harder and faster with every stroke. His hands slid up my thighs, over my belly, and cupped my breasts. He pulled and teased the nipples, causing me to cry out. Then, he let his hands roam again, down my sides to rest at my hips, grasping them as I rode him.

Ian pushed his hips up, meeting me with every thrust, until our breath was coming in ragged gasps. My body turned to fire, the place where our bodies joined the white-hot center. Every muscle tensed and coiled, every nerve burned, and I drove on, faster and harder, until finally, the last thread of sanity broke and white-hot light burst behind my eyes, pushing me off the cliff into a pool with wave after wave of pure pleasure. I felt rather than heard Ian's groan as he bucked under me, his hands digging into my hips as he thrust hard into me when his own climax rolled over him.

We lay there for a long time, quietly curled around each other, the night air cool against our heated skin, staring up at the stars while we caught our breath. "She abandoned me." The words came out of their own volition. It wasn't until they were out that I knew I needed to say them.

Ian's arms tightened around me. "Who?"

"My mother." I leaned my head back on his shoulder. I didn't look at him, just stared up at the endless sky as I poured out my heart, breaking down the final barrier between us. Breaking it down so that he could understand the truth that I'd come to realize while I sat up here alone tonight. The truth that making love with him had only reinforced. "Oh, she didn't drop me off on Pinky's doorstep and leave, not exactly. It might have been better if she had. She died when I was eight, but I really lost her when my father died."

We sat there in silence for a long moment and when Ian didn't comment, I kept going, knowing he was listening intently. "My mother was obsessed with my father. She couldn't let him go. She couldn't accept his death, and she refused to stop looking for his killer. Right after his funeral, she left the home we'd shared with him and brought me here, to Pinky's. Then she joined the Blades. She started going to necromancers, both for leads on my father's killers and to contact him.

"She became obsessed. Blades make decent money, but she spent every spare buck she got on necromancers. She was hardly home, and when she was, she spent her days lying in bed crying. If it weren't for Pinky, I would have starved, or worse. At the end, she'd been going to the same necromancer for almost a year on a nearly daily basis. The information the necromancer gave her had been getting progressively more accurate. Mom was sure she was getting closer and closer to the killer, and she owed it all to the necromancer who had been channeling my father.

"The last bit of information the necromancer gave her led her straight to leader of the smuggling ring that had killed my father. He was waiting for her." I paused.

"It was a trap?" Ian asked, his voice quiet.

"Yes. The so-called necromancer my mother had been relying on for months was a fraud. She'd actually been the girlfriend of one of the smugglers. They'd gotten wind of my mother and decided to take care of her. The woman had faked everything, pulled my mother in with her lies, and then sent her into a trap. In the end, though, my mother got her way. She died, but she killed them first." My mouth quirked in a sad, half smile.

Ian cupped his hand under my chin and turned my face towards him so that he could brush his lips against my forehead. "That's why you hate necromancers."

"Yes. No. Well, yes, it was." I tripped over my own words, not quite sure how to say what I was thinking and feeling. "I spent most of my life believing that if it hadn't been for the fake necromancer who cheated her, my mother would alive and here with me. But I was wrong. Oh, it's possible she would be alive, but she wouldn't be here with me. She hadn't been with me since the day my father died, not even when we had been in the same room together."

"I'm so sorry." Ian's voice was tender and full of emotion.

The tears that had been too stubborn to fall began streaming down my cheeks. "There is nothing for you to be sorry about. I'm sorry. I've been holding a grudge against you and an entire group of people for something no one had control over but my mother."

"I'm sorry that happened to you. I'm sorry you needed your mother and she wasn't there for you. I'm sorry I can't take away that pain." He kissed me again, this time our lips melting together in a passion so sweet and tender that it made my tears flow harder. I gasped and pulled away.

"Fiona, I love you and I promise…"

"No," I cut him off. "I can't." My heart thudded so hard in my chest that I was afraid it would explode any second. I pushed away from him and fumbled for my clothes.

"I'm sorry; this probably wasn't the best time to say that." Ian's voice was husky with regret.

I turned to him, my heart in my throat. "Don't you understand? There will never be a good time. I didn't tell you that to make you feel sorry for me or love me. I told you so that you could understand why I can't love you. Not like that." *I can't be like my mother.* The last sentence was spoken only in my head. I couldn't lose myself to him. Oh, but I could. I so easily could. I already had. But it had to stop.

"You don't love me?" His voice was thick with confusion and irritation.

"No, I can't," I nearly screamed. Why was he being so fucking calm when I felt like I was coming apart at the seams?

"Can't or won't?" His voice was hard.

"Does it matter? Ian, there is a sixteen-year-old girl out there alone and afraid, needing me to find her, and I'm up here lying under the stars, fucking you. I need to focus, and I can't. Perhaps if I had my head more on work and less on you, we would have found Bokor by now. Rangel would still be alive, and Millie would be at home safe with her family." I pulled my pants and shirt on, feeling a little braver fully clothed.

Ian pulled on his pants and stood across from me, his arms crossed over his bare chest. "I see, so you stopped blaming me for your mother's death so you can blame me for Rangel's death and Millie's kidnapping?"

"No, that's just it. I don't blame you. I blame myself. I'm too much like my mother. I let myself get so wrapped up in you that I failed to do my job. If I had been more focused, I would have caught on to Bokor's game in time to save Rangel. I should have realized Millie would be a target, I should have protected her." I couldn't quit sobbing, which pissed me off and made me cry harder.

"And who died and made you queen of the world?" Ian's voice was calm and steady.

"What?"

"I was just wondering when you became the omniscient ruler of Earth? When did the welfare of the entire population become your responsibility? When did your clairvoyant powers kick in? When did the world start revolving around you?"

Had he lost his mind? "Don't be a jerk. I know the world doesn't revolve around me."

"Do you? Because you seem to want to take responsibility for every bad thing that has happened. So you either came into some sort of powers that would make it possible for you to have prevented them, or you are incredibly arrogant. Or perhaps you are just scared." His tone was ice.

"Of course I'm scared. Millie could die," I said, wiping my eyes with the back of my hand.

"That's not what you are scared of. You say you don't want to be like your mother. You don't want to love me because I make you lose your focus. That caring about me makes you not able to do your job. But that is a load of crap. You aren't afraid of being like your mother. You are afraid I'll be like your mother," he said, sneering.

I wanted to protest, but he kept going.

"You already love me, but you don't want to because you think I'll leave you like she did. You think if you push me away now, it won't hurt as much as it would if I leave you later."

"Yeah, who's being arrogant now?" I shot back at him, not wanting him to know how close to the truth he was. "You are right about one thing. I am afraid. But not of you, Master Necromancer." I spat the last two words out like they tasted bad in my mouth. "I'm afraid because people are dead, and still more are missing. It is my job to stop this monster before more innocent people are abducted or killed." My voice had reached near-screeching pitch, but I couldn't seem to get it under control.

"It's not your job to save the whole world on your own. It's not even your job to save Millie alone. There is an entire team working to find her. And there's me. I'm your partner, Fiona." His voice was quiet, but hard as steel. He took a step towards me, but I stepped back, ramming my spine against the wooden workbench.

"You are right; you are my partner," I yelled, clenching my teeth against the pain in my back. "So, act like it and get to work. You've had your head stuck up my ass for days, when you could have been out doing something, anything, to find this creep. Instead, you've been too busy playing touchy-feely with me."

"That's crap, and you know it." He was shouting now, almost as loud as I was. "This asshole is coming for you, Fiona. For whatever reason, he has you in his sights. I was ordered, by Sam, to stick to you, to protect you. You know that what's between us has not affected my job performance. And since your memory of how things have been going down the past few days seems a little blurry, let me remind you that you came to me. You showed up at my home in the middle of the night, looking for a fuck."

I took a deep breath and forced my voice back into a calm, steady tone, despite the fact that I couldn't stop shaking. "You're right. I showed up looking for a fuck. A fuck, Barroes, not love." I saw him flinch at my words, but I didn't stop. I couldn't. "I'm a big girl, and I can take care of myself. Jarrett and Pinky are here to protect my sisters. You aren't needed here. Go home. I'll scry Sam tomorrow and ask him to assign us new partners. We need every person we can get on this case."

He bent to pick up his boots and shirt, but he didn't make a move to go.

"Leave."

"Fiona." His voice was soft again, full of defeat. "Don't do this."

"I said get out." Even I could hear the tremble in my voice. I turned away from him so he couldn't see the tears that had started falling again.

We stood like that, in complete silence, for several minutes, though it felt like hours to me. Finally, I heard the creak of the rooftop door opening, and then Ian's voice, "This isn't over."

I wasn't sure if he meant the fight, our partnership, or whatever else was between us. It didn't matter.

"Yes. It is."

June Stevens

The door swung shut, and a bone-deep loneliness settled over me. It was over.

TWENTY-NINE
Fiona

A NARROW PATH RAN AROUND THE TOP EDGE OF THE BUILDING, BETWEEN THE three-foot-high lip where River's jungle of trees and plants started. I paced it now. I'd gone down earlier, about half an hour after Ian left. My face had been fresh scrubbed of tears, and I plastered on a half smile as I let River, Anya, and Pinky fuss over me. I had dinner with them and Jarrett, as had been planned before the world had fallen apart. They tried to keep the conversation light, only once asking why Ian hadn't stayed for dinner. I told them he had work to do, and no one questioned it, though Jarrett gave me a raised eyebrow look.

River went to sleep, and Jarrett, Anya, and Pinky were downstairs in the pub, now clear of the aftermath of today's fight, playing cards, doing their best to enjoy a forced night off, despite the circumstances. I was on the roof, alone, walking miles around the building because I couldn't sleep.

Actually, I hadn't even tried to sleep. I'd taken one look at my empty bed and fled back to the garden. But once up here, I couldn't force myself to go in, to walk among the flowers, vegetables, and trees. Couldn't bring myself to sit in my favorite spot. I would probably never be able to sit beneath the apple trees again, not after making love with Ian there. Not after ripping him from my life there.

So I spent my evening between the ugly concrete wall that marked the edge of the building and the lush garden that made it more than just a roof. For what might have been hours, I walked and stared out over the city at the lights of candles, hearth fires, and crystal lanterns flickering like hundreds of fireflies. Somewhere out there, Millie Linton was fighting for her life. Maybe, just maybe, Farah Purcell was still alive and doing the same. And there I stood, in safety and comfort, utterly useless. I felt so completely powerless.

I hated that feeling, I hated it because it made me feel like I was five years old again, watching my mother as she lay in her bed in our apartment over Pinky's Pub, crying herself to sleep over my father, who had already been gone so many years I didn't even remember him. But she did, and she wept every night she was home, with such complete desperation and sorrow that I would tiptoe into her room, crawl onto the narrow bed with her, pat her on the back, and say, "It's okay, Mommy, I'm here." But she would pull away from me, curling into a ball, and scream at me in her tear-roughened voice to go to bed. And so I would, and I would sit there in the center of my bed, my knees hugged to my chest, listening to my mother sob, feeling alone and helpless, waiting for dawn. When dawn came, Pinky would close up the bar and go to bed. I would sneak down to his room and though I knew he only pretended not to hear me, he never sent me away when I crawled onto the foot of his bed, curled up at his back, and fell asleep.

I pushed the memory, and the sick feeling it invoked, out of my head and refocused my gaze on the quiet of the city. Well, it was quiet from up here, but not down in the streets. Even at this hour, people milled around, shopping or going to bars, or whatever they did. The night was the time of the vampires, the only time they could do the normal things everyone else did during the day. So, while in the outer edges of the city and off towards New Nashville lights started blinking out and settling down for the night, the streets right below me were bustling and bright with life and laughter.

I had always loved that strange contrast. All the streetlights and cook fires burning in the inner city, slowly fading out as you looked further out towards the wall. From my vantage point, I could just see the outline of the city wall. The Guards pacing their watch along it were tiny dots in the distance, backlit by the bonfires beyond the walls, which added another element to the beautiful contrast. Unlike the small fires flickering from inside windows or from rooftop or sidewalk fire-pits in the city, huge outdoor bonfires raged every night out past the wall.

Dozens of small communities existed in the few miles beyond the city, close enough for the inhabitants to work or trade in the city, but still live free of Nash laws, as well as Nash protection. Most of the little villages out there, consisting of anywhere from twenty to a hundred people, built huge bonfires at night for communal food cooking and for warmth. Up close, those communities were sad and dangerous, most home to gangs and outlaws, but from afar, their fires were like fireflies twinkling against the black velvet night. The sight always calmed me.

Oh, fuck. I was so incredibly stupid. The outlying villages were mostly home to gangs of thugs and outlaws. Of course! We'd searched the entire city and found nothing, because maybe, just maybe, Bokor's hideout wasn't in the city. The city gates were closed at twilight every night and few were let in, but anyone would be let out. If someone came into the city during the day, getting back out at night would not be a problem. I still didn't have a clue as to how he was getting the mages out of the city unseen, but I was suddenly positive that he was.

I ran downstairs, to the apartment. It was, as I had expected, empty except for River, who was quietly snoring in her room. I was as quiet as possible as I jotted down a note where I was going and headed out. I stopped in the back room and grabbed my cloak and hanbo, then quietly snuck out, releasing, then reinstating, the alarm wards on the back door as I slipped through it. Once outside, I paused for a breath. No screeching sirens sounded behind me. Pinky hadn't made good on his threat to set a keep-in spell. Of course, why would he? I had pinky-sworn not to sneak out. A wave of guilt rocked me in my boots, but I stood firm. There was no sense in getting everyone excited over this lead until I had something solid to go on. Besides, if I told them I needed to go out and why, Pinky would insist Jarrett go with me. That would leave my family unprotected. I was not prepared to do that. So, I snuck out, and hoped Pinky would be able to forgive me for breaking his trust.

I banged on the heavy door as hard as I could with my fist. "Carly, Matt, are you in there?" Though it had seemed like days had passed since my confrontation with Bokor, it was only ten pm. Way too early for Matt and Carly to be asleep. Perhaps they were out. I banged on the door one more time.

I heard the thud of boot-clad feet racing then the door was jerked open. Mateo and Carly Corsini stood in the opening, their eyes wide with alarm. "Are you okay? Are you hurt?" Matt asked as the door swung open, his eyes darting behind me, looking for trouble.

"I'm fine. I just need to get into the archives. You didn't hear me when I knocked at the front doors, so I came around to your private entrance," I said. They gave me blank stares, and I finally realized what they were wearing. Mateo had on a pair of pants, the top button still undone. His boots were unlaced, as if he'd just stuck his feet in them and ran. Carly was wrapped in a blanket, her hair wild. I hadn't expected to wake them; it was early by vamp standards. But then, they hadn't been sleeping. "Oh, crap. Oh, Carly, Matt, I'm so sorry. I wasn't thinking. I started to call on my way over here, but I left my scry-crystal at home. I wouldn't disturb you if it weren't extremely important. I swear."

Behind Matt, Carly's eyes softened. "Is it about the case you and Ian have been working on?"

"Yes. I think I might finally have a breakthrough on a location, but I need to take another look at that pre-Cataclysm list of churches and the maps. I would have waited until morning, but he's taken another girl, and he's killed a City Guard. I want this guy."

"We heard about Marcus," Mateo said, referring to Rangel by his little-used first name. He stepped back. "Come in. I'll take you to the map room while Carly gets dressed. She'll probably be more help to you in the actual research, though, since she lived in Nashville before the Cataclysm."

"I'll be right there," Carly called over her shoulder, already making her way into the depths of their apartment to get changed.

I followed Matt into the room where they kept old maps and other historical images. Mat went to a large, metal cabinet and pulled two ancient maps out of a drawer. He carefully unrolled them and laid the out, side by side, on the table in the center of the room. One was a street map of Nashville, circa 2012, the year before the Cataclysm started. The other was the same map, but with the city wall, gates, and other modern landmarks drawn in.

By the time Mateo had the maps set up, Carly had joined us. In her hands, she had a huge old book with extremely thin, yellow pages. "Okay, this should have what you are looking for listed. What exactly are you looking for? I think we covered every religious setting in the city."

"Within the walls of the current city, yes. But I think he is taking the mages outside the walls. What I'm looking for is somewhere of spiritual or religious significance somewhere in the O.Z., but still a part of the original city of Nashville."

"Holy smokes, Fee," Mateo exclaimed. "Do you know how big Nashville was?"

"Not to mention the number of churches?" Carly added.

"I know. Well, I don't know the number of churches, but considering the number there were just inside the walls, I can imagine. I know Nashville was huge. But, I think I can narrow it down," I said, sounding more confident than I felt. All I really had was a hunch, a feeling. Nothing solid to go on. This could just be a wild goose chase.

"Okay, I'm up for the challenge," Carly said, settling down in a chair at the table so that the maps were on either side of the huge book. She flipped it open until it said "Churches" on the top corner of the page. "Okay, give me your criteria."

I sat in the chair opposite her. Mateo still stood, leaning against the metal cabinet. "The first criteria is that it has to be within a couple of miles of the walls. I can't imagine he would be traveling very far with an unconscious mage. Whatever drugs he is using would have to wear off eventually."

"Okay. But that still leaves us with a pretty wide area, if we don't even know what general direction he's going in," replied Carly.

I shook my head. "No, still no witnesses. This is all pure speculation on my part, so no idea of direction. But, it needs to be a significantly large structure."

"Why?" Mateo asked.

"For one, it needs to be still standing. But mostly, and I thought of this on the way over, it needs to look religious or spiritual. I realized we are finding old religious spots by using the archives."

"Which he doesn't have access to," Carly chimed in, catching on to my train of thought.

"Exactly. So, it needs to be a structure that is still standing that looks religious. I also realized it might not actually be a church. I can't imagine that there are many still upright in the O.Z."

"No, there aren't many pre-Cataclysm buildings standing at all, at least not in the few miles surrounding the city. Those that weren't demolished by war, weather, and earthquakes were taken down during the reconstruction, to help nature reclaim some territory and make it friendlier to animals," Mateo informed us.

"It could be a cemetery, or a statue. There could be a more-modern structure built near it, or there is still the possibility that he is a part of a gypsy tribe," I said.

Carly began to flip through the book she'd brought in with her and we were all quiet, the tension thick in the room. After a few minutes, Carly leaned back in her chair, her face scrunched in concentration. "Wait a minute. You said possibly a statue? So it doesn't have to be a particular type of religion? Just has to seem to be religious or spiritual?"

"Yes. We don't think this guy is a vampire, so the likelihood of him having a strong grasp of pre-Cataclysm religion is pretty slim. It is more likely that he has adopted somewhere that he thinks is of spiritual significance as his home base. Which is why I'm thinking cemetery," I told her.

"I think I have an idea of the place we are looking for," she said. "It's not a cemetery. It isn't even a place of religious meaning or worship, at least not in the 21st Century. It was actually a part of a park. It is a replica of an ancient religious site on the other side of the world. Even then, the religion hadn't actually been practiced on a wide scale for thousands of years. But, I do think it would seem, to someone born after the Cataclysm, as somewhere sacred."

"That sounds like the place," I said.

"Hang on," Carly said and ran out the door. In a few minutes, she returned with several small, colorful booklets and papers. "This is where you are going," she said, handing me the papers.

While Carly filled me in on the basic layout of the building, Mateo drew a rough map from the closest city gate to the approximate area of the building.

"This was once a park," Carly said. "But, that was two hundred years ago. I have no idea what it's like there now. It could be that the building is in ruins or so covered up by vegetation that it hasn't had eyes laid on it in centuries."

I sighed. "That's a chance I'll have to take. At this point, I'll take any lead we can get."

I stepped out of the library and stood there for a moment, trying to decide where to go. Ian was still, technically, my partner, so I should go to him with the information I had just learned, first. But I wasn't sure

I was ready to be alone with him and after our conversation earlier, he might not even allow me in his building. The better thing to do would be to go to Headquarters and call Sam in. Then Sam could call Ian, along with the rest of the team. I had no doubt we could assemble a full assault team within a couple of hours. Nor did I doubt that he would, even when the information, the entire operation, was based on a hunch. But, it was better than spinning our wheels.

I laughed out loud. What a funny expression. I had heard it often and used it just as often, but I had no idea where it came from.

I shook my head to clear it. *Okay, on to the Blades building*, I thought. I started jogging along the quiet road, touching my hand to my thigh pocket again. I couldn't believe I had forgotten my scry-crystal. If I had it, I could call Sam now and he would get to the headquarters building shortly after me.

A rickshaw for hire ambled up the street towards me, which seemed odd considering the part of town we were in. Despite the bustle of Broadway a couple of blocks over, this part of town was quiet and deserted at this time of night. The driver stopped a few feet away and called to me, "Can I offer you a ride?"

I stopped jogging for a minute, considering. A cool breeze blew, so it was a good night for a run. Perhaps my mind would be a little clearer by the time I'd ran the few blocks between the library building and Headquarters. Besides, he was going the wrong way. By the time he went around the block, I would be almost to my destination, even at a slow, jogging pace. "No thanks," I called back and resumed my run.

I ran about another block, when I felt a sharp pain in the side of my neck. I stopped running, my hand flying to my neck. Something long was protruding out. I pulled on it, and it came out in my hand. Suddenly, the world was spinning. I stared at the object in my hand, blinking my eyes to try to clear my blurry vision. It was a feather. Why did I have a feather in my neck? Fog rolled in on my brain, but I fought for control. No, not a feather. It had a feather on it, but it was a dart. Someone had shot me with a dart. I tried to turn my head to see who could have done it, but I couldn't. I realized everything felt numb; I couldn't move my legs or even wiggle my fingers. Then, suddenly, the ground rushed up to meet me as my body crumpled. I landed on the concrete sidewalk cheek first, and my last blurry thought was, "Thank goodness I can't feel anything." Then, everything went dark.

THIRTY
Ian

IAN STARED UP AT THE CEILING AND TRIED NOT TO NOTICE HOW BIG AND EMPTY his bed felt without Fiona in it. It was strange how before he'd had her in it, the bed had been a soft, cozy place to rest. Now it was just a cold, flat place to lie down while he didn't sleep. Not that he'd gotten a lot of sleep over the past week. But, staying up half the night talking and making love to Fiona had been well worth the weariness the next day.

Now, all he could do was stare at the ceiling with bleary eyes and play their last conversation back in his head, over and over. He couldn't believe he had lost her. No, he refused to believe it. He was certain that though she may have meant everything she said when she said it… her motivations had been fear, weariness, and stress. Besides, she'd said she *couldn't* love him, not that she didn't love him. There was a very distinct difference. He would give her time and space, but he wouldn't give up on her. Not just yet.

She was hurting, and what he really wanted to do was hold her and comfort her, then go kick the ass of everyone and everything that had ever caused her pain. But all he could do was take a step back. He would do as she asked, get another partner on this case, and continue to try to find

Millie and the other missing mages. And when it was all over, he would go to her and try to sort things out... if he didn't die from the hole in his heart first.

With a sigh, Ian heaved himself out of bed and stumbled across the room to pour a stiff drink. It wasn't the first time he'd had to drink himself to sleep over Fiona Moon, and he doubted it would be the last. As he raised the whiskey to his lips, his large, wall-mounted scry-crystal began to buzz and pulse with color.

It was very late. Maybe it was Fiona. He half dropped the glass onto the table, whiskey sloshing over the side, and rushed to his desk. He waved his hand over the crystal to activate it, but when the fog cleared, it was Jarrett Campbell's face he saw, not Fiona's.

Ian scowled. "Campbell," he said, by way of greeting.

"Barroes." Jarrett returned the greeting. "I'm sorry to bother you so late, but Fiona left her scry-crystal here and I need to speak with her. We have a bit of a situation."

Confusion, and then fear washed over Ian. "Jarrett, Fiona isn't here. Why isn't she there? What the hell is going on?"

In the crystal, Jarrett went rigid. "I don't know. About half an hour ago, River woke up, terrified, from a dream. She's convinced it was a vision. She isn't completely coherent yet, but she refuses to go back to bed until she speaks to Fiona. We went up to her room, but she wasn't there. Her scry-crystal is on her dresser. She left a note saying she went to the library. But I just scryed the Corsinis and Mateo said she was there, but left just under three hours ago. I figured she would be with you."

"I'll be there in ten minutes," Ian snapped, slapping his hand across the crystal and cutting the connection before Jarrett could say anything. Clad in just his pants, he stuck his feet in his boots, leaving them unlaced. Grabbing his shirt, vest, and his rarely worn sword, he headed out the door, dressing as he went.

Ian's guard, Daniels, drove the rickshaw at breakneck speed while Ian sat in the back, dressing and peering out along the side of the road for any sign of Fiona. When Ian entered the pub, it was full of people. River and Anya sat side by side in two chairs pulled together. River was leaning against Anya, her head on her older sister's shoulder as Anya hugged and soothed her. Carly Corsini sat at the table on the other side of River, one of River's hands in hers, speaking in low tones.

Mateo and Pinky were at the bar, bent over a piece of paper, and Jarrett paced the far side of the room, speaking into his scry-crystal. "Okay," he said, and then snapped the crystal closed. He looked up and started walking toward Ian. "That was Sam. He's headed into Headquarters to start gathering a team for a search."

"A search? What the hell is going on?" Ian bellowed.

"We aren't sure, but we think Fiona went after Bokor, alone."

"What? How? She wouldn't even know where to look. Where would she have gone?"

Carly cleared her throat. "We think she went to the Parthenon."

Ian searched his memory for the word but came up blank. "What is that? Where?"

"It's a pre-Cataclysm building that was once a part of a park. It's a couple of miles outside the city walls," Carly told him.

"Okay, can someone start from the beginning?" Ian said, his irritation rising. Nothing they said made any sense.

Carly and Mateo recounted their conversation with Fiona. "When Jarrett called looking for her, I was afraid something had happened, so I redrew the map I gave her and brought it over," Mateo finished up the tale.

"Why didn't you go with her?" Ian raged.

"Hey, man." Mateo held up his hand. "I thought she was headed to Blade Headquarters to assemble an assault team. That is what she said she was going to do. I had no idea there had been a threat on her life, or I never would have let her go alone."

"It's true; she said she was going to the headquarters building," Carly reinforced.

"But she either changed her mind or didn't make it there," Ian said, suddenly very sure Fiona hadn't went after Bokor by herself. Despite her sense of responsibility for Millie, Fiona was too smart to put them both in danger by rushing in unprepared. "My money is on she didn't make it there. River, you had a vision?"

"Yes," she said, her face tear stained, and her voice creaky. "But it was just flashes. I saw Fiona; her eyes were closed. Her wrists were in chains. It was dark. I couldn't really see."

Fear gripped Ian so hard he could hardly breathe. "Was she hurt? Who else was there? Damn it, River. Is she alive?" His voice rose with every word.

"I don't know. I don't know." River dissolved into a fit of sobs.

Before Ian could blink, Pinky was in front of him. The man's nostrils flared and his eyes were wide with rage, but his voice was icily quiet. "Ian,

I know you are worried about Fiona, and that is the only reason your heart is on the inside of your chest right now. You need to take your voice down a notch. If I ever hear you speak to River, or any of my daughters, in that tone again, I will break every bone in your body before I rip out your throat."

Ian took a step back. For all that he looked like a harmless kid and had the easiest-going demeanor Ian had ever seen, the scrawny vampire was not someone Ian wanted angry with him. "I'm sorry," he said, meaning it.

"I know," Pinky said, clapping Ian on the shoulder. His normal tone of voice returned. "And I suppose I should take back some of that promise. I can't really blame you if you use that tone on Fiona once in a while; I think we all do. She kind of brings it out in a person."

"No need to worry about that," Ian replied. "She'll break my bones herself if I get out of line."

Pinky laughed. "That's true. Try to remember that. My little girl is tough as nails. She'll get through this."

Ian nodded, then walked over to River and knelt beside her chair. "River," he said, softly. "I'm sorry I yelled at you. I'm just frightened. Forgive me?"

River gave him a shaky smile through a wall of tears. "It's okay," she said, her voice tremulous. Then she leaned over and whispered into his ear. "You love her."

Ian kissed River's cheek. "I do. Try not to worry. I'll find her and bring her back, I promise."

River smiled again, this time a little more brightly. "I know."

"We should head over to the headquarters building; Sam said he would have the team ready to leave in an hour," Jarrett said.

Ian rose. "Mateo, you have the map. Can you draw another one?"

"Yes, from memory at this point. Why?"

"I'm taking that map, so can you go draw another one for Sam and make sure they get to the right place?"

"No problem. I have a general idea of where the place is, so I'll go with them."

Carly looked like she was going to protest, but then just nodded at her husband.

"Ian, you can't be meaning to go after her alone. Isn't that what landed Fiona in trouble?" Anya said.

"She didn't go off by herself. She wouldn't. She is too damned smart for that. I think Bokor got her some other way. He's already had her three hours. I can't sit around and wait another one while everyone gets ready. I'm going now," he said, determined.

"He's right. She is too smart for that," Jarrett agreed. "I'm coming with you." Going to the back room, he returned with a heavy, black cloak and a sword. He slid the sword into the scabbard at his waist.

"It may be well past dawn before we return," Ian said.

Jarrett grinned and held up the cloak. "That's what this for."

"Let's go," Pinky said, a cloak in his hand.

"Pinky, I've heard the stories, man. I know you can hold your own in a fight, which is why you need to stay here." He cut his eyes to River and Anya as they talked to Carly and back to Pinky. "I know Anya can protect herself and River, but she is no match against this guy if he comes back here."

Pinky sighed and tossed the cloak over a chair. "You are right. You just make sure you bring my little girl back to me," he said to both Ian and Jarrett, his voice hard. "If you don't, you may not want to come back yourselves."

"Understood," Ian said. If he couldn't bring Fiona home safe and sound, he would welcome Pinky's rage.

Ian and Jarrett went to the Blade Headquarters building first, but not to join the assembling team. They didn't even go upstairs. Instead, they went into the stables to get horses. "Wait a minute," Ian said, as a groom was on his way to saddle a horse for him. "Is Fiona Moon's horse here?"

"Mal?" asked the groom. "Yes. But he won't let you ride him; he won't even let any of us gear him up."

"You were right," Jarrett said. "She doesn't go anywhere outside the city without Mal. Ever."

"I was afraid of that," Ian replied. To the groom, he said, "Take me to him. He'll let me ride him."

They reached the stall, and the groom stood back as Ian entered. Mal snorted and pranced, not at all happy with the intrusion. Ian walked right up to the horse, running his hand over his nose. "Remember me?" he asked.

Mal snorted.

"Fiona is in trouble. She is missing, and I need you to help me find her. Do you understand?"

Snort. Stomp.

"I need you to let the groom get you all saddled up so I can ride you. Then we are going to go find Fiona and bring her home. Okay?"

Mal snorted and bobbed his head, turning to look at the groom expectantly.

Ten minutes later, the two men rode out of the stables, Jarrett on his horse, Davidson, and Ian on Mal.

THIRTY-ONE
Fiona

*E*verything hurt. My face throbbed, my arms screamed, every part of me ached. I tried to open my eyes, but even my eyelids hurt, so I kept them closed. Fog swirled in my brain. What happened? I was at the library, but where was I now?

Something tickled my face, and I realized it was my own hair. I tried to bring my hand to my face to push the hair away, but when I did, my arm wouldn't move. I tugged harder and a sharp pain shot through my wrist, radiating down my arm. I tried the other arm and got the same result. What the fuck?

I forced my eyes open, but for a moment, I could see nothing. Everything was a mass of dark blurs. Slowly, my eyes began to focus. Little pinpricks of light appeared, and then grew, until finally, my eyes cleared, but all I could see was a dirty floor littered with… Oh, crap! Were those bones? I jerked my head up and instantly regretted it. Pain sliced through my head, sending a wave of nausea into my stomach. My body jerked, but I couldn't move. Slamming my eyes shut, I took deep breaths to keep the dizziness at bay, but the putrid stench of the air around me made my stomach lurch even more. I gagged, and then coughed, trying not to puke my guts up.

"Ahh, it seems our guest of honor is waking up, Amos," said a creepy, high-pitched, nasal voice. "Check her restraints and the amulet. We don't want a repeat of what happened with our last visitor."

"Yes, My Lord," came another voice.

I opened my eyes again, just in time to see a thin man with stringy, brown hair dressed in a shapeless, gray robe walk towards me. Amos, apparently. My gaze followed him, still not able to completely focus, as he reached up and checked the iron shackles at my wrists. *Iron. Damn.* That would make pulling energy hard, but not impossible. But wait, the voice said, "and amulet". As I thought it, Amos reached towards me. I looked down to see him grasp a large crystal wrapped in wire strung on a length of leather that hung between my breasts. He tugged it once, and then let it go.

"She is secure," Amos said, backing away from me.

Unfortunately, he was right. There was no doubt in my mind the crystal around my neck was charged with a null spell, like the one I used on mages for transport. *Damn.*

My vision was clear now, and I could see the world around me. I immediately wished I couldn't. I was in the largest room I'd ever seen before in my life. It was dark, only dimly lit by torches attached to large, crumbling stone columns that lined the cavernous room. I was chained to one such column. Across from me was a row of cages. Some of the cages were empty, but some were inhabited by people. From the sounds coming behind me, there were more cages behind me, and they were also occupied.

My head swam. How many were here? How many had been here? I scanned the room, taking in the grisly scenery. Bones littered the floor, like cast-off trash, but I couldn't tell if they were human or animal. I could tell that the skeletons hanging from the columns and propped up in various positions around the room were all human.

"How do you like my temple?" the nasal voice asked.

Temple? I had already figured out this was Bokor's lair, I mean, why else would I be hanging here like human piñata? But, now that he said the word, I could really see that was what it was. It was set up as some sort of strange place of worship. I was chained, my arms spread out above me, my legs bound together, and my back against a stone column, about halfway between the two ends of the room.

One end was empty, save the tallest double doors I'd ever seen. A massive statue stood on the other end. It was cracked and huge chunks were gone, but I could tell it was a woman. Her long, flowing dress and elaborate headdress were flaked with large spots of dull gold, as if they had once been painted that color. A huge disc was leaning against one leg; the top of it was broken, as was her arm. She'd apparently been holding the disk, a shield, I thought. The top of a thin spear was attached to her shoulder, but the base of it was broken and gone. The other arm was bent at the elbow, extended outward, but also broken off between the elbow and wrist. This woman was a warrior, that much I knew.

The warrior woman stood on a huge, rectangular stone base. Around her feet and around the bottom of the base were more skeletons. They were spaced out, leaning against the stone. Dozens of skulls filled with flickering tallow candles cast an eerie glow.

"My Goddess is beautiful, is she not?"

My attention was caught again by the nasal voice that seemed to echo throughout the huge room, and I realized its point of origin was right next to the warrior statue. I blinked, trying to adjust to the dim light.

"Goddess? I'm having a hard time seeing," I said, making my voice sound as weak as possible, which really meant I talked with as much strength as I had. I vaguely remembered a feathered dart between my fingers.

This asshole had drugged me.

"Bring more torches," the voice called. Instantly, two gray-robed figures bustled from behind the statue with large sticks of wood wrapped with some sort of cloth. They lit them in the other torches and then stuck them in holders attached to the four corners of the base. Within moments, the entire statue was lit up with a golden glow.

That was when I saw him. It? A huge throne that looked like it was built out of rock and bone sat on the side of the statue's base that was furthest away from me. On the throne was a figure unlike anything I could imagine, even in my nightmares. It was a man, or had been once. Now, I didn't have a name for the mass of gray-tinged flesh. My stomach roiled. This had to be Bokor. He was at least four or five times the size of Rangel, who had been a bear of a man. But Bokor wasn't fat; it wasn't like he'd just eaten too many honey cakes. It was more like his entire body was bloated, misshapen, and mushy. His skin cascaded in folds and rolls, and he was only covered by strips of cloth across his groin. As I watched, his greasy, gray skin twitched and shuddered as if something was crawling beneath it, pushing out, trying to get free.

"What are you?" I screamed, my voice shrill with anger, fear, and disgust.

Pain exploded in my cheek as Amos's hand collided with my face. "How dare you speak to the master that way, you filth! Mind your manners in the presence of a God," he spat.

"That's enough, Amos. I said I want her unharmed," Bokor's voice boomed, echoing through the chamber.

Blood from my lip trickled down my chin, and I felt a strange giddiness start in my stomach and boil up into an almost-insane laughter. "A God? That is what all of this is about? You are kidnapping and murdering because you want to be worshiped?"

"My sweet Fiona," he crooned in a tone you would use with a petulant child. "This isn't about what I want; it is about my calling, my duty to the world. I walk among the unclean, consuming and purifying worthy souls."

I snorted. "I doubt you've walked anywhere in a very long time on those jelly legs."

My remark didn't seem to have any effect on him. He serenely replied, "It is true; my mortal body has its limitations. But I cannot be contained by this shell. My spirit can walk in any shell I choose."

"Really? Is that why I'm here? You wanna take my body out for a test drive?" I taunted, even though the thought made my blood run cold.

"No mere woman's shell would be strong enough to hold my energy," he scoffed. Then he added, "Though yours might come close. But no, I have no need for your body, delectable as it is."

"Oh, and what do you have planned for me?" I didn't really want to know; I had enough imagination without hearing the words. But I needed to keep him talking. I didn't know how long I'd been out, but surely, someone had noticed me missing by now. Sam would send a team of Blades after me. Ian would come after me. I had to hold out for a little while longer.

"You are as curious as a kitten. Very well, I have a few minutes before the ceremony begins. You see, my sweet Fiona, my avatars don't last very long. They are fragile, human. I can only use one for a short time before it depletes my energy and I must return to this body. As long as I am tied to this corporeal body, as long as I must come back to it to recharge, I am only a demigod. A half god still bound to the mortal world."

"Unchain me and give me back my hanbo. I'll cut those mortal ties for you really quickly," I jibed.

He chuckled and the sound made me want to scrub my brain out. "I love how feisty you are. But, of course you would be. No one with your power, with your state of grace, would be anything but. You are going to be the one to help me break my bonds, but you won't kill me. Not even you have that power."

"So, how am I going to help you become the god you always wanted to be? Is there a secret handshake or are we talking full-on virgin sacrifice here? Cause, I gotta tell you, the ship has sailed on that one…"

"Through no real effort of your own. I shall consume you, and with your power, I will no longer be forced to feed on the unclean. I shall consume the energy of the world. I shall ascend and finally be with my goddess as her equal. As her king."

This guy was completely off his rocker. He thought he was a god and was going to eat me? No, he was going to consume me. *Oh, fuck!* He planned to suck the life out of me. I looked around at the skeletons and realized he would probably eat me after he sucked out my spirit. Then, a sudden, gruesome thought occurred. More gruesome that being eaten, strangely enough. The way his skin crawled and pulsed—what if it was the spirits he'd pulled into his body and never let go? He had hundreds, maybe thousands, of people's life energy swimming around under his skin.

I was no religion expert, but nothing about anything he'd said, nothing about anything I'd seen in this temple, or whatever it was, sounded like the Voodoo religion I'd researched and learned so much about.

"So, Bokor," I said, conversationally. "Why do you call yourself Bokor? You don't seem like any Voodoo priest I've heard of."

He sneered. "Religion is a construct of mortals that have never been in contact with true divinity. I am the truest priest of my religion, because I know the truth of the universe. I once lived with a gypsy tribe. I was born into it through my mortal mother. We practiced Voodoo, and I was the loyal apprentice to the priest, until I was cast out of the tribe for being unclean and evil after I consumed my first soul. I tried to tell them I was divine, but they did not listen. Not until I consumed the priest and every elder in the clan. I formed my own tribe of worshipers who could see the truth of my divinity. I became their leader, their Bokor. When I found this temple, found my goddess, I knew this was where I would ascend. And now, it is time."

I opened my mouth again, but was silenced by the huge doors at the end of the room opening. Twenty or thirty grey-robe clad figures marched in. They silently strode across the dirty, bone-littered floor and knelt several feet away from the statue's base and Bokor's throne.

Amos went to stand in front of them. He cleared his throat, and then in a loud, carrying voice declared, "The Ascension ceremony will now begin. Bring in the girls."

THIRTY-TWO

Ian

The city wall had four main public gates, one each to the north, south, east, and west of the city that had been installed when the walls were built. The roads leading from those gates were the main thoroughfares of travelers and merchants in and out of the city. Few people dared to venture off those roads and into the wild overgrowth and ruins. Though some communities and villages existed in those wild places, they were generally inhabited by cutthroats and thugs. There were a few, well-guarded, smaller gates cut into the north and south walls, which were many miles long. The smaller gates were used primarily for guard patrols and emergencies, and the roads that led away from the city were little more than narrow horse paths that looped around to the other major roads.

Ian and Jarrett took the Charlotte gate. It was a supply gate used for official city deliveries from city-state run farm communities and prison compounds in the south. The gate was simply a double metal door set into the concrete wall, just wide enough for a horse and cart to get through. The path beyond, leading from the city, was just wide enough for two horses to ride side by side.

"According to the map," Jarrett said, "if we go about a mile, the

Parthenon will be about a thousand yards off to the east. But that undergrowth is so thick, we'll never get the horses through unless there is a path cut."

"If he is coming and going through the south gate, he would likely use the cut-through path to get to this road, so I'm hoping there is some sort of path already there," Ian agreed. *And I really hope this isn't a wild goose chase,* he added silently. There didn't seem to be any reason to voice it out loud, Jarrett was just as tense as he was.

Ian leaned forward, patting Mal's next. "If you see a path I don't see, you let me know. If you can sense Fiona, you find her, okay pal?"

Mal snorted, and Ian was positive the horse had understood him. He sat straight up and cut Jarrett a look, daring him to make a joke.

The vampire laughed. "Hey, no judgments here, man. I've seen that horse in action. He and Fiona have a bond like nothing I've ever witnessed. You should see the two of them in battle together; it's like they share a mind. Well, at least a mental connection. If she can be found, Mal will find her."

Ian hoped the big man was right. The thought of losing Fiona was more than he could bear. If she didn't want to be with him, he would find a way to deal. But if something happened to her... he didn't want to imagine the possibility.

They rode in silence about three quarters of a mile as fast as was safe on the rocky path when Mal abruptly stopped in the road and began snorting and prancing. Ian held out his lantern and scanned the tree line, but he saw nothing. "I don't see anything," he said.

Mal snorted again, and when neither Ian nor Jarrett responded, he walked to the edge of the trees and started nudging with his nose, then grasped on to some leaves and pulled. A large branch slid several feet as Mal backed up.

"I'll be damned!" Jarrett yelled as he hopped off Davidson. "A hidden path."

"Good job, Mal. Good job." Ian patted the horse's neck, and then jumped down to help Jarrett pull the brush aside to reveal a well-worn cart path. "Someone didn't want this path found," he said, heaving a large branch to the side. I'm going to hazard a guess that we are on the right track."

Once the path was clear, the men remounted their horses. The pace was slower now. While the path was well worn, the foliage overhead was so thick that no moonlight could get through. Jarrett took the lead, his vampire eyesight even better than the dim, golden glow cast by Ian's oil lantern. They picked their way through the winding passage for fifteen minutes before Jarrett held up a hand, signaling Ian to stop.

Ian pulled Mal to a stop and waited for Jarrett. He didn't want to speak in case Jarrett had sensed danger nearby. The last thing they needed was a fight in the tiny confines of the path.

After a few minutes, Jarrett dismounted Davidson and turned to Ian. "I hear something up ahead. We should check it out before going ahead with the horses."

"Right behind you." Ian dismounted, and then turned his lantern down until the flame flickered out. There was no sense in calling undo attention to them.

"Can you see okay?" Jarrett asked as they walked.

"My eyes are adjusting pretty quickly," Ian told him. In just a few minutes, the path opened into a large clearing. Just beyond the edge of the woods was a pond, the cart path continuing around it.

The moon was bright and it was easy to see that just beyond the pond was a small village of around thirty or forty rough-built huts and tents. Despite the late hour, there were fires lit and people moving about. A large group of gray-robed figures stood at the end of a wide, torch-lit path that led from the village up a small hill to what, at first glance, looked like a huge copse of trees.

With a harder look, Ian could see that it was actually a large structure, a building that had, over the years, been completely covered by ivy and other vegetation. Trees grew tall over it, creating a protective canopy. The brush and ivy had been cut back and cleared around the entrance and steps. That was where they needed to go.

Ian touched Jarrett's arm and nodded his head back towards the wooded path. They retreated and were quiet until they reached the horses. "That big structure, that has to be the Parthenon. I feel it in my gut—Fiona is there."

"I'm with you," Jarrett agreed. "So, do we head in or wait for the cavalry?"

The smart thing would be to wait for Sam and the Blades, but anything could happen in the hour or more it would take them to get there, if they were able to find them. "We go in," he said, his voice firm. He was positive he was making the right decision. "That much activity this late at night, something major is going down, and I have a feeling Fiona is at the center of it."

"Right on. We'll have to go in on foot though," Jarrett agreed. "There are too many of them to go in straight at them. We'll have to play it stealthy, and hope like hell we can get her out without being seen, or that back-up gets here in time." He pulled his sword from where he had it stored on Davidson's rump and slid it into the sheath at his waist.

Ian did the same with his sword, and then stopped with a thought. He turned back to Mal. "Okay, pal, I know you want to come with us, but I need you to go back down the path and wait for Sam and the other Blades. I need you to make sure they find this path. Will you do that?" He felt a bit like an idiot talking to a horse as if it were human, but he knew Mal understood him. To confirm his suspicion, Mal snorted, stomped once, then turned around and headed back down the dark path the way they had come in.

Jarrett laughed when Ian returned to him. "I've never seen that horse obey anyone but Fiona. If I were you, I wouldn't get on his bad side."

Ian agreed. "Well, let's go get her back for him so that doesn't happen." *And for me, too*, he added silently.

When they reached the clearing again, they kept low in the tall grass and skirted the pond, getting as close to the village as they could. The large group of grey-robes was gone, and now a low chanting was coming from inside the Parthenon.

"We've got to get in there, now," Ian whispered, almost frantically. He didn't like the sound of that ominous chanting. "But how are we going to get across that clearing without being seen? Edging the woods will take too long."

Jarrett was silent a moment, and then he nodded toward the village. There were still several men and women milling about. They watched as four men dressed in dark pants and light tunics went into a large tent. A couple of minutes later, four gray-robed figures walked out.

"You can't be serious. You think it will be that easy? Seems a bit obvious to me," Ian whispered.

"Better suggestion?" Jarrett countered, one eyebrow raised.

Ian sighed. "Nope. Lead on." And he reluctantly followed Jarrett into the village.

THIRTY-THREE
Fiona

I WATCHED AS SEVERAL MEN STOOD AND BROKE AWAY FROM THE GROUP. FOUR went around to the back of the statue base and came back with a long, wooden ramp. They placed it against the statue before going up. Grasping Bokor's chair, two on either side, they carried it, and him, down the ramp. My assumption that he was so grotesquely bloated because of the energy he was taking into his body was confirmed. His body was so massive that it should have taken twice as many men to carry him.

A sudden, terrible thought assailed me. If the spirit energies were still moving within him, were they conscious? Did they know what was happening to them? If so, Rangel was in there, floating around in that disgusting, vile body. The thought made me grind my teeth. If there was such thing as pure evil, Bokor was the embodiment of it.

A low, wooden altar was brought in next, and placed a few feet in front of Bokor. As soon as it was in place, the kneeling, hooded men began to chant.

"We praise the glory of Bokor.
Bokor alone is worthy of worship.

Bokor is the remover of all sin and evil.
Bokor will rain destruction upon the unworthy.
Bless us, Bokor, that we shall be worthy of your glory."

They repeated the verse in creepy singsong voices as five women were herded in. Despite the dim lighting, I immediately recognized Millie. Her clothes and face were dirty and her hair was wild, as if she'd been sleeping in filth. From the looks of the place, that was exactly the situation. But other than being grimy, she looked in decent health. Not so for the half-starved girl with stringy blond hair next to her. I couldn't be positive, as her face was much thinner than the sketches I'd seen of her, but I was pretty sure it was Farah Purcell. Millie had her arm around the girl's waist, helping her stay upright as they shuffled in and were pushed down to their knees in front of the altar.

As they turned, I saw the faces of the two men that had brought the women in. Sparks of recognition burned in my mind. One was the rickshaw driver that had stopped and asked if I wanted a ride. The other I'd seen many more times than that. He was a vendor at the market. He sold leather goods or something. I finally knew how Bokor had been getting the mages in and out of the city without a trace—how no one had seen or heard a struggle. No one paid attention to rickshaws or the drivers unless they wanted to hire one.

The loud chanting was reduced to a low murmur. Amos stepped up beside the altar, facing Bokor. "My Lord, Bokor, please accept these offerings of our faith and loyalty."

The chanting grew louder and louder as the kneeling worshipers stretched their arms out over their heads and brought their hands and foreheads to the ground in front of them, before rising back up and doing it again.

One of the gray figures stood and began chanting something that was different from his comrades, but I couldn't tell what he said over the noise and the sound of my own blood thundering in my ears. Suddenly, everything that was happening was very clear. Bokor intended to suck the life out of those girls, and then me.

Panic rose within me as the voices got louder, as if building up to some crescendo. I knew that once they reached it, the entertainment portion of this little show would be over and then it would all be over. I struggled against my bonds, but it was no use. Trussed up as I was, there was no way I could save those girls, or myself.

A lump welled up in my throat, but I refused to let it go. I couldn't believe this was the way it was going to end, the way I was going to go out. A wave of regret washed over me. I would never see my sisters or Pinky again. I had snuck out, violating a pinky-swear, and hadn't even told them I loved them. *Love. Ian.* My stomach cramped. I was going to die with Ian thinking I didn't love him. I had been such an idiot. Of course, I loved him. Nothing, not even my reluctance to open my heart to him, could change that fact. He was a part of me I would never get rid of, never be able to shake off. And I suddenly realized that I didn't want to. I wanted him to be a part of my life, a part of me, always. But now my life was about to be over, and I never told him how I really felt. I couldn't help the tears that rolled down my cheeks.

I was so engrossed in my little internal pity party that I didn't notice movement behind me until a strong hand cupped over my mouth. "Shhh," a low voice hissed in my ear as I stifled a squeak of surprise.

The hand moved from my mouth, and I gasped. "Ian?"

"No, Jarrett," replied the very familiar voice behind me.

Though a tiny spark of hope that I'd make it out alive burst to life, my heart sank. Ian hadn't come.

Jarrett continued, "Ian is on the other side, getting into position."

My heart soared. Ian had come to rescue me after all! Then, after having that thought, I mentally slapped myself. I wasn't some helpless princess from the stories Carly told my sisters and me when we were little. Though, admittedly, I did need a tiny bit of rescuing right now.

"Get me the fuck out of these chains," I vehemently whispered back to Jarrett.

"No can do, Fee. Not without making a ton of noise. We just wanted you to know we were here. Sam and a whole team are behind us, but it's going to be a bit before they get here. We need you to be cool and stall as long as you can."

"Be cool? Are you off your fucking rocker? Shit. Okay, can you at least get this crystal off me?" I hissed.

"Sure thing." He reached around and gave the crystal a sharp tug. I bit my lip to hold back a gasp of pain as the cord bit into my neck and then broke. "Hang on," he said. After a few minutes, the cord went back around my neck with something else tied to the end. I couldn't see what it was, and he quickly tucked it into my shirt so there was an obvious bulge.

"What is that?" I asked.

"A piece of bone. It'll look like the crystal slipped inside your shirt.

Now, I've got to go before I'm seen. Just hang tight, Fee, we'll get you." Then, a gray-robed figure walked from behind the pillar I was tied to, joining the other worshipers.

Very clever. They were blending in and biding their time. I scanned the praying worshipers as well as the few figures still walking around, but they all had hoods hiding their faces. I couldn't tell which one was Ian.

The chanting came to an abrupt halt. I pulled my attention away from trying to find Ian and back to the strange proceedings. Amos heaved Farah to her feet and pushed her across the altar.

"My Lord, our first offering."

"No," I screamed, before I could help myself.

Millie looked up, saw me, and her eyes went wide. "Fiona!" she shrieked and was immediately on her feet, running toward me. One of the worshipers easily grabbed her and pulled her back to the altar by her hair, Millie kicking and screaming the whole time.

"Stop it. Leave her alone," I ineffectually ordered.

"Silence, child," Amos said, standing over Millie threateningly. Millie immediately hushed, and I wondered at the abuse she'd already suffered at the hands of these monsters.

"Bokor, let them go. Take me instead. You don't need them." I began pulling in tiny amounts of energy, hoping he wouldn't notice.

Bokor's laugh grated against my nerves. "You have no idea, my sweet Fiona, what you ask. Oh, do not worry; I will take you. I will consume every last drop of your energy and feel you inside me. But, first, I must prepare. You underestimate your own power. I must be strong enough to take you and keep you. You are the main course. They are just the before-dinner snack."

My stomach lurched. "Oh, come on," I taunted. "Are you saying you aren't man enough to handle me?"

"Enough," Bokor thundered. "This is a sacred ceremony; you will not interrupt it again. Remember, my sweet Fiona, you do not have to be conscious for this," he threatened.

He turned his attentions to Farah. "Now, where were we?"

Millie jerked up again. "No, take me first. I'm stronger. She's half dead. I'm as good as two of these girls. Leave them and take me."

I didn't know whether to cheer or scream. Surely, she knew that she couldn't save Farah or anyone else. Bokor would still do what he wanted. Then, as I saw her eyes flit around, I realized what she was doing. She was trying to buy time. She thought that if I were there, help must not be too far behind. Millie was stronger than Farah, so she would buy her and the other girls time with her own life. The girl was ridiculously courageous and incredibly stupid. She reminded me of me.

"Very well," Bokor crooned. "Bring her forward."

Farah was pulled from the altar and shoved, unceremoniously, into a whimpering heap on the floor. Millie was pushed onto the altar in her place. I opened my senses just a bit. It was strange. There was a void of blackness around Bokor. I couldn't see any energy around him, though I knew he was filled with it. When Bokor began drawing energy off Millie, a thin stream of light began flowing off her into the blackness around him, making it darken and pulse.

I couldn't let this happen. I said a quick spell and tried my bonds. Nothing. I tried again—still no use. I didn't have anything to focus my energy with, so I would just have to do my best. I opened my senses as wide as they would go, sucking in energy and then pushing out as hard as I could, widening my bound hands and motioning towards the altar.

Gray-robed men went flying as the wave of magic hit them. The stream of light between Millie and Bokor stopped temporarily as he focused his attention on me. "Get her," he screamed, and all hell broke loose.

"Way to hang tight," Jarrett yelled as he swung his sword at my manacles.

I fell forward, my hands and knees hitting the grubby floor. I was free. I pulled myself up, my knees still weak from the effects of whatever drug Bokor had used on me. I started towards Millie and the other girls but was brought up short.

Bokor's eyes went wide and black, and his minions started pulling themselves up, their eyes were wide and dark as well. "Oh, fuck," I breathed. Now, this was like what I'd read. Somehow, Bokor was mind controlling his followers. The slow-moving horde coming at Jarrett and me were not just angry worshipers protecting their so-called God. They were full-blown zombies, doing their master's bidding even if it meant death.

All at once, they were on us. Jarrett started swinging his sword, and I started kicking and punching. As minion after minion came at me, I frantically searched for Ian. I thought I saw him once, but before I could be sure, a blow to the stomach sent me sprawling. I was back on my feet quickly, using every bit of my fighting skills to push back the men. But every time I made progress, two more popped up. I looked towards where the girls were. They were all huddled together at the base of a column in the far corner, all except Millie. She laid on the altar, unconscious, her life energy streaming out of her and into Bokor, fueling his attack.

I had to get to her. Another minion came at me, punching at my head. I ducked, catching him in the stomach with my knee, but he grabbed my ankle and I went crashing down in a tumble with him. We rolled around, struggling, and I finally got my elbow up high enough to land a blow across his nose. I felt a crack, and he stopped moving. I pulled myself from him, but before I could regain my feet, I noticed little wisps of energy floating across the ceiling. They were bright white, life energy. I followed the stream back to the source and I finally saw Ian standing at the back of the room, his face red with fury. He had his sword out, fighting minions as they crowded him. Tiny wisps of energy were flying off him like sparks. I watched as one of the wisps sought out a skeleton on one of the columns. It flew into it, and the skeleton, a tiny bright light glowing within, pulled itself off where it was hanging and jumped into the fray, fighting Bokor's minions. Within seconds, there were dozens of skeletons punching and hacking at the worshipers alongside Jarrett.

I pulled myself to my feet and began fighting, but was soon knocked on my ass again. I was getting too weak and making little progress. My mind whirled, and I tried to tamp down the rising terror. After all this, we were still going to die if something didn't happen. But what? There was no way to know when Sam would show up with the cavalry. Or, if he even would.

Bokor had to be stopped. He had too much power. As long as he controlled his disciples, we'd never get close, not with just three of us fighting, even with the extra help Ian was lending, which was both terrifying and amazing. If we both got out of this alive, I was going to tell him how awesome I thought necromancers were.

I looked where Millie lay unconscious on the altar. I didn't even have to open my senses to see the life force streaming from her body and into Bokor. It was getting thinner, weaker. Soon, there would be nothing left. He would have her entire life force absorbed, and Millie would become a dry, dusty corpse.

I kicked a child of about ten in the shoulder as she slashed at me with a knife. She fell back, her head hitting the stone statue hard. She lay there still for a long moment, and I felt sick. I had been reduced to hurting, possibly even killing, children. My rage intensified. But then her eyes opened and she blinked, as if coming out of a trance. She looked around, terrified, then hopped up and ran out. She must have been unconscious for just a moment.

"Knock them out," I screamed, but it came out in a hoarse croak. They couldn't hear me, and I didn't have the energy to make myself heard. I stumbled forward. The residual effects of the drugs Bokor had used on me had me weak, and the energies Ian and Bokor were using were churning up the atmosphere, making the magical energy fluctuate in a way that made it impossible for me to draw any energy from around me.

Suddenly, I knew what I had to do. I knew how to save Ian, Millie, everyone. It was dangerous, might even kill me. I knew Ian wouldn't let me do it. I looked over to where he and Jarrett fought the horde of zombified minions. They were surrounded. They slashed and hacked at the mindless men, but were losing ground as more and more people—women and children included—streamed into the cavernous room and began attacking. Even with Ian controlling the skeletons, they couldn't last much longer. His strength was waning; I could see it in his face. Soon, he would have to pull all of his energy back from the fighting skeletons just to be able to continue fighting himself.

I couldn't keep fighting, but I was sure I had enough energy to do what I needed to do. I took off towards Bokor. I tried to run but I was so weak it was more of a clumsy stagger, ducking blows from minions and getting out of the way of skeletons as I moved. I was only steps from the altar when I heard Ian scream, "Fiona! *No!*"

But it was too late. I pushed myself forward the last few feet, and then stumbled. I put my hand out as I fell, using Bokor's soft, fleshy mass to steady myself. The moment my hand touched his grey, slimy flesh, I opened my senses full force and began to draw in energy.

I heard both Ian and Bokor scream, "No!" in unison before a great thundering overtook me. White-hot energy filled me, seeping in through my hand and coursing through my entire body. I suddenly felt more powerful than I had ever felt in my life. I expected it to stop, but it didn't. It kept flowing in. It filled every cell of my being.

I could sense, rather than hear, Bokor's screams of pain and rage, but I ignored him and kept drawing in energy. Then I realized the thundering in my head wasn't thunder. It was voices. Minds. Spirits. I could feel the pain and confusion of every being from which Bokor had sucked the life essence. It was deafening. The sense of overwhelming power I had turned into immense pain. My body shook, I was being ripped apart, yet the energy, the spirits, kept flowing into me. I couldn't hold it. But I couldn't stop. If I stopped, their energy would stream back into Bokor, along with my own. He would be just as strong as before, stronger even. I couldn't let that happen. I had to make sure Ian had a fighting chance.

So I kept drawing the energy in. The feeling of power was completely gone and I was feeling weak, weaker than I ever had. I couldn't take much more. So I did the one thing I could think of. I clenched Bokor's spongy flesh with my right hand and focused harder on pulling energy out of him. Putting my left hand into the air and with the last bit of my strength, I opened myself up, letting all the energy built up inside me and flowing into me through Bokor, out. As the spirits inside me realized I was freeing them, I felt a sudden burst of elation when the energy burst forth. Not just from my hand but my entire body.

Every bit of me thrummed and vibrated, and I had the sense of a brilliant light surrounding me before darkness started closing in around me. I had done it. I'd saved Millie and Jarrett, and most importantly, Ian. As my body got weaker and weaker and the darkness moved in, I had a sharp pang of regret. My sweet, sexy, wonderful Ian. I would never see him again. But he was safe. I knew I had weakened Bokor enough that Ian and Jarrett could kill him. Ian would live. That was enough for me. That was my last thought before everything went black.

THIRTY-FOUR

Fiona

Fog filled my brain, and my whole body ached. I pried my eyes open and tried to blink away the dry, dusty feeling in them so I could see. After a minute, the world came into focus and I realized I was staring up at my bedroom ceiling.

"Wha...?" The dust in my eyes was also in my voice, and I started coughing.

River was by my side in less than a second, pulling me to an upright position and placing a cup at my lips. "Drink. It's water. Come on... drink a little. It'll help clear your throat."

Reluctantly, I took a sip. River's sickbed brews were not always very appealing. But, true to her word, it was just water. The cool liquid did indeed wash away the grit and soothe my throat and dry mouth. After draining the cup, I let River put some pillows behind me to help me sit up.

Unfortunately, the water did nothing to clear the fog in my brain. Why did I feel like I'd been run over by a team of horses? I looked around the room to try to fill in the blanks in my head, but came up mostly with questions. Why was I in bed in the middle of the day? Why was River hovering over me? Why was there a chair covered with pillows and blankets as if someone had been sleeping in here?

River followed my gaze to the chair. "Ian's been sleeping there. He insists, but he's almost as banged up as you are. I made him go get something to eat and lie down flat for an hour."

Ian. Ian was hurt. Memories slammed into me so hard I fell back against the pillows. The past several days flashed in my mind in pieces. *Making love with Ian in his bed. Rangel turning into a corpse. Making love with Ian in the rooftop garden, fighting in the garden. Bokor, fighting skeletons, Millie unconscious on the floor. Then, so many voices in my head.*

I sat straight and fumbled with the blanket, trying to get out of the bed.

"Oh, no you don't," River said in her sternest voice. "You are not moving for at least another day. You keep your ass in that bed. I mean it."

I relented and leaned back. "Millie?" I croaked.

"Millie is fine. She is at home with her parents, recovering quite nicely. I visited her this morning. She was chattering about getting back to work and starting the Academy in a few days. And before you ask, Farah is doing well also. She is still at the hospital, but she will make a full recovery. As will the other women rescued. No, don't talk, and don't glare at me. Sit there, rest. I'm going to go get you some mint tea for your throat, and if you are nice, some visitors."

Leaning back, I let the soft pillows and quilt envelope me. I was too weak to argue.

She bustled out and I heard her say, "She's awake. No, don't you all crowd her. I need some mint tea with honey. Anya can take it in to her. You can visit for five minutes, one at a time. She's too weak and tired to handle all of us blathering at her at once."

I laughed, and then groaned as a sharp pain ripped through my side. Okay, so maybe resting wasn't such a bad idea. I laid my head back and closed my eyes. A few minutes later, Anya came in carrying a steaming mug. She set it down and sat on the edge of the bed, wrapping her arms around me, being careful not to squeeze too hard.

"Fee, I'm so glad you are awake. You scared the crap out of us," she scolded gently, her eyes glimmering with unshed tears.

I smiled at her, despite the ache in my head. "It's okay, An. I'm okay." It came out more of a whisper than I'd meant it to. Anya handed me the cup of tea and I sipped it, letting the hot, sweet liquid slide down my throat. After I drank half the cup, I cleared my throat. When I spoke again, my voice was stronger, if a little scratchy. "How long was I out?"

"Three days."

"What?" I'd been unconscious for three days?

The tears in Anya's eyes finally overflowed and trailed down her cheeks. "We thought we were going to lose you."

I pulled her to me, ignoring the ache in my arms as I wrapped my arms around her. "It's okay. I'm not going anywhere."

"You better not," Pinky's voice sounded from the open doorway. "Anya, River told me to tell you that your time is up. But since I'm the adult around here, I say you can stay during my visit." Pinky raised his voice loud enough for River to hear the "I'm the adult around here" part. As usual, all three of us giggled. Poor Pinky, who was almost three hundred years old, looked more like our younger brother than the only father any of us had ever known.

Anya sniffled and wiped her eyes. "No, I'm good. I need a nap before work. I'll see you later." She bent over, kissed my cheek, and then was gone.

Pinky didn't sit. "I'm not going to stay long. There are some fellas out there who want to come in too." He bent down and dropped a kiss on my head. "You know, you scared the heck out of us, Fee-diddly-dee."

I couldn't help the tears the use of the nickname he hadn't called me since I was ten brought on. "I know, Pinky. I'm sorry."

"Forgiven." He smiled and walked to the door. "But if you ever break a pinky-swear again, soul-sucking bad guys are going to be the least of your worries. Got me?"

"Gotcha," I said, grinning as he left. I loved my family, but I was glad they got through their visits quickly. Butterflies swarmed my stomach. Ian would be next, and I needed to see him so badly.

But the next person to come through my door, though equally welcome, was not Ian.

"Jarrett," I said, trying to hide my disappointment.

"Don't look so happy to see me, Fee." He laughed and jerked his head toward the living room. "Sir Necromancer out there isn't so sure you want to see him. So, I'm testing the waters."

"Ugh, he's an idiot," I groaned.

Jarrett laughed and sat on the edge of the bed as Anya had. He leaned close and whispered, "He is an idiot. But cut him a little slack. He's an idiot in love. I've never been such an idiot myself, but I hear it's not all it's cracked up to be. Especially when said lover is kidnapped and nearly dies."

"Okay. Point taken. So, three days? What the hell happened?"

For the next twenty minutes, Jarrett regaled me with the story of how they'd figured out I was missing, the trail to find me, and sneaking into the Parthenon clothed in the robes of Bokor's followers. Then he told me that when I released the spirits from Bokor, I let loose a burst of energy so powerful that it hit the columns of the building and the whole building started collapsing around them.

"Luckily, Sam and ten Blades showed up just before you did whatever it was you did to Bokor. They had already started releasing the captives. The other women helped Farah out, and Ian and I grabbed you and Millie. We nearly didn't make it out. Ian took a hit from a piece of falling ceiling. Don't look like that; he's fine. Wow, Barroes isn't the only idiot in love, is he?"

"Shut up, Jarrett," I said, but I could feel my face turning red.

"Okay. Okay." He laughed at my feeble attempt to punch him in the shoulder. "Well, kiddo, now that I know you are gonna stick with us in the living world, I'm gonna head out. I met with my informant a couple of days ago, and I need to hit the road."

"Alright. Be careful," I said, turning my cheek up for a kiss. "And send the idiot in, will you?"

"Sure thing." And he was gone.

After several long minutes, Ian finally appeared in the doorway. His face was bruised, a bandaged covered a gash above his eye, and several other small cuts were sprinkled over his face and neck. His left arm was wrapped in a bandage and nestled in a sling hung around his neck.

I gasped. "Are you okay?"

He smiled shyly. "I'm fine. It looks worse than it feels."

"I'm sorry," I said softly.

"This isn't your fault. The ceiling fell. Well, sort of your fault, but you got the bad guy. Bokor's dead. And I'm just bruised."

Not what I meant, but I went with it for the moment. "Did you know I could do that? Pull the spirits out of his body, I mean?"

He sat in the chair River had sat in before. "No idea. I didn't even realize they were still intact inside him until you started releasing them. But, Fiona, that was amazing what you did. Are you okay? I mean, I know River says you are going to be fine, but are you okay? Having that many life energies, that many spirits, flow through you had to have been a strange experience."

"It was, though I only really felt what was happening for a moment.

I could feel them and hear them. It was terrifying. Then, when they realized I was releasing them, the only thing I could feel was their joy. After that, everything went black. Now, I don't feel any of that left over, so I'm guessing there won't be any permanent effects."

Ian's face grew serious. "No one else really saw what happened; there was a lot of confusion, trying to free captives, and fighting off Bokor's minions. Jarrett saw, but has no idea what it was. The general consensus from the rest of them is that Bokor tried to take your energy and it backfired. It's probably best for people to keep thinking that."

He was right. I didn't know if I could do what I'd done to Bokor a second time, and I didn't want to find out. And if anyone suspected I might be capable of draining the life out of a person, it would be very dangerous to be me. "I understand," I told him. Now we shared one more secret.

"Fiona," he started in a choked voice.

"No. Stop. Let me talk first," my words rushed out, drowning his. "I need to say this and if we keep talking about this crap that doesn't really matter, I won't be able to get it out."

"Okay."

"Ian, I'm sorry. Really sorry. I didn't mean what I said on the roof."

"Yes, you did." His voice was matter of fact.

I sighed, wishing he weren't right. "Okay, maybe I did, at the time. But I was wrong. I was scared. But I was more scared when I thought I'd never see you again. And terrified to the tips of my toes when I thought you were going to die if I couldn't stop Bokor. Frankly, I'm still scared. You've quickly become the most important person in my life. You are as much a part of my family as Pinky and my sisters. Somehow, you've become a part of me. I can't bear the thought of losing you, and for the first time, I can understand the pain my mother must have felt when she lost my father."

I paused, knowing there was more to say, but I couldn't find the words. I didn't need to.

"I know. I love you too," Ian said. In an instant, he was over me, our mouths locked. Heat surged through me. I wrapped my arms around him, trying to pull him towards me, but we both cried out in pain. He pulled back.

"Now might not be the best time to have make-up sex." He grinned.

"Probably not," I sighed, disappointed. "I suppose River will be forcing you out of here and into bed pretty soon, anyway."

"I'd like to see her try." He grinned again, and then came around to the other side of the bed. Pulling back the covers, he slipped in next to me, his good arm going under me and his injured arm resting on my belly. He pulled me close. "I'm not going anywhere."

I rested my head on his chest. Being in his arms felt safe, right, and like it was where I belonged.

"You know, I can't promise I won't be a hardheaded bitch in the future."

I felt his grin against the top of my head. "I can promise you will be. And I'll be a pompous ass. It's who we are. But I love you, and I'll do everything I can to make sure you know that every day."

"So, you are going to be all girly and touchy-feely?" I laughed.

"Yes, as a matter of fact, I am."

"Okay," I said. "I can live with that." And I realized I could, and I was looking forward to it.

About the Author

June Stevens is the pen name of DJ Westerfield.

DJ uses the pseudonym June Stevens to write ROMANTIC fiction in a variety of genres including contemporary, suspense, fantasy, paranormal, urban fantasy.

DJ is a wife, step-mom, sister, auntie, daughter, daughter-in-law, sister-in-law, friend, and Mommy to four adorable and mischievous four-legged babies. She writes non-fiction, blogs, and co-hosts an internet radio show as DJ Westerfield.

Acknowledgements

So many people helped me bring this novel from idea to the form you are now reading. It seems almost impossible to thank them all, but I will do my best to hit as many as I can without this turning into another novel.

My first thank you has to go to my husband, Steve, and not just for his undying support and tolerance of 3 am writing sessions. If it weren't for him there wouldn't be a book, quite literally, because there would not have been a bad guy. I needed a bad guy for Fiona to beat, but I had no idea how to write a bad guy, or even come up with a good idea of one. Luckily my husband is a fan of horror and has a brilliant mind. While I wrote Bokor and all of his scenes, the basic idea was Steve's. And every scene was run by him with me asking, "Does this sound right? Is he evil enough?" Also, thanks to my husband the kitties were fed, the puppies were walked, dinner was cooked (thank goodness for pasta and sauce) and dirty laundry didn't pile up around our ears while I was on deadline.

I will never be able to thank Sherry Ficklin enough for her support, but I'm going to try. She has been my go-to girl throughout this entire process. She has listened to me whine, she has read, re-read, and edited. She cheered me when I deserved it and she chastised me when I needed the push to get back to work. She has been my best friend and confidant and if she hadn't believed in me and the book, I might have given it up long ago.

In life we are each given one mother, but if we are truly lucky we get to pick another one. I couldn't have picked better than my mother-in-law

Patricia Westerfield. There is no doubt she was meant to be in my life, so it is really lucky that I love her son. She believed in me when I didn't believe in myself and she and my father-in-law, Al, have been unbelievably supportive. I will never be able to thank them enough.

I must also thank everyone at Crimson Tree Publishing. The journey for Voodoo Moon has been long and winding and I'm so glad to have found such a wonderful home for it and the rest of the series. Of all the choices I've had to make, signing with CTP was one of the easiest. Thanks ladies!

And last, but certainly not least, all of my friends, fans, and readers that have followed my progress, read my stories, and encouraged me to write more. I couldn't do this if I didn't know there were a few people out there that would actually read and enjoy my work. So thank you, from the bottom of my heart.

www.ingramcontent.com/pod-product-compliance
Ingram Content Group UK Ltd.
Pitfield, Milton Keynes, MK11 3LW, UK
UKHW041305180426
11947UKWH00009B/690